Ed & Lily

Happy Travels!

Soph #2

Ed&
Lily

DEPARTURES

Sofia Due

The Book Guild Ltd

First published in Great Britain in 2021 by
The Book Guild Ltd
9 Priory Business Park
Wistow Road, Kibworth
Leicestershire, LE8 0RX
Freephone: 0800 999 2982
www.bookguild.co.uk
Email: info@bookguild.co.uk
Twitter: @bookguild

Typeset in 12pt Minion Pro

Printed and bound by CPI Group (UK) Ltd, Croydon, CR0 4YY

ISBN 978 1913913 298

British Library Cataloguing in Publication Data.
A catalogue record for this book is available from the British Library.

For my family present and passed

1

Lily

23 December 2017, 18.00

The coloured lights on the sustainably grown tree in the corner were blinking out of sync with the LEDs on Lily's sweater. Her vision was starting to blur.

If she was going, she'd better do it now. While there was still time to make the train. Before anyone else asked how she was spending the holiday or the heat in the boardroom overwhelmed her and she wilted like the poor tree.

Lily squeezed around the table and back towards the door, pulling at the neck of her jumper, hand-knitted from oddments of wool with appliquéd felt reindeers and snowmen and fluffy white pompoms. Another couple of sequins fell off. That was the thing with working for a charity with an environmental ethic. The only garments with credibility on Christmas jumper day were horrors your mother gave you years ago or things you made yourself.

Money spent on anything finer would be better donated to the homeless.

What remained of a mince pie crumbled in her other hand. There was nowhere to leave it, the bins had all been emptied and the cleaners had finished for the day. She crammed the sticky mess into her mouth and the wave of nausea sent her stumbling down the stairs and into the bathroom. The sweater was suffocating her. She dragged it over her head, catching on an earring which skittered across the floor, and then leaned against the basin, gulping air until the sensation passed. Nerves, that was all.

She couldn't tell Ed she didn't want to go. It was much too late for that.

The sound of voices got her moving again, out of the bathroom and into her office, where her coat and bags lay next to her chair in an untidy heap. There was another pile of stuff on her desk, but the filing would have to wait. She swept the paper into her drawer, grabbed her belongings and ran for the exit.

'Lily?'

If Maggie was on her way, Matt wouldn't be far behind.

'I'll call you,' Lily shouted.

She shoved the door open with her shoulder and paused on the step, testing the weight of the sweater in her hand. The zips on her suitcase were already stretched and there was no room in her rucksack. Unless she left the jumper on the doorstep, or tiptoed back inside, she'd have to wear it. Iceland was bound to be cold – in more ways than one. The jumper might come in handy. She yanked it over her head again, lifted her chin and set off for Cardiff Central Station, trailing her bag behind her.

It could be fun. Travelling with Ed usually was. Or had been. He liked to discover hidden gems, an odd little bar down a side street or a cove accessible only by boat. Or a lone cottage on a glacier with a wood-burner and no WiFi, which would be spectacular. Lord knew why Ed fancied it, though.

He wasn't what you'd call naturally outdoorsy. He was urban through and through. It wasn't only the job – all those designs in glass and steel, any green spaces marked out with a ruler – it was his wardrobe too. Ed dressed for Clerkenwell, not boulder-strewn fjords. Always in black Chelsea boots, sleek and elastic-sided and ordered from a classic bootmaker. He must have about eight pairs. She'd learned to recognise the style differences, details so subtle almost no-one would notice. He even wore them on site, come rain or shine, along with his hard hat, ignoring everyone else in their rigger boots.

Seven days in a cottage, the longest time they'd managed together since the summer, entirely on their own.

She stopped, breathing deeply while her stomach churned, and counted her days again. It was probably nothing, but if it wasn't, it would add a whole other level of awkward into the situation. There was a chemist along from the station. It wouldn't hurt to check. Put her mind at rest.

An assistant blocked the door. 'We're about to close,' she said.

'I'll only be a sec,' said Lily, with a grimace. 'It's kind of an emergency.'

The assistant sighed and waved her in.

The pharmacy section was at the back, past stacks of pampering products in shiny gift boxes, huge three-for-two stickers all but obliterating the contents.

Lily scanned the shelf. It didn't matter if the results were announced in numbers, lines or pictures of bunny rabbits. She just needed to pick one – and fast.

The cashier slid the packet into a discreet paper bag.

'Good luck,' she said, the right response whatever the result.

Lily nodded and stuffed the package in the pocket of her coat, smiling weakly as she backed up and manoeuvred out of the shop.

The ticket machine was uncompromising. The booking reference wasn't sufficient; a payment card was required. Lily stood before it, passing the crumpled paper bag helplessly from one hand to the other as she emptied her pockets. Here was another uncomfortable conversation she'd be having that evening. It didn't require the most vivid imagination to picture her bank card left lying on the shop counter while she hid her purchase and hoisted her rucksack onto her shoulders.

The chemist had closed, its shutters down, windows hidden. Lily pressed her face and hands against the door, straining her eyes for signs of movement, but the place was horribly dark and silent.

There was no point going back to the station. Her train would be long gone and she didn't have enough cash for the next one. She knew that because, as Ed would be sure to remind her, it wasn't the first time she'd missed a train. This close to Christmas the ticket price would be eye-popping.

Turning circles on the pavement was making her dizzy. What she needed was a plan. Or a bus. She stopped and consulted her phone. There was a coach to London in twenty minutes. If she couldn't afford a ticket on that, she'd have to give up and go home. It wasn't as if she had many options: all her other bridges were now smouldering.

Ed picked up on the third ring.

'Don't go mad,' she said.

'Why are you out of breath? Are you running?' She heard the pause, the sigh. 'You missed the train, didn't you?'

'It's no big deal. I'm getting the bus.'

'The bus? Why the bus, Lily? Get the next train.' He was using that tone with her, clipped and precise.

'I can't get a ticket at the moment. It's easier to get the bus.'

It was a long story and there was no way to make it short. Nor was she running. It was more of a power walk through the city centre.

'How can it be easier to get the bus?' There it was again, that tiny note of sarcasm.

'It'll be fine, Ed.'

'But how long's it going to take? You won't be here for hours.'

'Don't worry, I'll get there. You won't miss your plane.' She regretted it as soon as the words left her mouth. There was no point to this trip if it made things worse.

'Li—'

He hung up, which he didn't have to. It was petty. Lily slowed down. The window displays in St Mary Street must have been there since Halloween, but she hadn't had a chance to admire them. Strings of sparkle suspended across the street. Snowflakes or stars? Lily couldn't tell. It wasn't important. What mattered was the illusion. It didn't take much; a bit of glitter was enough.

Ed was right about one thing. The coach took almost twice

as long as the train and she wouldn't reach London until after ten. Better late than never... She pushed away the thought as she trailed her bag past Cardiff castle and onto the patch of churned-up grass which served as a terminus. A bus was waiting, a group of baggy-eyed youths wielding huge holdalls shuffling forward to put their luggage underneath and climb on board.

'I can't take cash,' said the driver when Lily reached him.

'What do I do, then?'

'Use the website. Download a ticket.'

He switched his attention to the passenger behind. Lily was bundled out of the way as the next in line pushed forward to prove his right to travel. She stepped back onto the verge, walking boots sinking into the mud, and fumbled for her phone. What was wrong with her? She could have done this at the station. A bar code appeared on the screen and Lily mounted the steps again, waving her phone at the driver.

There was some luck – a seat by the window. She could curl into her coat and pretend to sleep while she worked out what to tell Ed. A young man slid into the space beside her and pushed his rucksack down between his feet. He grappled with his earbuds, untangling the wires as the beats bounced from his phone. It was nothing Lily recognised. It might only be a few years since she'd left university, but time moved fast.

She took out her own phone and dialled again.

'Ed?' She wasn't sure he'd pick up. 'Eddy?'

No-one else was allowed to call him that.

'If you don't want to come, just say so,' he said. He didn't have to sound so weary.

'How can you say that? I got held up at work.'

'I get that,' Ed said. 'Last day before the holiday, Secret

Santa and so on. What I don't understand is why you're getting the bus! It's like you're delaying your arrival.'

'I'm not,' she said, feeling the heat reach her face. He had a point. 'I told you, there was an issue with the train.'

'What, like a derailment?'

'No, it's more an issue with the ticket. I'll explain when I see you.'

'If you bought the right sort of ticket, it wouldn't matter if you missed the train because you could take the next one,' he continued, now sounding all reasonable. He got quieter when he was angry.

'Is this going to be another lecture?'

'Well, if you bought the tickets in advance... Or let me book it for you if you're short of time... You live your life in denial.'

She disconnected and glared at the lock screen and the image of the laughing man with the dark hair and even teeth, holding her in close for the selfie, summer-tanned cheek pressed to hers. When did he get so pompous? She was on her way, wasn't she? She ran a hand through her hair, separating the waves with her fingers. Now was not the time for second thoughts. She'd made her choice and she had to see the thing through, however it turned out. The alternative was worse. She turned towards the window. The boy beside her was still fiddling with his headphones. He fidgeted in his seat.

'Am I disturbing you?' she asked. He shouldn't be listening.

'No.' He shrugged. 'It's fine. Your bag's blocking my seat belt, though.'

'Oh, sorry.' She tidied her belongings around her, abashed. 'Are you going home for Christmas? To London?'

'Yeah.' He lifted his headphones to put them in his ears

and stopped halfway, made self-conscious by her attempts to converse with him. 'Erm, are you?'

'No. I live here. Cardiff.'

Where was home anymore?

'Oh,' he said, waiting for the sign their exchange was over and he could return to his private world of grime and hip-hop.

She nodded and eased her arms out of her anorak, trying not to reveal too much of her sweater as she rolled her coat into a makeshift pillow and tucked it next to her ear.

A cottage on its own surrounded by snow. Ordinarily she'd have loved that. But Christmas on their own, miles from everything and everyone? With no family or friends to relieve the tension, at the time of year when everyone else would be busy eating, drinking, kissing, dozing in front of the television. When all the public buildings would be shut and all there was to do was walk and talk. Would it turn into one of those conversations, the sort that went on for days, starting and stopping, dotted with silences full of unspoken truths, to be resolved only when one of them made a decision? *Your choice, not mine.* She wasn't ready.

2

Ed

Ed sat on the edge of the bed and inspected his feet, not quite recognising them as his own. He turned the huge grey walking boots from side to side, tracing squeaky arcs on the parquet as he pushed first the toes together and then the heels. They made his legs look like twigs and he wasn't what you'd call skinny, and really, how could you possibly need that many eyelets? He hated laces, always had. They were such a waste of time. He'd made his style choices when he was a teenager and he was sticking with them – black trousers, black boots, black coat. It cut the time needed to get out in the morning.

Whatever the boots looked like, the whole thing had been pointless. At this rate Lily wasn't going to get there in time to recognise his efforts. Her accusations that he was treating Christmas as an endurance test, as an opportunity for self-imposed exile (she hadn't said 'self-pity', she hadn't been that unkind) rather than embracing the adventure, had hit a nerve. He had something to prove. Now all those hours badgering his Scandinavian colleagues for footwear recommendations, the day spent buying clothing fit for clambering around geysers, would have been in vain.

He carried his bag into the sitting room, testing its weight. He'd left room for all the things Lily would be sure to decant from her bag into his. It was a good job airlines fixed limits, otherwise who knew how many coats she'd take?

There wasn't much to do to prepare the flat for his absence. No pets to feed or plants to water, nothing to keep him busy while he waited. He closed the curtains on the balcony doors and sank in his coat onto the old leather sofa, which, after fifty years of use, had enough give in it to be comfortable. It was like the rest of the place – somewhat scratched and worn but holding its own. So little had changed since his uncle Martin lived there, it still felt like Ed was housesitting for him. The bedrooms were full of the glass lamps, heavy mahogany wardrobes and dressers Martin had plucked from the clutter in his Portobello Road shop. Only the kitchen was new, updated to brushed steel when Ed was offered something fancy fallen off the back of a builder's lorry. Neither he nor his brother Kit, when he lived there, had ever felt the impulse to replace anything else – not the threadbare armchair or the chaise longue, last reupholstered by one of Martin's lovers in something that resembled the Bayeux tapestry. In fact, Ed was sure that the reason Kit popped back so often was to discourage Ed from changing too much too soon. He could be sentimental like that.

Ed pushed his glasses back onto the bridge of his nose and

checked his watch – plain gold case, battered leather strap, another of Martin's legacies – then picked up his phone.

'She's always late,' said Kit. 'Don't know why you're surprised. She'll turn up eventually. Good job you built in a decent buffer before the flight.'

'Suppose it's more than that?' said Ed, finally giving breath to his misgivings. He almost never told anyone anything, least of all his younger brother.

'What did he expect?' yelled Anisia from the background.

And that was why. His brother's marriage to Lily's best friend reduced his usefulness, ensured that information was only shared if he wanted it fed back, drip by drip, to Lily. His brother wasn't indiscreet. He was quite good at keeping secrets, mainly because he remembered little of what you told him, but Anisia was a master eavesdropper. She had hearing like a bat.

'Why Iceland? Why not Paris or New York?' she continued.

'How...? Kit, am I on loudspeaker?'

'No,' his brother said in low tones, covering the lie. 'You know what she's like. But she's right, there's not a lot of cheap shoe shopping in Reykjavik.'

'I guess I panicked. I wanted to try something different, and you know Lily, she's not into that. She likes small boutiques that sell products made by women's cooperatives in Peru or design start-ups from Glasgow. She's not bothered by all the label stuff. Like some people.'

'I can hear you,' bellowed Anisia.

'Well, why not Iceland? It will be beautiful. Anyway, we've been to New York, and trust me, Paris isn't always romantic. Last time we went, I suggested taking a look at a new housing project in the suburbs and she wanted to go to a concert by a band from the Congo raising awareness of FGM.'

Kit laughed. 'I'm guessing Lily won.'

'Worst evening of my life,' said Ed. He shuddered. 'If you'd seen that slideshow, Kit.'

Lily hadn't enjoyed the evening either, but she'd never say so. He'd danced around her on a Parisian pavement, nudging and teasing her as she shook her head, nose in the air, refusing to admit she'd hated it too.

'You don't fancy a pint, do you, Kit, before I head off into Central? Or a Highland malt for a bit of adventure?'

'No, he doesn't,' yelled Anisia. 'He's on call.'

'That's a "No", then, is it?' Ed groaned. 'What can I do, Kit?'

'He could find something Lily actually wants to do,' said Anisia, whose voice seemed uncomfortably close. 'She seems really unhappy at the moment.'

'Are you suggesting I'm what's making her unhappy?' asked Ed.

He abandoned the pretence he was having a conversation with anyone but her. Anisia and Kit came as a pair. When she entered Kit's life, Ed hadn't lost a brother so much as gained a sister, the sort who'd point out all his failings in the way only a sibling could and get away with it.

'No. At least not entirely,' she said.

'Ha! Well, guys, thank you for your support. As ever, you've been splendid. Both of you,' said Ed.

'You know, bro, if it all goes tits up, you're welcome to spend Christmas with us. You can have the baby's room. She doesn't use it. She's pretty much permanently in with us.'

'Thanks. Appreciate it. You're not heading to Dad's at all then?'

'Hell, no,' said Kit.

'Baby's got a cold,' Anisia added hastily. 'Wouldn't want to pass it on to Samantha.'

Samantha. The new wife. A stepmother, for God's sake. At their age.

'No, that wouldn't do,' said Ed, blandly.

'Seriously, Ed,' said Anisia, 'do something nice. Spoil her.'

So they were back to that again, were they? Ed glared at the phone. 'Just out of interest, if it's not entirely my fault, whose fault is it?'

It couldn't have anything to do with Anisia, could it, cooing non-stop over the perfectness of her baby?

'Well, it's that guy, isn't it?'

'What guy?' He said the words, but they didn't seem to come out of his own mouth. His blood ran cold, ice starting in the pit of his stomach and gradually burning through to the ends of his fingers. He hated that sensation.

'See? You need to pay more attention, Ed.'

She was probably joking, but she couldn't see the effect she was having. His skin felt clammy. It wasn't at all funny.

'It's all since she moved to Cardiff,' Anisia went on, oblivious.

He wished she'd stop. It was typical of Anisia. Even if there was nothing to make something of, she'd pretend to know all the details. He wasn't going to ask. The thought of someone else, particularly Anisia, poking their fingers into the cracks in his relationship was unbearable. As was the idea she might know more than he did.

'How d'you put up with her, Kit?'

His brother didn't react.

'Well, that's when it started,' she insisted.

13

3

Lily

18.40

Streams of travellers journeying east, keeping pace with the bus. Like a real Christmas story. Lily wiped the window with the sleeve of her jumper and looked up at the sky, but no stars were going to make it through those clouds.

If she had something Christmassy to listen to, that might get her in the mood. Ed used to send her a song every Friday. He'd message her a link to liven up her journey and kick start the weekend. When was the last time he'd done that? Maybe the day she said she'd saved the song so they could listen to it together. He didn't say anything, just looked at her over his glasses. He hadn't been fooled; he knew she'd forgotten and spent the train time reading emails. It was what he always did and what she was going to have to do now. She still had a couple of queries from her fieldworkers to deal with. They needed responses before everyone packed up for the holiday.

She couldn't leave them hanging. They'd be the ones holding the fort in destinations where Christmas cheer would be in short supply. People didn't stop having medical emergencies because some others had a roast dinner to eat.

She'd call Ed before she got too involved.

'Lily?'

Why did he have to sigh?

'I said I was sorry. I am. I'll get there soon enough.'

'Soon enough for what? Or for who? You or me?'

'What d'you mean?'

He groaned now. 'You'll miss dinner,' he said eventually.

'We'll find something. It's London, somewhere will be open.'

'I booked a table.'

'Oh.' Her stomach clenched. 'Why did you do that?'

'I thought it might be busy, two days before Christmas. And I thought it might be nice, okay? Nice hotel? Nice dinner?' Voice rising again. 'No big agenda, Lily. I thought we'd hang out and chill this evening. Acclimatise before we head north and freeze.' He laughed. It was short and hollow, but at least he laughed.

'Yeah, chilling would be good.' She leaned back in her seat and managed a smile.

'Call me when you're close. I'll come meet you. It's Victoria, is it?'

'Yes. What will you do 'til then?'

'I expect I'll find a way to amuse myself.'

'You usually do.'

He paused again, probably gritting his teeth. 'Sometimes you leave me no choice, my lovely. Maybe I'll call my dad. See if he fancies a drink.'

He rang off.

Lily hid her cheek in her hand and leaned against the coach window, wrinkling her nose at the griminess of the glass. Empty threats. Ed wouldn't phone Laurence, not just because he was at least partly responsible for this thing, the great Christmas escape. No-one would ever say so, though. They'd blame Samantha. Admittedly she'd caught Ed off guard, but he had said the first thing that came into his head, giving no thought to the consequences or what it meant for Lily. It was a test, a straight-up choice – Ed over her job, Ed over her family. There was no other way to see it.

He must know he'd made things difficult for her. She could still picture the last time she'd seen him, framed in her bedroom doorway, black-suited and severe, as he left for London on Monday morning. He turned to look at her and she pulled the duvet up to her ears, hiding her face.

'See you Friday?'

4

Ed

The hotel was only about five miles from his Kentish Town flat. It'd seemed such a good idea. A way to restore some neutrality. It was Lily's sort of place – four-poster beds, log fires and heavy brocade, utterly different from the energy-efficient, minimalist places he usually booked. She'd like it. Or so he'd thought. A chance to escape the agonies of her day job, an invitation to sink into the cushions and close her eyes. *There!*

At this rate, she'd never see it because she was making every excuse not to get there. He could have stayed at home, feet up, toasting Christmas alone with anything vaguely drinkable remaining in the kitchen cupboard. Cup-a-soup, probably.

He padded across the deep pile carpet to peruse the contents of the minibar. Still an hour or so until his restaurant booking. He might as well keep it, even if he sat alone, looking like the guy who'd been dumped two days before Christmas and drinking the cover charge in gin. They'd sting him for the deposit anyway.

Waiting in this room was like a slow descent into hell. Everything had a gold fringe or a coordinating blue velvet cushion. Wherever he turned, fleurs-de-lys and tassels teased him with their frippery. He couldn't stay there, standing up and sitting down, checking his messages, clicking the television on and off as the plush closed in.

No way would he call his dad. What could he teach him about relationships?

Perhaps he should have stayed at work and headed to the pub with the rest of them. If he went back now, they'd laugh. *Late again? She avoiding you or something?* They knew what Lily was like. There'd be banter about which time zone she inhabited and then they'd make room for him and send him to the bar to stand the round they accused him of running out on, and he could smile and pretend to be looking forward to Christmas.

It didn't sound so bad and he wouldn't rule it out, but he needed some air first. A walk would also give him a chance to try out the new boots. He grabbed his coat and room key and made his way down the thick-carpeted corridor, testing the length of his stride. The boots looked ridiculous with his leather overcoat, but there were only so many concessions a man could make in one day.

The coat, swaying heavy and unbuttoned, was his trademark, as useful as it was distinctive. He never had to hunt for his keys or his phone. Everything he needed was already tucked deep into its pockets, inside and out. An

18

honest man wouldn't describe it as black anymore, but it held on to a faded gleam. He had spruced it up for this trip and tonight it smelt pleasantly of wax, rather than the old rhino Lily once complained of. It was a coat worth looking after, warm and waterproof. It never let him down.

He'd found it the summer he left school, rummaging for cheap suits at a fashion house fire sale. It was chucked casually over the end of a rail, the only one of its kind, too fine for the company it was in. When no-one else showed an interest, he ducked between the raised elbows of the hot and bothered bargain hunters and took it to a quiet corner to examine, sliding his fingers over the careful overstitching and silk-satin lining, which had needed replacing every few years. The coat cost him a month's rent, but he didn't think twice. It was the only thing in his life – apart from his relationship with Lily – that he'd decided on instantly and never had doubts about.

When Martin saw the coat, he drooled with pleasure, dragging it off his nephew's back to try it on.

'I had one like this,' he said. 'In the '80s. But not quite as nice. Mine was so heavy I needed shoulders like an ox to carry it off. I used to stride about like "I" in '*Withnail*.'

Ed couldn't imagine his skinny, bespectacled uncle ever having ox-like shoulders. He needed help to open a jar of olives. Neither did Ed have any idea who or what 'Withnail' or 'I' were and wasn't interested enough to ask. Months later he came across a DVD in his uni flat-share and watched it over and over with grisly fascination. He even summoned Kit to join him for the weekend and confirm the movie hadn't secretly been filmed in his father's kitchen – a place where pots and pans built up like abstract sculpture and the ivy growing up the red bricks at the back pushed its tendrils through the cracks between the windows and their frames. The chaotic male landscape of the film had too many parallels with his own life for comfort – though happily, his own uncle, Martin, was a benign influence.

Putting a mirror up to his own world was instructive, if painful. Ed made up his mind. He'd never let things slide like that.

5

Lily

19.10

A message flashed onto Lily's phone.

Did you make it?

She replied before she thought better of it.

Missed it. Won't get into London until late

The response was instant.

Still time to change your mind

Her fingers hovered over the keypad. She couldn't give the idea space to grow.

Don't. I'll see you next week x

This was absolutely the last message she'd send him. She tucked her phone back into her pocket and nestled her head against her coat, closing her eyes.

It took her a while to realise that the bus had stopped moving and was sitting by the roadside.

6

Ed

September 2012

Anisia was planning a party for Kit. It was to be a surprise. And not only for his brother. Ed had also been taken aback. Kit hadn't been seeing Anisia very long, but how naturally she'd slotted herself into his life. Sunday brunch with the family, Tampax in the bathroom, a cleaning rota in the kitchen. Few girls had got this far before. His younger brother must finally be growing up. It got Ed thinking. He was so used to keeping an eye on Kit and it being just the two of them, but it was looking more and more as if there was someone else ready to do a better job of it.

Ed quickly recognised there was little in the world Anisia would ever require his help to do. Like Kit, Anisia was training to be a doctor but, unlike him, she was scarily competent, the sort of person who completed her 'to do' list each day and still had time for half of Kit's.

Now, though, she was after a favour. She needed a venue.

'Yeah, sure, use the flat,' said Ed. 'We've had some pretty good nights here. The neighbours are chilled and not much is breakable and what is, doesn't matter too much.'

'That's not it, and it won't be like that,' said Anisia, bundling him into the kitchen alcove off the sitting room and running the taps so they wouldn't be overheard. 'If it's here, Kit's less likely to suspect anything.'

'Honestly, you don't need to work that hard to keep a secret from Kit. He doesn't notice much. Even if you told him, he probably wouldn't remember.'

Anisia shook her head. 'You're wrong about Kit. He's got real emotional intelligence. He's so intuitive, it's almost scary. It's going to be difficult to hide this.'

Ed didn't want to upset her. He decided not to tell her about the hour Kit spent the previous evening pontificating about Jaffa Cakes. *They're clearly biscuits. They want to be biscuits,* he said, insisting on proving his theory with the dunk test. It took a whole packet. Ed declared the results inconclusive. It wasn't a proper comparison when dunking cake wasn't a thing. You didn't see old ladies in tea rooms dipping chunks of lemon drizzle in their Earl Grey. You might as well say a fish finger was a biscuit because you could dip it in tea. Kit was dismissive. What did Ed know about what old ladies did in tea rooms when he only drank coffee out of insulated mugs? According to Kit, it was the temperature of the tea which was the problem variable. He needed to do the whole experiment again with a different type of biscuit. Then he'd be sure.

Anisia asked two things of Ed – to give her free access to the flat and make sure the bathroom was clean. He did both, helpfully hoovering the carpet as well, and then threw himself into preparing for the party, as he did for every house party. He bought beer and a couple of bottles of good vodka and donned his Hawaiian shirt. Even if Anisia only invited him because she had to, he'd earn his passage. He'd also be one of the few people there able to recognise his brother in time to yell, 'Surprise!'

And Kit was bound to be surprised, not least because he'd know hardly anyone there. Anisia had invited about three of his friends, the only ones she knew – as he'd been keeping her under wraps – and all of hers.

Anisia brought her own tableware in jewel-coloured plastic. She wasn't happy with the random selection of cut glass and crystal the flat offered, odds and ends collected by Martin over the years. They didn't match, she complained. Ed thought that was sort of the point. She bustled around clearing surfaces and positioning bowls of snacks on the coffee table – Art Deco and broken before it ever arrived in the flat.

'What's that?' she asked.

'It's beer,' he said, nudging her dip selection to the side to make room for a bucket of ice on the sideboard.

'No, not that, though we won't need beer, we've got cocktails. That! Where's your black T-shirt? You always wear black.'

'It's a party, not a funeral. This is my bowling club shirt.'

She tutted and then squealed as the intercom buzzed.

'Get the door,' she said, and dived into Kit's room to change.

'Oh, didn't you get the message?' Ed asked two girls in short, tight dresses. 'It's Hawaiian-themed.'

'It is not,' said Anisia, pushing him out of the way and ushering the guests into the flat.

'You look nice, though,' he said, flattening himself to the wall as she swept past in something bright and shiny.

She blessed him with a smile, flicking her long hair over her shoulder.

'Find out where Kit is,' she ordered. 'Think of something that will keep him out of the way for twenty minutes.'

Ed messaged his brother.

Hey, you on your way home?

Yeh. Unless you want to go out?

Nah, I'm beat and got an early start. Where's Anisia?

Night shift

Pick up some beer then. I'll see if the guys wanna come over

He winked at Anisia and gave her a thumbs-up. She frowned in reply.

Someone missed the surprise. By the time they rang the bell, the party was in full swing and only Ed was free to answer the door. He was impressed anyone had the audacity to arrive late. Anisia's event may have had no dress code, although she'd set strict rules on alcohol and heels on the parquet, but the instructions on arrival time had been quite clear.

'Hello,' said the newcomer, caught in the act of rearranging her hair – just past her shoulders and dead straight, so dark it was almost black. 'I'm guessing you're Kit's brother. You look like him.'

'I'm guessing you're... not Anisia's sister. You're nothing like her.'

Ed was already having second thoughts about his shirt. He dragged his eyes from the girl and settled on the bicycle she'd managed to haul up the stairs and was holding in front of her.

'That's particularly generous and you really shouldn't have.'

'I didn't know where to leave it. I must've left the lock at salsa class.'

'You can lock it up with mine,' he suggested, grabbing his keys from the coat hanging by the door and pointing her back down the stairs.

He hadn't bargained on Anisia having nice friends. He thought they'd all be like her, pretty but hard to keep up with. He offered to take the bike from her.

'I can manage,' she said. 'It's really light.'

'Carbon?'

'Mostly.'

'How d'you like the Shimano on that?'

She had huge brown eyes and he was talking to her about groupsets. He shook his head at himself.

As they stood outside under a security light, looping the bikes together, Ed was jumped by two men and almost wrestled to the ground. The girl stepped back in alarm.

'It's okay,' he gasped.

It was only Tom and Bob. The Hawaiian shirts flapping over their T-shirts gave them away.

'Oh, was there a theme?' asked the girl, moving to the side to avoid the men bouncing around the pavement. She unzipped her backpack and started rummaging. 'I didn't realise. I might have some silk flowers in here. Maybe I can make a lei.'

'No, no theme,' explained Ed, a little breathless as he freed himself from his friends' beery embrace and wondered how she'd missed all the Facebook party chatter. 'Just the shirt of choice for the bowling club.'

For some reason he was keen to get her back upstairs without further delay.

26

'Who's this, Ed?' leered one of his friends as the girl stuffed bits of clothing and a string of LED lights back into her bag.

'Good question.' Why hadn't he asked her yet? 'Who are you?'

'I'm Lily.'

She wriggled a little as she smoothed down her short black dress. She held out her hand.

'She's Lily,' explained Ed, smiling as he clasped her palm. 'I'm Ed. How d'you do?'

His friends pulled it together enough to introduce themselves.

'Come on,' said Ed, shoving Tom towards the front door. He knew that look; he'd seen it before. This girl deserved better than that.

'Yeeaah!' shouted Kit when his friends appeared. 'Wait a sec. Lemme get my shirt.'

He rushed into his bedroom and appeared a minute later, buttoning a crumpled pineapple-patterned shirt. The jumping and hugging started all over again.

'She did all right, your Anisia. She got four of us here, that's not half bad,' said Ed, clinking his beer bottle against his brother's.

Kit still looked stunned, his grin fixed as if someone had pushed it into place on his face.

'Four of who?' asked Lily.

She was back at Ed's elbow. He pretended he hadn't been watching her every move; the way she smiled at everyone, the way she praised Anisia's party staging and the candles in the grate. How she was drinking beer from the bottle Tom had handed to her.

'The bowling club,' he said. 'There's eight of us, though it's difficult to get together nowadays. Everyone's scattered.'

'One's in Brazil,' explained Kit.

'And Rory's all the way up in Manchester,' added Ed.

'True,' said Kit, raising his bottle in acknowledgement. 'I'm Kit, by the way.'

'I know. We've met. I'm Lily.'

'Have we? Sorry.' He put on his thinking face. 'Oh yeah, best friend from uni. You were at Bristol with Anisia.'

'Oh?' said Ed, widening his eyes and miming edging away from Lily.

He wondered at Kit. His brother could be useless, but he must be seriously into Anisia to have forgotten meeting this girl – unless he was playing dumb on purpose. He wouldn't put it past him.

'Don't judge me,' said Lily, laughing. 'Anisia tells everyone off. She's always been like that, but she has a heart of gold, believe me.' She turned to Ed. 'So, how often d'you go bowling?'

'Bowling? Never. We play football occasionally.'

'And darts, now and again,' added Kit.

Lily screwed up her face.

'It's our festival uniform,' Tom explained, rushing to help out. He hadn't taken his eyes off her either. 'And when we went travelling. All in the same shirts, like a bowling team.'

'Yeah, I know, totally lame,' said Kit, 'but it was funny when we were eighteen.'

'So… salsa class, Lily?' asked Ed. He was losing the edge.

'What about it?'

'When d'you do that?'

'Today. Sunday afternoons. We have a class and then they open the club to all-comers. And we dance.'

'And you do that every Sunday?'

'I do the class. I don't always stay to dance. Depends if there's something better going on.'

Ed looked around the flat at the small groups of people, chatting as they sipped their drinks and nibbled cake. The music was Sunday evening low.

'And this was your "something better going on"?'

She lifted her chin when she laughed. It was having a strange effect on him.

'Do you dance, Ed?'

'Not in any recognised capacity.'

She met his eyes briefly.

'But I'm always up for trying,' he said carefully.

If this lovely girl really was one of Anisia's friends, his best hope of getting to know her was away from the flat and somewhere Anisia couldn't put her off.

'She may never forgive me but come on. It's not far, just Camden. We can get the tube.'

'Maybe I should change,' said Ed, pausing in the act of lifting his coat from the hook as he remembered the green and orange shirt.

'You're good as you are. You'll fit right in.'

Was a place where a Hawaiian shirt would blend in really his thing? Not necessarily. But for Lily, he'd take the chance.

7

Lily

September 2012

The man who answered the door wasn't in black, as Anisia had promised. Nor was he weird – though Lily could see why her friend might think so. He didn't fit the mould. His shirt was truly horrible, the sort you'd pick up at a music festival and only then if you were very drunk. You wouldn't wear it again, unless you were decorating or all your other clothes were at the launderette. When he lifted a hand covered in silver rings and leather bracelets to sweep his hair out of his eyes, she saw that the sides were clipped short and only the top was long. He needed more gel to hold it in place. She empathised. The guy was, however, unmistakeably Kit's brother. Same colouring and expression, but slighter and more thoughtful-looking.

She probably had a product to sort out the hair, but she wouldn't check in her bag yet. He might take it the wrong way and she needed to get into this party, if only to show Anisia she'd kept her word.

Lily had met Kit a couple of times. He wasn't Lily's type, but Anisia was so into him and they were a good match. His cheerful dopiness took the edge off her sharp perfectionism. It seemed someone had finally convinced her that it was possible to live without planning for every unforeseen circumstance.

One of Ed's friends handed Lily a drink and she raised it to her mouth, using the moment to get her bearings. The flat was strange, like somewhere a time traveller would rest up when taking a break between dimensions. Leather bound books and candelabras, binoculars hanging on a hook on the wall, a shelf stacked with straw hats by the front door. It would make a great stage set.

She took another sip of her beer and checked out the other guests. She didn't know as many as she'd expected but give Anisia her due, she'd put together an impressive-looking gathering. The room was full of well-turned-out, hard-working professionals, nagged into their party clothes and too scared to misbehave. The only ones who appeared unconcerned were Ed and his friends. What did it say about her that faced with a group that could have been put together by an elite dating app, she preferred to hang out with the lads wearing the scruffy, patterned shirts? Anisia would sigh and tell her she didn't know a good thing when she saw it. She was pretty sure she did though, and it was the guy joking with her as he balanced a tray of drinks at shoulder height on the tips of one long-fingered hand.

It was how Ed behaved around Anisia that made her laugh, the way he treated her with utmost care and consideration while she responded with thinly veiled suspicion. He didn't seem bothered; it was part of the fun. Even so, he kept his friends in check, shutting them down when they complained the chocolate brownies were just cake.

'Eat them,' he insisted. 'It might be a girl thing, actual cake at a party, I don't know. What d'you think, Lily? Do you bake?'

'Where are the beer glasses?' asked the one called Tom, opening cupboards in a kitchen so modern, there were no handles or visible appliances. It was utterly at odds with the rest of the place, as if a doorway had been knocked through to a different flat entirely. Lily stared at it as if it was an observation test. Where did you turn the oven on?

'Why d'you need beer when you have cocktails?' said Ed, answering Tom and pointing at the selection of spirits and liqueurs, each one a different rainbow colour. He inhaled sharply, as if about to face an endurance test.

'Can I have beer later?' Tom asked, sniffing at a bottle of mandarin gin.

'If you're good,' said Ed.

'And if I'm not?'

'I'll call your mum and tell her to come and collect you.'

'She'll be delighted to hear from you. She's always asking after you.'

Tom helped himself to a beer and offered another to Lily while Ed dutifully sipped at something in a red-stemmed plastic glass with sugar round the rim, clearing his throat after each mouthful.

Lily took a cocktail from the tray. She would do right by Anisia, and not only so Ed would notice. She circulated, pursued at a gentle distance by Tom, chatting to the old friends she knew and Kit's junior doctor friends whom she didn't. Each time she gravitated back to Ed, he smiled and found something to say to her, a question about her work or an offer of a drink. She watched as without making it obvious, he inserted himself between her and Tom, a move in a game he'd already won, even if he didn't yet know it. It saved her having to rescue herself.

It was easy to entice him away. She had no plan, but he didn't seem to mind. That was almost the thing she liked best about him.

8

Ed

September 2012

Ed scanned the room, taking in the black walls and floor and the red-shaded table lights in the booths around the edges. A DJ, hidden behind a rostrum at the far end, introduced each new track noisily but invisibly. The female ratio in the club was in his favour, which was good (though he mustn't let Lily see he thought so) and there were as many people jostling at the bar as on the dance floor, which was better. He waited while Lily dropped their belongings in the cloakroom and checked out the competition. The standard of dancing varied from the clearly proficient to the flailing around. Dubious-looking men, the sort Ed wouldn't trust with his sister (not that he had one), were taking advantage of the situation to grasp their partners too tightly.

'I'll need a drink,' he said, when Lily returned.

'Mojito?' she suggested. 'You get a free drink with your

entry. It's probably more soda than rum, though.'

Please, no. No more cocktails.

'I'll stick to beer,' he said. 'I'll get them.' He darted towards the bar and joined the longest queue.

'Don't you want to dance?'

'Yeah, course,' he said, not managing even to convince himself.

Her smile had faded a little. She probably got this all the time. He wouldn't be the one to disappoint.

'Okay, okay, but you might have to remind me which foot goes first. It's been a while.'

'But you've done this before?'

'Only in Cuba.'

Lily raised her eyebrows. Her eyes were so huge, it was off-putting. 'In Cuba, is it?' She tugged him out of the queue and took his hands in hers. 'And were you wearing that shirt by any chance?'

Ed thought for a moment as he shifted his feet into gear. 'Very possible, now you mention it, Lily. Very possible.'

She slowed, dumbing down her act for him, which was kind, if not exactly complimentary. He glanced down to check on his feet and she lifted his chin with a soft fingertip. Just where was he supposed to look? He focussed on a spot to the left of her cheekbone so she didn't catch him gazing at her face. As he turned and caught her again, he sneaked a quick peak and was relieved to see she was smiling. He must be grinning like an idiot.

'Put your hand here,' said Lily, mouth close to his ear as she moved his hand to her lower back and placed her hand on his shoulder. 'It's easier that way.'

As a rule, Ed liked dancing – in tight-packed, laser-lit clubs with drunk friends. This was different. There were spotlights and space, no shoving or jostling. No anonymity. He could sense the eyes on him. It helped that he had to concentrate on what he was doing but not that he could feel Lily's vertebrae moving under his fingers as she swivelled her hips or that her hair flicked out and tickled his cheek each time she spun past him.

Just as he was starting to relax and enjoy himself, two women came over and demanded to cut in.

'Sorry,' said Lily.

He thought she was apologising to them, but he was wrong.

'They're in my class,' she said, moving aside, offering him up as a partner with no resistance.

Any technique he'd picked up evaporated instantly. He hated it, but how could he refuse without risking wrecking the mood?

'You should come to the class,' said the first one in what sounded like a Polish accent.

Ed grunted. He would rather stick pins in his eyes.

'Lily is a great teacher,' she continued.

'Sorry about that,' said Lily, reclaiming him when each had taken a turn. 'You didn't mind, did you? There's a shortage of men who can dance. And who actually want to dance.'

Ed tried a bit harder and held her closer, casting a last look at the bar before abandoning the idea. He'd have to forego another drink unless he wanted someone else getting in the way.

'You didn't tell me you teach the class.'

'Would it have put you off?'

It would, but he shook his head. 'I might have watched a couple of YouTube videos as a refresher first.'

'I'm only the substitute teacher. I'm filling in for my friend.'

'Where's she?'

'He. Adam. He's rehearsing for a show. He'll be back when the run ends or he needs the money, whichever happens first.'

'I see.'

Her turn to shake her head. 'I've known him for years. We live together, I mean, we share a house. He isn't going to give up a gig lightly.'

When the DJ changed the rhythms and went back to his club night mixes, Ed got to show Lily some of his own moves. She seemed to like that, laughing and matching him beat for beat, but now it was getting late and he was sweating through his party shirt. Surely, he'd done enough to pass the test?

'Lily, I hate to play grandad, but I've got to be at work early. I should probably head off.'

'Oh yeah, the architect. I remember.'

'Architectural assistant,' he said, flattered that she knew that much about him. 'Still training. Which way are you going?' he asked, feeling that he ought to see her home.

'Stoke Newington. It's not too far from here, I can cycle,' she said, pointing him in the direction of the cloakroom.

Her hand flew to her mouth. 'Oh no I can't, I left my bike at yours.'

He wondered whether this was something she did often, leaving her things here and there. Was she marking her territory or leaving clues for anyone following?

'You can pick it up tomorrow if it's easier,' he said as they gathered their coats.

And perhaps they could squeeze in a drink – or a coffee – or something? Or if not then, maybe lunchtime? Or after work?

'Yeah, okay,' she said, perching on the edge of a chair as she laced her trainers and stuffed her dance shoes into her rucksack. 'Oh...' Her hand flew to her head this time. 'I've got visits tomorrow afternoon for work. It's going to be a pain without my bike. Can I come and get it now?'

'Of course. We can still get a tube.'

They walked a hundred metres down the road before he remembered she'd left her bike lock behind again. He jogged back to collect it.

The tube journey was too short to settle into a proper conversation and almost before he realised, they were at Kentish Town and exiting the station. He was the one slowing now, matching his pace to hers. She seemed in no hurry and wandered along as he told her about his plans to design and build his own house. From the bare ground up. He usually kept it to himself, but her assumption that he became an architect because he had some sort of fascination with preserving derelict buildings forced it out of him. She'd seen the flat, with its chandeliers, marble fireplaces and wooden window shutters, and drew conclusions. But that wasn't him; he wanted to create something new, not patch up the past. He was obliged to defend himself.

He unlocked her bike, holding it as she zipped herself into her fluorescent jacket. What would she do if he kissed her? ... too soon?

'Ed, I couldn't use your loo, could I?'

She'd done it again, knocked him off his stride. With a flick of the D-lock, he relocked the bike. He made it to the entrance before her and leapt up the stairs, heart growing heavier with each step. The bathroom wouldn't be in anywhere near the pristine state it had been in when he handed control of the flat to Anisia. Girls cared about things like that, in his experience. Anisia certainly did.

The soft music and loud voices were audible as he opened the door to the flat, but only the members of the bowling club remained, lounging on the sofa, drinking beer and chatting to two girls.

'Mate! Hey, where you been?'

'Dancing,' he said. 'You remember Lily?'

They started laughing and Ed joined in.

'You gotta try, I guess,' said Tom.

Bob looked at Lily and put his bottle down. 'We'll leave you to it,' he said.

The men helped the girls find their shoes and bags, and took their leave, with many hugs and 'love you, man's.

'Where's Kit?' asked Ed, suddenly aware there was no-one else in the flat.

'He left a while back, with Anisia,' said Tom. He flicked his eyes towards Lily and dipped his chin, a nod of respect, which Ed ignored.

'He left? What'd he do this time?'

Tom laughed again as he clattered down the stairs. 'Anisia had to go to work. She told so many people she was working, the hospital believed it and called her in. Kit went too. Think he felt bad carrying on without her.'

Ed stood in the entrance hall, surveying the debris of paper plates and cake, half-full glasses and bottles covering every surface, and felt cheated. It wasn't Anisia's fault. In fact, if you were having a medical emergency, you'd be mighty relieved if it was Anisia that showed up. Your chances of recovery would definitely improve. He looked at Lily, still pretty in her reflective jacket, black hair sticking out from under her cycle helmet. It was only his chances that had taken a dive.

He sighed and slid out of his damp Hawaiian shirt, screwing it up and tossing it across to the sofa.

'I didn't anticipate this,' he said, striding to the kitchen alcove and hoping there'd be dustbin bags under the sink.

'What did you think would happen?' asked Lily.

It didn't sound like banter. More like curiosity.

Ed found a crumpled black bag and sniffed inside, uncertain of its origins. It would do. He looked up from where he was squatting beside the cupboard.

'Well, I thought I might get your number, maybe even a goodnight kiss, and then congratulate Anisia for her delightful party.'

'Two out of three isn't bad.' She held out her hand.

He gave her the bag.

She laughed. 'I was giving you a hand up.'

'Sorry,' he said, snatching the bag back. 'I'll do it later.'

'I'll help you.' She unclipped her cycle helmet and handed it to Ed while she unzipped her jacket again. 'You do glasses, I'll do cake.'

Then, with a dustbin bag in one hand and a cycle helmet in the other, Ed kissed her for the first time. It made sense, he'd had his arms around her for most of the evening, and it brightened the prospect of clearing up hugely. He also got his first chance to examine her face in the light, its width across the cheekbones, smiling mouth, even white teeth. He smiled back at her.

'Let's leave it.'

'Come on, it won't take long. We owe it to Anisia. She'll be devastated to have left the place like this. She'll never live it down. Where's your hoover?'

Ed apologised to the tired old machine as he dragged it from the cupboard in the hall again. It would be the second time that day that Martin's ancient Persian rug had been cleaned. Neither might cope with the attention. When Lily had dealt with the carpet, she turned her attention to picking icing out of the sofa. She was impressively industrious. Ed occupied himself wiping down all the surfaces.

'You can always stay if you don't fancy the cycle back,' he said.

It was almost 2.00am and he felt bad turning her out into the dark, especially as she'd done such a good job of the flat.

'I mean, you can have my bed, I'll crash on the sofa.'

'I don't want to put you out. I'll take the sofa,' she said.

Ed's pulse quickened at the idea she wasn't leaving. He hoped it didn't show. He glanced towards his brother's door. Kit probably wouldn't be back.

'I'll use Kit's bed. I wouldn't offer it to a guest, though.'

He gave Lily a T-shirt to sleep in (black, no visible logos) and offered her his toothbrush (with due health warnings and hoping she didn't take him up on it), and then shut himself in his brother's room. He shoved the mess of paper, clothes and birthday gifts on the bed to one side to clear space to lie down. He felt exhausted but strangely exhilarated, too wired to sleep. It was dark enough, even with the open curtains, but it might as well have been daylight, he was so alert. He rifled through Kit's clutter, hoping for a book to distract him, and found a game of beer pong. He wedged a paper cup between his feet and started flicking balls towards it, but his aim was off and the balls clattered to the floor and pinged around the parquet.

What was he waiting for? Obviously, Anisia would yell at him and it might screw things up for Kit, which would not

41

be at all good. And he'd learned to be more cautious as he reached the second half of his twenties and avoided tangling with anyone he didn't really like. On the plus side, he was pretty certain he was going to really like Lily, but unless she turned tail and fled, she'd still be there in the morning. In which case… what was the rush?

There was a crash from the sitting room. He charged out in his own black T-shirt and shorts to find Lily in the near dark, fumbling on her hands and knees.

'What happened? Are you okay?'

He ran a hand through his hair. To end the night with a half-naked Lily being tended to by Anisia in A&E would also be disastrous.

'Sorry, I was trying to find my bag. I need my eye drops, but I've knocked something over.'

'You're allowed to use the lights, you know.'

'Couldn't find the switch. What have I broken?'

He started picking things off the floor.

'It's only Kit's chess set. It won't break, it's quartz or something. You might have lost his place, though. He's been playing the same match for the last five years.'

She joined him on the parquet, scooping up the stone figures.

'Online against a Kung-Fu master?'

Ed grinned.

'You can't fool me. I know Kit doesn't have time to play chess.'

'You're right. And it's a stupid place to leave it.'

He put the board back on the side table and piled the pieces on top.

'You look different without your glasses,' said Lily, kneeling beside him.

'So do you. You're a bit blurry.'

'That's how I feel.'

'Go to bed then,' he said, touching her arm. He so wanted to kiss her. 'It's late.'

She didn't move.

'Lily, we've got to be smart about this. There'll be consequences.'

'What do you suggest then?'

'Cup of tea? Cold shower?'

He couldn't believe he was hesitating. It must be those eyes. Could she see what she was doing to him?

'What about a hot bath? I wouldn't mind a bath, I'm really sticky. And don't worry about Anisia,' she said, climbing into his arms. 'I'm in it too if she finds out.'

'Oh, it's the risk, is it?' he asked, realising suddenly that an essential quality in a prospective girlfriend was someone unintimidated by Anisia.

His hands knew the shape of her already, where her ribs ended and her hips began, the curve of her spine. She didn't feel like the stranger she was.

He lifted her up and carried her to the sofa – as far as he dared go without counting the chess pieces to make sure there wasn't another one waiting to stab him in the foot. The sofa wasn't ideal; it was all deep cushions and awkward angles, but Lily said she was fine.

'No more dilly-dallying?' he asked.

'Please, no,' she said.

He thought they'd done a good job of cleaning up the flat, but when he went to run Lily her bath, there were still crisp crumbs sticking to the balls of his feet.

He climbed into the tub and wrapped his arms around her as she folded herself in against his chest.

'So, this flatmate of yours,' he said.

'Which one?'

'How many are there?'

'Four. One's a girl.'

He felt better. 'Are they all dancers?'

'More or less. Acrobats, gymnasts, all-round performers. When they're not at the gym, the house is full of semi-naked men practising routines or waxing their chests.'

He was glad he'd wound a towel round his waist when he went back to fetch her for the bath. He glanced surreptitiously at his own chest and flexed his shoulders, grateful for the dim light.

'I've known two of them since school,' she continued. 'Adam and Menassi took me in when I came back from university. Actually, they begged me to move in, as they needed help with the rent. That's why they work me so hard. Gotta pay the bills.'

He turned her round to face him. 'You're telling me they force you out to teach salsa?'

'That's not the worst of it.'

He tensed – he'd seen the customers in the club – but she was smiling.

'They have this performing arts company. They provide entertainers for events – stilt-walkers, living statues, that sort of thing – and sometimes, they're short-staffed and they make me fill in.'

'How often are they short-staffed?'

'Pretty much every week. Basically, all the time.'

'What do they make you do?'

44

'Juggling sometimes, but mostly I have to do living hedge.'

Ed sat up straighter in the bath. 'Living hedge?'

'Yeah, you know, dress up in fake privet. It's difficult to explain. It depends what we've been booked to do. Stand still or leap out at people, or just dance around decorated like a Christmas tree.'

'The fairy lights!' He laughed and kissed her. 'Have you got the costume with you? I'd love to see that. Or maybe just the lights.'

She sat up straight. 'Ed, I don't mind helping them out, but it's not what I planned to do with my life.'

He touched her shoulder. Offending her was the last thing he wanted. 'Sorry, I'm not laughing. Well, I am, but not like that. What do you want to do, then?'

'I want to make a difference.'

'Entertainers make a difference.'

'Only temporarily. I want to make a difference long-term.'

'You've made a difference to me already.'

He shouldn't have said that. The water she splashed at him was now cold. He helped her out of the tub and back into his bed. He was glad he'd made the effort to tidy up before Anisia came round; tidied in the sense of opening the heavy wardrobe doors and shoving everything inside.

'That's better. Your sofa still smells of beer and cake,' said Lily as she rearranged herself around him.

'It always smells of beer. It's the cake that's new.'

Lily, on the other hand, smelled warm and lovely, and it was only slightly disconcerting that, as he'd tipped in a generous quantity of his brother's Noir Extreme when he ran the bath, she now smelled quite like Kit.

Ed didn't think he slept at all, but he must have dozed off because he was woken by his alarm. Lily was sleeping and barely stirred as he carefully separated himself and wriggled out from under the duvet, one limb at a time.

He showered and dressed and leaned over his bed. 'Lily, I've got to go.'

'Ah, okay,' she said, shaking herself awake. 'I'll get my stuff.'

'No, it's fine. Stay as long as you want.'

'Oh, good.' She settled back down again and closed her eyes. 'Don't leave, stay a bit longer.'

'I've got to be on site by 7.30. I can't be late. What time do you need to be at work?'

'Ten, but I'll have to go home first.' She snuggled in a bit deeper.

'Here, put your number in my phone and missed call yourself. Then you'll know who you're avoiding.'

'I won't be avoiding you,' she said, handing the phone back.

It was a good feeling.

'Help yourself to whatever you can find. Leave the bike lock on the rack. My code's 2787.'

'My date of birth,' she said.

'Is it?'

'Almost. Seventh of February.'

'Must be a sign,' he said, hand to his heart in his best girlfriend impression.

'Is it weird to high-five you?' she asked, offering up her palm.

He grabbed her hand and hung on to it. 'Best party ever,' he said, kissing her three or four times before tearing himself away.

9

Lily

September 2012

Someone in the house was singing – with the sort of fully committed but patchy tuning that said he thought he was alone. Lily opened the front door and winced as the top notes were missed again. If she was fast, she could be in and out before the culprit noticed. She raced up to her room and plundered the pile of clothes on her bed for combat trousers and waterproofs.

It would not do at all if the first of the volunteers turned up for their day of community engagement, regenerating green space in East Ham, before she did. It was the sort of fluid arrangement which wouldn't get off the ground unless the facilitator arrived early to marshal the crew and hand out yellow vests with a winning smile. Why did she do this to herself? She should have left when Ed did. He would probably have lent her a T-shirt to pull over her leggings – if she'd asked him. Was it too soon to ask? It would have given her an excuse to go back. If she needed an excuse.

She ran back down the stairs.

Menassi was standing at the bottom, in joggers and bare feet. He couldn't have been up long. His curly dark hair was squashed flat to one side of his head. He had a teapot in one hand. Her teapot.

'I thought I heard you. Where d'you get to last night?'

'Anisia's thing,' she said, avoiding eye contact as she attempted to brush past him. 'I messaged you. You making tea?'

'Yeah, borrowing some, sorry. Couldn't face coffee this morning.'

'It's fine,' she said, ignoring his cue. She rummaged in her bag for her travel cup. 'As long as you put some in there.'

'Good night?' he asked, pushing back against her attempts to hurry him into the kitchen.

'Hmm,' she said, stomach full of butterflies. What did that mean?

Menassi nudged her with his elbow.

'Gotta go. Absolutely cannot be late,' she said, grabbing her empty cup back and heading for the door.

10

Ed

October 2012

Lily swept into the cinema. Her jeans and trainers were spattered with paint, and she leaned to the side under the weight of a huge bag for life.

'Finally,' she said, dropping the bag and giving Ed a quick hug.

He was relieved too. He'd begun to think she was giving him the brush-off. How many times could a date be rescheduled before the smart thing was to back away and move on? Ten days had never felt so long.

He kissed her cheek. 'How've you been?'

'Can you hang on to this for a sec?'

Lily nudged the bag in his direction and was gone again, running to the bathroom with her rucksack. Ed took his phone slowly from his pocket and scrolled through messages he'd read already, giving all his attention to appearing unconcerned by her sudden departure. He needn't have worried. She reappeared in minutes in a short dress and ballet pumps, smiling and wafting a cloud of something citrussy.

'Wow,' he said, impressed not only by the speed of her change but by just how much stuff she must carry in her bag.

'Yeah,' she said. 'I wiped away some of the grime.'

'No need on my account,' he said. 'Paint and grime are my kind of thing. You look great, though. I mean, you did before... as well.'

He lifted the bag, which seemed to be full of forms and clipboards. 'Work?'

'Yeah, I can't leave it on the bike,' said Lily as they made their way into the darkened auditorium. 'It contains the personal details of forty-five people.'

They wedged the plastic bag into the space between their knees.

'Are you hiring for a show?' Ed asked.

'What? No, this is for the volunteer databank,' she explained in a whisper. 'Skills and availability.'

'I thought you were a dancer.'

'Only evenings and weekends. This is my real job. The community in Newham doesn't want to lose the momentum generated by the Olympics and so they're harnessing support for a range of community initiatives.'

'What sort of initiatives?' he murmured back, keeping one eye on the advertisements. He'd heard the film had an explosive start.

'Well, that's why this project's so good. It's less about what they do than engaging the community. They see what people are interested in and then help them organise themselves to do it. There's been huge investment in infrastructure and now they want to make sure people use it.'

'Clever. I suppose it cuts crime and so on.'

'Exactly,' said Lily, patting his arm with approval.

It all sounded a bit fluffy to Ed. He wasn't sure that would-be burglars could be redirected into renovating community gardens – not unless their sentences required it and there were penalties if they didn't turn up.

'So how did you get into that?'

'I did a bit of volunteering at uni and then a couple of internships with volunteer programmes before I got this job as a community organiser. I've been there about a year now.'

She carried on whispering as the pre-credit sequence of the film started to roll.

'The idea is it builds communities. People meet their neighbours and get to hear about things that are going on. It grows use of other services, green spaces, libraries, leisure centres. It'll only pick up a percentage of new people – the others would get involved anyway. It's always the same people who are active. My stepdad calls it obsessive compulsive volunteering syndrome. He thinks I'm a prime example of it.'

It was something Ed had never considered before. He'd always assumed volunteering was something people did randomly, replying to a message on Twitter or Gumtree and turning up to lend a hand, collecting jumble or sweeping up after a flood. According to Lily, there was usually a plan and often a volunteer coordinator, recruited to manage the process and channel goodwill into the project in the form of money, manpower and publicity.

'D'you have to wear dungarees and smile a lot?' he asked in an undertone.

'Sometimes, mainly if I'm working with students. Then I put rags in my hair and spend the day eating hummus while we work out how to organise the furniture swap-shop when the only transport they have is bicycles and skateboards and it would be much better if they did a clothes swap. But the point is they get to that place by themselves. We just facilitate it.'

'Yes,' he said, taking hold of her hand and hoping she'd get the message. He didn't want to shush her, not on their first real date.

'Did you always want to be an architect?'

'I'll tell you later,' he mouthed.

In fact, he'd only decided on architecture when he was in the sixth form at school and had to fill in some university application forms.

'Don't forget.'

Ed leaned in close. 'Lily, d'you want to watch the film?'

'Yes,' she said, taken aback. 'Of course. But I want to get to know you too.'

'Who's in it?'

'What?'

'The film. Who's in it?'

'Isn't it…? I can't remember which one we chose in the end.'

He grabbed the bag with his free hand. 'Let's go.'

'We can't go now.'

The couple in front turned around to glare at them.

'Come on,' urged Ed, tugging Lily behind him as they edged their way past the knees of the other moviegoers, less irritated by their bumbling exit, he guessed, than they would be if they stayed.

'Where are we going?' asked Lily when they burst into the foyer.

'I don't know. Someplace else. Anywhere.'

'What about the film?' she asked.

'We'll go another time. Have you eaten?'

She shook her head.

'Let's find somewhere quiet and I'll tell you about my long journey into design, which will take about two seconds, and then you can explain to me the difference between a service user and a beneficiary. And over pudding, I need to hear more about the fire eating.'

And then hopefully she'd come back to the flat with him, although if she'd rather do something different, he'd be up for that too. First, though, he was going to kiss her.

11

Ed

20.00

Wherever Ed looked, there were throngs of people in tinsel and Christmas hats pressed into pubs and restaurants. Usually, he'd be with them, starting the festivities crammed inside a sweaty bar or spilling over the pavement into the road, raising a glass to the holiday and shouting to be heard above the hubbub of drunken voices. At some point, he'd join them; he'd need to fortify himself for Lily's arrival and what must now be inevitable.

Loud shrieks caught his attention. He looked up to find he'd passed Hyde Park Corner and was halfway along Park Lane. The lights of Winter Wonderland were to his left, the jumbled rumble of rides and music and cheerful screams competing with the traffic noise. An hour ago he'd craved lights and company, but he was no longer tempted. There was enough confusion inside his head already.

What had happened at the weekend? It made no sense. Lily was cold, and she was never cold. He could have told her he loved her, probably should have told her, but at that moment, he couldn't. He was paralysed. She'd accused him of horrible things, of using her. He was scared to touch her, any move he made might be misinterpreted. He'd lain awake, barely able to breathe, straining his ears for any sound from her. Suppose he'd told her he loved her and this time, for the first time, she didn't respond in kind? Well, she didn't need to draw it out for his benefit. If she couldn't bring herself to do it, he'd cut the ties himself. Make it easier on them both.

He sped up, putting as much space as possible between himself and that idea.

How could she say they didn't talk? They did, didn't they? Sure, there were days when he didn't call her, days when he was crazy busy or times she was travelling and told him to wait for her to get in touch – which he did, though it wasn't easy. And when she called, he did his best. There were topics he skirted round – but that was normal. No-one wanted a row. And he listened, even when it was hard to keep track of who was who and what they did, and tried to make her laugh. In other words, he did what he'd always done. But if they talked now, what would she say? He wanted to know, and as soon as possible – why prolong the agony? – and at the same time, never wanted to hear the words.

How could he have been so blind? Believing it was all about her job because it was tougher than she expected and, being Lily, she couldn't admit that sometimes she hated it. Not the hours or the people, but all the politics and jostling for position. That's what the move to Cardiff had been about, hadn't it? Or so she said. Maybe he didn't always understand, but it didn't mean he didn't care. The opposite, in fact. Her work stories scared him.

And he did nice things, whatever Anisia thought, but maybe she was right and what Lily wanted was stuff, pretty things and trinkets, not adventures. Her life was full enough with life-or-death experiences, as it was. Well, if that was the case, he still had time to remedy the situation.

He increased his speed again, turning right at Marble Arch and into Oxford Street. It was still bustling at seven. Clearly, there were plenty of people with the same idea.

A doorman in brocade and cap was managing traffic at the entrance to Selfridges. Shoppers collided with Ed's back as he stopped to check the list of departments. Where to start? Kit would go with a bag, but that wasn't right for Lily. It would send the wrong sort of signal, imply she should use it to pack her stuff and move even further away. And definitely not a watch. That would not be well received. In fact, any jewellery was problematic right now. When the moment came, and it wasn't looking like it would be today, she'd want something handmade from Hatton Garden. Ed could thank Martin for that. All the afternoons Lily spent with him in his shop, learning about hallmarks and carats, had shown her what was possible.

He studied the list again. J... K... L... Why not? It was worth a try. He headed for the escalators.

He got quite far into the rows of fancy underwear before an assistant intercepted him. 'Christmas shopping, sir? Do you need some help?'

Ed circled away with a noncommittal smile. 'I don't know exactly what I'm looking for, but I'll know it if I see it,' he said.

The assistant followed.

'Okay, kind of like that,' said Ed, and pointed at an undergarment he'd spotted amid all the racks, rails and displays. It looked to be about the right length and style.

'Can I ask who it's for and when they're going to wear it?' She tipped her head to one side as she smiled. Her name badge said she was Luisa. She appeared to be in her early fifties with lots of make-up and a Southern European accent. 'It's best to ask. It's that time of year, darling, and people have some interesting parties. I never judge.'

Ed laughed. 'Not me, unfortunately. It's for my girlfriend.' Even the word felt sore. 'And I hope she'll wear it when we go away together.'

'I hope so too. Let's see what we can find.'

The assistant directed him past the racks of slips, short and long, lacy and sheer, to another section, full of nightwear. She stopped at a row of satin-look nightdresses, thin and strappy, printed and plain. 'Something like this?' She pulled out a bright red number, edged with black lace.

'Yeah, a bit like that. Only not that colour. Or that.' He pointed at the purple cat print next to it. The material didn't feel quite right either. He'd stand a much better chance of finding something if she left him alone to wander, but she was glued to his side. Maybe they didn't let stray men loose among the underwear. He looked around and pointed at the pale green glass of the counter. 'More that sort of colour.'

Luisa looked him up and down, her eyes lingering over the battered leather coat and slightly straggly beard, offset sufficiently, he hoped, by the sharply clipped short hair and designer glasses.

'I haven't got anything like that but... follow me.' She

beckoned him towards the other side of the rail. 'Do you know her size, darling?'

'Yeah, she's usually a 10. Do you need her bra size?'

'Not really, but do you know it?'

He nodded.

'Good man.'

Luisa selected a hanger from the rack and offered him a pale grey version, edged around the top and bottom with the smallest band of cream lace.

Ed felt the fabric between his fingers and thumb. It was so light, there was barely anything to grab hold of. The colour was close enough too. 'Yeah, that's better. That's right,' he said.

'How much are you looking to spend, though?' she asked gently. 'This is more expensive.'

'What's the damage?'

The assistant turned the tag to show him. At that price, it ought to have been hand-spun by elves.

Ed puffed out his cheeks. 'That's okay. It might be make or break.'

'If it's break, bring it back, darling.'

'And change it for something I can wear to one of your interesting parties?'

'We'll go together,' she said as she placed the slip of silk on the counter to wrap it in tissue. 'I'll put it in a box.'

He left the shop swinging the yellow carrier bag. Would he have time for a drink before dinner? He smiled grimly to himself. The condemned man deserved a hearty meal. His phone buzzed in his pocket.

'Hey, Lovely,' he answered, heart pounding. 'How's it going?'

'You're not going to believe this. We've broken down.'

He heard the crack in her voice.

'What? Where?'

'I don't know exactly.'

Ed stopped by a dustbin and dangled the bag above it before snatching it back from the brink. Even if Lily wouldn't be wearing it any time soon, its price tag earned it a reprieve.

12

Lily

20.20

'Where are you going to go, Ed? What are you going to do?'

'I'm going to eat. Are you coming with me?'

He must be walking. His breathing was heavy.

'Of course. Where are we going?'

She leaned her head against the window and gazed at the steel grey barrier alongside the motorway. It was doing a poor job of holding back the weeds. If she was there much longer, they'd start pushing through the glass to swallow her up.

'It's called "Terra Mare". It's like a Mediterranean version of surf and turf. Shellfish and red meat arranged in arty shapes.'

'Have you been there before?'

'Yes, with clients. I thought you'd like it. Amazing flavours. You can have watermelon with your shrimp. I told you about it.'

She didn't remember. 'Sounds nice, though.'

'It would have been.'

'I'm sorry, Ed.'

'Ah Lily, Lovely, let's not sweat the small stuff. It's one dinner, right?'

That didn't sound like Ed. He was happy with a burger. If he'd booked something special, he wanted her to notice. Her heart lurched. If he was scared, there must be something to worry about.

Someone was speaking over the public address system. It sounded important.

'Ed? I'll call you later, when I know what's happening.'

'Sure thing, take it easy.'

The noises coming over the intercom were garbled, but Lily got the gist. They had to leave the bus and take another. The muttering and sighing which had been the soundtrack for the past twenty minutes swelled into discontent. The driver was now making more effort to be heard.

'I don't know when,' he shouted. 'They said the bus would be along in a couple of minutes... No, you're not coming back here. You need to gather your belongings together... You're going to the service station and the London bus will pick you up from there. And take everything with you.'

Lily re-zipped her backpack, slipped her phone into her coat pocket and, chin tucked down, slotted into the queue to troop off the bus. The passengers stood in a depressed line on the embankment waiting for their luggage. A light drizzle fell. Lily shrank further into her parka, down-filled and bought for all those times she had to stand outside, stamping her feet against the cold, mouth turned up to appear positive and encouraging. It was someone else's job tonight and her turn to look cold and miserable.

Luggage off, luggage on. Join the line, head down, shuffling aboard.

Lily found the student, her neighbour from the previous bus, and slid into the seat next to him. 'Hello again.'

He pulled one earbud out. 'Oh, right. Hi,' he said, shrinking against the window.

Before they could get settled, the bus stopped again to decant them. The driver remained trapped in his seat, hemmed in by anxious passengers, bombarding him with questions. Lily squeezed past only to get stuck at the top of the stairs.

'Can you let the driver off, please?' yelled a woman with a teenage boy, hauling on the handrail to climb back into the bus. 'We need our bags out.'

The driver stood, straightened his company-branded fleece and waded into the mob. Lily slipped out in his wake like someone chasing an ambulance and waited at the kerbside, collar pulled up around her ears. A sprinkle of sequins lay around her feet. She was shedding Christmas one bauble at a time.

She turned her eyes from the growing chaos by the luggage hold. If things turned nasty, she'd lose any chance of dinner with Ed, but this was a community there was no point trying to organise. At some point they'd work out for themselves that if they carried on arguing, they'd get nowhere.

If Ed was there, he'd be unable to resist pointing out that if her bag was smaller, she wouldn't have to keep standing in line to collect it. It wasn't her fault. The bag was full of things for his family – little gifts for Anisia's baby and the proud parents as well as scarves and scented candles – peace-keeping trinkets for Laurence and Samantha. She may as well not have bothered. There'd be no time to pop in for coffee or a drink. They'd have to drop them off in the middle of the night, post them through the letter box or push them down the chimney like a proper Secret Santa. Honestly! She really was losing her mind.

A little girl stood next to her. She was crying, the breathless gulps suggesting it'd been going on for some time, her hand clutching the coat of her exhausted-looking mother. Poor thing was probably scared – or maybe there was a Christmas treat she'd been looking forward to and would now miss. Lily remembered days like that, but she learned early to hide the disappointment. Perhaps she could help with this, though. She shrugged her shoulders out of her parka and bundled the coat at her feet.

'Look,' she said, and reached inside her sweater to flick the switch on the battery pack.

The reindeers' red sequinned noses were now mostly on the floor, so some of the effect had been lost, but the jumper still did its job. The girl watched the white and red lights flick between the animals and snowmen, and her sobs turned to sniffs. She held out her hand, showing Lily her own toy, a small glitter-encrusted ball which changed colour when she touched it.

'That's pretty,' Lily said. 'Hang on, let's see what else I've got.'

She rummaged in her backpack, delving deep to find a satsuma, an apple and one of her old juggling balls, which she'd repurposed as a stress reliever. She tested the weight of each.

'Here, look after this,' she said, handing the orange to the little girl in exchange for the toy.

Lily tossed the glitter ball in the air, followed by the apple, and showed off a few tricks as the ball flashed its neon colours in time with her jumper. A few other passengers turned to watch and the presence of an audience spurred her to aim higher, throwing the balls above and behind her, even spinning on the spot before deftly catching them as they descended. She was a little rusty, encumbered with the baggy jumper and clumsy boots, and her foot got stuck as she tried to wrap one leg around the other and turn, something she could usually have done blindfold. It made her smile for what felt like the first time in hours.

'I want to do that,' said the child as Lily handed back her ball.

'If we're still here in an hour, I'll teach you,' said Lily.

'Please God, no,' said her mother with feeling.

They both laughed.

By the time Lily made it inside the service station, a queue had formed at the coffee shop. The girl behind the counter made a fuss when Lily handed her a £10 note. Lily smiled her sweetest smile and stuffed the change into her coat pocket. She had enough to deal with as she wrangled her rucksack and her case, and moved to the other end of the counter to wait for her tea. Sometimes, there was no point trying to explain, and anyway, there must still be a hefty proportion of the planet which didn't have chip and pin and wasn't contactless.

Her phone buzzed. A message from Ed with a picture of the menu.

What do you fancy? Sea Bream en papillotte?

She sent him a miserable face back.

He replied instantly.

Or the duck? They're doing it specially for Christmas.

Okay, she'd play, though the prospect of food made her feel a bit sick.

Are we going starters or puddings? she asked.

Whichever you like, he messaged. *Both?*

She sent him a picture of the cold cabinet with its array of sandwiches.

Ooh dear. No thanks. What are we drinking? Couldn't decide red or white so I started with gin.

Choosing the wine was her job. She liked to find something that would match their food choice. Or else something she'd never tried before. He wasn't fussy.

Good call, she said. *Never drink wine alone.*

But gin's okay? he asked. *Or is it the drink for drowning sorrows? Mother's ruin etc*

You drowning your sorrows?

A bit. Maybe

And then, after a minute, another message.

Shall I order one for you?

This shakiness was unlike him. He was looking for a way in. Had he finally realised? It was about time. She wouldn't make it difficult.

Can I share yours? she said.

Always. But we might need another

People were waving at her.

Got to go. Bus here, she messaged, and then, in case she'd been too abrupt, sent him a row of hearts.

She trailed her fellow travellers to where a man in a bus company jacket was standing, shouting into his mobile phone. A bus waited in the bay, engine growling, doors firmly shut.

'It's full,' came the word down the line. 'The driver won't let us on.'

Lily went straight to the man with the phone. He turned to shake her off before she had a chance to pull on his sleeve.

'When's the next one? Will we get on that?'

'I'll make sure of it. I want to go home too,' he said.

The crowd started to gather round him, but Lily wasn't staying for the row. She dragged her suitcase back inside and flopped into a seat near the fish and chip concession. Her phone was buzzing in her pocket again. What was the point in answering if she had nothing good to report? Ed was going to need another gin. Perhaps the restaurant could make one for her as a takeaway.

Her phone fell silent only to ping a second later with an incoming message.

Lilleeee where are you call me need your help

13

Ed

November 2012

At least on Saturdays they got a day to themselves.

The girl worked crazy hours. Unless she grabbed an evening off, the only time Ed got to see Lily during the week was if she turned up at bedtime with greasepaint smears around her hairline. Which was great. Just wasn't enough. He wanted to know more about her. She didn't have to make the trek to his flat if it was a problem. He could go to her, bring food, cook even. Maybe. She kept putting him off. Something about her housemates, the mysterious, larger-than-life characters that dictated her day. He didn't doubt they existed. All the clues were there – the website, the clothes, the make-up – and Lily could certainly juggle. There were juggling balls in her bag, though she didn't need them. She'd juggle with anything that came to hand – lemons, water bottles, hairbrushes – instinctively, as if she hadn't noticed she was doing it.

Why did he care? He didn't usually need to test things.

'What d'you wanna do today?' he asked, stroking her hair as she lay next to him.

'I don't mind,' she said. 'You choose. Though d'you mind if we pop by my house?'

'Course not. Really?'

What had changed?

'I need to pick up a jacket,' said Lily.

He had to clench his whole face to avoid flicking his eyes to the side where a large pile of her clothes lay tangled on the armchair and dropping onto the floor. There were certainly jackets in amongst the heap. The sleeves gave them away.

'Yeah, sorry,' she said. 'I promised to lend it to someone. She's in a band. They're playing tonight. We can go along, if you like.'

The exterior of the small terraced house suggested it wasn't much of a cut above the places he rented as a student. The front garden had been concreted over and now housed dustbins and an earthenware tub that once held plants but now served as a giant ashtray.

'The boys take a conditioning class on a Saturday,' Lily said, turning the key in the door. 'With any luck, they won't be back yet.'

There it was again. Why was she so reluctant? He'd never regarded himself as too undesirable to take home. Ed combed his hair off his face with his fingers and gave his reflection the quick once-over in the bay window before following Lily inside.

The hallway was narrow. Ed ran his hand along the wall, calculating how much work had been needed to convert the two-up two-down into a dwelling for five people.

'Where's your room?'

'Back bedroom,' said Lily, pointing up the stairs.

'This is where I find out if you're as tidy as you claim.'

His hand was already on the bannister when the door to the front room sprang open. A head wrapped in a pale green towel popped through the gap. It raised its thickly arched black eyebrows.

'Ahh. The big reveal. The hot new boyfriend,' it said in a voice deeper than Ed was expecting.

The rest of the creature's body followed, slithering through the doorway to stand before them dressed only in cycle shorts. Ed had difficulty keeping a straight face.

'We meet at last.' The man pursed his lips and scanned Ed from top to toe. He held out his hand. 'Adam.'

'Ed.' Ed shook the offered hand.

'I'd better give you the tour, then,' said Lily with a sigh.

She pushed Ed ahead of her into the kitchen as Adam danced behind.

'Ooh, come in, come in,' he sang. 'Menassiii! Make yourself decent, we have a visitor.'

'Adam, shut up and take your meds,' said Lily. 'This, Ed, is the kitchen.'

The back room and kitchen had been knocked into one and extended to make a decent-sized living room, the sort of thing that in estate agent blurbs was described as a large kitchen and family room. If the roof lantern had been a metre to the left, it would have given more light, but it was a great place for a party, still, in his view, the best way to judge most living space.

'Nice room.'

His eyes lingered on a rack of costumes which ran the

length of one wall. Beneath them, huge plastic cases were stacked clumsily alongside cardboard boxes overflowing with props. It was clearly a bigger operation than he'd realised.

'And this is Dennis Menassi,' said Adam, who had somehow wormed his way around them and into the room. He indicated the man with the scruffy black hair propped on the sofa by the window, examining his big toe with torchlight from his phone.

'Just Menassi,' the man said, leaning across to extend a hand. 'No-one calls me Dennis except Adam.'

'Not even his mother,' said Adam, leaping over the back of an armchair and landing on the seat. He lifted his buttocks to pull a bunch of clothes out from under him and dumped them on the floor.

'Because my name's Gianluca so that's what she calls me,' said Menassi. 'Ignore Adam. He's a dick, but harmless. Mostly.'

'Why are you two home anyway? Why aren't you at class?'

Lily worked her way around the room, picking up shoes and bits of clothing and piling them in a corner.

'Workplace injury,' said Menassi. 'Those fucking stilts, Lil. I hit a pothole and fell off. I think I've got splinters in my toes.' He peered again at his feet. 'Can you see anything?'

Lily took the proffered phone and examined his toes. It wasn't a job Ed would have wanted. Menassi's feet were calloused and knobbly and already covered in plasters, like the feet of a man who'd worked barefoot in a quarry.

'There's nothing there,' she said. 'All I can see are blisters. What've you been doing?'

She picked up a couple of mugs and a dirty plate from the coffee table and took them into the kitchen. Ed followed. There was a lot to process. He needed a minute to catch up.

'Dennis, like the cartoon?' he whispered.

'Exactly. Tea?'

He nodded. It would be some sort of green tea with whichever flavour had taken her fancy last time she went shopping. She was slowly converting him.

'It's that tightrope,' explained Adam. 'He can't do it, he's rubbish, but he won't wear the right shoes. Here,' he said, whipping the towel off his head, 'what do you think of the colour?'

Adam's hair was white blond. The black eyebrows, white hair and surprised expression reminded Ed of something, but the image was just out of reach. He turned his laugh into a sniff and pinched his nose, hiding his face with his hand.

'You look like that character from *Madagascar*,' Lily said.

A lemur. That was it. Ed gave up trying to stifle his laughter, but Adam wasn't offended. He seemed pleased to get a reaction.

'It was the only way I could get rid of the pink,' he complained. 'It's not that bad, is it?'

He stood to examine his reflection in the mirror above the boarded-up fireplace. He turned his chin this way and that and fluffed his hair into spikes. Menassi shook his head at Ed. *Say nothing*, said his expression, but Ed had to ask.

'Pink?'

'He dyed it for a gig,' said Lily. 'Everyone else wore wigs but now the show's threatening to sack him.'

'They're saying no-one had pink hair in 1930s Berlin, but I bet they did,' said Adam. 'You can't see it when I've got the hat on, anyway.'

'So, how's business?' asked Ed. 'Working tonight?'

'Busking while I wait for him,' said Menassi. He nodded

towards the other side of the room and all the stage gear.

Ed walked over to the rail, which bowed under the weight of wooden hangers and stiffened garments, many sprayed with metallic paint. They certainly had the appearance of old bronze, if not the feel. The fabric was sticky to the touch.

'I'll do the pirate,' said Menassi, 'that way I'll get to stand on one leg and rest my poorly toes.'

The costume was easy to spot. It was the one with the ridiculous parrot wobbling on the shoulder, it too covered in black and brown paint. Menassi wouldn't need a lot of disguising. With the hair and multiple piercings running up and around his ears, he was storybook pirate already.

Ed quite fancied the frock coat himself – if he could get rid of the bird – until he realised his fingers were covered in something shiny. It explained the glittery sheen on his pillows each time Lily stayed over. Paint. Not angel dust.

Lily handed him a wet wipe from a box on the table. 'Here. The stuff gets everywhere. We need a better way to fix the colour,' she said.

He could probably find a product to help them. A spray varnish, maybe.

'We might go out after,' said Menassi. 'D'you wanna come?'

'No,' said Lily.

'But thanks for the offer,' added Ed.

'Can I try your coat on?' asked Adam, already on his feet and peeling the coat from Ed's back. He was surprisingly tall and broad, well over six feet, and the coat was too tight across the shoulders. He went to admire his reflection again.

'I could rock a coat like this.'

'You'd give strangers nightmares,' said Menassi, shaking his head again.

'What's in the diary?' asked Lily, grabbing the black book from the table before Menassi could stop her.

'We'll need you on Tuesday,' he said.

'It says Trafalgar Square,' said Lily.

'Some exhibition opening. We're doing the paintings again. They seem to like that.'

Lily dropped the book and went back to the clothes rail, where a huge picture frame was tucked behind the costumes. She dragged it out on its castors, selected an ugly, brown dress from the end of the rack and held it against her as she squatted inside the frame, folding her hands in front of her.

'Look, Ed.'

'*Mona Lisa*,' he said, nodding. 'I suppose you can't really do *The Hay Wain*. Do you sit and look mysterious?'

'Mainly, and now and again say stuff like, "Ooh, I like your shoes," or, "D'you want to know why I'm smiling?"' With the Estuary accent, her whole demeanour changed. 'I have an easier time than the others. Oliver and Maxine do "American Gothic" with greased-down hair and sour faces and have to think up new things to bicker about.'

He wasn't sure about the whole talking picture concept, but he got why Menassi needed her. Lily was good at this stuff. When she danced, when she spoke, when she moved, she was the only one you saw. He was never the only one who couldn't keep his eyes off her.

'Trouble is, guys, I have other plans for Tuesday,' Lily continued. 'You see, this is what he does, Ed. He takes the gig and doesn't tell us 'til the last minute and then nags at us until we give in.'

Who was she kidding? They both knew she'd honour the booking.

73

'Sounds 'bout right,' he said instead. 'Sell the service to the customer and then find a way to deliver it.' He tested the weight of the picture frame. In MDF it was heavy for its size. 'Who makes your costumes?'

'My mum makes a lot of them,' said Adam. 'Some we buy and some we make ourselves.'

'Let me know when you replace the frames. I might be able to find something lighter for you.'

'Don't,' said Lily. 'Once you offer, he'll never let you go.'

'Welcome to the family,' said Menassi.

'I knew this would happen,' said Lily. 'I knew you'd get on. Now there's no escape – for any of us.'

'It's too soon,' warned Adam. He flopped back in his armchair, hand shielding his brow, still wearing Ed's coat. 'Help me, I'm in love again. How many times have we heard this?'

'That's not me, that's you,' said Lily, just in time to stop Ed's heart sinking into his boots.

'Is it?' he asked.

'Yes,' said Menassi. 'She's never done this before. You're the first one she's brought home to us. Actually, you're the only one she's ever talked about.'

It was what he wanted to hear, but it was odd hearing it from them. He let his eye wander over to the stack of stilts in the corner. There were old-style wooden ones with long crutches to match, as well as the modern, spring-loaded variety favoured by the plasterers on site.

'Which are yours?' he asked Lily.

'We take turns,' she said. 'I like the decorators' ones. Sometimes we take them out the back and shoot a few hoops.'

74

'You do that too?' He glanced through the kitchen window to the small yard beyond. Shame they didn't have time.

'The jacket?' he asked.

Lily's room was what he'd expected, an Aladdin's cave of sequins and trinkets and small rainbow-coloured pots of make-up and lotions, crammed into nine square metres. There was an illuminated mirror and more shoes than he'd ever seen in one place.

'Oh, God,' said Lily, and rushed around, scooping brightly coloured clothing from the floor.

He averted his eyes and snooped through the pile of books on the table. Volumes on eighteenth-century dress mixed with texts on twenty-first-century economics. A couple looked quite interesting. When he thought she'd done with the panicked tidying, he turned to face her.

'Okay, what am I looking for?'

'It's gold satin,' she said. 'Might be in the wardrobe.'

A pink feather boa was draped over one corner. He lifted it off and wound it round his neck before opening the doors. He stepped back.

'Wow.'

A gold jacket would stand out amongst anyone else's clothes, but not Lily's. There wasn't a maxi dress or blue denim jacket in sight. Lily slid past him, pulled the jacket off the hanger and slammed the doors shut, pressing herself against them.

'I know, I know. It's a lot. But don't judge me by this.'

'Are you kidding?'

She was more than anyone else he'd ever met.

'You were wearing a Hawaiian shirt when we first met,' she said.

'And you were in black,' he reminded her. 'But this is better. Really.'

He pulled her into a tight hug.

'It might be time to introduce you to my family.'

14

Lily

November 2012

Ed leapt to his feet and peered down through the French windows into the street. It made Lily jump. He'd been lying on the sofa with his iPad while she sat cross-legged in front of the bookcase, pulling out each volume in turn.

'What happened?' she asked, expecting flashing blue lights and sirens.

'Come on,' he said. 'It's not that wet. We can take the bikes.'

'Where to? Where are we going?'

'Portobello Road.'

'What for?'

'You've been sitting there moaning that there are no images of picture frames in my books, so I think we should go check out some paintings.'

She hadn't been complaining that much, and if she had, it was Ed's fault. He'd got Menassi all stirred up about the quality of their props. She'd thought she'd be bound to find some ideas in one of the vast collection of works on art and antiques lining the shelves of Ed's flat, but none were any use. Especially not Ed's books, which seemed to consist mainly of monochrome works on the architecture of Berlin. He had literally no portraits of anything living.

'You mean the market? Will it be open today?'

'We're going to my uncle's shop.'

'You have a shop?'

'He does.'

She looked at the holes in the knees of her jeans and glanced towards the door of Ed's room. She probably had a dress or two in one her bags.

'You're fine as you are,' said Ed, picking up their cycle helmets. He might have been laughing.

Lily associated Portobello Market with Notting Hill Carnival, heaving crowds and second-hand clothes. She rarely ventured further south than the Westway and into the bustle of fruit and vegetable stalls and antique arcades. Closed and shuttered on a Sunday morning, with no yelling or people clogging the street as they worked the tables outside the shops, the area made no sense.

Ed led the way, freewheeling along the pavement, a thing it was impossible to do on any other day. He stopped before a blue-painted shop front, the darkened window displaying a couple of seascapes on wooden stands behind a brass-coloured security screen.

'Martin's an antique dealer?'

'That's what he tells people, but trust me, Lily, if he hadn't had money to start with, he would never have made any.'

Ed locked up the bikes while she peeked in through the window. He leaned on the doorbell. There was no sound of ringing. Ed took out his phone and dialled.

'You going to let us in, then?' he said into the handset.

The man who opened the door had a cigarillo in one hand and a cut-glass tumbler of what looked like whisky in the other.

'Bit early, isn't it?' said Ed, kissing the top of the householder's head.

'Morning to you too, darling. I would offer you a martini, but I put all the vermouth in the risotto.'

'Martin, this is Lily,' said Ed, pulling her round in front of him. 'She'd like to see your collection of uninspired and poorly executed paintings.'

Martin grinned. He was in slippers and blue jeans, the sort of man who wouldn't have looked out of place with a cravat tucked into the neck of his linen shirt. 'Art lover, are you?'

'Not really, I—'

'Thank God for that,' said Martin, rolling his eyes behind his tortoiseshell glasses.

Lily searched for a family resemblance. He had Ed's expression, that spark of interest in what was going on around him, but apart from the glasses sliding down the bridge of the same straight nose, that was it. Ed was taller and darker.

'It's the frames she's interested in,' Ed said, 'for her act.'

'Come on in, then, my dear,' said Martin with a sweep of his arm. 'I have a whole roomful of pictures where the entire value is in the frame. And you have an act, do you?'

Lily caught the look Martin shot Ed – the raised eyebrows, the shrug in reply – and cringed.

'I do hope you'll tell me about it,' said Martin, as he switched on the internal lights and ushered her into his showroom. 'Some of my closest friends tread the boards.'

The first room was orderly. Paintings hung floor to ceiling, mahogany tables and cabinets displaying just the right amount of silver and crystal. It was the sort of place Lily would usually be scared to enter in case she touched anything and instantly reduced its value. There was a second room to her right which was chaos. Furniture piled haphazardly and pictures leaning here and there against the wall. Cardboard boxes lay all over the floor, newspaper spilling out, revealing enough of the china inside to tempt you to delve further. Clever. Let the bargain hunter think they had discovered some hidden treasure. Martin must have catalogued exactly what was in each box.

'I'll let you loose in here,' he said, 'while I crack on upstairs. But don't look too closely at the paintings, the brushwork won't stand up to scrutiny. You'll stay for lunch, won't you?'

Lily slid her feet out of her trainers and handed them to Ed before clambering over the sofas to reach a couple of the larger canvases stacked against the far wall. She had to lean across the tables to pull them towards her to measure and photograph them. Ed was right. The oil paintings were surprising light. It was the watercolours, sandwiched between layers of glass and board which were heavy. When she got stuck dragging a frame from where it was wedged behind a wardrobe, Ed came to lend a hand, easing the furniture aside for her. She slid the painting out and ran her fingers over the gold painted frame, tracing the nubbly indentations with her forefinger, memorising the pattern.

'Seen enough?' he asked, when he shoved the wardrobe back into place.

Lily nodded and flicked the dust off her shirt. She held her filthy hands out to Ed. Ordinarily she'd have wiped them on her jeans, but she was about to eat with his family. She couldn't leave grimy marks on the napkins. Martin was bound to have napkins.

'Is there a bathroom?'

'Sure. Upstairs.'

He beckoned her to follow him towards a desk at the back of the first room. The row of lever arch files suggested this was where the real business took place. Ed pushed against the wall behind and a doorway appeared, the outline and handle cleverly concealed by the elaborately patterned wallpaper.

Hidden doors! Lily clapped her hands. How much better could it get?

The flat upstairs was an extension of the shop, an over-furnished and cluttered magpie collection of art, carpets, jewellery and tableware. It was a resting place for beautiful, and mostly unnecessary, relics of the past, biding their time, waiting to be dusted off and rediscovered. It wasn't obvious where the merchandise ended and Martin's possessions began. Lily flitted about, picking up bits and pieces to examine them, neither man objecting if she put them back in a different place.

'What's this?' she asked.

'Waterford decanter,' said Ed, picking up a rainbow-coloured feather duster and flicking it around the crystal without making much impact. 'I used to work here on Saturdays when I was at school. That's where I developed a dust allergy, I'm sure.' He coughed unconvincingly.

'Let me know if you find the stopper,' said Martin. 'I put it down somewhere and I can't sell it without.'

Lily grabbed the duster from Ed and started sweeping it

across the surfaces of the side tables and around the figurines. She tickled his neck with the feathers.

'I suppose you're going to tell me you like it here,' he said, batting the duster away.

She loved it. She skipped into the kitchen. 'I can help,' she told Martin.

'Lay the table, if you must,' he said, and pointed her towards a corner cabinet.

She lifted a pile of blue-and-gold-banded plates down.

'Ed has some like this,' she said, 'but his are red instead of blue.'

'Royal Worcester,' said Martin, turning a plate over to show her the mark. He paused. 'Perhaps we'll use the silver plate. In honour of your visit.' He opened a drawer and pulled out a battered wooden box. 'I've lost a couple of coffee spoons along the way, but we're mostly intact.'

'Does Ed come for lunch often?'

'Not a lot… Is that about to change?'

He put his head to the side and raised an enquiring eyebrow. The gesture reminded her so much of Ed and Kit that she laughed and bumped her shoulder gently against his.

'You two gossiping already?' said Ed from the doorway.

'Not with you here,' said Martin.

Ed rolled his eyes, in a decent impression of Martin, and grabbed a bottle of wine from the counter.

'I'll open this then, shall I?'

Lily waited until Ed had left again. 'Will you tell me about Cat?' she whispered. 'He doesn't talk about his mum.'

Martin nodded and squeezed her arm. 'Pop in sometime. If you're passing. It's always nice to have someone to share a pot of tea with.'

Lily put an arm around him. She could do with someone like Martin in her life. Maybe he could adopt her? Her relationship with her stepfather was good now, but it had taken her a while to appreciate him. Mick had many fine qualities, but they didn't stretch to deep heart-to-hearts. His standard answer to everything was *Dunno, love. Ask your mum*. It used to annoy her, the way he avoided getting involved, preferring to hover somewhere in the background, never expressing an opinion. Now she recognised him for the genius he was – holding the back line, keeping her mother occupied while she and her brother got on with things, a man who'd perfected the art of sleeping with his eyes open. He was a lot more use than her 'real' dad. She'd never found much to say to him.

15

Ed

December 2012

Ed slipped into the club after Lily's salsa class had started and found a place at the bar to wait. Jess, who worked the afternoon shift, cracked open a beer and plonked it on the counter for him before he'd even sat down. His new Sunday routine.

'Cheers,' he said. 'One for yourself?'

She poured herself a Coke.

Ed draped his coat over the back of the stool and sat, sipping his beer and minding his business, surrounded by images of Lily reflected in the mirrors which lined the walls and the back of the bar. She stalked the floor, all sinuous hips and shoulders, demonstrating steps, counting rhythms and offering advice, correcting the dancers with a gentle hand on a back or arm. She was total concentration; he was utterly gripped. He caught her eye and she strode over.

'You have to dance,' she said as she pulled him off the stool. 'It's too gangster the way you sit and stare.'

'I'm not staring. It's difficult to avoid you, you're everywhere.' He had a horrible thought. 'Is it gangster? Is it creepy?' He got to his feet in panic.

'Yes,' said Jess.

'No,' said Lily. 'I quite like that people think you might be dangerous.'

'You're glad I'm not, though, right? It's the coat. It happens all the time. When I sit at a bar, people think I'm there to collect money.'

She was trying to nudge him into position, but his feet seemed to be made of lead. 'I thought you liked dancing.'

'I like dancing if I'm dancing with you,' he said, which was a soft thing to say but it might buy him some time.

What it bought him was a smile and a kiss. Salsa was never going to rank as his number-one favourite activity, but so long as he knew he wouldn't be offered up as a partner to anyone else, he could relax, maybe even enjoy it.

Things were going so well, he was having doubts about his plan for later – introducing Lily to the only other tradition the Black family observed – Sunday night jazz. He'd ducked out recently, but now that Lily and Martin had met, he was running out of excuses. It was a relic from the dark days, the Sunday evenings during their teenage years when he and Kit would run out on their father to hide out at their uncle's. Martin would make them cheese on toast and let them loose on his liquor and his voluminous record collection. Since Martin handed over the flat, roles had been reversed. Martin came to them, with a bottle of his favourite blend under one arm and a stack of vintage vinyl under the other.

85

Ed stopped Martin on the doorstep and checked through his record selection. There could be no twenty-minute drum solos. Lily's initiation must be gentle.

'Trust me,' said Martin, handing him his coat. 'I've got this.'

He settled on the sofa next to Lily and beamed at her. Ed left them to it. He knew the drill. He filled the ice bucket and placed it on the coffee table along with four cut-glass tumblers, mismatched but not chipped. Kit arrived on cue, bringing boxes of pizza, and Lily shuffled along to make room for him. As Ed picked the top disk from the pile and queued it on the turntable, Martin filled the glasses with ice and poured two fat fingers of whisky into each. He handed the first to Lily.

'My dear,' he said.

'You can have something else,' said Ed, taking the armchair next to her, but she clinked her glass against his and lifted it to her lips.

He toasted her in return and kicked back as the first piano notes filled the space.

'Is this Monk?' asked Kit.

'Mary-Lou Williams,' said Martin.

'She taught Monk,' said Lily, who was reading the sleeve notes.

Ed took another slug of whisky. It wasn't only the alcohol warming his insides.

16

Lily

21.00

It had to be Menassi. The charge on her phone was dwindling, but even with a full battery, she wouldn't be rushing to phone him. If he or Adam were calling today, it could only mean one thing – they were short of a juggler or a dance partner for some booking on Christmas Eve. If she called Menassi, the master blagger, he'd talk her into something, with all his, *You know I'd do it for you, Lily. Anything you need, anytime. No word of a lie, I'll be right there.* And he meant it, he would be there, but he was negotiating from a position of strength. He'd never have to return a favour because she'd never have an emergency need for a fire eater or stilt walker. Not many would.

Lily rummaged in her bag, spilling the contents onto the seat beside her. Where was her wireless phone charger? She had her laptop, hair straighteners, a book and her mini rucksack with her valuables and the receipt for Ed's snowmobile safari – because it turned out that was a thing in Iceland – but no charger. Or was this it, right at the bottom, tangled in her headphones? She plugged her phone in, scooped everything back into the bags and left them lying alongside. She stretched out her legs. All those hours she'd spent in uncomfortable locations waiting for transport which was invariably delayed, if it turned up at all, should have been good preparation for this, although in her hot and itchy wool socks and heavy boots, she was rather overdressed for this terrain.

It was too soon to call Ed again and she had no intention of phoning Menassi. Her mum would be home, though, deep in preparations for her Christmas Eve Open House, unpacking a supermarket shop large enough to feed the entire street, while Mick kept out of the way, digging out extra chairs from the garage.

'Hi, Sweetheart. Where are you? Are you going to pop in?' Her mum sounded breathless, her words punctuated by clattering. She was probably counting plates with the phone tucked under her chin.

'I'm sorry, I'll get into London too late.'

'Oh, Lily. Couldn't they have let you off early?'

Lily picked at the stitching on her jumper before catching herself. She smoothed over the damage. 'Not their fault. I missed the train and now I'm waiting at a service station for a bus.'

Lily waited for another round of, 'Oh, Lily,' but her mother sighed instead.

'I knew this was a bad idea. I'll speak to Mick. He'll come and get you.'

'It's fine, Mum, don't worry.'

'You could come here for the night, keep an eye on your nan. I don't know what she's up to. She keeps taking these little walks and it's got nothing to do with her physio. I bet she's still smoking. Hang on a minute.'

'Mum—'

She was too late. Her mum was calling up the stairs, not bothering to mask the phone with her hand.

'My mother's offering to send someone to fetch me,' Lily announced drearily to the other passengers who'd straggled back into the building and were slumped in a loose group around her, silent and resigned.

'My dad's coming,' said the student. 'He said he'd rather do it now than get a call in the middle of the night.'

'He's got a point,' said Lily.

Her mum burst back on the line. 'Mick's asleep, darling, sorry,' she said. 'He went for a drink after work. I'd come myself, but I can't find my glasses.'

Her mother's diction was also a little slurred. No wonder she couldn't find her specs.

'Well, what about Ed? What's he doing? Maybe he'd like to come round for a bit. He can wait for you here. Shall I give him a ring?'

'No, Mum, don't. Please.'

'Your brother's here. He'd like to see him, I'm sure, and there's loads of food.'

'Ed's not in a good mood.'

'Well, what about tomorrow? Can you come by on the way to the airport? I don't see why you should miss out just because he won't spend time with his family.'

'We're not missing out. We're going away. Like an experiment.'

89

'At what? Being miserable? Cutting yourself off from your family?'

'We've been over this.'

'You'd probably both feel better if you ate something.'

'That's not it, Mum. It's…' Oh God. Where to start? 'He booked a table for dinner and I won't be there.'

'He booked a table?'

'Not like that.'

'How do you know? He might surprise you.'

She knew because he'd told her it wasn't, and anyway, Ed didn't do things like that.

'I don't think we're—'

'You don't want to let him get away, Lily.'

Lily gritted her teeth. Wasn't it Ed who'd let her go? That box was still in his pocket where it had been for over a year. He couldn't have forgotten it was there, jumbled among the loose change and door keys. His fingers would feel its velvet shape every time he reached for a pencil or a steel tape. Yet he didn't say a word.

'I worry about you,' her mum continued. 'It's no fun being on your own this time of year.'

'Oh, Mum, let's not,' Lily murmured, screwing her eyes shut, willing herself to stay quiet while her mother got it out of her system again. Once a year she'd let her do this.

'I suppose if the spark's gone, the spark's gone. There's not a lot you can do about that. People change. They move on. Keeping that connection going isn't easy. You have to work at it.'

'It's fine, Mum, still sparky enough.'

'Perhaps he needs a bit of a nudge. Shall I ask Mick to have a word?'

What she'd give to be a fly on the wall during that conversation. Even the idea made her smile. Nonetheless, she'd have to call Ed before her mother did and keep the line busy until she got distracted by something else.

Ed picked up straightaway. 'How's it going?' he said.

'I'm back in the service station with the plastic seats and the strip lighting and I'm tired and cold and hungry. Don't say you told me so.'

'It's nice and warm where I am. You'd like it. Red walls and lots of candles. Paintings everywhere. Mainly still lifes, if you're interested. There's a scary one of a lobster. He's glaring at me with one beady eye. I hope he's not dish of the day. Don't you wish you were here? I certainly do.'

The bitter edge had gone and he was just Ed, Ed at his sweetest and best. Tears pricked her eyes. 'Yeah, I do, actually.'

'Thought it'd be safest to stay in the restaurant 'til you arrive, go straight to the bus station. The waitress agrees, though she won't sit and have a brandy with me.'

'Sounds like you're doing fine on your own. Are your sorrows all drowned?'

'You weren't drinking your share. Couldn't let it go to waste now, could I?'

'Course not.'

'Did Menassi get hold of you?'

So it was Menassi. Piling on the pressure – along with everyone else.

'I missed him. Did he say what he wanted?'

'No, just really insistent you call. Even more than usual. No-one else will do, he said. I know what he means.'

She pictured him at the restaurant table, hunched over

his phone, drunk and sentimental, talking too loudly for the neighbouring diners.

'So, Lovely Lily, are you going to get here tonight?'

'I hope so,' she said, lowering her voice, although there was no-one close enough to hear.

'I got something for you.'

'Yes?'

'The hotel room's got one of those canopies behind the bed and it reminded me—'

'Your brother's wedding—'

'When you were late leaving work—'

'Sorry.'

'S'okay, and you had to choose between going home to get the rest of your stuff and picking up your dress from the cleaners.'

'I remember.'

'And, of course, you chose the dress but you didn't have the right underwear so we had to stop off on the way to the station while you tried on half the shop.'

'It's important it fits right.'

'And we had to run for the train.'

'And you bought me that nightdress—'

'I couldn't find the same colour but I got pretty close,' said Ed.

She could hardly breathe, the memory was so vivid.

'It might not be warm enough for Iceland.'

'I'll wrap you in my love,' he said, pronouncing the words carefully. 'You won't need anything else.'

'Ed? Is that you?'

He laughed. 'Hurry up.'

Lily plugged her phone back into the charger and thought

about that night, the night before Kit's wedding, when they hid out in their room, recognising each other's need to cocoon themselves away. Living in that moment, blocking everything else out. They hadn't managed to reach the same place since – that closeness, the total understanding. Was he having the same thoughts, sitting at the restaurant table, swirling the ice in his drink, wondering what they'd lost?

He didn't have the beard then. Strange that when she remembered the best times with Ed, he was cleanshaven.

17

Ed

23.00

If he had to describe the restaurant decor, Ed would probably say baroque fusion – if that was even a thing. Fortunately, the food had been designed by someone else. Covent Garden's other top spots were going for something more subtle – pre-war dining room with soft overhead lighting and Rennie Mackintosh-style chairs or Asian canteen with huge plate glass windows – but Terra Mare didn't hold back. There were wall hangings, cherubs in the bathrooms and fiery torches in wrought-iron brackets outside. Lily would have laughed. That was the plan, anyway. Neither could walk past a flaming torch without thinking of Menassi. There was a time Ed saw almost as much of Menassi as he did his brother, but it was months since they'd got together.

The waiter arrived, replacing Ed's empty amber glass with a fresh cocktail.

'Would you like to order some small appetisers, sir? Some olives or perhaps octopus? While you're waiting.'

'Oh, we may as well get on with it,' said Ed, picking up the menu again and avoiding the waiter's eye. 'She's not going to get here.'

Should he do like Lily and pick something with an ingredient he'd never heard of just to see how it tasted? Or go safe with steak? There really were few ways to make this evening enjoyable.

The waiter must have said something to his co-workers, as Ed seemed to be getting more than his fair share of table service. In his work suit – with a fresh shirt – he must still look like a decent date. He couldn't say it wasn't reassuring. His suspicions were confirmed when he turned down a dessert and his double espresso came with a small liqueur.

'Compliments of the house,' said the waitress.

'Are you able to join me?' he asked.

He offered her the glass. He needed to string things out a bit before he paid up, collected his things and headed down to Victoria.

'Not until we close,' she said.

'I may well still be here then,' he said. 'My girlfriend's late.'

She nodded and walked away but was back after a few minutes with a small tray of truffles which she placed on the corner of the table.

'It's Christmas,' she said.

'It certainly is. Help yourself.'

He pointed to the chocolate. The girl shook her head, as if it was more than her life was worth. She was sweet-looking with a few curls escaping from her messy blonde bun and very young, probably at university still.

'You working this weekend?'

'Only tomorrow and Christmas Day. Then we're closed.'

She rearranged the glasses on the table as she spoke, fiddling with the dessert menu, picking it up and putting it down. Looking busy, he guessed.

'And what're you going to do then? Hang with your family? Or have you got exams coming up?'

'Yeah, I should be revising but I'll probably just sleep. That's all I do – work and sleep.'

He lifted his glass. 'Sweet dreams, then.'

That's how it was for people starting out in London. Working long hours, balancing the price of the commute against the cost of living in the city, catching up on sleep at the weekend. It's what he and Lily used to do. Work all week, squeezing in as many hours together as possible, even if it meant meeting her after a gig with a green chai latte and a change of clothes. Then holing up at the flat at the weekend to catch their breath. It had been like that the whole time they'd been together. Now Lily complained they never did anything anymore, but it was hard to plan when they had to fit themselves around all their other commitments. And hers were constantly changing.

Unless it was their Sundays she missed. If there was nothing else going on, they'd surface slowly. There'd be a run on the Heath or a late breakfast in one of those cafés with stripped oak tables and fancy scrambled eggs. Then they might drop in on Laurence before they headed up to Camden and salsa class. It was fun. All the twisting and turning, the not quite touching, the laughing when he lost his place and tangled them both up. And if he missed that, she must be bereft. She loved to dance.

When they stopped dancing, they stopped moving in the same direction. Why hadn't he seen that before? Well, there was no way of going back, of recreating that time. They'd all moved on in one way or another, but if it was dancing Lily wanted, he could fix that. There were bound to be salsa bars in Cardiff, but why stop there? Lily's birthday was coming up. How about Mardi Gras or the Rio Carnival? He popped a chocolate into his mouth and opened the search engine on his phone.

18

Lily

February 2016

Lily had missed lunch again. It was a bad habit because now her stomach ached and there was no time to go home before dance class. She'd have to eat something soon or she wouldn't make it through the ordeal Adam would have planned for them. If she hurried, she could pick up some pad Thai and drop by the shop. Martin always let her upstairs to make jasmine tea and freshen up, especially if she brought him spring rolls.

She swung off the road onto the pavement outside the shop and stopped, straddling her bike. There was something strange about the place. Why was it so dark? She tested the door with one hand and found it unlocked. The little bell above tinkled as it swung open.

'Hello?' she called.

Gavin, Martin's business partner, emerged from the gloom.

'You okay?' said Lily. 'Shall I put the lamps on?'

Gavin looked surprised as if he hadn't noticed the fading light. It had been a bright morning, but it was still a way to go until spring and night fell early at this time of year.

Lily took her bike through to the back of the shop. It was her special privilege; Ed had to lock his up outside. Gavin shut the door behind her and returned to the desk. He still hadn't said a word. What was going on? Usually if he or Martin were in the shop, every light was blazing and the door was propped open for any wandering browsers – even if they were only sheltering from the cold. Neither of them could ever let a customer leave without sharing their knowledge about some collectible or other, whether it led to a sale or not.

'Martin gone out?' asked Lily, feeling already that this was a loaded question. She pushed away the sense of foreboding.

'He's not back yet,' said Gavin. 'And if he's not called by now, it must be bad news.'

What did he mean? Her expression must have given her away.

'Didn't you know? Isn't that why you're here?'

Lily walked slowly upstairs to the kitchen and made tea for herself and Gavin, stirring her teabag so long that it burst and she had to boil the kettle again.

'Why didn't he tell me?' she asked Gavin, placing a mug on his desk. 'I'd have gone with him.'

'He wouldn't have let you,' he said. 'He refuses to talk about it. He's not been right for a while, but he wouldn't get himself checked out.'

The weight loss. She ought to have realised. Martin had

said he was pleased about it and she'd believed him. How could she have been so blind?

'Don't tell him I was here,' she said as she left.

It was late when she reached the flat. Ed was already asleep and barely stirred as she slid in beside him, tucking in as tightly as she dared without waking him. She brushed her lips against his bare shoulder. Would it be wrong to tell him? What did she really know, though?

Waiting for Martin to speak was driving her mad. She'd put all her skills to work to create the right opportunities – getting Ed home early on Sunday evenings (feigned twisted ankle), making herself scarce if Martin came round (early bath) – but he said nothing. Unless he didn't need to tell Ed because Ed already knew, had known all along. But if that was the case, why hadn't he told her? Perhaps Gavin had been overreacting and it was nothing. That would be better. She could relax then. There was only one way to find out, but if she asked Ed and voiced the words, she'd give the idea substance. She didn't want that at all.

'Are you okay?' said Ed.

He was on the balcony, drinking coffee, feet propped on the railings, enjoying the first sunny Saturday for weeks. Lily paced up and down.

'Yeah, sure,' she said. 'Just need some air.'

They rode over to Camden Lock and sat by the water. Lily reached for his hand. 'If there was something I knew and I wasn't sure if you did, would you want me to tell you?'

Ed frowned. 'That's kind of a weird question.'

'Well, would you?'

'How can I answer that? Do you want to tell me this thing?'

'Yes.'

'Okay, I want to know it.'

'Oh, Ed, you don't. Not really.' She rubbed her forehead with her free hand.

'Lily, just tell me.' He looked worried now.

She took both his hands in hers and told him the thing she wanted him to know without having to tell him. 'I could be wrong,' she warned.

'No,' he said, shaking his head. 'You're right. He's not going to Montreux this year and he goes pretty much every year, has done for as long as I can remember. He's also not smoking.'

Lily hadn't noticed. The smell of black tobacco hung around the shop as if exhaled by the faded wallpaper.

'I just thought he'd given in to all the nagging.' Ed rolled his eyes. 'So dumb.'

'Should I have told you sooner?'

Ed shook his head again. 'It's his thing. How bad d'you think it is?'

Without the diagnosis, it was impossible to guess. All she had to go on was what Gavin had told her – the night-time vomiting and the liver biopsy. Her haphazard internet searches hadn't helped much.

'Probably not that bad,' she lied. 'And treatment's really good nowadays.'

She held his hand tighter. Ed didn't resist, but he didn't grip her fingers back.

'Oh, he won't want treatment. That's why he hasn't told Kit. He avoids doctors.'

He lifted his chin to the weak March sun, breathing

deeply. Lily did the same, but the air still carried the hint of the last year's leaves rotting by the side of the canal, and it didn't make her feel any better.

19

Ed

March 2016

Kit was in the kitchen when they got home, shovelling microwaved rice into his mouth.

'You off to work?' said Ed. He was trying to act casual, but relaxed people didn't usually open and shut drawers like he was doing.

'Might be the last time I eat for a while,' said Kit through a mouthful of food.

'Look, before you go...' Ed leaned against the counter. He picked through the words crowding his head, discarding plenty, selecting a few. Lily was bustling around the sitting room, noisily straightening cushions and drawing the curtains.

'It seems the Old Love's sick,' he said, slowly.

Kit looked up. 'Really sick? Properly sick?'

'I think so.' Ed nodded. 'So, if you still want him as your best man, you'd better get a move on.'

They'd shared some scary moments growing up, he and Kit, but he'd never before seen terror in his brother's eyes. He drew his brother into a hug and patted his shoulder.

'I'm sure it's gonna be fine. I mean, you're the medic, you know how these things go. We'll just get him to a good doctor...'

Just hold the line, he willed him.

'Okay, said Kit, nodding rapidly and clearing his throat. He wiped his fingers across his eyes. 'I'll speak to Anisia.'

Ed stayed in the kitchen for a minute after his brother left. He identified an ache. It was quite sharp and started in the centre of his chest before moving up into his throat, where it lodged. Long-remembered pain. A sob that refused to be expressed.

No need to ask why Martin hadn't told them he was ill. He was the one who broke the news to them about their mother. He couldn't be responsible for unleashing all that fear again.

Well, it would be different this time. He and Kit would see to it. They'd make it easier for him.

20

Lily

June 2016

Lily pushed the front door open with her shoulder and swung her bags into the hall. She heaved the two holdalls the extra distance into Ed's room and dumped them on the floor.

The June effect. Sometimes she wanted to issue a public service announcement and let people know it would all be fine, no-one need worry, their summer sporting event or corporate garden party would go just as well without stilt-walkers or living statues. Whatever her opinion, she'd keep it to herself. She needed the money and so she spent her days running in circles between bookings, starting each morning crouched on Ed's floor, rummaging through her bags for the tools of whichever trade she was plying that day, piling up clipboards, dance shoes and clumsily folded costumes to squeeze them into her bicycle panniers as Ed checked his watch. He held out his hands for the overspill, packing it into his own panniers to take in with him in the morning. Often, she only had time to dive into his office to change and kiss him quickly before racing off again, grinning clown-face painted in place, leaving her day clothes stuffed in the drawers of his desk.

She flopped into an armchair and kicked off her shoes.

Kit was sprawled on the sofa opposite, still in his work clothes, tie tucked in, sleeves rolled to the elbows, too tired even to close his eyes.

'Where's Anisia?' she asked.

'With her mum. Or aunts. Planning something or other.'

'Isn't there anything you need to do?'

Lily pulled the phone from her pocket and showed him the page of messages requiring her input. *Is old gold too yellow? What about champagne? Too beige? How about lilac for the chairs?*

'Nope. She doesn't want me wrecking things. All I have to do is turn up.'

How did he get away with it? He never ventured into the fairy-tale land of Brideworld. Nor Ed. They swerved the maelstrom, Kit with his lazy smile, Ed with the expression he reserved for Anisia, the slight frown that said he had to concentrate on something really urgent right now but would be with her in a minute.

'Why aren't you dancing? It is Sunday, isn't it? Or have I missed a day?'

They'd stopped dancing. Ed wanted to be home when Martin got there. They hadn't discussed it.

'Still Sunday,' said Lily.

She'd always thought she was good at facilitating dialogue, it said so on her resumé, but she could find no way into this

106

subject. Was this how they'd managed Cat's passing? With calm acceptance?

When they were home, the brothers spent their evenings and weekends in the way they always had – music on, balcony windows thrown open, beers with the bowling club, denying that the world as they lived it was about to change. Nothing was said but it was understood. Leave your troubles at the door.

'Can I have the bathroom first?' she asked.

'Go for it. Is Martin coming?'

'Ed's bringing him.'

He was bringing him, but he was unlikely to stay long. There'd be some excuse like having promised to drop in on a friend after supper. He'd leave the bottle of Chivas Regal on the table and insist on making his own way home.

'D'you think he's looking better?' asked Kit.

Lily thought not but she nodded. 'Yeah, of course.'

Anisia was waiting when she emerged from the bathroom.

'Martin's speech,' she said. 'We need to talk.'

21

Ed

June 2016

Kit might be getting married, but it was Anisia's wedding. Down to the minutest detail. Who else would use a Gantt chart? He was a fool to have shown her the software. Every time she saw him, she waved her phone at him.

There was really no need. He knew what she wanted from him. To stay out of her way and keep an eye on Kit. He'd keep the other on Martin.

On which subject, what would Martin eat?

Ed wandered the aisles of the supermarket, picking up packets and putting them down again. Omelette? Pasta? He stopped at the deli counter, scrunching his face as he stared at the cheeses, before moving back to check the fish laid out on a blanket of ice. Prawns, maybe. And spaghetti?

Portobello Market was quiet, as was usual on a Sunday, but the empty boxes cluttering the entrance to Martin's shop suggested he hadn't opened up the day before, either.

Ed suppressed a sigh. He put his shopping down on the pavement and picked up all the cardboard, squashing it into a pile and leaving it by the kerb for the recycling van. When the doorway was clear again, he leaned on Martin's doorbell and waited. Each time he visited, it took longer for his uncle to make it down the stairs, and each time he opened the door, Ed prayed he'd have the strength to haul himself back up again.

'I expected you sooner,' said Martin when he opened the door. 'This is an emergency.'

Ed laughed. 'I stopped for supplies,' he said.

Martin led him through the shop to the desk. He stood for a moment, gripping the leather top.

'Sit down,' said Ed. 'I'll chuck these in the kitchen and then we can take a look at what you've got so far.'

When he returned, Martin was sitting in front of a blank sheet of paper. His fountain pen was lined up alongside.

'Is that it?' Ed put his iPad on the desk and pulled up his chair.

'It should be you, Ed,' Martin said. 'I don't know why he asked me.'

If he'd said it once, he'd said it a hundred times. It was nonsense. They both knew he was delighted about it. If, though, he was trying to apologise, for his illness and all the rest of it, he didn't need to. He should know that.

'It's your own fault,' Ed said, instead. 'You always bang on about how you'll make the best speech, how you have all the quotes and jokes ready, but you've never had the opportunity because none of your friends got married. Well, this is your chance. And it'd better be funny.'

He lifted his hand to pat his uncle on the back but lowered it again without making contact. Martin was so thin his shoulder blades protruded through his shirt.

Ed dragged himself up the stairs to his flat. He felt utterly drained. Martin, though, seemed to have found a second wind.

'Give me the bag,' he said as they reached the front door.

He extracted the bottle and, brandishing it as if he'd won some major prize, made his entrance. 'Hello, hello,' he called, beaming, although to Ed's ears, his voice sounded reedy and weak, and the grin looked forced. 'Anyone home?'

Kit and the girls were gathered around the coffee table. Lily and Anisia jumped to their feet and rushed to take Martin's things.

'I'm utterly exhausted,' said Martin, lowering himself carefully onto the sofa as Lily fussed over him. 'He's a complete slave driver, but no matter, it's done now. Polished to perfection.'

Ed stepped into the bathroom to relieve himself. He washed his hands, carefully avoiding his reflection in the aged mirror above the basin. He would have smashed his forehead against the glass, but it was an elegant piece, mottled at the edges where the silvering was wearing away, and it would be a shame to destroy it. Instead he pressed his face for a moment into Lily's satin dressing gown which was hanging on the door and took a long, slow breath.

Lily, in person, was waiting by the kitchen for him.

'Okay?' she asked.

'Never better.'

She laughed, which made him smile, and when she wrapped her arms around him, he smiled some more.

'Why's Anisia here?' he asked, nose buried in Lily's neck. 'She hates jazz.'

'It's the speech, Ed.'

'The one I spent all day on?'

'Yeah, that one. She's wondering whether it might work better as a two-hander, you know, you and Martin?'

He held his breath. Where was she going with this?

'It's only a precaution,' she said. 'It might take the pressure off him a bit.'

He nodded, but it was a nod to say he'd heard, taken it on board, not that he agreed. Sometimes you needed a reason to carry on. This was Martin's.

'I wouldn't have let him keep those jokes in if I thought I'd have to deliver them.'

'Well, hopefully it won't come to that.'

'It won't,' he said. 'He's ready. And willing. He'll be there.'

22

Lily

June 2016

Lily ran around Ed's bedroom, finding shoes and wraps and make-up and chucking them onto the bed. Where were her curling tongs?

Ed watched from the doorway, overnight bag at his feet. Was he tapping his toe?

She surveyed the pile. There was no time to fit it all in a case for him to take to work for her. It was all right for him. He had an office. She worked out of a large backpack.

'Pack later,' he said. 'It'll be okay as long as you leave work early.'

She wasn't disorganised. He shouldn't think that. Packing in advance had felt too much like tempting fate.

'Meet me at Martin's at four-thirty. Don't be late. I want to avoid the traffic.'

'I'll be there,' she promised.

She would. She wouldn't keep Martin waiting.

Ed called her at lunchtime. 'Change of plan. Meet me at Victoria.'

'Station? What about Martin? Will you collect him on the way?'

'He's coming down in the morning.'

Her heart contracted. Was this it?

'Should we wait for him? Go down tomorrow?'

'Nah, no need. He'll be fine.'

'What about the dinner? He'll miss the dinner.'

The night-before dinner at the Sussex country house, carefully planned by Anisia to kick off the celebrations.

'He says there are too many members of the family he's fallen out with.'

Lily screwed up her face. Martin was the peace-broker in a family that never seemed to row.

'Does Anisia know?'

'He spoke to her.'

'Shall I call him?'

'You'll see him tomorrow.'

'Ed?'

'See you later. Don't forget your stuff.'

She called him at four from a coffee shop.

'Can we get a later train?'

'She's your friend.'

True, it wouldn't be Ed who was huffy and turning his back on her. Or Kit. He wouldn't mind what time they showed up. He would wrap them in a bear hug, demand they had a drink with him and introduce them to people they already knew.

'It doesn't feel right. Leaving Martin.'

It was the only way to explain the inertia that had gripped her since lunchtime.

'But he insists, so let's get a move on.'

Lily rummaged in her work bag, dumping the contents on the table as she spoke. Would she need tights? The neon fishnets would never do, but the weather was warm, she would manage without. She had her dance heels, clean knickers and more than enough make-up to get her through. Someone was bound to have some rollers or straighteners she could use on her hair.

'Oh, God. I'll need to fetch my dress from the cleaner's. And could you pick me up a toothbrush?'

'Sure.'

The drycleaner's assistant slid her dress across the counter to her. Now she remembered why she ought to have gone home first. The dress was fuchsia satin, clingy and spaghetti-strapped. She pulled at the neck of her T-shirt, borrowed from Ed for her day motivating young offenders clearing weeds and fast-food wrappers from a communal garden, and checked what she had on underneath. There was no chance the lime green sports bra could have morphed into something elegant and underwired, was there? More urgently, she couldn't possibly wear her bridesmaid's dress tomorrow, the one so carefully chosen by Anisia, without the coordinating strapless, seamless, neutral-coloured underwear which was still in the pile on Ed's bed.

Meet me in House of Fraser, she messaged him.

The lingerie section stretched before her; carousels, rails and racks of every imaginable type of undergarment in sensible shades of white, black and beige, with occasional exciting flashes of bright patterns in scarlet, purple and turquoise. This could take a while. Lily looked in vain for an assistant and then plunged in. Ed arrived, suit bag slung over his shoulder, while she was still flicking frantically through a row of plastic hangers. He kissed her cheek.

'This looks interesting. Can I help you choose?'

'Here,' she said, waving a handful of strapless bras at him. 'See if you can find something like this in my size.'

He wandered off to stroll between the aisles of pastel-coloured garments, while she continued to rifle through the rails. Too big, too small, too fancy. Ah, finally.

'Ed,' she called, and ran to the till.

'How about this?' he asked, dropping something on the counter.

'It's not… It's not exactly what I was looking for,' she said, pushing his choice gently to the side. Her fingers lingered on the fabric.

'I like the colour,' he said.

She did too, a shimmering eau-de-nil. She touched the material again.

'Will it fit?' he asked.

She checked his expression. What was he saying? He shrugged. She checked the size and held it against herself, a simple strappy shift.

'Should do.'

She smoothed the silk down with her hand and fingered the narrow band of lace trimming the bottom. She didn't own anything as delicate as this. Then she saw the price tag and stared, wide-eyed, at Ed.

'No way. It's more expensive than my dress. It's actually more expensive than my bike.'

'I'll get it.' He handed his bank card to the assistant.

Lily hesitated. 'Ed—'

'Come on. I know the crazy stuff that's in that bag of yours and I don't fancy sharing a bed with a Christmas tree. Anyway, we haven't got time to argue about it.'

He took the plastic bag the assistant gave him and zipped it into his suit carrier along with her dress in its protective cover, his smile the promise of something better later, when all the festivities were done.

They left the party early with excuses that Ed needed to work on the best man's speech, the one he was still insisting Martin would deliver, and locked themselves away in their room with its canopied bed.

Ed had a way of stepping aside from the main action, playing a part without stealing the scene, that Lily loved. He could say the right things, turn up when he was expected to but still somehow keep himself to himself, or rather keep himself for her. And tonight, he was all hers, restraint abandoned, all the feeling they'd been holding on to for months spilling wordlessly into each other. He wasn't asking for comfort but she gave him all she could, holding him, stroking him, kissing him. They didn't talk about the following day, they talked about that day and the past and themselves and all the things they hoped to do. But what she really wanted to do was stay there in that room with him, not moving forward, not going back, living those moments over and over.

In the morning, Ed was dragged away to go and perform his duties. Lily steeled herself as friends and relatives gathered for the main event. Whatever happened that day, there'd be tears for sure. She'd be fine; she could switch on a performance. She put her arm around Anisia's waist as they were zipped into their dresses and laughed as they practised their eyes-and-teeth smiles in the mirror.

Martin crunched up the gravel drive in his old convertible and straw hat.

'Aha,' said Ed, and ran out to meet him.

He turned halfway to look back at Lily and give her a nod and a smile, finally admitting relief, as if she'd been party to his secret fear. But she hadn't been, not really. He hadn't shared.

Ed leapt around, laughing with the group in the courtyard, but all Lily heard was the sharp intake of breath at the sight of the stooping figure who stepped out of the car. Martin's linen suit hung off him as if there were weights in the pockets. Ed was pulled aside to be interrogated in less than subtle whispers. Lily rushed to lend a hand, beaming at everyone who came into her sight line, encouraging everyone else to join her in pretending everything was fine.

She carried on smiling as she followed Anisia up the aisle of the function room, between the rows of little gilt chairs and swags of bougainvillea. Kit was at the front, next to Martin, hand hovering protectively under his uncle's elbow. She winked at him and he gave her a thumbs-up in reply.

All under control. She took her seat at the end of the front row. Martin eased himself onto the chair beside her. That was wrong. He was supposed to be on the other side, next to Ed. She turned to smile at him.

'Okay?' she mouthed.

He dropped a leather jewellery case into her hand. She clicked it open. Inside was a string of pearls.

'Something old for when it's your big day,' he whispered, looking straight ahead, not at her.

'I don't... we're not...' she said, taking his bony hand, careful not to squeeze his fingers.

It was there in the air but neither she nor Ed had given voice to it. One day. Probably.

'I'd rather give them to you now.' He nodded towards Anisia, who was wearing something similar.

Lily rested her chin gently on his shoulder and closed her eyes to stop the tears flowing. If she tried to speak, she wouldn't get through a sentence.

'Look after him for me,' he said.

She walked back up the aisle with Martin, past Samantha who sat at the end of the second row. It was only the second time they'd met. She looked Lily up and down, registering the red leather box in her white-knuckled hand.

'You won't be long,' she said.

Ed was right behind her. He must have heard.

23

Ed

June 2016

Martin stood by the car as Ed squeezed his and Lily's bags into the boot for the drive back to London.

'Well, that was fun but I'm glad it's done,' said Martin. 'You can write that on my gravestone, if you like.'

'Don't,' muttered Ed, shaking his head. This was really not the time to start talking.

'It was fun, though, wasn't it?' said Lily.

She hugged him tightly, which he appreciated, and then tipped the seat forward to climb into the back of the car.

Martin wouldn't let up. 'It's better if you drive,' he said, and handed over the keys. 'I might still be over the limit.'

Ed wanted to tell him to leave it, but how did you say that to a dying man? Martin had drunk almost nothing, a glass of wine only. It was close to miraculous the man had made it there at all. If it had been anyone else's wedding, Martin would have stayed away. He was probably as scared of the stir he'd cause as the disease itself. He'd never enjoyed being the centre of attention. Martin had turned up for Kit, and that moved Ed more than he could say.

His nostalgia only deepened as he took the wheel of the ancient soft-top. It was the car he'd learned to drive in. Another thing he owed his uncle. Another thing not to think about as he settled into the leather seat, cruising north while Martin dozed alongside.

Ed followed Martin up to his flat, carrying his bags and halting on every other step as his uncle paused to catch his breath.

'Can I get you anything?' he asked.

He hovered as Martin removed his jacket and dropped into a reproduction Queen Anne chair. His skin was a grey yellow, a decent match for the upholstery.

'Oh, that's very kind. I'll have the usual.'

'Are you sure...?' Ed said and frowned. Shouldn't he be encouraging him to eat something first?

'You're not going to fuss, are you?'

Ed did as he was told and fetched a tumbler of ice and a half-empty bottle of Chivas Regal from the kitchen, as he'd done many hundreds of times before. He moved a cut-glass rose bowl from a side table and squeezed it onto the mantelpiece to make room for the drinks at Martin's elbow.

'Trumpets, I think, don't you? Something celebratory.'

Ed nodded and went to look at the alcoves either side of the fireplace, where vinyl LPs lined the shelves from floor to ceiling. Celebration? If Martin could do it, then he could too. He pulled out a few albums to check the sleeves. His mind was blank, unable to recall the name of a single jazz trumpeter. Maybe the cover art would help.

'Kenny Dorham?'

'Why not?' said Martin.

Ed queued the disc on the record player and then picked up Martin's suit carrier and took it through to the bedroom.

'What are you doing?' called Martin.

'Putting your stuff away.'

'No need, I can manage. Come here.' He extended a thin and shaky hand to his nephew. 'Look, I wanted to give you this.'

'What is it?' said Ed.

He took the red velvet ring box from him and opened it, wincing when he saw the contents. Trumpets squealed in sympathy.

'Woah! Where in hell did you find this?'

'I thought you could make use of it. For Lily. Make your dreams come true.' Martin grinned, his face all wrinkles now.

'By giving her nightmares?' said Ed. 'That's an absolute disgrace. No thanks.'

He tried to hand the box back. Martin pushed it away.

'Don't be an idiot, the diamonds are good. You can use them in something else.'

Ed opened the box again. It was so out of context with what he was feeling, he couldn't quite take it in. He got that weddings made people sentimental and Martin had more reason than most, but this ring really hit a low point. The setting was bulbous and garish, intertwined leaves and flowers, sacrificing style in an attempt to be pretty and managing neither. It was hard to see what could be done to improve it.

'I've got no-one else to give it to,' said Martin.

'That's no excuse.'

'I want you to have it.'

'I can't think about this now.'

'Take it, and then take Lily home. You can bring the car back tomorrow.' He closed his eyes.

'Martin…?'

'You still here?'

Ed picked up the whisky bottle and carried it into the kitchen. He went to put it in the top cupboard but stopped halfway and allowed himself a long gulp, coughing as the alcohol hit the back of his throat. He placed both hands on the edge of the sink and leaned forwards, closing his eyes for a moment before pulling himself up, lifting the bottle onto the shelf and flicking the door shut.

By the time he returned to the car, Lily had moved into the front passenger seat and was curled against the window with her eyes closed. He let himself into the driver's side and sat for a moment.

'Lily?' he said softly, touching her arm. 'You awake?'

She sighed but didn't open her eyes.

'Lily?' he tried again.

He wasn't even sure what he was going to say, something about not making it through without her. When she didn't reply, he dropped the box in the pocket of his coat, chucked it on the back seat and started the engine.

24

Lily

23.10

Lily stuffed her phone in her pocket, grabbed her rucksack and suitcase, and headed for the car park, her head still full of images of Ed, quiet and loving in the half light of a hotel bedroom. It seemed so long ago.

'Happy Christmas,' she called to the student who remained at the table, watching something on his phone.

'Oh, right, yeah, you too,' he said, eyes darting here and there.

It was getting old, this queuing to load her bag in the hold, queuing again to board the bus. Christmas goodwill was evaporating like the steam fogging up the windows. Lily had to ask someone twice to move their bag so she could squeeze into a seat. The driver wasn't hanging around either. As soon as he'd reached his passenger limit, he shut the doors against further boarders and sped back onto the motorway before anyone gathered enough wind to complain.

Lily scrunched her anorak on her lap. Her fingers traced the outlines of the coins in the pocket. It wouldn't do to lose them; it was all she had left. She collected the money into her palm and reached with her other hand down and under the seat to drag her rucksack up onto her lap, taking care not to elbow her neighbour, who sighed each time Lily moved. The top zip of the backpack was level with Lily's nose. She wouldn't have to open the bag fully, just wide enough to pull out the smaller bag, find her wallet and tuck the coins away.

She swapped the coins to her other hand and dug deeper, identifying each item with her fingertips. It was ridiculous. Why couldn't she find it? The mini rucksack had to be there because if it wasn't, and it didn't bear thinking about, it meant that neither were her wallet or her passport. Lily squeezed down to the floor and felt wildly around, bumping against her neighbour, who yelped every time she touched her feet. All she came up with was an empty juice box and a screwed-up tissue.

Then she remembered. She'd taken the bag out when she charged her phone. Of all the stupid things she'd done that day. The bag must still be there on the plastic seats next to the fish and chip shop. She grabbed her coat and rucksack and pushed past her neighbour again and out into the aisle, bouncing off the backrest of every seat until she reached the driver.

'Can you stop the bus? I have to get off.'

He ignored her.

'It's an emergency. I left my bag at the service station.'

'Sit down, please.' He didn't take his eyes off the road.

'I have to go back. Please.' Her desperation was making her tearful. 'If you stop here, I can walk back.'

'I can't let you off, it's the motorway. And I can't stop to take your luggage off.'

It needed less than a second's thought. She could travel without make-up and spare shoes, but without a passport, she'd be going nowhere.

'I haven't got luggage. My bag's at the service station.' She grabbed the driver's door.

'Don't do that! It's dangerous,' said the driver, eyes firmly ahead. 'If you do it again, I'll call the police. Go and sit down.'

'Okay.'

She sat on the steps and rested her head on her hands. Things couldn't really get much worse. The driver had probably already pressed his panic button and they'd be met in London by police vans and men with handcuffs, looking forward to locking her up over Christmas. She wouldn't need a passport then.

'I meant in a seat,' said the driver. 'You are one problem I don't need this evening. Go sit down and I'll let you off at the next service station. I'm not taking you back, though.'

Lily scrambled back up the steps and scanned the front seats for any gaps to park herself in. The other passengers averted their eyes until a man five rows back shuffled across enough for Lily to perch on the edge.

'Thanks,' she said, shrinking into her coat.

The driver swerved into the inside lane as soon as the sign for the exit appeared. He opened the doors almost before the coach reached a standstill, closing them again with a swish as Lily's boots hit the tarmac.

She looked around. The car park was poorly lit and hidden from the road by foliage. There were a few cars dotted here and there. The lorry park to the right seemed busier but she wasn't inclined to venture over. Hitching a ride might be marginally safer than walking along the hard shoulder, but this was the sort of situation that all her personal safety training would flag up as red. She put her hood up, swung her one remaining bag onto her shoulder and walked past the petrol pumps to the shop. She picked up a bottle of water and went straight to the till.

'Hi,' she said. 'D'you know how I can get to the other side of the road? Is there a subway or walkway round here?'

The teenager behind the counter looked at her like she was mad. He picked up the bottle and scanned it. Lily looked at the price and slid some of her precious coins across the counter.

'How can it be that much? I could buy two for that anywhere else.'

He shrugged.

'I need to get to the service station before this. D'you know how I can get there?'

A man had joined the queue behind her.

'Well, love,' he said, 'we have this fantastic invention called a roundabout. There's one up ahead and one back the other direction. D'you think if you get in your car and drive it on that road there, you'll be able to manage that?'

'I expect I could if I had a car,' said Lily, too weary to deal with the rest. 'But I haven't, so is there another way to get there?'

'How did you get here without a car?' asked the boy who couldn't have left school yet.

'I drifted in from outer space,' said Lily, taking her water and stalking past them to the door.

'Hang on,' said Mr Know-it-all, following her out of the shop. 'If you really need a lift, I've got my van over there.'

'Which way are you going?' asked Lily, not believing the words were coming out of her mouth.

'Well, I wasn't planning on going to Mars.' He leered at her. 'But I'll take you somewhere else.'

'I get it.'

She backed away towards the comparative safety of the shop, waiting in the doorway until the man had driven away past the fuel pumps. Her options were limited. Her mum would be sympathetic, even if her brother wasn't, but it was unlikely anyone in the house would be in a fit state to help her. Uber! Ed's favourite solution whenever she'd missed the plane/bus/last tube and had to get somewhere fast. Could she get a car out here? She went back to the counter.

'Where am I, by the way?'

'Earth,' said the boy.

'Funny,' she said. 'Postcode?'

She picked up an A-Z from the rack and opened it on the counter, following the motorway route with her finger.

'You buying that?'

'No, I don't intend to stay in these parts long enough, but can you help me?'

'Sure,' said the youth, pointing out her location. 'You're here. You don't want to go with that other guy, though. He don't look right.'

'Oh, you spotted that too.'

She took her phone and wandered outside, pacing the car park like a water diviner until she caught a decent signal.

Simon would be with her in twenty-four minutes in his silver Toyota, said the app – but there'd be a surcharge. Naturally. It was Christmas.

'Ed?'

'Hey, how are you? Are you here?'

'It's a bit complicated to explain. I think I'm going to be quite late, so don't wait at the bus station. Go to the hotel and I'll find you there.'

'Wha's 'appened?'

'Oh, it's not a big deal. I left my bag at the service station—'

'Lily!' he groaned.

'It's your fault.'

'My fault?'

'I was thinking about you and that hotel room.'

'Oh yeah?' He laughed. 'Me too, me too.' He was barely coherent. 'Wha' were you thinking?'

'I was thinking you didn't have that beard then. As soon as I moved away you grew a beard.'

'I had to. I held out s'long as I could. Everyone at work has a beard. Don' you like it, then?'

'Yeah, course I do, it's fine, but when I think about you, I imagine you without.'

Why she was even telling him? The beard wasn't important. It was only that all their best times together, all the memories that were precious, dated from over a year ago.

'Anyway, I'm going back to get my rucksack. I'll do it very quickly.'

'Why? Wha's in it?' he said, suddenly alert. 'Have you got your passport?'

'Yeah, yeah, of course. But my wallet's in the bag.'

'Don' worry 'bout that. Stop the cards. S'long as you've

got your passport, s'fine. I've got money. Get on the bus, I'll see you soon.'

'I can't. The bus doesn't stop here. Look, I won't be much longer.'

She rang off before he could ask more questions. He'd offer to pick up the tab and she'd be beholden to him again. He wasn't mean and he'd never make a thing of it, but he seemed unable to understand why she couldn't let him pay for something until she knew she'd have the money to pay him back.

'It's because you've never been poor,' she'd told him the last time it came up.

'Neither have you,' he retorted. 'You went to private school.'

'It was different. It was a theatre school and I had a bursary, but my mum had to save to pay the rest of my fees. I've always worked. For everything.'

'You think I haven't? I never turn a gig down either.'

'That's not what I mean. What I mean is you knew you had choices. There was money there if you needed it.'

'What I had was a trust fund set up by my mum to pay for my education and then Martin in an emergency,' he said. 'And you know what that taught me? Money is a means to an end. That's all.'

She didn't want to upset him by arguing about it. In many respects, her childhood had been less deprived than his.

Simon was at the service station in twenty-four minutes as promised, but it took him another twenty to find Lily. She watched him on the app driving in circles around the perimeter.

'It will have to count as waiting time,' he said.

'Fine, fine,' said Lily. 'Can we go?'

25

Ed

24 December 2017, 00.00

Ed walked the long way back to the hotel. He hadn't intended to. He was almost down at the Embankment before he noticed. He cut back up to Trafalgar Square to divert along the Mall, past Buckingham Palace and the night-time tourists peering optimistically through the gates for a glimpse of the royals in their pyjamas. It wasn't an unpleasant walk, apart from the annoying yellow bag swinging and knocking against his knee.

What to do? Lily wasn't picking up her phone. There could be many reasons for this, not all of them bad. If he knew where she was, he'd borrow the car from Kit and go get her – or he could if he hadn't drunk so much. Perhaps Kit would drive? Might be a tough ask at this hour.

What did she mean when she said the buses didn't stop there? Why didn't she get a cab? At least to the bus station. If she was worried about the cost, he'd pay. He stopped under a streetlight and messaged her.

You okay? Can you get cab from there? Send postcard and I'll get you Uber.

He squinted at the message again. **postcode*, he corrected. There was no answering ping.

'The bar's still open for residents, sir,' said the night porter, buzzing him into the hotel.

Ordinarily he would have been tempted, but drinking alone had lost its appeal. He headed upstairs, relying heavily on the bannister. The room was as vacantly pretty as when he'd left it five hours earlier – curvy lines and gold-edged patterns just waiting to be admired. Ed wagged his head at them. They couldn't fool him. He designed spaces for a living. You could do what you wanted to a place, but it was the people that made you want to stay. Ed threw his coat on the chair and sat on the edge of the bed. The new boots were a big disappointment. So much for symbolising hope and escape. He kicked at his heels, but the boots didn't budge. They were laced too damn tightly and bending down to undo them seemed unwise for the moment.

He leaned back against the pillows and checked his phone. Still nothing. He messaged again.

Love you. Was that too needy? Anisia, the great expert on his and Lily's relationship, told him he was needy. It may have looked like that at one time – the perfect storm of events. He'd once asked Lily if he was too needy. Not nearly enough, she'd said.

The carrier bag lay on its side on the dresser. He winced at the sight of it. What did Lily mean about his beard? He stood to examine his reflection in the mirror above the desk, gripping the polished edge to keep his image in focus. Fair enough, the beard wasn't in great shape, but there were guys in his office whose beards wouldn't look out of place in an adaptation of Tolkien. Lars, for instance, who divided his beard into three sections, plaited and threaded with coloured beads. He rarely made it on site, though. Ed could imagine what the steel crews would say if he turned up with beads in his beard. They took the piss enough already.

I see the Grim Reaper's here again. Who've you come for this time? they said when he arrived, black suit buttoned up beneath the fluid black coat. One of their favourite tricks was handing him a pickaxe or a stake. *You left this behind, Ed.* Half the labourers thought he was called 'Mister Black' for a joke. They didn't realise it was actually his name.

It wouldn't hurt to trim his beard, but his washbag contained no scissors or razor, nothing that might end up in a bin at airline security. All he had were nail clippers. He ventured into the bathroom, twisting them between his fingers. Hell, the light was bright. He shut one eye against the shimmer, leaned closer to the mirror and took a tentative snip, losing his balance and banging his forehead on the glass.

His phone pinged. He dropped the clippers in the sink and rushed back into the bedroom, knocking his shoulder on the door frame as he went.

x

It wasn't much, but she was alive, at least.

He planted a kiss on his phone and sat heavily on the bed. Bloody boots with their bloody laces. It was time to sleep, but if he lay down, his head would spin, and if he closed his eyes, he'd think of Lily, Lily in that pale green shift with her nearly black hair and her olive skin. He couldn't get her image out of his mind. Or the feel of her as he slid his hands over and under, kissing her body through the silk. Was that what she meant about the beard? He shook his head to rid it of the torment and paced the room again, tripping over his toes as his boots snagged on the thick carpet.

If it was cleanshaven she wanted, he could do that. He opened the door and made his way carefully along the corridor to the stairs, using the dado rail as a guide rope.

'Hi,' he said as he approached the receptionist at the desk, casually grasping one corner of the counter in case he swayed. 'I need to get hold of a razor. Do you have a spare one by any chance?'

'We don't tend to hold them, sir. Or lend them out. Hygiene reasons.'

'Yes,' said Ed, drawing out the syllable. 'I see. What about the spa? Could I get a shave there?'

'Not at this time, sir. Can it wait 'til the morning?'

'I don't know. Maybe not. I'm going to Iceland and I need to shave my beard.'

'I'm pretty certain they allow beards there,' he said.

'Turns out my girlfriend doesn't like it.'

The receptionist finally looked up and gave him a long, hard stare, no doubt wondering whether this girlfriend, the one who hadn't yet appeared, really existed. Ed didn't blame him. He was starting to wonder too.

'Tell you what, sir, there's an all-night chemist in Old Brompton Road. They can probably sort you out. Shall I find you a taxi?'

26

Lily

00.30

The bag wasn't on the chair. Nor was it on the floor beneath. Lily climbed on the banquette for a bird's eye view, but the rucksack wasn't lying on a table or tossed in a corner. She toured the seating area, weaving in and out of each concession, hunting under tables and around every chair, boots pounding in time with her racing pulse. Where was it? The whole place was way too orderly, with only a couple of food trays on the tables and a discarded paper cup here and there. If the bag were there, she'd have seen it – and so would whoever had tidied up – but if a well-intentioned someone had found it and handed it in, where would they take it?

Lily ran to the coffee outlet, where a tired-eyed assistant with a black shirt and barista beard was cleaning the coffee machine.

''Scuse me,' she called. 'Is there a lost property here?'

'Yeah,' said the assistant, barely turning to acknowledge her presence, 'but it won't be open 'til the morning.'

'I can't wait 'til then. I've lost my bag.'

'Have you asked the cleaners? Sometimes they pick things up.'

'Where are they?'

'They're usually in the toilets,' said the man. 'Can I get you anything?'

Lily jangled the change in her pocket. She was hungry, but the lump in her throat was putting her off eating and probably the only thing she'd be able to afford was a flapjack, which didn't rate as comfort food as far as she was concerned. She gulped some water from her bottle instead.

It was easy to work out the way to the toilets by following the smell. A cleaning trolley was also parked outside, unattended.

'Hello,' Lily called into the white-tiled doorway. 'Is anyone there?'

A middle-aged man exited, re-zipping his jacket as he passed.

'Excuse me, did you see…?' Lily started.

He gave her a funny look and walked away.

She tried again. 'Hello-oh.'

A man in blue overalls and rubber gloves, carrying a yellow fold-away sign, appeared. He jumped at the sight of her.

'Are you the cleaner?' said Lily, smiling as brightly as she could manage. 'I wanted to ask if you'd found my bag. It's quite small, like a rucksack?'

He shook his head.

'I lost it this evening. An hour or so ago.'

'I didn't find it,' he said finally.

'Are you sure? It's really important. Is there anyone else I can ask?'

'I didn't find it,' he repeated.

He looked at her curiously, running his eyes over the unravelling jumper and her hair, which must be standing on end from the number of times she'd raked her hands through it.

'Are you the only cleaner?'

'The others finished already,' he said. 'We didn't find a bag.' He shook his head again. 'Just jacket, umbrella, like that.'

'Can I leave you my number? You can call me then if you find it. It's black, with a leather flap and leather straps.'

Lily scrabbled in the bottom of her bag for her notebook and tore a page out to draw a picture of the missing rucksack. She wrote her number underneath. The man shrank from her as she tried to press the paper into his hand.

'In case you find my bag,' she said.

'It's not nice,' he said, 'staying there, by the toilet.'

He pointed her in the direction of the shopping zone and gave his trolley a small shove. It didn't touch her, but the gesture was clear.

Lily allowed herself to be shepherded back to the central area and sat obediently on the closest chair. She waited until he'd gone before putting her face in her hands. It was an effort not to wail or rock on the chair like a small child. She'd managed to lose her wallet, and all of her clothes. Her bank card was somewhere in Cardiff. She had a credit card, but it was all but maxed out and was at home, safe in the drawer of her bedside cabinet. Buying a bus ticket was pointless as this place wasn't an official stop, and if she gave up on London in favour of returning to Cardiff, she couldn't get into her flat. The keys were zipped safely into the bag she had lost.

Then there was her passport. Without ID, she'd have no chance of sorting any of this out. She took her hands from her face and pushed them down into the pockets of her coat. She turned the remaining coins between the fingers of her left hand. With her right, she traced the lines of the cardboard box and the pregnancy test. It might be all she had left.

27

Ed

03.20

So there was some guy, was there? Ed checked his watch. If he called Anisia early, he might catch her off guard, but he mustn't wake the baby. She woke up early, didn't she? Wasn't that what Kit moaned about? What was early, though? He'd sort of lost track. On the other hand, if he called Anisia, she'd assume he was worried. And he absolutely wasn't.

If only he could sleep. But what was the point? When Lily arrived, she'd need his help getting past the night desk manager, that's if she even found her way to the hotel.

Where was she?

Ed fetched his laptop from his bag and settled back on the bed, great fat boots on the coverlet. It had been so long since there'd been anyone to point out stuff like that and no-one here who would care – apart maybe from the housekeeper. He slid his feet to the side, heels and soles hanging over the edge.

Where to begin? He started with his Facebook page, a place he hardly ever visited. In the old days, this would have been easy. Lily's page was permanently open on his computer, her life laid bare for him – if he cared to look. Now when he got Facebook alerts from her, he barely gave them a glance. Most of it was about her work anyway. If anything was that important, she'd tell him, wouldn't she? He switched to her page and scrolled down the timeline, registering all the messages from people he'd never heard of, far outnumbering the friends he recognised. It wasn't a good sign, but even so, nothing out of the ordinary, no cryptic clues, nothing he could see… Suppose she'd reset her privacy settings and what he wanted was restricted and invisible to him?

Lily's own account was password-protected, but he could make a guess; she only ever used variations of her cat's name. *Fluff1ngt0n* got him in. He was sweating. It was awful, like rifling through her bags, a thing he'd never do, though she went through his pockets often enough. Half the contents belonged to her, all the hairbands and lipstick and so on.

He flicked through the messages. Most were invites, feedback or thank-yous, and virtually all were from women. He moved on to the photos. There were enough of him to be reassuring but apart from a couple from the summer, few recent ones. They still took photos, didn't they? Perhaps they'd stopped smiling in them. One caught his attention. A picture of him, with Kit, holding Kit's baby, both laughing as the little girl opened her mouth to yell. Why had that one been given such prominence? The obvious wasn't necessarily that obvious with Lily.

The recent uploads were all about Medic48. He hadn't

appreciated how much she now defined herself by her work. There were links to demos about doctors' pay and hospital closures, peace demonstrations, petitions and citizens' campaigns. The hyperlinks to the company website took him to photos of Lily and her team in green tabards, loading and unloading medical supplies, meeting and greeting teams at airports. Her mate, Matt, was everywhere in them, wearing that expression that said concern-but-also-empathy. Was anyone taken in by him? Then, there were the images of the medics at work, the makeshift field hospitals and people wrapped in bandages and on drips. Part of him wanted to turn away from it, the other half drew him closer.

The photo-stories were compelling. He sat up straighter, immersed in the narrative. Lily's work had everything – excitement, urgency and emotional reward – and Medic48 were lucky to have her. Not everyone had the skills and charisma to produce results like this. Each intervention was crafted to respond to an immediate need before a longer-term strategy was put in place, like the sort of thing he had to design in refurbs to make each stage of a project safe and viable, a bridge to the next phase. The missions were planned like a pop-up shop. As soon as they found a venue and had permission to enter, they were there. If they couldn't source a place ready equipped with a bombproof basement and a generator, they'd build their own field centre. He knew that because he'd built one for Lily once.

According to the legends splashed across the cover photos, the charity got most jobs on the road within thirty-six to forty-eight hours, making sure everything hit the ground at the same time. Every mission statement bore the same boast. Medic48 were first on the ground, filling the gap until a more permanent response, national or international, arrived. They were in and out of a site within six weeks.

Well, there was something wrong there because they must have been in Serbia for at least a year, sending in wave after wave of volunteers. Lily had been there loads of times and here were the photos to prove it. Here was Matt and Andy, even that weird Hassan. Wonder what happened to him.

Ed closed the Facebook page and deleted his search history.

He wasn't going to look for anything else. Lily had been to Serbia four or five times, way more often than to her other medical centres. He'd never asked her why.

28

Lily

June 2016

Menassi drove into the grounds of the Hurlingham Club and parked next to the caterers' trucks. Lily propped her make-up mirror on the dashboard and smeared black and gold paint across her face, neck and shoulders before climbing over the seats and into the back of the van. She pulled off her T-shirt and stepped into her raggedy dress, turning her back for Adam to fasten the hooks and eyes. Next she tugged on her wig and painted gloves before checking her reflection again in the mirror and climbing out, dragging her theatrical chains behind her.

'Hang on,' said Adam, and put a bit more paint on the back of her shoulders. 'Yeah, you're good.'

The perfect lawns were populated with small groups of prosecco-swigging partygoers who parted with a graceful shudder each time Lily's renegade, dead-eyed slave drifted past.

Lily didn't envy them exactly. What she envied was the downtime. Ed and Kit worked long hours, Kit especially, but there was a purpose to what they did. She wanted her days to be filled with the same conviction. Her sort of busy was a trap, never paying enough to develop her skillset or buy time to look for something else. She couldn't do this forever, spending her working life with a pair of green and yellow tights hidden under her day clothes. If she'd learnt anything from Martin, it was that life was short. There were things he'd never do now, places he'd never see.

Lily stopped behind a tree and pulled her phone from her stiffened lace sleeve.

'Hey, Kate,' she said, when her friend answered. 'Were you serious about sneaking me onto one of your marketing courses?'

'Absolutely,' said Kate. 'As long as you'll choreograph my wedding dance.'

'You're on.'

Lily stood to the side of the break-out room, holding her cup and saucer and trying to decide if she was enjoying the sight of someone else standing at the front trying to motivate people or whether she was going to struggle to stay awake. She almost never spent an entire day indoors, let alone three in a row. Maybe it wasn't for her. She felt conspicuous in her leggings and trainers among all the suited and booted marketing execs. There was nothing in her wardrobe, most of which was on the floor of Ed's room, which would pass for office worker, even on a dress-down Friday. Everything she owned was too sparkly, scruffy or slutty.

The programme looked good, though – *Defining and*

delivering messages – even if it was being delivered by a psychologist pushing his latest book.

A man in jeans and a crumpled T-shirt looked over at her. That was the second time. A herbal tea label was draped over the side of his teacup. Maybe he recognised a kindred spirit. She smiled encouragingly and he wandered across.

'So, er, Lily,' said Matt, reading her name badge. 'Are you going to get what you want from this?'

She'd heard worse chat-up lines.

'Too early to say, Matt,' she said, checking the name of his employer under his own. She'd heard of them, an international development organisation. 'Are you?'

'Definitely. I'm after a couple of days where I'm not standing around in a muddy field, pretending I know what's going on. It's already looking good.'

'You too?' She laughed. 'What d'you do, then?'

'General logistics specialist. I'm working in food security right now. In West Africa.'

What had been happening there recently? She'd have to look it up before the next break – or call Ed. If he didn't know, he'd find out for her.

'And you came all that way for this?'

'Continuing professional development. Twice a year, they fly me back for meetings and training courses. At least I get to sleep in the same bed for a fortnight.'

'Wow. How long have you been working there?'

'A year or so. I was doing supply coordination before for a medical charity. What about you?'

'Oh… I specialise in community engagement, legacy projects, that sort of thing.'

'Interesting,' he said, nodding his approval.

She wouldn't tell him she spent most of her time handing out dustbin bags and litter-pickers. Here was someone who could open up the world of aid coordination for her. A bit of gloss could do no harm.

At lunch, he told her he was looking for a project manager job.

'Are you going to stay in Africa?'

'I hope so. I like the travel, and if you want to work in this field, you need to be free to move around.'

'But there are jobs in the UK, aren't there?'

'Sure, but the best jobs are elsewhere.'

She stored that thought away.

They finished for the day and it wasn't a surprise when Matt suggested going for a drink.

'Ah, sorry,' she said. 'I've got to work.'

She shrugged, letting him think she was extraordinarily dedicated to the population of Newham, not spending the evening wrapped in netting and green plastic leaves. It was terrible timing. In one day, she'd learnt as much from Matt as from the trainer – a whole new lexicon, the vocabulary of humanitarian assistance. There had to be a way to make this connection work.

'I'm meeting my boyfriend first, though. Why don't you come for a drink with us? Ed never needs an excuse to go to the pub.'

They left the university building together and walked out onto the street. Lily waved at Ed, who was leaning against the wall opposite. He was holding onto her bicycle to prevent it toppling over from the weight of the panniers bulging on either side. She so wanted to introduce them and for Ed to understand what else might be out there for her.

'There he is,' she said, but when she turned back to Matt, he'd walked off in the other direction.

Ed was wearing a nylon cap pulled down over one eye. He showed her a moody profile.

'Where did you get that?' Lily asked, laughing as she kissed him. She pulled the hat down over the other eye, knocking his glasses down to the end of his nose.

'Menassi dropped it off with your stuff. He said I look like a young Marlon Brando in it.'

'Do you? I'm not sure what he looks like.'

'Neither.' He lifted the hat from his head and put it on hers. 'Suits you, though. Good day?'

'Really good. At least I thought so.' She reached her arms inside his coat and hugged him tight, squeezing the air out of him.

'That good?' he gasped. 'So, what are we doing? Food? Or something else?'

'Food, but easy on the carbs. I mustn't bloat, privet is so unforgiving.'

'Can't tempt you with noodles, then?'

'Always.'

She climbed onto the seat of the bike, holding her hat with one hand and Ed's coat pocket with the other as he stepped over the crossbar and took to the pedals.

Lily arrived the next morning with a list of questions for her new friend. She slid into a seat at his table, expecting to pick up their conversation where they'd left it the day before.

Matt offered her a bland smile. 'Hey, you okay?' he said, before turning to the woman on the other side and joining a conversation she was having with the next table.

146

'Yeah,' she said, taken aback. 'You?'

It was a little disappointing that the most interesting person she'd met in a while should turn out to be so superficial, but not necessarily fatal. It could even make things easier. She'd find a way to pick his brains while he got over any notions he might have had about how he was going to spend his home leave.

'Hey, let's keep in touch, yeah?' said Matt, when the course broke up. 'I'll look out for something good for you.'

29

Ed

August 2016

The sudden silence got to him. He'd forgotten what that was like. Martin was the one who'd always filled the gaps, sliding gently into his dead sister's shoes to restore some order to his nephews' lives, along with vitamins and green vegetables. He was the link between the past and the future. Without Martin, there was no dialogue. And no-one to interpret his parents for him.

Ed's memories of his mother were fading, but Martin kept her alive for him, even if half the stories were made up. Whether or not he was supposed to believe his mother hated smoking, loved playing chess and never turned the corner of a book, Ed appreciated the effort. He would match Martin's tales with some of his own. Cat playing gin rummy, for instance, cigarette jammed in the corner of her mouth, one eye shut against the smoke, cheating so her boys could win. And no-one who cared about their property would ever have lent her a book. She lay them face down on her studio table, curling pages threatened by the pool of ink spreading from a spillage nearby. His father followed her round, picking them up and closing them. He'd banned her from touching anything on his shelves.

With Martin gone, Ed had no-one to talk to about Cat, and worse, no-one to remember his uncle for him. He yearned to speak to his mum in a way he hadn't for years.

Did Laurence feel the same? Martin had been family, but he'd also been a friend. He had to be suffering his loss, although he'd never say anything. Ed knew his father's limitations in that department. If it was philosophy or literature you were interested in, he'd chat for hours, but if it wasn't on the written page, it might as well not exist.

Ed wouldn't let him suffer. He'd reach out to him.

He had a key to his father's house, but he rang the bell anyway. His dad and Samantha were newly-weds and you never knew. Weird, that.

Samantha answered the door.

'We thought it best to change the locks,' she said. 'Martin won't be coming and going anymore, and Lord only knows how many people still have keys to this place.'

Why had she told him? If she'd said nothing, he'd have been none the wiser.

His dad sat at the table, engrossed in the review section of the paper. He waved his son into the chair opposite and passed him the travel supplement.

'Here you go. I won't be a moment,' he said.

Samantha brought a pot of coffee and placed it in front of

Laurence along with three floral mugs. Where was the willow pattern? Surely she hadn't binned all the old china.

'It might be better to call before you come over,' she told Ed. 'In case we're not here.'

She stood behind her husband, hands on his shoulders, as Laurence poured coffee for them all.

Ed had never called ahead. Apart from anything else, his father couldn't be guaranteed to answer a phone even if he was in the house. Laurence relied on people just rocking up. He wouldn't turn anyone away. Ed searched his dad's face for clues, but Laurence's expression said nothing. He was preoccupied looking for somewhere to place his wet teaspoon. The man couldn't cope without a saucer, let alone organise coffee invitations.

'I don't mind,' Ed said. 'It's not far. If you're not in or you're busy, I'll come back another time.'

Samantha squeezed Laurence's shoulders. If her hands moved any higher, they'd be around his neck.

'Your dad might have plans,' she said.

Ed frowned. Plans? Samantha might have plans, but not Laurence. He didn't plan. He did what he liked, always had done. The only constant in his behaviour was how he avoided committing himself to anything. It probably wasn't the best time to point it out.

'That's good, Dad,' he said instead. 'I'm glad you've got plans.'

He sipped his coffee and flicked through the reviews of winter breaks to Chile and New Zealand. What was Samantha worried about? He didn't exactly burden his father with his company. Usually, he felt the old boy was due a bit more attention. Still, if she wanted him all to herself... He glanced round the room, taking in the faded wallpaper with the water stain from when the gutters had leaked and he'd had to fix them, the scuffed wooden floor that he and Kit had sanded and finished. *You're on your own now*, he told the place.

His father looked up, smiled and slid the newspaper across the table. 'Seen this? Someone got there first.' A biography of the politician whose memoirs his father was ghosting.

'Might work in your favour,' Ed said. 'You can put the record straight.'

They were back on familiar territory, even if it wasn't exactly where he wanted to be. Laurence talking, Ed paying half attention.

If plans were the order of the day, he could make some too, exercise some agency, as Anisia would say – even if she preferred to organise Kit's life for him and deny him independence. For starters, he should ask Lily to move in. She was there more than half the week, he could make it official. Let's face it, it was about time and it was what he wanted. But she had to want it too and not worry she was filling the void left by Kit, because that wasn't it. Would she even want to live in the flat? It was so much his family's place, his and Kit's inheritance, yes, but also the place where all the clutter of their childhoods, actual and psychological, was stacked up. If she came in, she had to be free to rummage through all the drawers. Not a pleasant thought. She shouldn't have to clamber over the past to get to the future – and someone else's past at that. She deserved better. Kit had taken the easy option, moving his love elsewhere, but Ed would have to deal with all the crap before he let someone else in.

30

Lily

September 2016

It wasn't stalking, not really. All she did was check Matt's profile on every site where he had an online presence. And he sent her the links. If anyone could help her land the right job, it was him. He knew everyone and went everywhere.

Lily tracked his travels through Africa, poring over the photos. Lorries ploughing along red sand roads, deliveries to corrugated shacks where Matt stood waiting, Matt playing football with smiling villagers. It was her guilty pleasure, a window to another world. If Matt could make a career out of coordinating people, maybe she could too. All the days spent in community centres and fly-tips reasoning with truculent teenagers and angry neighbours could be serving a purpose.

An email dropped into her inbox.

I've got a new job, Matt wrote. *Project manager for Medic48.*

They're recruiting, expanding ops to Europe. Do you want the application pack?

Lily's fingers hovered over the keyboard. What did he mean by Europe? Even France would be a stretch right now. Ed couldn't travel – not when he was so near to qualifying. She sneaked a peak at the job description and her stomach churned. True, they were hiring for a project in Central Europe, coordinating volunteer doctors for disaster relief, but the job itself was based in the UK. Not London, but Bristol. If it had meant a move to Cyprus or eastern Ukraine, she could have pushed it out of her mind, but Bristol, that was doable.

There was no easy way to break this news. Filling Ed with feel good food would take her only so far.

She waited until they'd almost done clearing up the kitchen, moving every item from the polished surfaces and back into the cupboards, the only room in the flat where that was possible.

'I've been offered a new job.' She showed him her phone with the congratulatory message.

'Well done,' he said, barely glancing at it. 'When d'you start?'

'Depends if I take it.'

'Why wouldn't you?'

'It's in Bristol.' Lily placed her phone in his hand. 'I'd need to move there. I couldn't commute every day.'

He recoiled slightly, then frowned as he lifted the phone to read the details. 'Oh.'

He was looking for the right thing to say, she could tell. She felt a heat start beneath her ribs and move outwards as if she'd taken a hit to the chest.

'It all happened much faster than I thought it would,' she said, rushing her words. 'I didn't think I'd get it. I was just, sort of, testing the waters.'

He was still reading.

'I should have told you sooner. It was just that you had so much on your plate, with all the wills and trusts and stuff, and I didn't want to disturb you. Especially if it didn't go anywhere. I know the timing's really bad.'

He smiled finally. 'I've got nothing to say to you about timing. D'you want to take it?'

She hesitated. What would he do? What would he say? What she didn't want was for him to think she was forcing his hand. Everything was still so raw. It wasn't the right time.

'I don't know. I think so. It's an amazing opportunity. I don't know when I'll get another chance.'

He exhaled heavily. 'Then take it. We'll cope. It's not that far. We'll see each other at weekends.'

'Could you, maybe, get a job in Bristol?'

'I'll try,' he said, with no enthusiasm. 'I'll look for some competitions to enter.'

He looked like someone had switched off his energy supply. His smiles had no power behind them.

She put her arms around him and squeezed him as tightly as she could. 'You're not glad to get rid of me, are you?'

'Course not.' He kissed her cheek though her hair. 'You know I'm not.'

'This is the thing I've been looking for.'

'I know, you've worked hard for it. You deserve it.'

'But you don't want me to go?'

'No, I'd like it better if you stayed.'

They stood, arms around each other, until Lily relaxed her

grip and offered to make them a cup of tea. If he'd only speak. But what was it she wanted him to say? It would be awful if he made going into an issue.

He released her and stretched.

'Nah,' he said, 'not tea. Let's go for a drink. Celebrate your new career.'

31

Ed

October 2016

He'd known Lily was applying for jobs. It was how she spent her spare time. That and shopping for shoes. If she was going to leave him for a job, it had to be this one. It was hard to argue against. She'd be coordinating a medical response to emergencies abroad – all the earthquakes, wars or outbreaks of disease in hard-to-reach locations where, if they could get doctors there swiftly, it would make all the difference to survival. The sort of work celebrities made films about for charity fundraising. He was proud of her. And said so. When he got a chance.

Mick drove them to Bristol. Ed would have preferred to do it himself, but it was Mick's van and he wanted to come along. Ed sensed Lily's mother's part in it. It made for an awkward journey, the three of them squeezed into the front seat, Lily holding on to Ed's hand while Mick listened to the football on the radio. Ed wished he'd stayed at home, but it would have looked like he was sulking, which he absolutely wasn't. It would have been much easier to do this with just the two of them and no witnesses. He felt like he'd been turned to stone.

Could he have asked her to stay, for his sake, in a job that was taking her nowhere? It wouldn't have been fair.

More crucially, suppose he begged her to stay and she refused?

This was something she had to do and he wouldn't make her feel bad about it. It would deny everything he loved about her and he would tell her that – as soon as he got a bit of breathing space.

Mick was unloading the van, hurrying them along, insisting on breaking for pizza. Ed swallowed what was before him without tasting it. Suddenly everything was unpacked and arranged and Mick was worrying about the traffic. It had happened too fast. Ed hadn't had more than five minutes alone with Lily. He hadn't told her how he liked that she'd push her limits and give anything a go, whether it was juggling flaming batons, eating snail ice cream or moving to Bristol for a job helping people in places she'd somehow never heard of. Her school must have been a crazy place. In between all the dancing and voice coaches, she'd learnt a lot of maths and drama but seemingly no geography.

'You could stay the night,' said Lily, hugging him goodbye. 'Go back in the morning?'

Mick was jangling his keys. It was too late for any of this. Ed shook his head. 'Early meeting,' he said. 'I'll call you later.'

'And I'll see you Friday,' she said.

She was smiling. He walked away backwards.

'Yeah, and good luck. I know you'll be great.'

32

Lily

December 2016

Sundays were better when Ed came to her for the weekend. When she went to London, she'd only get as far as lunchtime before she started dreading the evening and the station barrier goodbye. Did he know how hard it was to leave him on a Sunday night to go sit on a half-empty train as it trundled west through the dark and cold, while he went home alone? Sundays had been about music and laughter and eating cheese. Now there was only instant ramen and a hot water bottle.

Ed paused at the entrance to the platform and Lily hugged him tightly, trying to squeeze a week's worth of love into his bones. He kissed her and nudged her towards the gate.

'Off you go then. Go and be inspiring,' he said.

She caught him checking the clock.

'It's fine,' she said. 'I've still got a few minutes.'

'I was thinking,' Ed said, hesitantly. 'You know how you're always saying we should do something worthy at Christmas?'

'Worthwhile, you mean.'

'Whatever. I think this might be the year.'

Lily gave him an extra kiss and let him get away with it. Ed's family had never been big on Christmas, and without Kit and Martin, there'd be even less reason. She wouldn't force him to admit he couldn't bear to see Samantha in the family home at the head of the Christmas table, even though his mother had been gone for almost twenty years and Lily had never seen Ed's family set the table for anything other than poker. That was the point, according to Ed. Everyone had their own traditions.

'Okay,' she promised. 'I'll see what I can find.'

Monday morning started with a briefing. Specialists on transport, logistics and human resources crammed round the table with the medical advisers to pore over the pleas for emergency medical help which seemed to come in every day from Southern Europe and the Middle East. The brief was simple – get the medics and equipment out to the site within forty-eight hours. Lily stayed quiet as the CEO reviewed the previous week's activities and fixed the new priorities. She was glad she wasn't sifting the requests or making the decisions; she'd never have been able to turn anyone down. All she had to do was grab her project sheet and find a way to get things done once the CEO and the board had agreed to assist.

The buzz was contagious. Everyone on the phone, hushing their colleagues who were yelling in the background, scrolling through the database, scrambling willing volunteers. Today's job was easy. An obstetrician for a refugee camp. What took longer was reaching the team in the field to do the risk assessment and agree on medical kit. Satellite phones, lags on the line, time differences. By the time she got through to the coordinator, she would pretty much have agreed to anything – until she surveyed the list of requested items. It was more like a Christmas wish list than an emergency response. If it were up to her, she'd give them everything, but there were limits. It had to fit into a 25kg bag and meet a test of being reasonably necessary. She was getting better at identifying medical equipment, but she looked up a couple of things so as not to seem stupid when she got back on the phone to the doctor to negotiate down, separating the essential from the desirable, ditching the totally impractical.

In her old world, she'd have been the one at the front delivering the programme, with gear provided by whichever not-for-profit was employing them that day. Now her job was to run down to the warehouse, fill in the requisition sheet for the kit and wave off the medics before going back to the office, doing the filing and organising a resupply. The need seemed to be endless. Lily had been sending medics and psychologists out to pop-up clinics in war zones and disaster areas on an almost weekly rotation. She'd thought it would be difficult to find anyone to go, but the doctors were champing at the bit to put their skills to use.

Her debrief with the previous week's volunteers was fixed for five o'clock. The questionnaires didn't take long – standard questions rating travel, facilities and tech support on a scale of one to ten, but it was the stories they told. She couldn't get enough of them. What was it like? She needed to know.

There was one more thing on her list. She called Ed.

'Still want to do this?' she asked.

'Definitely.'

'Okay, then,' she said, leaning forward in her chair and starting a computer search.

It would be great to get him doing some mentoring at one of the colleges – or partnering a school in designing learning environments. Better ease him in gently. She scrolled down a database of volunteer requests. What could she find to suit him? Three or four days long, minimal training, zero experience required.

'So what d'you fancy? Sponsored fast? Foodbank collections? Soup kitchen?'

'What's available on Christmas Day?'

Her heart sank a little. If Ed could bear to pop into his father's for an hour or so, and swap presents over drinks and snacks, she'd go with him, but if he'd made up his mind, there was no point in asking. She refined her search, looking now for something she'd be willing to do too. It wouldn't do to turn up for work after the holiday and confess she'd sent her boyfriend off to a refuge at Christmas while she sat on the sofa in her pyjamas, peeling satsumas.

'Homeless shelter in Southwark?' she suggested.

'Count me in,' he said and then, as if an afterthought, but she wasn't fooled, 'Can you make it too?'

'Course I can,' she said, forcing a smile. 'We'll dish out the Brussels and roasties together.'

33

Ed

December 2016

It wasn't the best Christmas he'd ever had, but it was far from the worst. It was knackering, to-ing and fro-ing from the kitchen with huge trays of food and dirty plates, but that wasn't a problem. He did feel bad for Lily, though, and if she'd bailed on him, he wouldn't have blamed her, or even been surprised. She didn't appear to be having a bad time. In fact, she seemed completely at ease, chatting to everyone as she handed out toiletries and clean underwear, handy gifts from Santa.

He took his break with her. They ate leftovers in the kitchen as other volunteers started to stack chairs and mop the floor in preparation for the following day. He ought to say something, but it was hard choosing the right words.

'Thanks for doing this with me.'

It went nowhere near covering what he felt, his depth of appreciation for her presence, for her sheer all-round competence, but he'd have had to write a speech to deal with all that.

'Don't be silly. It's fun,' she said.

He laughed and put his arm around her shoulders, knocking her Christmas hat sideways as he kissed her.

'Have I got you in trouble with your mum?'

'A bit, but you know what she's like. Things can never be Christmassy enough for her.'

'This from someone whose entire wardrobe is covered in glitter.'

'Yeah, but it can get too much.'

He put his plate down and pulled her closer, resting his chin on the top of her head as he rocked her gently.

'I know, I know. Sometimes it's easier to swerve.'

Lily's mum sighed when he delivered her daughter late and tipsy for Boxing Day dinner with the family.

'Someone had some cider,' Ed offered by way of explanation, 'and one turned into two.'

No alcohol was allowed in the shelter, but it didn't stop people sitting on the steps outside sharing a can or two. Nor did it put Lily off taking some plastic cups outside (because it would look better) or leading the group in some Christmas songs.

Jo looked the pair of them up and down. Their jeans and T-shirts were still splattered with grease and gravy.

'If I'd let her go home to change,' said Ed, by way of apology, 'we'd never have got here.'

'It's fine,' she said as she kissed them both and ushered them into the house. 'As long as you're happy now you've finished all your do-gooding.'

34

Lily

February 2017

When she had no trouble getting a flight from Istanbul to Bingol, Lily assumed the worst of the earthquake damage had been contained. She knew there'd be devastation, but two weeks on, she'd expected the initial shock to have subsided. She was unprepared for the sight of dazed householders picking through the snow-covered rubble lining the village streets.

Her taxi raced through the roads on the way in from the airport. Lily craned her head, unable to ignore the struggle between the bulldozers and the people, still desperately searching, two weeks on, for any remnant of their belongings. It was unbearable to watch, but it would have been worse, rude in fact, to turn away from the suffering.

Medic48 hadn't promised Lily overseas travel, but she'd talked them round. She'd make a better job of the evaluation and recommendations for future volunteer rotations if she

could visit the site herself and she needed to see it early on –
before the first wave of medics gave way to the second.

She couldn't turn back. People were depending on her.
She sat up, tapped the driver on the shoulder and reminded
him to take her straight to the local hospital.

Lily waited by the reception with her wheelie suitcase and
huge bag of medical kit, shrinking into the wall as trolleys
rushed past. All but the most seriously injured had now been
discharged, but the place was still busy. She had hoped to
catch up with her volunteer doctors, two traumatic injury
specialists, but they were held up in the operating theatre,
battling to save crushed limbs. The head of the medical staff
was summoned. He took Lily into his office to park her bags
before insisting on taking her on a tour of the wards, although
he must have had a thousand more important things to do.

They started at the bedside of a toddler who'd been
pulled from the rubble and was under sedation while the
local Red Crescent staff scoured the surrounding villages for
any surviving family members. Lily listened and racked her
brain for something she could do to help. She had no medical
training, no language skills and no vehicle. All she could do
was pass the message back to Bristol that they needed more.
More money, people, equipment. More everything.

As the day wore on, she didn't feel any more useful. She
was a hard worker, but these people were on another level.
They never stopped moving – round the clock, exhausted
and hungry, in the same clothes they'd been wearing for three
days.

If she could only speak to Ed, he'd tell her she was doing
okay. Or he would if he answered the phone instead of sending
an auto-message that he'd call her later. He was probably in

a meeting and he wouldn't have been expecting her to call. She'd warned him she might not get a chance.

In the evening, she tagged along with the aid workers as they drove back through darkened streets to the Grand Hotel, the nearest one with a generator and functioning restaurant, before heading back to the more modest place where they'd been billeted. Her room was cold, but it was winter, and the bed was hard, and she'd slept on much worse. At least she had a bed. There were people still camped out in a school while they waited for the all-clear to return to their homes. Aftershocks could be just as devastating as the main event, she'd been told. She wrapped herself in her jacket, propped herself up in her bed and tried to distract herself with spreadsheets, calculating the numbers of persons assisted against the statistics for met and unmet need.

Her phone buzzed.

'Hey, Lovely,' said Ed's flickering image.

She grabbed her phone and ran down in her socks to the lobby where the signal was better. If she'd known he'd videocall, she'd have wiped the smudged eyeliner from under her eyes.

'Hey, you,' she said, smiling at the sight of him.

He hunched over the phone, peering at the screen. 'Are they pigtails?'

She twisted one of her plaits in her hand and made a sorry face. Usually she only French-braided her hair when it needed a wash or she was planning to wear a wig.

'No straighteners,' she said.

'Ah. They rationed your luggage.'

'One change of clothes. I had to save my baggage allowance for the medical equipment.'

'Well, in all fairness…'

With Ed, she could laugh at herself. He knew how hard it was for her to travel light, to spend a week in a single pair of shoes. He'd even be sympathetic. It wasn't a thing she could admit to the others; certainly not the medics giving up their holidays to volunteer or the poor people whose homes had been flattened. It was irrelevant to them that she found it easier to deal with things when she felt like herself, over-equipped and overdressed with patent leather boots and a huge holdall. It was inappropriate, ridiculous.

'How's it going?' Ed said.

'It's kind of…'

'Yeah, I can imagine. Just seeing innocent buildings ground into the dirt would do for me, let alone the rest.'

It was the thing she hated when she was home, the way he knew when something hadn't come out the way she expected and would turn the tables, take the heat for her, like some kind of pain-eater. It was nice of him, but so annoying. This was the life she'd wanted and it had to work for her.

She missed him when she was away. It was fine while she was busy, debriefing her doctors, chatting to beneficiaries at their bedside, but when night closed in and she was back at her hostel on a road where the streetlights were still down, her itchy fingers reached for her phone.

It sounded like Ed was in a bar, a noisy one at that.

'Hang on,' he yelled. 'I can't hear you. I'll go outside.'

If she'd left it longer, would he have called? What did he do when she was away? Did he miss her or did he have more fun without her?

35

Ed

March 2017

The flat above the shop was still full of Martin's belongings, not just his clothes, his furniture, his chipped crockery, but all the childhood souvenirs that he couldn't bring himself to throw out. A childhood shared with Ed's mother. Ed had no desire to lift the lid and Kit was no help. In six months, all they'd managed to do was rescue Martin's record collection and move it the five miles across town to Kentish Town. Ed could imagine it being the only thing he and Kit would ever argue about – who would be custodian of the vinyl. Kit wanted it to stay in their flat with Ed as curator – or expected Ed to stay in the flat as its caretaker, Ed wasn't sure which came higher up the order.

He called by Kit's on his way home from work. It was the best time to catch his brother – before the start of the baby's evening rituals. He had his own key now since the use of the doorbell had been banned. Anisia believed in establishing routines, but perhaps she hadn't told Kit as he lay sprawled on the sofa with the baby asleep on his chest. Ed made some tea and gently edged his brother's feet across so he could join him on the sofa and prop his legs on the coffee table.

'Hey, how's it going?' asked Kit, pulling himself up and rubbing his face.

'It's knackering,' Ed said. 'It's Monday and I'm already done. I spend half my life on trains. There's nothing wrong with Bristol but—'

'You don't know what knackered is, love,' said Kit, who never missed a chance to play the junior doctor card. 'Even if I cloned myself, we'd both be exhausted. And I don't know why you're wasting your weekends in Bristol. I'd travel while I had the chance. Trust me, you'll miss it when it's gone.'

Ed played the world's smallest violin for him, but it rankled when Kit was right. A proper break was an excellent idea. More reasons to be out of the flat. Where would Lily like to go? Somewhere she wasn't going for work, at a guess.

Gavin called again. He'd started calling during the working day. Ed hesitated before picking up. He owed the man an answer. He'd been very patient so far.

'We've got a potential tenant, Ed.'

'Sorry, sorry,' said Ed, tracing small circles on his desk with a forefinger. 'I'm stuck at work this evening, but I'll try for tomorrow.'

'You don't even need to come and get the stuff. I'll drop it round in the van.'

When the coast was clear and it was too late to do anything other than go home, Ed went back to the flat. He reached into the fridge, grabbed a beer, peered at the meagre food offerings within – the lone bagel, half jars of mustard and mayonnaise, and almost-out-of-date chicken – and closed the door again. He flopped onto the sofa, rising only to change the record on the ageing turntable, dragging himself off to bed when he was woken, frozen, at two in the morning by the curtain flapping against the balcony doors, which he'd opened when he got home and forgotten.

This was what his evenings had become. At least there was music. He'd been working his way through Martin's vinyl in alphabetical order, applying strict rules. No skipping a selection because he wasn't in the mood for ska or a four-piece baroque ensemble where the harpsichordist was one of Martin's mates. Some transitions worked surprisingly well, like when an evening of BB King led the following day to Bauhaus and then straight on to the Bee Gees. He'd managed to cook himself pasta that night while dancing round the flat. The evening spent listening to John Coltrane was more difficult. Too many memories of heated arguments about socialism and bass lines. It was a good job so many of his Sunday evenings were spent in Bristol. No chance to wallow.

Kit didn't seem to have a problem. The tell-tale jazz piano recordings he left on the turntable gave him away, quite happy to move on himself so long as nothing else changed and he could drop back in at will.

Ed helped Gavin unload the van. They carted it all up to the first floor, lining the grey cardboard boxes along the hall like a pathway. To where? Nowhere Ed wanted to go. While Gavin took a break, Ed made a start on one of the boxes. So many books. He flipped the first one open, found his mother's handwriting and froze. He stood for a while, tracing the 'C' of Catherine with his eyes. It was similar enough to the 'Cat Black' signature he remembered from her illustrations, but not quite there yet. Still a character in development, flirting with a calligraphy pen before abandoning it for her trademark fat, black, marker.

Why had Martin kept all this stuff? And why had it fallen to him to sort it all out? Ed didn't collect clutter. He and Kit had burnt their schoolbooks and now he was suffocating under sixty years of other people's memories.

They moved all the boxes into Kit's room.

'Don't look at any of it,' said Gavin, shutting the door. 'Just chuck it all out. He was a terrible hoarder, worse than my mum, and she was bad.'

Ed lived alone, but the flat was far from empty. If he opened the door to Kit's room, he'd surely be drowned by the flood of Martin's paintings and photos, paperwork and old books. He didn't believe in ghosts, but the place was full of them.

'Ed?' Lily was breathless when she called. 'Something's come up. I can't go to Italy this weekend, I'm really sorry. I've got to go to Serbia.'

'Okay,' he said slowly, swallowing his sigh. It wouldn't help things. He reached for his iPad and started scrolling through the booking confirmation and cancellation details.

'Yeah, we've got to sort out something for the refugees who are stuck there. The weather's awful and there are kids with broken bones and injuries from the war in Syria.'

As excuses went, it was unbeatable.

'No prob,' he said. 'I'll change the tickets. We can go some other time.'

It felt like a nudge from Martin in the hereafter – or the tax man in the here and now. Probate couldn't be put off much longer. A couple of days of forced solitude in the flat might be the only way to get down to it. Truth to tell, he was finding it difficult to motivate himself to do anything, and if he spent the weekend reading and drinking beer in his dressing gown on his balcony, who would know? It really didn't sound bad at all.

'I don't know when I'll be able to go away with you. It's all got so complicated. I could be there for a while as I've got to do another recruitment drive. They said they wanted two medics, but now they've asked for three and they want a surgeon too.'

She was talking too quickly.

'You okay? Should you lay off the coffee?'

She didn't laugh. Was he losing his touch?

'How am I going to get it all done in time?'

'Can't you do it from here?'

'I can find doctors, but they also need somewhere to work. We've got a caravan for the medics, but it can only be used by one of them at a time. There are crowds and crowds of people stuck there. It's stopped snowing but it's still cold. You should see the pictures, Ed. Women and children sitting on the ground covering their faces while the men are arguing and fighting. It's chaos and everyone's sick or dehydrated.' She paused for breath. 'We need more consulting space.'

'Can you get more caravans?'

'D'you know how much they cost? And it takes time to transport them. If we drive them from here, it will take three or four days minimum, and we'd have no way of towing them right now. Our two vans are leaving tomorrow with all the equipment.'

'What about building your own treatment centre?'

'I've got permission for a tent, nothing permanent.'

'That's a start. You can construct something quite decent with enough wood and canvas.'

'Then I'll need manpower. I've only got one guy on the ground there and he's the driver. I could go earlier and try and recruit some locals, I s'pose. I should be able to get some people off a site for a few days. What d'you think?'

What he thought about his lovely Lily walking round a building site with wads of cash to hire day labourers wasn't something he'd share with her.

'D'you want me to volunteer?'

He was only half joking. What were they doing to her? Lily wasn't the panicking type. She was the one convinced she'd have enough time to squeeze all the things she'd signed up for into her day and all would be well. Give her her due, when she turned up late with a cheeky smile and a crazy story, it usually was.

She hesitated. 'Would you? Could you come out with me? And bring a builder or two?'

He laughed and then thought better of it. 'Seriously?'

'I've got a budget. I can pay your fares and expenses,' she said.

She sounded so hopeful suddenly, he couldn't disappoint her.

Persuading anyone else to go was another matter. He knew a lot of builders, but the unskilled workers barely earned enough to keep themselves and, while the skilled workers earned a decent wage and might spend a weekend helping out a mate or doing private work on the side, they weren't likely to give up their free time unless the cause was close to their hearts, which limited it to family, money or football.

Ed dropped into one of his sites to have a word with the Albanian foreman.

'Don't s'pose it's your mother's birthday, is it?' he asked him. 'Would she welcome a visit from her son if you could nip across and see her from Serbia?'

'I'll do it if I don't lose any pay,' said Oz.

'I'll see to it,' said Ed.

The only thing left was to work out how. He doubted the main contractor had a volunteering policy. He'd have to suggest one.

Lily missed the Friday lunchtime train into Paddington and Ed's phone was full of messages apologising and changing their meeting point. At least she was behaving normally again. He caught up with her at Liverpool Street Station. She was stuffing a baguette in her mouth and waving frantically as he strolled across the concourse towards her.

'I was getting worried,' she said through a mouthful of bread.

He checked his watch. They still had ten minutes before the train, which was pretty much a record for them. He eyed the sandwich. 'Did you get me one?'

'Course.' She handed him the bag and wiped the crumbs from her mouth to kiss him. 'Chicken, bacon and avocado?'

'Good as it gets. You okay?'

'I am now,' she said.

He steered her towards the platform for the express train to the airport. She resisted.

'Where's Oz?'

'Meeting us there.'

'Okay!'

She took his hand and allowed herself to be led away.

'Hard hat?' she asked, indicating the bright yellow item swinging from the side of his shoulder bag.

'Set dressing,' he said.

Ed rarely travelled unprepared, but Lily was so jumpy, he didn't dare ask questions. He bit his tongue again when they arrived at Belgrade and the promised minibus was nowhere to be seen. They had a long way to go, and without transport, they were going to struggle to make it out of the capital, let alone to the border with Macedonia. That much he knew. Oz looked at his feet as Lily darted up and down in the arrivals lounge, phone clamped to her ear.

'Where's the driver? He should be here,' she kept saying, over and over.

Ed strained his eyes for any signs with her charity's green and white logo and wondered whether Lily could claim back the cost if he hired a car. He was pretty sure, though, that now was not the time to offer an opinion. Or make suggestions.

'Can I do anything?' he said instead.

'Wait here. I'll look outside,' she said, and ran towards the exit.

The minibus, when it turned up, was one of the big ones, so they spread out and took a row each. Ed kicked off his boots, lifted his feet onto the upholstery and leaned his back against the window, readying himself for sleep. He could usually drift off without too much difficulty and it was comfortable enough. It was impossible, though, with Lily fidgeting in the seats in front, rustling around and kicking the armrest. Ed leaned over the seatback.

'Sorry,' she said, shifting some more as she tucked her coat in around her. 'I can't seem to—'

'Where's your neck pillow?'

'Forgot it.'

Ed took a hoodie from his bag and balled it up to make a cushion for her. 'Here,' he said. 'Try and sleep. There's nothing for you to worry about for a few hours.'

It was advice he would do well to follow himself, but every time the bus hit a bump or Lily stirred, he jolted out of his dozing state, alert for any sign of trouble. He guessed they were nearing their destination when Lily stood and pulled her bag from the rack, although to his tired eyes, there was nothing up ahead but farmland.

'Don't worry,' Lily whispered. 'This isn't where we're staying. I booked a hotel in Presevo, it's the next biggest town. I know it's early, but I'll call them if you like, see if we can drop our stuff off.'

'No need on my account,' said Ed. He wasn't the one with a lot of stuff.

They drove off the road and into a rocky field. Ed reminded himself that a spring dawn light didn't flatter every environment, but what met his eyes resembled a scene from a disaster movie after a tornado had passed through. Makeshift tents formed from plastic sheeting were dotted between piles of discarded rubbish. Broken-looking people shuffled forward to queue at a single water tanker parked in the mud.

He sucked his teeth. The sooner they got something built for this lot, the better.

He climbed out of the minibus, shivered and stretched to hide it. It was chilly and he hadn't had enough sleep, but it wasn't that. He was used to cold, early starts.

'I only need to pee and then I'll be good to go,' he said, pulling the collar up on his coat and heading towards the bushes visible beyond a heap of rubble, glad of the moment to gather his thoughts.

Lily's other van, emblazoned with logos and loaded with equipment, was parked nearby, guarded by two wary-eyed men in anoraks and jeans, sipping from tin mugs. They must be the advance party.

'D'you want a brew?' asked one of them when Ed returned. He pointed to a kettle plugged into the cigarette lighter. 'I can offer you a biscuit too. I'm Andy, by the way.'

'Ed,' said Ed.

'I've never seen anything like this,' said Andy's mate, 'and from what I hear, it's only going to get worse. They're saying there are thousands of people in the town the other side of the border and they'll start pouring through as soon as it opens. According to one of the interpreters, the police have been ordered to stop people heading west. If that's true, this'll be a bottleneck.'

'We'd better crack on then,' said Ed, rubbing his hands together with an enthusiasm he didn't feel.

Andy and his mate unloaded their van, and Ed and Oz took stock of the building materials they'd been given. Lily traipsed to and fro, looking for a phone signal.

'Where are all the others?' she asked, wandering back to them. 'They were supposed to be here to meet us.'

'Having breakfast in a cosy hotel, I expect,' said Ed. 'But don't worry, Lovely, we're fine. What exactly d'you want us to build and where?'

'Where's the caravan?' said Lily. 'We should build the centre close to that. I got someone to put a plan together.'

She rummaged in her file, pulled out a folded sheet of A3 and handed it to Ed. He smiled to hide his trepidation, but he needn't have worried. The plan was nothing more complex than a design for a big tent with plywood boxes inside, more like the instructions for assembling a wardrobe than the structural drawings he was used to.

'What's that barn?' asked Oz, pointing to a wooden structure with a corrugated roof. 'If there's a water source there, that would be a better place to build this. We can run a tap through. I'll go take a look.'

'Here,' said Lily. 'Take this.'

She handed him a green bib, emblazoned front and back with white crosses and Medic48 in huge letters. She threw one towards Ed as well.

He tugged it over his leather coat. Better not court trouble. The last time he'd seen that many armed police in one place was travelling in Latin America. This lot stood around in groups, looking as cold and unhappy as the families drifting about, gathering their children to get an early start on a journey further into Serbia. Ed beckoned Oz to follow him and, holding the plan, strolled across to speak to the police officers.

Oz hung back, head down, scuffing his boots in the mud while Ed struggled to make himself understood, stitching together snippets of all the East European languages he had picked up at work. The word for water was pretty much the same, wasn't it? He pointed at the design and at the landscape and did his best to convey that they had permission negotiated by the local UNHCR to construct an emergency medical centre and they were going to build it alongside the barn. The police shrugged and muttered to each other, none addressing him directly. The young officer on the end looked behind Ed and said something to Oz, who finally seemed to wake up. He nodded and addressed the policeman in his own language. Then another officer joined in and before long all three were laughing. The police translated for their colleagues, who smiled drily. Ed looked from one to the other. He had no idea what was going on, but if they were laughing rather than ordering them off the site and out of their country, that had to be a good thing, right?

One of the older officers, perhaps the most senior, raised his hand in dismissal.

Oz held out a hand and the young officer shook it cautiously. The others kept their hands firmly in the pockets of their vests and resumed their stony-faced staring.

'What was that about?' asked Ed as they walked back to the pile of wood and canvas.

'They wanted to know why I was helping these people. I won't repeat the language they used.'

'What did you tell them?'

'I said I was a builder.'

'Are they Albanian, too?'

'Two of them are. It's mainly Albanian around here. There was a lot of fighting in the past. That's why the army has a base. They asked if I was smuggling in more Albanians. I said I was bringing in my army.'

Ed flinched. 'And they laughed?'

'The Albanians did. Anyway, they said get on with it and go.'

Ed suspected that if the commander of the unit turned up and demanded they stop what they were doing, anything previously agreed would count for nothing. The police were armed; no-one was going to argue with them.

'Okay, then. Let's get on with it,' he said, and patted Oz on the shoulder in matey fashion.

They started by staking out the ground, marking the perimeter and the examination cubicles. Andy and his mate came to help. It was a while since Ed had sawn wood by hand using a workbench. It was like being back at school. He was a little out of practice.

Another minibus with the distinctive green and white logos arrived. A big guy in jeans, boots and 'doctor' written on his green bib, jumped out and headed straight for Lily, who, lacking anything more constructive to do, was holding string straight for Ed.

'Lily Kane? Good to see you. I'm Sam. These your builders?' He pumped Ed's hand enthusiastically. 'Welcome, welcome. How're you getting on?'

He could only be a couple of years older than Ed, but he had that air about him, as if he was used to making decisions and being listened to – a proper doctor, not like Kit, who thought he could make a career out of medicine because of his skill syringing vodka into watermelons. Sam seemed more in charge than anyone else in the muddy field, so Ed summoned Oz and the two of them started to explain the logic of building where they'd chosen, even if there was a twenty-metre gap between the consulting caravan where medicines were kept and the tent with the other examination cubicles.

Oz pulled the design from his jacket pocket and the four of them huddled over it.

'So,' said Oz, shaking his head doubtfully. 'If you want the doors there like that…' He jabbed a finger at the wide barn-style doors on the drawing. 'Then we need an extra batten across the top.'

'Because you've got this extra bit on the end,' explained Ed. 'We're also a bit worried about the ventilation. We could put a hatch here.' He pointed at the back.

'And we'll see if we can sort out a water supply for the other end,' said Oz.

'We could get some troughs for washing,' suggested Lily, who had brightened up when Sam arrived.

'Sounds great!' said the doctor. He nodded towards the queue of people forming outside his caravan. 'Better open up. I'll come and help when I've sorted out this lot. Did you bring supplies, Lily? Have you done the inventory?'

'I'll do it now,' she said, and scampered after him.

Another man in a green bib came over. This one had a clipboard.

'Morning, guys. Thanks so much for coming out. How was your journey? Good, yeah? I'm Matt. I run local operations.'

So this was the famous Matt.

'Ed? Oz?' He shook their hands. 'Guys, listen, I'm sorry to do this to you, but we'll need to move the tent over there, behind the caravan.'

Ed glanced at Oz. He didn't want to go through it all for a third time.

'Thing is, Matt,' said Ed, 'the ground's not level there. If we build it there, the entrance will be either upslope or downslope, and if it rains, you won't keep the water out.'

'And if it's here,' added Oz, 'we can get a piped water supply into it.'

'Maybe,' corrected Ed.

'Well, the plan was to put it there,' said Matt.

He pointed back to the caravan and the uneven ground alongside strewn with rubble. Andy and his mate stopped what they were doing to listen.

'Can you get Lily?' Ed asked them.

He wasn't going to argue, especially on someone else's job. He would do what any sensible contractor did – fetch the client and hope they'd see it his way.

Lily ran back from the caravan. 'What's up?'

'It's about the position of the tent,' said Matt.

Ed registered Lily's anxious face. He touched her shoulder. 'Look, we don't mind at all. We think it's better here, but you decide.'

'Breakfast?' said Oz.

The builders' standard response when there was a row brewing: make yourself scarce and come back when it was all sorted. Oz revved the drill in his hand like he was gunning an engine. Ed nudged him to stop, though the idea of food was certainly appealing. He was very hungry now.

'There's a town nearby,' said Andy.

'You coming with us?' Ed asked Lily. He smiled at her. 'Or shall I bring you something back?'

Lily looked from Ed to Matt and back again.

'We won't be long,' said Ed softly, holding her gaze. He wasn't going to upset things for her by having a fight with an idiot with a clipboard who wouldn't know a spirit level if you knocked him out with one. 'Honestly, Lily, it's fine. It makes no difference to us. We'll move it if you like. Someone has to make a decision is all.'

When they returned armed with coffee and cheese pastries, Matt was nowhere to be seen, so they carried on building the tent where they'd staked it out. Lily – or Sam – must have prevailed. Ed went back to the van and reappraised the contents. They'd been supplied with a fairly decent range of materials. It seemed a shame to build something as basic as a reinforced tent. After all, the vans weren't likely to be taking much of it back with them. They'd need the space for the medical equipment.

'I think we could do it better,' he told Oz.

Oz compared the plan against the pile of timber. Sam joined them, clinic over.

'We're thinking of going bigger,' Ed said.

'Do it,' said the doctor, slapping him on the shoulder.

Ed grabbed the pencil from behind Oz's ear and drew a few more lines on the plan. He had in mind a sort of summer house, partitioned inside, with windows and decking and covered water troughs behind. The tent could go alongside, like a lean-to.

Matt reappeared in the early evening to inspect progress and rushed to assist. Everyone wanted to be Sam's friend. Ed could see why. He was a bit of a hero. While Matt fumbled to fix a cassette into the staple gun, the doctor finished attaching corrugated plastic to the roof of the water point. Some people could turn their hand to anything. He appeared just as happy helping Ed fix tarpaulin and heavy canvas to the posts as he was following Oz around, sawing wood and screwing down planks.

Ed paused for a moment on the roof of the structure, testing its stability. It felt like a good day's work. He surveyed the scene below and spotted Lily by the caravan, chatting to a man who was sitting on the steps. A handful of patients had already gathered for the evening clinic.

'What's that guy's name again?' he asked the doctor.

'Hassan,' said Sam. 'He's great. He's been interpreting for me. My Arabic's not really up to the task.'

Hassan leant forward, hunching over his knees, and Lily laid a reassuring hand on his shoulder. There was something about the man which made Ed uneasy, and not only because he was exactly the type of sorry individual to spark Lily's interest. Ed had no illusions about what first drew Lily to the flat. It was Anisia's stories about the two lost brothers with the dysfunctional family. He'd got her to admit later that she hadn't expected to like Ed as much or discover that he and Kit managed perfectly well without Anisia's intervention. Kit just pretended not to.

Lily must have felt his eyes on her because she turned towards him, blew him two kisses and sent him a thumbs-up.

Hassan didn't look up.

36

Lily

March 2017

The storm they'd all been dreading came in at midday. The sky, until then a cheerless grey, suddenly turned black and the heavens opened. In minutes, the ground, rubbed bare of grass and vegetation by thousands of trampling feet, became a sea of slithering mud. Matt's band of volunteers had been weaving gently among the crowds of recent arrivals, making new friends and handing out hygiene packs. Now they ran from the pelting rain for the only shelter available, cramming themselves into the minibuses as their beneficiaries, the families they'd gone there to assist, huddled together in the open. Lily ran towards the medical caravan. There were polythene sheets in one of the vans, she was sure. They'd be better than nothing.

She heard a yell. Ed was crouched on top of the tent structure, coat collar turned up against the rain, fastening tarpaulin and corrugated plastic to every surface as fast as he could, but the sound hadn't come from him. A row was developing by the buses, between the older hands who thought they should take a break until the weather passed and the younger ones, the enthusiastic gap-year interns that Ed meanly referred to as the Mattellites, who wanted to stay outside in solidarity with the travellers. Matt trotted across to mediate. Lily ran back to help Ed.

'What can I do?'

'Go inside and check the seals are watertight,' he shouted, walking the roof and counting off the sections for her as she ran a torch and her fingers over every seam and join, checking for seepage.

Andy ran over with another roll of plastic for the roof. Lily helped him pass it up to Ed. When she lifted her head, she had to close her eyes against the rain which ran inside her jacket and down her neck.

'We'll only be able to lay the plastic out and weight it down until we can use the power tools again,' Ed shouted down.

Andy rolled his eyes towards the minibus, whose occupants kept entering and leaving, slamming the door after each exit. Lily could imagine the dialogue within. It was one of Matt's strengths, making people feel they were doing the right thing. If you had doubts, he would take the time to talk through your insecurities, but right now, they didn't have time for that. As one minibus left, Lily was sure the occupants felt good about their choices even if the group who stayed behind on the ground hated them with a passion and it would be days before they could bring themselves to speak to them. Matt's way, the *sometimes there's no right answer, there's no shame in discovering that something isn't for you,*

you've learnt something about yourself way, had taken her a while to appreciate. It was as calculating as it was kind. He would rather put in the hours at the start to get the people he wanted.

Meanwhile, the rain was still pouring down. Lily had to stop herself banging on the door of the second bus to tell those on board to stop yacking and get their tails outside. If she was honest, she preferred Menassi's management style, although it was never going to feature in any 'how to' manuals. If there was a job to be done, you pulled together, gritted your teeth and smiled. Ed was the same, the type to finish what he was doing before downing tools and rowing about what to do next. How he felt about it was never going to feature in the discussion. It was one of the things they had in common.

'Those poor people,' wailed one of Matt's younger crew members who stood in her wellies and raincoat, gesturing helplessly at another family struggling to drag their bags through the puddles.

'Get them inside then,' shouted Ed.

She squelched off to help as he jumped off the roof, spattering mud over Lily, who was marshalling the travellers towards the tent.

'Can you take over?' she said.

She ran back to the medical caravan and rummaged through the box of green bibs for the flags – the white one with the red cross and the green one with the Medic48 logo.

'Marketing?' asked Ed when she returned.

'No,' she said. 'Not marketing.'

She was struggling to fix the flags to the poles. The string was wet and tangled, and her fingers were too cold to tie any knots. Ed tried to help, but his glasses were steaming up like when he cycled through the rain. She rummaged in her pocket for a tissue and wiped them for him.

'We have to put the flags up, so people know it's safe. Otherwise no-one will go in. They're scared we'll try to process them in some way.'

The rain was now running off the end of her hood and down her nose. Ed handed her his hard hat.

'What about you?' she said.

'I'm soaked, it won't make any difference.'

They stood on either side of the tent flaps as the crowd started to trickle inside. Another crash of thunder rolled overhead. It sent shivers down Lily's spine.

'Look at them. They're so wet,' she said. 'How will they ever get dry?'

Ed looked through the entrance to the structure inside. 'I can't see how we can safely rig up a heat source, though, unless we can get a generator from somewhere.'

He was still concentrating on the practical rather than the personal, carefully avoiding staring at the occupants. Sometimes it was the only way to cope. He probably didn't realise she'd noticed. She smiled at him, her eyelashes now so wet she was viewing him through a film of water.

The hostel receptionist was reluctant to hand over their key. Lily couldn't blame her; she wouldn't have wanted the two of them in her house either. They looked like they'd been rolling in mud. Removing their coats and boots didn't make much difference, Lily's jeans were sodden and the rain had soaked through to her underwear. She took off her socks so as not to leave damp footprints along the corridor to their room.

Ed peeled off his wet trousers and flopped onto the bed in his T-shirt and pants.

'Do we have to go out?'

'Not hungry?'

'Strangely, no,' he said, 'but I could murder a beer.' He put his arms around her as she pressed herself against him, damp T-shirt and all. 'Some of the people in that tent, Lils... the kids. You could hear they were crying, but their faces were so wet, you couldn't see the tears. And the adults, they have a sort of look about them. Looking but not seeing. D'you know what I mean?'

She did. The thousand-yard stare.

She kissed him five or six times. 'I love you and I'll find you a beer,' she said. 'We have to be discreet because this town's mostly dry. But you've got to self-care, right?'

If Matt was disappointed by anything that had happened that day, no-one would know. He waited until everyone was seated at the table with a drink in front of them and then offered a toast, clinking his Coke against Ed's.

'People like you make a big difference,' he said. 'This is what we want to get to, where we bring in the skills we need at the point we need them. Focus the commitment. It's so much better, isn't it?'

Everyone nodded. It was impossible to disagree.

'Are you glad you came, Ed?'

It wasn't like Matt to ask a question he didn't know the answer to. Lily felt a flutter of nerves.

'I am,' said Ed, with a nod. He turned to Lily, who was sitting alongside him. 'Thanks for asking me.'

37

Ed

March 2017

Ed stretched out on the bed, propped just high enough that he could drink beer from the bottle without lifting his head. He was losing the battle to keep his eyes open. Lily lay on her side, pillow tucked under one ear.

'Hassan was telling me about his family,' she said. 'It's so sad.'

Ed's brain nodded, but the signal might not have reached his head. It was all sad. And horrible, like the story Sam told him about the woman who walked miles and miles on a broken ankle rather than get medical treatment and hold her family up. He took another swig of his drink.

'His family left Iraq when he was a child. They were in Turkey for a while and then settled in Germany. He's lived all over the place, that's why he speaks so many languages, even Serbian,' Lily continued. 'But he went back to Iraq after the war because he wanted to help rebuild the nation, fell in love and got married. Then, after they had a baby, things got dangerous again and he had to run, leaving his wife behind. He's trying to get them out.'

Ed grunted to show he was listening. Why, with all the thousands to choose from, was she sympathising with this one?

'Can you imagine how that feels? To lose your country twice over.'

'He must have been chucked out of Germany. He wouldn't have gone back to Iraq otherwise.'

'You can't say that. If you left your home because of the war and then suddenly everything changed and there were new people in charge and a sense of hope for the future, you'd want to go back and help build a new country.'

Ed wasn't sure he would. If he walked away from something, which he rarely did, he wouldn't go back and help the new guy create more problems. There was something about Lily's tone, though, that forced him to concentrate.

'Tell me, why did he leave Iraq again?'

'He had to. His life was in danger. Haven't you been listening?'

'Okay, well, supposing that's true, why is he hanging around here? If he was legal in Germany, he could go home. It's not that far, he could probably get a bus.' Ed gestured vaguely in the direction of the street.

Lily shook her head. 'He's given me his parents' address in Germany. I'm going to try and contact them and see if they can find a lawyer to help him get back. Until he's safely in Germany, he won't be able to bring his family out.'

It wasn't only that the guy was moving in on Lily, there

was something off about the whole story. He was just too tired to process it properly.

'Don't get involved, Lily. You've got enough to do. What's that thing? "Do no harm"? You're doing a fantastic job here. You should feel proud. I'm proud of you. Let someone else do the other stuff.'

'But if there's something else you can do, you should do it.'

'Not at the expense of your own job.'

All the good feeling they'd had earlier seemed to be evaporating. He rolled over and reached an arm around her, but her shoulders were more rigid than his stiff back.

'Lily.' He hoped he sounded soothing. 'What you're doing here is really good. It's professional and necessary and ticks all the boxes on your codes of conduct. You can see the difference you're making. Getting caught up in something else might jeopardise that.'

She relaxed a little.

He kissed her and tried a joke. 'For all you know, he could be on the run or something.'

'Ed!'

She sprang away from him as if she'd been burnt. She was angry now, her sweet mouth set in a firm line and her eyes bright and narrowed.

He raised his hands defensively, but it was too late to apologise.

She stood and snatched her coat. 'I'm going to ask Matt to help.'

Ed lay back and counted down to lifting his heavy limbs off the bed to follow her. Matt wouldn't help with this. No way. From what he'd seen, Matt was the type of person who made a thing out of taking time, building consensus, making sure everyone was on the same page. It might work with all the female volunteers who flocked around him, hanging on his every word, which seemed to consist mainly of *You're all okay here, yeah?*, and he was alright-looking, if you liked guys who left their hair long because they said they hadn't had time to get it cut. How long does it take?

Ed's days were spent surrounded by demanding, single-minded individuals, and any one of them would have left halfway through one of Matt's explanations, saying, *Okay, I get it*, and gone to find someone who could make a decision. By the time he'd sat everyone in a circle and they'd introduced themselves with a fun fact and described what they hoped to achieve from the day, even Hassan would have got bored and fucked off.

38

Lily

04.00

Four o'clock in the morning. A bad time to realise the only person you can call is the one person you can't because you've wrecked it all for him. The dinner, the hotel, the holiday. Everything. What could he do, anyway? The passport office wouldn't be rushing to open on a Christmas Eve Saturday. Not for her. Not for someone so chaotic. And Iceland might well take the view they'd be better off without them.

People were staring at her, the few who were left in the service station. They turned away when her meanderings around the concourse brought her closer, as if she were one of the invisible homeless, hanging out there as an alternative to sleeping in the park. She'd like to reassure them she wouldn't be tapping them for change; but it might yet come to that.

She wiped her eyes, smudging her eyeliner some more, and scrolled down her phone, hoping it would throw up some ideas. Menassi would be awake. He wouldn't have made it home yet from whichever club night he'd wormed his way into. He'd certainly come and get her – on condition she took part in whatever mad event he'd signed the group up to and could wait for him to sober up. That's if she could bear to tell him what had happened. He was boss, but he still thought of Lily as the clever one. She couldn't disappoint him. It was almost worse than telling her mother.

Adam was different. She could confide in him. He thrived on heartbreak. He'd open the door with a flourish and a sad smile and tuck her into his bed with tea and sympathy, as she'd done so many times for him. Unfortunately, there was no way of contacting him without alerting Menassi.

There was no point putting it off any longer. It was time to find out quite how much trouble she was in. Lily took the paper bag from the pocket of her coat, grabbed her rucksack and headed for the bathrooms.

39

Ed

June 2017

Ed read the email again. It had to be a joke. How could he have been shortlisted for an award? And for Ludlow Square, of all places. Everything about it was a horror show. He'd only got the gig because the managing partner, who'd won the bid and done the first drawings, had fallen out so badly with the client he refused to speak to him except through an intermediary. When he handed the project over to Ed, Mr Philippou hadn't been the least impressed. He'd accused the firm of handing his job to the teaboy. Ed was slow to take offence but even he'd been taken aback, especially when the man said it to his face. He shrugged his shoulders and told his new client that if he'd like tea, he'd make him some, but in the meantime, his team, under his direction as senior architect, were waiting for them with coffee in the boardroom. Pastries too.

Only one person could be behind this. Ed left his desk and

went in search of his boss. He found him in the kitchenette trying to make sense of a maquette.

'*Architecture Now!?*' said Ed.

'Ha! Yes,' said Olav, grinning. 'That should shut Philippou up. You know, he emailed again about restructuring his bill. This nightmare is never going to end. Unless, Ed, you win and we can persuade him to sell the site to a reasonable human being.' Olav's eyes shone with a crazed desperation. He wasn't faking it.

'I see,' said Ed. He reached across the counter and realigned the small white cubes. 'I think it goes like this.'

'Thanks. Why couldn't I see that? It's that man. He's doing it to me again.' He clenched and unclenched his fists like a cartoon villain.

Ed backed out of the room and clicked the door shut after himself. He rested his head on the frosted glass. This was nuts. His buildings weren't even completed and wouldn't be anytime soon. The builders kept taking sections of it down, thanks to Mr Philippou. That's why Ed had made the film. To show his client what the square could be like – if he'd only let them finish it. It had taken time, but he had plenty of that. The hours he couldn't spend with Lily, the hours he couldn't bear to spend at home. Work was undoubtedly more appealing when the alternative was an empty flat. Even so, the film had been a bit of an indulgence, an opportunity to show that given the chance, he could make the south side of the square so attractive and aspirational everyone would want buildings like it, or at least one as individual in the same distinctive way – maximising light and space, respecting history and functionality through a vigorous environmental agenda. Olav had loved it and put it on the website, and Mr

Philippou had loved it and put it on his phone. His single complaint, unusual in itself, was that he wasn't in it.

It hadn't stopped there. The Royal Academy was showing the film to its students. You had to laugh. He assumed they got it and understood that he'd only had to fall back on terms like juxtaposition and positive conflict to explain away the mismatch between the agreed design and what had actually been built.

He was already looking forward to the awards ceremony and the prospect of Christos and Olav putting aside their differences for the evening, forced to sit together and smile for all the photos, outdoing each other for backslapping and insincerity. A win was a win. For everyone. The building could sell for much more than its market value and an award for the firm made every person working there a desirable property. It was an evening that would be stuffed to the gills with prospective employers.

Ed walked back into the main office, high-fiving his colleagues pretty much every step of the way. He'd never been so popular. Whereas a year earlier, each one would cheerfully have denied any responsibility for Mr Philippou's build, now they were all claiming involvement, however minimal. Roll on the party. Shame the firm wouldn't spring for tickets for partners.

40

Lily

04.30

The packet said two minutes, but Lily had been in the cubicle for over twenty and the wand was still in the box.

It was not an inspiring environment, with its white-tiled floors, empty toilet paper dispenser and claustrophobia. She could almost touch the fibreboard walls with each elbow. Certainly not the place she'd have chosen to discover her fate – if she even wanted to find out. The future would happen whether she opened the box or not. The real question was whether she wanted the decisions she made now – today, tomorrow, next week – and the decisions made by others, to be dependant solely on what was in the box. At some point, they might have to be, but there were other things to think about too, other determinatives, such as where and how she would be spending the next twenty-four hours.

She put the packet back in her pocket, unlocked the door

and went to wash her hands. There was a pile of green paper towels behind the basins so she dampened a couple, pressing them to her face and the back of her neck as she surveyed herself in the mirror and wiped the clogged mascara from the corners of her eyes.

'So, me and you, then,' she said to her reflection, the shadows in her pale face even greyer in the harsh fluorescent light.

She hoisted her rucksack onto her shoulder, trod on the pedal of the waste bin and tossed the screwed-up tissues in. She could scream if she wanted. There was no-one to hear. The lid clanged shut as she left the bathroom.

Something stopped her in her tracks. Was it possible she'd glimpsed a thin black strap? She turned back, heart thumping. There was no point being squeamish, but still she pushed the doors of every cubicle to make sure there was no-one else about before opening the dustbin and tipping it on its side, dumping all the bits of paper towel, sanitary protection wrappers, food packaging and god-knows-what on the floor. She poked about in the mess with her boot and there it was. The little rucksack. Her heart was still pounding as she wrenched the bag open. The interior was empty and her wallet was gone, but it was just possible that whoever stole it hadn't looked in all the pockets. Lily undid the inside zip and traced the dark red spine of her passport with trembling fingers. It was a shame about the wallet, but she'd lost nothing else. Her bank cards were all elsewhere. Poor thief, wasting their efforts robbing a person who was so chaotic.

Braver now, she had a further delve in the rubbish. Here was her hairbrush, her lip balm and her keys. No-one would be burgling her flat tonight which, all else considered, was a good feeling. She tossed the lip balm back in the bin and scooped the rest of the mess off the floor and dumped it on top.

'See?' she told her reflection as she washed her hands again. 'We can do this.'

'Ed? You awake?' She was whispering, which was mad because he'd picked up the phone, so she'd already disturbed his sleep.

'Yeah, yeah,' he said, though he sounded groggy. 'What time is it?'

'About five.'

'What's happened? Are you here?'

'No, no, I'm still at the service station. I just wanted to tell you that I found my passport so it's all okay, but I might need some help getting out of here.'

'What do you mean you found your passport? Had you lost it, then?'

The blood rushed to her face. So stupid to have been caught out like that.

'Yeah, I told you, I left my bag at the service station.'

'You told me you hadn't lost your passport,' he said, now sounding completely alert.

'Well, I didn't want to worry you. Could you look up the nearest train station and tell me how to get there?'

'Yeah, sure.' She heard rustling. 'Wouldn't it be easier if I got the car from Kit?'

'Could you do that?'

'Course, I'll go get it now. You'll need to tell me where you are, though.' He kept cutting in and out, must be moving around again. 'I knew you'd lost your passport.

'Yeah, well, I've found it now.'

201

'I know when you're lying, Lily.'

After everything that had happened, was he going to make a big deal of this?

'You think I don't, but I do.'

'And you always make a point of telling me.'

'Most of the time I don't say a word. Even when I'm pretty sure you don't believe what you're saying.'

'D'you think you're being nice, telling me all this?' She was gritting her teeth. Couldn't he just sound happy?

'I'm trying to say you don't have to pretend with me. You don't have to pretend you like something when you don't or that you don't like something when you do.'

'Like what, for example?'

'I dunno, like food, for instance.'

'Maybe I'm being polite.'

'Okay, what about other stuff then? Things you've done, people you've met? You can tell me the truth, Lily. I'll understand.'

'Me? Who are you kidding?' Now she was shouting, her voice amplified as it bounced off the tiled walls. 'You think I don't know when you're lying? You lie the whole time.'

'I don't.'

'You lie about how you feel.'

'It's not lying. Sometimes I can't explain because I don't know how I feel. But I know how I feel about you.'

He wasn't getting out of it like that. She shook her head, although he wasn't there to see it.

'More to the point, you lie about where you go and what you do!'

He said nothing for a moment. 'Is this about that night again? Lily, it's so long ago. I thought we were over this.'

'Clearly not.'

'I told you what happened.'

'Yes, you did, but it's funny how your version is so different from everyone else's.'

'What do you mean, "my version"?'

Now was the time to stop. She could hang on until they could talk about it properly, calmly, in Iceland even, but her anger, now it had been released, seemed to have a life of its own.

'Funny how everyone says you went to her house but you're the only one who says you left again.'

'Who's everyone? There was no-one else there. Who's been telling you things?'

'No-one. I haven't spoken to anyone.'

'Well, how d'you know what I did?'

It was difficult arguing with Ed. While she got heated, he stayed cool and rational, but she couldn't let it go.

'I asked Kit what time you came home.'

'I see.'

'And your phone was on silent. Why was that?'

'If I'd known you'd call, I would have kept it on loud.'

'I was phoning to congratulate you!'

'Well, I'm flattered you followed the result.'

'What's that supposed to mean?'

He hesitated. 'Okay, if we're doing this, let's do it. It means that before you went away, I'm not sure you could have cared less if I was there or not, you were so full of your project.'

'It matters to me and it takes a lot of time.'

'I know.'

'I didn't think you were interested.'

'I am, but you're so defensive. When I ask, you say

everything's fine, and if I question it, we end up in an argument, so I stopped asking. You won't tell me and I don't push it because there's no point. It's clear what your priorities are.' He sounded tired, resigned even.

'Hey!'

There were too many words fighting to be said, struggling through her sleep-deprived brain. Why shouldn't she have other priorities sometimes? Then she remembered why she'd called him that morning in June.

'I felt bad about it. That's why I checked the awards results and called you.'

'Well, I'm sorry I didn't pick up. We stayed out, that's all. We wanted to celebrate.'

'Obviously.'

'Aagh, Lily! D'you want me to come and get you or not?'

'Not.'

She said it without thinking. It still didn't make sense to her. How could it have taken him three hours to walk a mile and a half? And she wasn't being defensive, no more than he was.

Sometimes you have to accept a thing. This wasn't meant to be. *It is what it is*, as her mother would say.

At least with keys and a passport she had choices again.

41

Ed

05.10

'Fuck.'

Ed chucked his phone onto the bed and pressed his fists into his temples, grinding them against his skull. He groaned again, caving in on himself so his elbows touched his thighs. It was a clumsy attempt to get Lily to tell him what was going on and it was risky, but he really hadn't expected it to backfire as badly as that. All right, the timing wasn't great – awful, in fact – but sometimes the only chance you got was late at night after too much gin. Didn't she get that he loved her? No matter what.

Why had she reacted like that? Was it a serious accusation or some strange admission of her own?

She couldn't know what she thought she knew.

42

Lily

07.00

'Matt?'

'Lily? Hey! How are you?'

She must have woken him. It was seven in the morning on Christmas Eve. Yet he behaved like she'd wandered into his office midway through a dull Wednesday afternoon. He didn't allow himself to get flustered. Sometimes, those times where she couldn't work out how to get everybody to the right place on the right day and her palms started to sweat, his control irritated her. She once asked the medics to check his pulse for him. He'd taken it in good part, as he took everything. *Everyone needs a way to de-stress, Lily. I'm fine with it if this is yours. Self-care, yeah? Remember?*

'I need a bit of help,' she said, and then stupid, gulping sobs got in the way.

'Oh, Lily, mate! It's okay, what d'you need?'

'A ticket or a lift home,' she managed.

'Are things that bad?' he said with a sort of sympathetic chuckle.

'I'm serious.'

'From Iceland?' He'd stopped laughing.

'No, from somewhere near Chippenham. Iceland doesn't seem to be happening for me.'

'Chippenham? I see,' he said without a flicker, enunciating each word with care. No doubt he was checking the quickest way from Cardiff to Chippenham on another electronic device as he spoke. 'Well, don't you worry, Lily, we'll get you home. Really, not a problem.'

The service station was refilling. Lily moved to a corner table and wrapped her arms around herself. Now there was a realistic prospect of escape, she couldn't get out of there fast enough.

'Are you eating anything?' said a girl in a blue-and-white-striped tunic as she sprayed a dribble of cleaner across the red plastic surface and wiped it away with a stale-smelling cloth. She nodded her head towards the line of people carrying loaded breakfast trays, looking left and right for a place to sit.

Lily jangled the coins in her pocket. If a beverage would buy her a chair for a couple of hours, it was money well spent.

When she'd sat over an empty cup for long enough, she moved to wait at the entrance, staying far enough from the automatic doors to avoid continually triggering the mechanism but sufficiently distant from the odour of stale chip fat.

Matt trotted across the car park towards her, a familiar outline in his blue Puffa jacket and jeans. To reach her within two hours, he must have jumped in his silver hatchback within minutes of her call. Or driven like the wind. Either way, his speed was impressive.

He hugged her, which was brave. She'd been in the same clothes for the past twenty-four hours and hadn't seen a toothbrush in all that time.

'Does this mean what I hope it does? Have you had a rethink about coming to Turkey with me?' he said.

'Hmm.'

Where she really wanted to be was her flat, with the door slammed shut, but it seemed a little ungrateful.

'No pressure.' He raised his palms. 'Let's get you sorted out first.'

'I expect you had plans for today.'

'Nope, packing's all done. Got nothing 'til this evening when I've got a drinks thing at my mum's. Until then, I'm all yours.'

Lily pushed away the sinking feeling.

'So, should we get some breakfast before we set off? D'you need a cup of tea?'

'No, no more tea,' she said with a shudder. 'But you get something if you like.'

'I will, if that's okay with you? Sure you don't want something to eat?'

She readied herself for the pep talk. She could probably quote every one of his mantras. *Make space to recognise your needs. You're no good to anyone else if you're no good to yourself. Take some time to process how you feel, accept the validity of your feelings.*

He pointed her towards his car. Lily waited by the passenger door as he walked round to the boot, coffee cup in one hand.

'Where are your bags?'

'Long story,' she said, opening the door as soon as it was unlocked.

She settled in her seat and reclined the backrest. Her eyelids were already closing. Would he be offended if she slept while he drove?

'You don't have to tell me what happened, but you know I'm a good listener.'

It was true, but he was also a good talker and she had no energy for conversation.

'I'm processing my negative emotions,' she said, eyes tight shut.

He did at least laugh. 'You go for it, my friend. And when you've worked through the negative, see if you can't find some positive in there too.'

Lily doubted she could. She tucked her chin into her anorak. She felt tired and foolish, less solid than when she'd set out, as if she'd faded on the journey. And she couldn't escape the creeping sense of betrayal. Was it wrong to feel like that? Like her own body had let her down. Ed too. Would it take something like that to make him pay attention? Really pay attention.

Other people appreciated her. Like Menassi, for instance. True, he took advantage, but he made her feel necessary. And Matt. He valued her. See how he'd whacked up the heating in the car and turned the radio down to a low buzz of music and voices? She took off her coat and laid it over herself like a blanket, tucking it in around her shoulders. She snuggled back down.

'Okay?'

'Yes,' she said.

'Feeling better?'

How she was feeling now was warm – and safe. And free. She closed her eyes again.

'You're good at this,' she murmured.

43

Ed

09.30

Ed blinked to get some moisture into his eyes and took stock. He was in bed, stretched out starfish-style, still in his clothes (and boots) from the evening before, slotted into the envelope between the bedcover and the undisturbed sheets. Apart from the empty screen on his phone and absolute silence from Lily, he wasn't feeling too bad.

He pushed himself up to sitting, loosened the bootlaces and gingerly released his feet, wiggling his cramped toes with a sigh. He ran a hand over his jaw. It felt sore, as well as a bit chilly. Drunk shaving was definitely something to add to his 'not-to-do list'. Shaving, in general, was off his daily schedule. Living mostly on his own now, there were few witnesses to how minimal his routines had become. When was the last time he'd been clean-shaven? It really could have been Kit's wedding. He hadn't done a great job of it this time and it wasn't entirely the fault of the cheap razor or the too-bright lighting bouncing off the shiny walls and making him squint. He was out of practice.

Making more effort could do no harm. He wiped a hand across the bathroom mirror to clear the condensation and took a critical look at his reflection. The hair was fine; he never neglected that. Or his eyebrows – which were mostly hidden by his glasses. He'd been in the habit of popping into the barbers for a weekly beard trim, a legacy from when he'd get a proper wet shave on a Friday, but he'd stopped bothering. Seems it hadn't gone unnoticed after all.

Using his fingers to judge which areas still needed attention, he picked up the razor and had another go. Good job he'd brought aftershave with him, for the scent rather than any soothing qualities. He tipped some onto his fingertips and patted it about cautiously. It wasn't especially comforting. Neither was his phone, which lay on the counter beside the basin, fully charged but showing no sign of life.

'Breakfast, sir?' asked the receptionist when Ed took his bags down.

It was the friendly one, not his suspicious colleague wondering why a lonely man needed razors in the middle of the night.

'It's included in your room rate,' he added.

'Oh, er, maybe. Look,' said Ed, 'my flight's not 'til two thirty. Can I leave my stuff here? Just for an hour or so. While I get some air?'

'That's absolutely not a problem,' said the receptionist, unlocking a cubby hole to the side of the desk. 'It's at your own risk, though.'

Ed handed over his bag and then the walking boots. Not abandoning, just taking a break. As soon as Lily arrived, he'd pick up the challenge again. As long as she did arrive. He tested the notion of her not turning up at all and his stomach filled with dread. He grabbed the boots back and executed a swift footwear swap. It was a pathetic gesture, but anything that sent positive vibrations in her direction was worth a try. While he was at it, he switched his phone to loud before venturing into the street. Who said he was incapable of change?

Strange to be in Central London on a Saturday morning and treading the tourist route. He wouldn't usually venture into town at this hour. Not without plans. His preferred option for killing time would be to get on his bike, race up to Hampstead Heath and ride the perimeter for a while. He could put his head into the wind and burn off all the bad stuff. Or he could actually call his dad and see if he fancied company on his route through the park and buy him a coffee on the other side.

Laurence's mobile rang for a long while before it was picked up.

'Hello,' said a woman's voice. 'Who's that?'

Ed checked his phone display. It certainly said '*Dad*'. Surely Laurence had saved his number?

'It's Ed. Is Laurence there?' he asked.

'Oh, no. Sorry, he's out. I don't know where he's gone. Hang on.'

Ed could hear the distant but unmistakeable tones of Samantha, which meant the person he was talking to must be one of her daughters.

'He's walking the dog. D'you want a word with Mum?'

He didn't, really. 'I expect she's very busy,' he said. 'Better not disturb her. Did Laurence forget his phone?'

'Must have,' said the voice.

What was his dad up to? Laurence wasn't daft; he didn't leave his phone behind by chance, though whether he chose to answer when you called was a different matter. His standard response time was when it suited him. Perhaps he'd gone to meet Kit. Ed wouldn't put it past Anisia to have engineered something.

Before he knew it, he was back at Marble Arch, caught up in the tide of people sweeping through the underpass and along Oxford Street in a last bid for Christmas sale bargains. Surrendering to the flow was easy, following the crowd until suddenly he was outside Selfridges again. He sidestepped the carol singers and the artificial snow being pumped into the air and stepped into the lobby. There was no escaping it; the air was heavy with the scent of Christmas – pine and cinnamon room fragrances, to be precise, being sprayed by an assistant at the door.

'Hello, there.'

A woman was smiling at him. It took Ed a moment to place her.

'Oh, hi, er, Luisa.'

'How are you today?' she asked as he gained his bearings, buffeted by each new arrival pulsing through the revolving doors.

'I'm fine, thanks, how are you? Busy day ahead?'

She laughed. 'Let's hope so. But you must tell me, is it make or break?'

'It's not looking too good right now,' he said. He felt a strange pressure in his throat and swallowed, fearful of what might happen if he said more.

'Darling, don't give up.' She patted his arm. 'What you

214

need is some retail therapy. Lucky for you, you're in the right place.'

'No, really. There are some things I've got—'

Luisa held his arm, quite tightly, and looked him up and down. 'There must be something I can offer you. Male grooming? Footwear?'

'Not the boots,' he said firmly. 'I can't change them. They're new. Seems I make no effort so I bought boots.'

'Very nice,' she said.

'They're not what I usually wear.'

'I'm pleased to hear it. What about leather goods? A belt? Or gloves, perhaps?'

'I... my girlfriend's lost her luggage. I could replace some of that?'

'You want to buy her a suitcase?' said Luisa, wrinkling her nose.

'What about a jumper, then? We're going to Iceland.'

This time she sighed. 'Come with me.'

She released her grip on his arm only to grab his wrist and drag him towards the perfumery department. He couldn't get away without turning it into a wrestling match.

'Don't you have to work?' he said.

'I'm on my tea break. I am also an authorised personal shopper. So, tell me, your girlfriend, does she wear make-up?'

'Yes, I guess so. Not as much as she used to.'

He shrugged, disinclined to explain that the make-up Lily no longer wore was face paint and green body glitter.

'Show me a picture.'

Even checking his phone screen was painful. There were no message alerts, no missed calls. Ed grimaced and flicked through his photographs, stopping at an image that on any other day would have warmed his heart – Lily in shorts, tanned and smiling, sitting on a wall in a cobbled town square, empty ice cream tub in one hand. She was carrying her flip-flops and pleading for a piggy-back.

'Her hair's a bit longer now,' he said.

'Is it still that colour?'

He nodded.

'Eyes?'

'Light brown.'

It was like he was describing a missing person, which, in a sense, he was.

'She's lovely.'

He groaned. She was. Lovely Lily.

Luisa pushed him towards a make-up counter. She started opening sample lipsticks and trying them on her hand to show him.

'When I was younger, my hair was that colour. Almost black.'

Her hair was now an unreal shade of blonde. Mostly. If he had to describe it, he would say Lucozade with streaks of copper. She picked out a pink lipstick.

'Cyclamen. It will suit her. And these are new. Bronzer and highlighter, like giving your skin a natural burnish of gold and silver.'

If she said so.

'He will need a complimentary pochette,' she told the girl behind the counter. 'And some samples.'

'Shall I gift wrap?' asked the assistant.

'Just cellophane and a small bow,' instructed Luisa. 'They're flying. We'll be back in a moment.'

She pointed Ed in the direction of the lift. 'Come on. What's the "E" for? Edward? Eliot?'

'Ed,' he said, not bothering to ask how she knew. He gave up pushing back. It wasn't as if he had anything else to do.

'Ed,' she repeated as they waited for the lift doors to open. 'I like that. So, Ed, there's knitwear and there is knitwear.'

'Not jumpers?'

'Not jumpers. Did your mother not explain this to you?'

'She's not around.'

Luisa scrutinised his expression and then squeezed his arm again. This was more physical contact that he'd had in days.

'Long time?'

He nodded.

'I know how that is. I lost my mother when I was sixteen so I came to England and made all my mistakes by myself.'

She took him to a display counter and lifted a cardigan to his face. He flinched.

'Feel how smooth it is against your skin. Cashmere.'

He tentatively placed a closely shaved cheek against the soft wool.

'Now the only question is colour and style.'

The counter held piles of neatly folded garments in all shades of the rainbow plus a few others. There were at least three shelves' worth.

'Do you want to go for cream or toffee? Or mink?' She pulled a series of woollen items from the stand and placed them in front of him. 'Or petrol? Or saffron?' She added green and yellow to the selection of grey and brown jumpers.

He assumed she was taking the piss, but she smiled encouragingly and nodded in the direction of the display.

'I like that one,' he said, pointing towards a dark, smokey blue jumper.

'Lavender,' said Luisa.

'I thought lavender was purple.'

'Could be, but this blue one is lavender. And would she prefer crew neck, roll neck, slash neck, V-neck or a cardigan?'

This was way more than one question. He guessed at a roll neck.

'I'm sure she'll love it. But she can change it if she doesn't. Could you run to a matching scarf as well?'

She took his arm again to push her way through to the cash desk. He was getting used to it now.

As they waited for the assistant to wrap his purchases, Luisa turned her attention again to Ed. 'Now, what about something for you? The lovely girlfriend can't have all the fun.'

Ed shook his head. There really was nothing he wanted now other than to hear that Lily was at the station.

'How about the coat? Can we do something about the coat?'

She brushed a hand across his shoulder and fingered the tired leather of the lapel. The coat had stylistic limitations, admittedly. He couldn't wear it with work boots or Dr Martens without resembling an extra from a dystopian fantasy. Worn over sweatpants and a hoodie, he was a wannabe rapper, and he had to be careful with a suit. If the cut was too sharp, it was only the coat's bright lining, purple-flowered originally, which prevented him looking like a relic from the Third Reich. He'd had one or two nasty encounters walking down the Holloway Road in the early hours as a result.

'Maybe something with a hood, a fur trim, perhaps?'

'A parka? You want to put me in a parka?' His voice must have gone up at least an octave.

'Let's see what we can find,' said Luisa, and took a firm hold of his elbow.

44

Lily

11.20

Matt pulled into the kerb outside her flat.

'So, back to Plan A, then?' he asked.

'It's Plan B, isn't it? Plan A was Iceland.'

He nodded, with the sort of sympathetic expression he must have practised in the mirror. 'Would you like to talk it through?'

'Not yet,' said Lily. What was the point? She knew what he'd say. 'I'm going to clean up and then I need to get some food, as I have nothing at all in the fridge.'

'How about I come back in an hour with some lunch? Does that sound okay?'

It was a classic Matt question, one that was impossible to answer other than in the affirmative. He left her to make her way up the stairs alone. You couldn't fault the man, he knew when to give a person space.

She dropped her bag and phone on the kitchen counter and filled the kettle. It was little more than twenty-four hours since she'd last been in her flat but seemed so much longer. She was a stranger in the place, without her own tea, even. Hers was in her suitcase, the one that, unlike its owner, would have reached London. It would have to be Ed's tea, builder's variety, drunk black as she'd thrown out the last of the milk before she left, and dry breakfast cereal. She reached into a packet for a handful of granola. A message flashed onto her phone screen.

Hey Lovely where are you? Did you get a ticket? x

Her insides contracted. She dropped the cereal back in the box. She had to tell him at some point.

Cardiff

Her phone sprang into action, bouncing across the counter as it vibrated with the incoming call. She watched it fidget until the answerphone kicked in and the handset fell still again, followed a second later by the ping of a message.

????

She searched for a way to explain, thumbs hovering over the keypad.

I… she started, and then deleted it. Whatever she said had to make sense to her, too.

Ed got there first.

As the plane leaves in 3 hours I'm guessing you're not coming.

Set out like that, in black letters, it was brutal.

Call you later, she sent, and then, *x*.

She rested her head on her forearms, her tears wetting her skin, and pictured him staring at his phone, rubbing his fingers against his forehead in confusion. His hurt was palpable from there.

When Matt returned, she was sitting curled on a wooden kitchen chair, still chilled from a shower that never got beyond tepid. It turned out that home was no comfort if the heating took six hours to warm up, her hair dryer was lost in transit and the pressure from the water trickling from the shower rose above her head barely matched what was streaming from her eyes. Her wet hair trailed down her neck and stuck to the back of her T-shirt.

He put a paper carrier on the table and started unpacking plastic tubs of brightly coloured salads and dips.

'Wow. What's this?' she said, trying to muster some enthusiasm. 'A feast?'

'Yep, the vegan Christmas. I got everything the café had to offer. You'll re-use the containers, yeah?'

'Sure. Let me know what I owe you.'

'No prob. And I got you a plane ticket. Just in case.'

She knew it! How dare he? But she was so hungry and the roasted peppers smelled divine. She slid off her chair in search of plates and cutlery.

Matt stayed quiet as she tucked into her food, but he was watching, waiting. Lily knew what was expected of her.

'It's difficult to explain,' she said finally. 'It's like one half of me is fighting with the other to make sure I never get to London.'

Matt chased some pine nuts around his plate. 'What does that say to you, Lily? Trust yourself. Have faith in your instincts.'

Lily shovelled some quinoa and pomegranate salad into a flatbread and stuffed it into her mouth. She was feeling lightheaded again. Probably the calorific rush.

'I think you've had doubts since Serbia,' he said.

'Yeah, I did, but I'm through that now. For a while, I was scared because everybody talks about playing their small part in the bigger picture, but I started to think the picture was just too big for me to deal with.'

'What?' Matt frowned. 'No, that wasn't what I meant, exactly. I meant Ed wasn't supportive of you and it highlighted the differences between you. Your approach, how you think about things.'

'He was supportive,' Lily said slowly, 'but he had his own stuff to deal with. And anyway, it wasn't... You and Maggie said—'

'Well, exactly. He had his own stuff. Don't you think he puts too much on you?'

Lily paused, forkful of falafel halfway to her mouth. Was that right? Did everything always come down to Ed's issues? Flashes of conversations came back to her: Ed telling her how strange it was to come across his mother's art school portfolio in Martin's belongings and have no clue what to do with it. Evidence of a twenty-year old Cat, someone he'd never known. Lily didn't know what had happened to it. She'd never seen it. Ed mentioned it only afterwards, when he'd cleared out the flat and it stopped resembling a charity shop drop-off point. He hadn't waited for her help. He hadn't expected it.

'Lily?'

'Sorry.' She pulled herself back to the present. 'I thought you liked Ed. You said you did.'

'Yes, I did. I do.' He didn't sound sure. 'I didn't mean—'

She looked around for something else to eat. Matt passed his plate to her and she wiped up the last of his hummus with the bread as he continued his musings. 'He's a nice guy and talented, obviously.'

'But?'

'But maybe a bit set in his ways, that's all, less open to new ways of working than you are.'

'You're still hung up about the tent,' she said.

'I'm not.'

For the first time that morning she felt like smiling. If it wasn't the tent, then it must be the coat. And the bib. *Make him wear this so it doesn't look like the secret police have come to town, yeah?* Matt could shake his head, but he was stinging from the way Ed and Oz had made him look like an amateurish civil servant, striding around with a clipboard and mobile phone pressed to his ear, while the workers got on with the job.

'Did you bring pudding?'

'Ice cream,' he said. 'They only had vanilla in non-dairy. You like that, don't you?'

Maybe she'd leave it. She picked up the plates and carried them to the sink.

'Anyway, you're wrong about Ed. New approaches to solving old problems is his thing. That's what he wins awards for.' She made quote marks with her fingers. '"*For innovation in retrofitting, maximising the potential for solar engineering, air and water recycling.*" He'd rather design from scratch, but he gets a lot of commissions for listed buildings, finding ways to preserve them and make them sustainable, as energy-efficient as possible.'

Why was Matt making her remember all this? It wasn't the time to catalogue all the things she liked about Ed. The thought of what she'd miss left her feeling hollow, despite the huge quantities of lunch she'd put away.

'I should have told him about Hassan, Reem and the baby.'

'I thought you had,' said Matt, noncommittal.

She stared at him. As someone who'd sworn her to secrecy, he knew very well she hadn't. The move to Cardiff was the fix cooked up to avoid ever having to tell anyone about Hassan.

45

Ed

12.00

This had to be the very definition of déjà vu – walking along Oxford Street following another gut-churning exchange with the person he considered his soulmate carrying another haul of purchases that stood an odds-on chance of being returned in two days' time.

Astonishing that twenty minutes ago, he'd felt so positive. A couple of hours with Luisa choosing presents she was convinced an olive-skinned brunette with a social conscience would love while he resisted (most of) her attempts to make him over into her ideal (if not his) of metropolitan desirability had left him hopeful. So hopeful he'd invited her for coffee – and cake – in the store restaurant.

They found a table and he immediately shrugged off the parka she'd talked him into – dark green with a quilted lining and huge pockets inside and out. Ed had conceded on colour, hood and lining, but he'd never give up on pockets. He felt for the press studs around the hood and popped off the fur trim, pushing it across the table to Luisa. She slid it back.

'You may need it.'

He shook his head. Never. There were limits. He checked his phone again, less than a minute since the last time, measuring Lily's silence against the countdown to take-off.

'Sorry,' he said, placing it back on the table.

'It's fine, don't worry. I used to be like that. My first husband was a wine importer and I never knew where he was. I was always waiting for him to get home from some trip or other, and just as he was home, he was off again.'

'First husband?'

'Yes, we divorced. I stopped caring whether he was cheating on me or not and then I knew it was over. If you still care, there's life in your relationship.'

It wasn't exactly reassuring.

'So, was there a second husband?'

'Yes, there was Derek.' Luisa rolled her eyes. 'I think he married me for my staff discount. He was so shocked when I started divorce proceedings. He said, *Darling, we are so good together. We have the best parties.* It was true, we did. We shopped well, we cooked well. We never argued. He thought that was enough.'

'And it wasn't?'

'Not for me. He preferred to spend time with his best friend who was bald and fat. It isn't good for self-esteem. I want to feel attractive. Don't you?'

Ed didn't know. He supposed so. What he mainly wanted was for someone to tell him what was going on.

'You're still young, you don't know anything yet. Let me tell you. Everyone wants different things and at different times. When you're young, it's all about excitement and suddenly you want security. You get married and want to settle down, or at least you think you do, but when you're my age, you want excitement again. To feel alive, to believe someone still wants you. You don't want to spend your life shopping for quail's eggs and cocktail napkins.'

'Do you get a discount on those, then?'

'Yes, but you can't build a life on that.'

He liked Luisa. She reminded him of Pam, his dad's old girlfriend. There was another middle-aged woman who'd tried to talk to him about relationships, mostly her own and mostly in vain, usually when he walked in on her slamming pots and pans round in his father's kitchen and felt obliged to chat sympathetically for a while. She also spent her time sourcing quail's eggs and napkins, but then she had a home catering business. It was Pam who taught him how to pour wine on all those occasions during his student years when she pressed him into service waiting tables for her. He was one of the few who could always be relied on to have black trousers and a shirt.

He left the shop with two large shopping bags, the bulkier of them containing his leather coat. Lily was cutting it fine, but that wasn't unusual. It was the silence which was out of character. His phone would usually be flooded with apologies, excuses and rearranged meeting points. He stopped in a doorway to send a quick message. Her response was a punch in the solar plexus.

What was she doing in Cardiff?

He shielded his ear from the racket of the Christmas carollers striving to be heard above the traffic and dialled her number, barely able to make out a ring tone above the hubbub. The call rang out. What was going on? The people jostling past him dissolved into a swirling mass as he put the bags on the floor between his feet and took his phone in two hands to steady his fingers sufficiently to type a sentence.

What did she want? Was he supposed to go there and fetch her? He could hack down there, but suppose he did and there was some other guy with her, some other existence which had been happening in parallel with his own? He'd give up on Iceland willingly if there was a point to it, but how could he be sure? He'd have to warn her he was coming because it would be ridiculous to go all that way and miss her. But if he told her, she might hide the evidence, not because she was dishonest, she wasn't, but because whatever else, she wouldn't deliberately hurt him. She wasn't cruel. If she did that, if she hid the truth, he'd never find out what was going on.

On the other hand, did he really want to know? Right now, Iceland might be the perfect place to be.

He messaged his brother. *Can I come get the car?*

Kit didn't keep him hanging. *Anisia's got it. She'll be back in a coupla hours. Can you wait til then?*

For the second time in twenty-four hours he felt like throwing his phone in the nearest bin. He forced his feet into motion instead.

46

Lily

19 June 2017

Lily had been summoned to a meeting with the trustees. There was no agenda attached to the email. It wasn't a good sign. How did they even know who she was? Maggie usually dealt with the board. Alone. Lily rose slowly from her chair. Robyn, the clinical lead, and Charlie, the transport manager, were also heading up to the boardroom. She tucked in behind them.

'D'you know what this is about?' she asked.

'Serbia.'

'Oh.'

Lily slid into a seat next to her colleagues and as far as possible from the chair of trustees, a man everyone referred to as Teddy, although his title on the letterhead was Sir Edward.

She didn't need it spelling out. Their medical point on Serbia's frontier was becoming more permanent than anyone had anticipated. Or desired. Each week, Lily sent out new rotations of doctors, who took more and more kit with them, requiring bigger and better containers. What else could they do? The people kept coming through the border in larger and larger numbers.

'This was always the risk,' said Teddy. 'We assumed regional governments would honour their agreements. You told us we could count on that. Our commitment was to provide emergency medical services to fill the gap before local teams moved in, and there's still no sign of that happening.'

Lily kept her eyes fixed on the surface of the table, like the child convinced that if they don't look at anyone else, they can't be seen. Surely Teddy couldn't hold them responsible for the mass influx of people or for offering them medical care? That could never be wrong. Robyn, seated next to her, was fidgeting. Maggie, on her other side, placed a restraining hand on the clinical lead's arm.

'The political landscape has changed,' she said, before anyone else could speak. 'No-one predicted this... this level of activity, the sheer numbers... and now, the surrounding states are demanding a Europe-wide solution. They won't allocate resources otherwise.'

'Exactly,' said Teddy. 'It's no longer a job for Medic48. We deal in immediacy, not longevity.'

'But we can't just leave,' interrupted Robyn. 'If we do, we'll leave a vacuum. That would be a disaster. The people on that border are vulnerable in every way possible.'

'We won't be leaving them with nothing. There are hospitals nearby. Anyone needing immediate care won't be denied access.'

Lily doubted any of those waiting at the border would set

foot in a local hospital – even if their lives depended on it. She kept her views to herself. How could they think about stopping now? It was all running so smoothly. There was no problem with resources. They had doctors signed up for the next few rotations, and now they'd made the commitment, they wanted their turn. It would be such a waste.

Maggie spoke again. 'Clearly we mustn't be drawn into rows about providing a magnet for refugees—'

'No, we don't want to be rated on migrant Tripadvisor,' said Teddy. He made a noise which could have been a snort, or maybe was a laugh. No-one seemed sure. They all smiled politely.

'But,' Maggie continued, her cool tones at odds with her hunched shoulders and tight jaw, 'leaving suddenly will create its own problems. We can't write off all our gear. We have so much invested in that site.'

Teddy thought for a second. 'Well, okay, let's agree that the centre can continue while we put in place an exit strategy, but we need to be clear about our intentions. Have we got that?'

Lily looked up to check everyone else was nodding and stood along with the rest of the operations staff. She paused by Maggie's chair on her way out of the room. 'Erm, will you have a minute this afternoon? I'm not sure what to do.'

Maggie stared at her as if the answer was obvious. 'Go to Presevo. Schedule our exit.'

Lily travelled out with the inbound medical crew, still pondering the concept of a 'planned exit'. Whether they left suddenly or with a month's notice could make no real difference. They needed all sorts of authorisations, assurances, insurances to be where they were, doing what they were doing, but they needed no permission to stop and leave. That was the exit part, but surely 'planned' meant something agreed on, wished for? And how could she make arrangements without an end date? Running down the supplies defeated the object of the programme – the fully stocked medical point that vanished as quickly as it arrived. Her operating manual had no guidance on what to do when your project stopped following the rules. She could hardly switch the red cross flag for a blue cross and flog off all the kit at bargain prices.

Then there was what to tell her volunteers. They'd suspect something was up. She didn't usually revisit a site after it was set up. Apart from anything else, the teams weren't supposed to be on the ground long enough for a return trip. Even restocking was outside their usual scope, although that was the easy bit, checking inventories and loading boxes onto a van. Staying on message was harder. How could they be both a reliable presence and yet temporary? If the need wasn't temporary, it was hard to explain why the help couldn't continue.

The minibus stopped at the perimeter of the field. Lily climbed down and took a moment to get her bearings. The site had trebled in size since her last trip. The first caravan had been joined by another and both were parked up against Ed's shelter, still standing strong against the elements. An outdoor kitchen had been added at one end for the big vats of stew and bread which arrived in a van once a day from the local town. Another charity stepping in.

The thing that hadn't changed was the air of panic and desolation. Spring had turned into summer, and the trees and bushes were now in full leaf. It was the sort of bright June day that wedding planners held their breath for, but no-one would be holding picnics or garden parties at this place. The groups that made it through the frequently closing frontier crumpled in an exhausted heap on the other side, before grabbing their belongings and the small amounts of food they held on to and scuttling as far from the border guards as possible.

Lily helped the new doctors over to the caravan with the weighty medical bags – a flying kit, not a resupply, she reminded them. They had to get the comms right.

Hassan was waiting by the steps. 'Lily!' He shook her hand warmly and held on to it while he spoke. 'I'm glad to see you.'

'I'm glad to see you too, but I suspect it's a bad sign.'

'It reminds me how long I am waiting.'

'Is there no news of your family?'

'Every day I hope to see my wife.' He shook his head sorrowfully.

She wriggled her hand from his grip and patted his shoulder. 'Well, let's hope it won't be too much longer. Let me introduce you to Dania. She's another of our Arabic speakers so we won't be taking advantage of you this time.' She stepped aside to bring the doctor into the conversation.

Hassan looked the medic up and down, taking in the hijab, long shirt and jeans, under the green bib of authority, and stopped short. He recovered swiftly, placed a hand to his chest and dipped his chin. 'Welcome. I'm Hassan. Anything you need, ask me, I will get it for you. I know everyone, I am here so long.'

From the look on Dania's face, Lily guessed she wouldn't be relying on Hassan's services anytime soon. For someone so tiny, she could be quite intimidating.

Just as the silence became awkward, Lily spotted a familiar figure by the entrance to the other caravan. 'Oh, look, there's Matt. Come on, Dania, we'll do your handover in a minute.' She pulled the doctor away to where her friend stood, hands in pockets, watching the latest group of arrivals.

'Everything okay? Good trip, yeah?' He hugged Lily, shook Dania's hand and, almost without taking a breath, got straight on with filling them in on the day's stats – the times of the border openings, the numbers crossing, ages, nationalities, needs. He didn't usually rattle through it like that. Lily couldn't keep up.

'When did you get here?' she asked, when he finally paused for breath.

'Yesterday. I was in Turkey for a bit, then Greece.' He opened the door to the caravan and lifted the rest of the bags into the vehicle. 'We'll let you get on with it then,' he told the doctors. He tugged Lily to the side and lowered his voice. 'It's not looking good. I'm not sure how much longer this is sustainable. The borders are closing again and the police are starting to make things difficult.'

Lily rubbed her hands over her face. Being evicted from the site was not the solution she was looking for. Medic48 was apolitical; they'd drummed that into her, above everything else. They were the people who were invited into an emergency, the ones with no agenda – apart from saving lives.

'Matt, you have to help me with this,' she whispered. 'Maggie wants us to plan our departure, but the medics are complaining about leaving when there are still people here needing help. Every time I raise it, they talk about credibility and abandonment. I don't know what to tell them.'

'We're not leaving. We're just finding a better place to meet the urgent need. That's our mission. We'll pull out the caravan and pop up again at the next crisis point, yeah?'

He nodded, eyebrows raised, waiting for her answering nod.

Better place to meet the urgent need. She fixed the words in her head and turned her attention to the visitors approaching the medical point. This was something that didn't change. The worried expressions and tentative enquiries; the women lifting their sleeves to offer bracelets in exchange for bandages and painkillers; the tearful smiles when Lily refused payment, pushing their jewellery back towards them together with a queue number for the clinic.

'Please?'

A woman with a toddler clutching at her tunic rushed towards them with a baby in her arms.

The look on her face told them all they needed to know. Matt jumped to the side while Lily poked her head into the caravan where the doctors were still catching up and briefing the interns.

'Looks urgent,' she said.

Lily was in the minibus, taking advantage of a few quiet moments to go through her paperwork. It usually needed more than one attempt to match up the inventories of equipment on the ground against numbers despatched.

Dania popped her head through the door. 'The baby, the one you saw, he should really go to hospital,' she said. 'We've given analgesia and fluids, but he's very dehydrated. I think he has pneumonia, which is not best treated in this environment.'

'That's fine,' said Lily. She was back on solid ground,

operating within the framework of her handbook. 'We can take them there. To the hospital, that is. I'll speak to Andy. We have to transport them with a medic and they'll have to make their own way onwards after treatment—'

'The mum's scared to go,' said Dania. 'Her husband thinks they'll end up in a transit camp. Can you talk to them?'

Lily followed the doctor back to the caravan. The parents and their other child were huddled around the bed where their baby lay, listless and connected to a drip. One of Matt's volunteers hovered nearby, pressing water and biscuits on the family.

'Hi, I'm Lily,' she said softly, nodding at the adults.

'Reem, Omar, Sara and Bilal,' said the volunteer, pointing to the parents and children in turn.

Bilal's parents spotted Dania behind Lily and the conversation started again in urgent, whispered Arabic.

'What will happen if they don't go?' Lily asked.

'Mum's a pharmacist. She knows what her baby needs.'

Lily touched Dania's arm. 'We can't take the whole family, though, only the patient and his mother. That's what the rulebook says.'

'Okay,' said Omar with a huge sigh. 'I stay here. Take him.'

Reem fell against his chest, tears flowing freely.

'Here, Lily, hold this,' said Dania, handing her the bag of saline as she started to prepare the baby for movement. She continued speaking softly in Arabic. 'I'm telling them it's the best thing, the right thing. It's what I would do.'

They walked slowly to the minibus, Omar carrying his baby, accompanied by the doctor holding the drip aloft. Lily followed, carrying Sara and supporting Reem, whose energy seemed to have entirely evaporated.

The minibus was packed with people. Some sort of crisis meeting, as everyone was there – Matt, the medics, the interns and various other hangers-on, including Hassan, presumably in his role as self-appointed patient representative. Lily wasn't getting involved. She opened the rear doors and helped Dania settle Bilal on the back seat with his mother.

The conversation in the front half of the bus had become heated. Matt was insisting that a re-distribution of resources wasn't the same as a pull-out, but he was never going to persuade everyone. Tonight, they had more important things to do, and the sooner the better. Lily walked round to the front to have a word with Andy and the other, locally hired, driver. It would give Reem and her family a moment of privacy to say their goodbyes and plan where and how they'd meet again. Where would you start a conversation like that?

The police were standing in a line in front of their own vans. It wasn't new, they'd been there all day watching them, but now, for some reason, their staring was unsettling. Lily opened the door quickly and climbed into the middle of the bus just as two of the officers wandered over, hands on their holstered guns. One rapped on the side panel, making Lily jump.

'Time to go,' the officer said.

The driver didn't need to be told twice and scrambled round to face the front, hand on the ignition key.

Matt was cooler. He stepped onto the footplate and leaned out with an easy smile. 'Yes, of course, Officer. Have a good night. See you in the morning.'

The driver had started the engine before Matt pulled the door closed. The minibus rocked as it rode over the rutted ground. Lily squeezed onto the edge of a seat before she lost her balance and fell into someone's lap.

'They can't do that,' said a voice behind her. 'They can't just order us to leave.'

'It's not worth the argument,' said someone else. One of the doctors, by the sound of it.

'But if we run, they'll think we're scared.'

'Aren't you?' reasoned another voice.

'We have to leave now anyway,' Lily said, turning to face them. 'We've got a medical emergency.' She flicked her chin in the direction of the back seat and the occupants of the first two rows swivelled to take a look. At least they'd quietened down.

They reached the hospital and Lily climbed over her colleagues to be the first off the bus. She ran to the back, flung the doors open and came face to face with Omar. He was squatting in the luggage compartment holding firmly to the bus with one hand and his daughter with the other. That was bad, but maybe the rules could stretch to two chaperones. There were two children after all, even if one was well and had no need of hospital treatment. She'd barely finished the thought when she heard Hassan's voice. He was leaning over the back of his seat, his forehead creased in a frown.

'Shall we get a stretcher?' he asked.

Lily felt the blood drain from her face and gather somewhere near her feet. There was no way of explaining this man's presence in the van. She could do as much planning for their departure as she liked. It would make no difference. It was all unravelling anyway.

47

Ed

24 June 2017

The day stretched before him, empty bar a couple of things, and they wouldn't take long. He read the morning news on his phone and checked the forecast for Serbia, satisfying himself there were no imminent cyclones or revolutions. Lily complained he didn't notice when she was away, but he absolutely did.

For instance, what was he going to do with the evening's tickets for the Camden fringe and a play written by one of her friends? He could go alone, but it made no sense without Lily. It wasn't the sort of thing he'd ever have thought of attending himself, although it didn't actually look too bad. Tom might be up for it, but he was bound to be busy. He messaged Bob instead.

No thanks, answered Bob. *We're going to a club in Mile End. Wanna come?*

Sure, Ed sent back, and emailed the Fringe box office to enquire about returns.

He should get his dinner jacket cleaned. It hadn't seen the light of day since he'd stuffed it back in its bag after Kit's wedding. It wasn't so different from what he wore every day, but a big event warranted the satin lapels, he supposed. He went to his room and opened the wardrobe. You could tell which side was his. It was like a comment on the twentieth century and the advent of technicolour, a sudden transition from monochrome order to colourful chaos, two or three garments on every hanger, things spilling onto the floor. He picked up a couple of items, but they seemed to have more holes than necessary to accommodate the average number of limbs and insufficient structure to support them. He watched them slither off the hangers and back down to where they lay. He wanted to join them.

48

Lily

24 June 2017

Matt joined Lily at the back of the minibus. He was wearing his professional smile. All teeth, no eyes.

'Right,' he said, rubbing his hands together.

Lily flicked her eyes towards the occupants of the van.

'Ah shit,' he said, tucking his chin down and speaking through his teeth so only Lily could hear. 'Down to me, I'm regional manager, my call.'

Whether it was or wasn't, now was not the time to argue about it. Lily scooped up the toddler while Omar climbed out of the minibus and gently lifted baby Bilal from his mother's arms.

'I'll take them in,' said Dania, continuing to hold the drip aloft.

Alex, one of the other doctors, appeared. 'I'll come with you,' he said and grabbed the emergency medical bag from the back of the bus.

'Call me when you're ready and we'll send Andy back,' said Lily.

She stood, watching, until the group was safely through the automatic doors, hanging on as long as possible before re-boarding the minibus. While they remained outside the hospital, it was a mercy mission, but the second they moved off with Hassan in the vehicle, they were transporting migrants. It was only a short drive to the hotel, but it wouldn't matter if were ten metres or ten thousand; it was still a criminal offence.

'Matt?' she said as she took the seat next to him.

He shook his head. 'Not here.'

'What about him?' Lily flicked her eyes towards the driver. 'Can we let him go now?'

'Wait 'til we get to the hotel.'

Lily sipped at her water bottle and fidgeted in her seat. She had no idea how far the charity would go to protect local contractors. There might be nothing they could do anyway. The police would say he should have known better.

'I didn't check before we left the site,' Matt whispered, relying on the noise of the radio to mask his voice. 'I didn't check we had everybody we ought to have, let alone anyone we didn't.'

Lily had never seen Matt worried before. He was the one with the breezy not-a-problem attitude. If he lost it, there'd be no-one to show her how to make this right. She mustn't crack. Matt wasn't to blame for this. Hassan was always hanging around. None of the volunteers would have thought to bar him entry. They were all about inclusion and no-one was ever quite sure whose job it was to do stuff like that, anyway.

It seemed to be taking forever to reach the hotel, but perhaps the evening traffic had always crawled along like that and she'd never noticed. Matt stayed on the bus, waiting as each passenger disembarked.

'Well done, guys,' he said. 'Great day today.'

Hassan also hung back. It occurred to Lily that it was Hassan who'd stayed in the van when the driver started the engine. No-one trapped him there. The door was still open, he could easily have left. Why would he do something like that? It made no sense.

'Hassan,' said Matt when their stowaway finally emerged. He placed a hand on the other man's shoulder. Lily could barely watch.

'This is where we have to leave you. We can't take you any further and we can't take you back to the border. It's unfortunate, but this is how these things work. Can you make your way from here?'

Hassan withdrew his wallet from the inside of his jacket and opened it. Lily reached instinctively into her own pockets to find money for him and missed what he showed Matt, but whatever it was had him frozen to the spot, his hand still hovering above Hassan's arm.

'Don't worry about me,' said Hassan. He smirked and set off casually down the road.

'What was it?' asked Lily.

'His police card.'

'What do you mean, police?' Lily stared after Hassan. 'Serbian police?'

'Seems so.'

'I don't understand. What's he going to do? Is he going to arrest us?'

Matt ran his hands through his hair. 'I don't know, Lily. I need to think.'

Andy reappeared. 'Hey, they're asking about the "debrief".
I'm getting the beer. Are you coming?'

'Yes, of course,' said Lily, forcing her face into a smile.

'Sure,' said Matt, more slowly. 'Come up to my room.'

They followed Andy into the hotel and up to the second
floor.

'He can hardly arrest us for smuggling a police officer,'
Lily whispered. 'Can't we say we always knew? Or at least
suspected?'

'We can certainly try. But what do we do about the
family?'

'I thought about that. We say we had to bring them all
because the other child was showing symptoms too.'

Matt nodded and Lily exhaled, feeling the tightness in her
chest finally start to release its grip.

The last thing she needed was a team meeting, but the
others wanted to pick up their earlier conversation and it was
impossible to refuse without an explanation. Matt wasn't at
his best. The discussion degenerated into a free-for-all. Lily
knew she wasn't helping. She couldn't seem to focus and tried
to cover it by handing out drinks and snacks, like an over-
zealous party host.

'Isn't that right, Lily?' Matt asked, not for the first time. He
placed a hand on her arm. 'I think we've got enough crisps
now.'

'Oh, okay.' She sat down on the edge of the bed but kept
one eye on the door. The police might burst through at any
moment.

Her phone rang and she sprang back up.

'I'm outside,' said Dania. 'Can you… erm…? We've got a
bit of a problem.'

Lily looked imploringly at Matt. He went straight to the door and held it open as if he, too, had been waiting for the axe to fall and wanted no witnesses.

'Well, I think we've managed to explore some ideas, don't you think? A starting point for us to build on. Let's call it a night.'

The old hands looked surprised. Abrupt wasn't a word usually associated with Matt. He encouraged hanging out and sharing experiences. Lily wasn't staying to explain. She raced back down and out of the hotel, leaving Matt to sort out the rest of the team. Dania was around the corner by the fire exit, standing in a huddle with Alex, Omar and Sara. Omar was wearing Alex's green bib. It was a decent disguise, as long as no-one asked him for medical assistance.

'I didn't know what else to do,' Dania said. 'They couldn't stay at the hospital and it's too late for them to go to the transit camp.'

'Can't we get them a room?' asked Alex.

Lily shook her head. 'They'd need ID and guests have to be registered with the police.'

She looked at Omar, face grey with exhaustion, and Sara, sleeping against his shoulder. She and Matt were in trouble already. Whatever she did now wasn't going to make things much worse.

'They'll have to use my room,' she said. 'We just have to get them inside.'

She ran her nails around the fire exit. The door was closed and probably alarmed. The metal stairs of the fire escape were no help. They went nowhere near her first-floor window.

'You know,' said Alex, 'I couldn't get the aircon in my room to work earlier. How about I go to the desk and lure the receptionist away to check it? D'you think you'll be able to sneak them in?'

It sounded too much like a student prank to Lily. She looked at Dania, who shrugged and apologised again, so she followed Alex inside and hovered while he did his best impression of inept tourist. Somehow, he managed to persuade the man that he didn't need the maintenance team, just a demonstration of control switches as Lily stood at his shoulder, grimacing at her colleague's embarrassing uselessness.

As soon as they left the lobby, she messaged Dania.

'Smile,' she ordered the medics, real and fake, as she opened the door. 'Look as if we have nothing to hide.'

They met Matt on the stairs. He opened his mouth to speak, but Lily put a finger to her lips and tugged his arm to take him back up with them. When they reached the first floor, he shook his head and pointed them up another flight.

'My room,' he said. 'It's quieter.'

Matt's room had twin beds pushed against opposite walls. As Dania helped Omar settle Sara in one, Matt beckoned Lily towards the tiny cubicle of a bathroom. He pulled the door closed behind them.

'We couldn't leave them to sleep in the street,' Lily said before he could say anything.

'I know, I know,' said Matt. 'It's what we're going to do with them in the morning that bothers me. Who else knows about this?'

'Only the four of us. Me, you, Dania and Alex.'

'Let's keep it that way, yeah? Whichever way you look at this, we're people smuggling. If they catch us with Omar here or in the van, they won't let us off lightly. It's bad enough doing it once by accident. I don't want to spend my prime years in a Serbian jail.'

It wasn't in her career plan either. Nor was ruining refugee assistance for every NGO operating in Europe.

Matt let her back into his room. 'Don't let anyone in,' he told Omar. 'There are snacks in the wardrobe – fruit, crackers, cereal bars, that kind of thing. Help yourself. Feel free to take a shower. I'll be back early in the morning.' He collected his sweatshirt and his phone and ushered the two women out of the room. 'You hungry? Shall we get a pizza?'

Lily was hungry, she almost always was, but nerves spoilt her appetite. As did the way Matt put an arm across her shoulders when they returned to the hotel. He steered her along the passage and up the stairs to her room. Lily wriggled free. She looked around for Dania, but she'd already vanished.

'Don't panic,' Matt said. 'You don't know who's watching. There needs to be a reason why I'm not staying in my own room. It has to look plausible, doesn't it?'

Lily rolled her eyes as he put his arm around her again. She had no desire to start any rumours, but at that moment, it would be less of a risk than the truth getting out. 'I'm having the bed,' she said.

It was a large double, room enough for two to sleep in comfortably, but she needed to be clear; she wasn't offering any invitations. She took her shoes and sweater off and climbed under the covers in her jeans and T-shirt.

'I should've realised there was something funny about Hassan. There's not a single other person I recognise from my last trip. Everyone else has moved on. And Dania says he has a strong accent when he speaks Arabic, like he's spent a long time out of Iraq. If he's ever been there.'

Matt sat down on the end of her bed. 'This isn't his fault, Lily. It's ours.'

Sometimes his reasonableness drove her mad. She sat up again. 'I know, I'm just saying. All that work I did finding him a German lawyer… He let me do it and all along he was a fake.'

'Lily, have you been in contact with Hassan?' Matt was stern now. 'I know it's easy to become invested in these situations. The people, their stories, can be very compelling, but—'

'Of course not. Not directly. I'm not that stupid. I sent the details out with the volunteers at Easter. I should've known something was wrong when the lawyer told me he hadn't contacted him. How could he do that?'

'You're really grouchy when you're tired.' Matt rubbed her knee through the blanket.

She glared at him and pulled her knees up. 'And scared, Matt. What's he going to do?'

'I don't know.'

'We'll have to call Maggie.'

'Let's not think about that now.'

'Why did he stay on the bus? He knew it was wrong. D'you think he's done this before?'

She arranged the pillows behind her and leaned against the wall, closing her eyes again as exhaustion and despair closed in. What happened when she wasn't around? Were her volunteers routinely ferrying migrants around the Serbian countryside? It didn't bear thinking about. It must be a trap. Ed had been right. Hassan was as manipulative as he'd said he was, worming his way into their trust just to catch them out.

She woke, hot and uncomfortable, tangled in the

bedclothes. Matt lay sleeping on the other side of the bed. There wasn't room to turn over without rolling into him. She pulled off her jeans and curled into a tiny ball once more, clamping her eyes shut.

When she opened her eyes again, there were chinks of light at the edges of the curtains and Matt had now manoeuvred himself into an L-shape around her. Lily arched away and slid out of the bed, stretching as she looked through the window at the brightening morning. Not a cloud in the sky. An empty street. Empty apart from the man standing on the corner, phone to his ear and smoking a cigarette. Why was Hassan there? Was he waiting for someone? Had he called for back-up and right now, the place was surrounded by riot gear-clad officers inching towards the front door and blocking all exits? Lily shrank behind the curtain again, but she was too slow. Hassan looked up. He waved and blew her a kiss. Her squeal disturbed Matt.

'What time is it?'

'Just gone six.'

He pushed himself upright and flexed his shoulders. 'Better see what's happening, then.'

'I can give you the highlights,' Lily said. 'Hassan's out in the street.'

'Oh God.' Matt went to the window and sneaked a look. 'Are you sure? There's no-one there now.'

Lily stood limply in the middle of the room, raising her hands in a helpless shrug. She hadn't imagined him.

'I'll go see to our guests, then,' said Matt.

He stopped on his way to the door and hugged her. She didn't want a hug, but she didn't push him away. Nor did she hug him back. When he kissed her cheek, she didn't move.

'We'll get through this,' he said, and left without another glance.

Lily went back to the window. She moved the curtain aside with one finger and peered down through the gap. Hassan wasn't on the corner, but it didn't mean he wasn't lurking somewhere nearby. Her phone rang.

'They've gone,' Matt said.

'How? Gone where?'

Had Hassan somehow managed to spirit them away? The chills were back.

'To the hospital,' Matt said. 'Dania left a note. She must have sneaked them out before it got light.'

Lily felt shamed by her relief. It was still their problem; Dania couldn't take it all on herself. The doctor was so brave and dedicated. She had to do more to protect her. Lily opened the window and leaned out into the street. There was a man in the distance, but too far away to be sure who it was. It was possible, if they were lucky, that Hassan had missed them.

49

Lily

26 June 2017

Lily held her breath each time the phone rang, in case it was Maggie, summoning her up to her office, where a warrant from the Serbian police was waiting, smoothed flat by fingers that were preparing her dismissal notice. It was ridiculous. She was safe at her desk, an average Monday morning with a list of supply movements to organise, although this time she was sending the transports out empty to return loaded. A normal day. Nothing to see here.

Matt called. 'Any chance you can come out again?'

Her stomach contracted. It was becoming a familiar sensation. 'Is it urgent?'

'Could be.'

She had the feeling he was saying less than he wanted to.

'Okay.' Her heart was thumping. What if the only reason

she hadn't been arrested so far was because she wasn't on the territory? 'I'll try for Saturday.'

'Hmm. We may have to move one of the caravans before then.'

'I see,' she said, barely able to get the words out. 'Friday?'

'Thursday would be better.'

She sat for a moment with her head resting on her forearms and then called Ed.

'I'm sorry,' she said. It seemed to be all she ever said to him. 'I've got to go to Serbia again. It means I'll be away this weekend, so I won't be here to celebrate your award.'

'Probably won't win,' he said. 'So, nothing to miss.'

She wanted him to complain and question why she was having to go back so soon, force her to own up to what was so important that she had to go back within a week. It was the only way she'd be able to tell him. Too many careers were at stake to give up the information freely.

'It's not long 'til Italy,' he said. 'We'll make up for it then.'

'Can't come soon enough,' she said. The sigh escaped before she could stop it.

'You okay, Lovely? Job giving you trouble?'

Could she tell him? Who was listening? She poked her head out into the corridor to see if anyone was about. You never knew who might wander in, but shutting the door looked suspicious.

'Bit tired of the travelling, is all.'

'Interesting. Tired of travelling but you want to go away. Immersion therapy?'

He could always make her smile.

'You know what I mean. So, what are you going to do this weekend?'

'Oh, I'll find things to keep me busy. I'm up to "Q" in my alphabetical listening. Surprisingly rich pickings with "Q". It's not just Quincy Jones, in case you were wondering.'

Matt couldn't meet her at Belgrade; he was at the other end of the country. Nor could Medic48 spare a driver so Lily had to hire a car. It was the first time she'd made her way to the border alone, unaccompanied by a van full of eager volunteers, and it wasn't a prospect she relished. She tuned the radio to some cheery East European pop and put her foot down, determined to reach Presevo before nightfall. There wasn't a lot of street lighting in the villages and the country roads weren't in great shape. Breaking down or sliding into a ditch in the dark, apart from being dangerous and generally undesirable, would certainly attract the wrong sort of attention.

The traffic dissolved as she drove south. Without the company of other drivers, she felt exposed. It was a moment for one of Matt's inspiring talks, such as, *With each experience, you learn more about yourself, and that's as important as anything else.* What she was learning now was that being able to juggle flaming batons didn't make you brave. It meant you liked the *oohs* and *aahs* of the crowd, but you preferred it when you had a mate nearby with a fire extinguisher.

There was no-one at the hotel at Presevo so she dropped her bags and headed straight back out to the frontier. She parked away from the camp on the last bit of made road and, stuffing her valuables into the pockets of her denim jacket, walked the remaining half a mile.

The site had that end-of-the-day tension about it. People milled around, filling water bottles and repacking their belongings, exchanging bits and pieces of information, worried about where they were going to sleep that night.

Matt was standing near the border post, talking to a police officer and a man in plain clothes with wispy grey hair and a paunch. He acknowledged her with a nod but didn't interrupt his conversation.

Lily picked her way across the uneven ground to the medical caravans. One was closed and padlocked, and the other was in disarray – ripped cardboard boxes and plastic packaging all over the floor. Andy was inside, sorting through the debris and putting anything that was salvageable in a plastic box.

'My God, what happened?' asked Lily, leaning in to get a better view. It looked to be hundreds of pounds' worth of damage. All that goodwill wasted.

'When we got the order to leave, one of the volunteers went postal and opened all the donated medicines, basically handing them out like they were sweets.'

'Where is he now?'

'She. The doc went mad and ordered her off the site. I've never seen anyone so angry. He said it was more dangerous to give out the painkillers like that than to give people nothing. He's gone to get his bags. He's going to help me drive the caravan back.'

'Back to where?'

'Ain't that the million-dollar question? You need to speak to Matt.'

Andy stood up and Lily got another shock. There was a large red swelling on his cheekbone and his eye looked bloodshot.

'What happened to your face?'

He shook his head. 'It's fine. Things've been getting a bit heated, is all.'

'Are you…? I mean…'

It couldn't end this way. Andy had been with them from the start, the month's sabbatical from work which had somehow turned into six. What sort of reward was this?

'I'm fine, Lily,' he said, laughing. 'Dania's checked me out and I've had the talk from Matt. It's cool.'

Matt was still deep in conversation. Lily looked around the camp trying to get a sense of what had changed in the last few days. She saw a man standing by the tent flap and froze.

'What's Hassan doing here?'

'Interesting story, that,' said Andy. 'He disappeared for a couple of days and everyone breathed a sigh of relief. For him, you know. We thought he'd managed to make it through. Then, late last night, he came back. He says all the borders are closed and it's impossible to get any further.'

Lily studied his expression. If he knew more, he wasn't giving anything away.

'Was he by himself?'

'Far as I know.'

The sick feeling she thought she'd got rid of was creeping its way back. She'd returned to the scene of the crime and Hassan was on home soil. He could do what he liked. All her instincts said run, but her feet were glued to the spot.

Matt finally took his leave of the two men. He shook their hands, although they didn't look altogether willing, and headed straight for Lily. He gave her a comradely hug.

'You could've warned me,' she said.

'I didn't know he was back until this afternoon,' he muttered. He was doing his best to appear relaxed, but beneath the early suntan, he looked tired and drawn. 'But it's good you're here. They've closed the crossing and they're bringing buses in to take the people who are still here off to the transit camp. It's mainly people with small kids and old ladies – the ones who can't make it any further. I've managed to negotiate safe passage for our gear.'

'Oh, okay. Great.' She forced herself to concentrate. 'Where are we going to take it?'

'Italy, I think. Fancy a road trip across Europe?'

Lily smiled – as he needed her to – but it took effort. 'How are we going to move the other caravan?'

'If we can't get a car with a tow bar, I'll have to hang around here 'til Andy comes back or we get another driver.'

'Hang around?' She stole a look at Hassan.

Matt nodded.

'By yourself?'

'We'll look at logistics,' said Matt, still holding on to his neutral tone. 'If it's safe to stay, then the rest of this week's rotation can stay until the weekend, but it's your team, your call.'

He was right. It was her call. She took a deep breath and ran down the risk matrix in her head, the one they'd rehearsed, checking for red light indicators. Apart from the sirens sounding around herself, Matt, Dania and the driver, there was no good reason to pull the others out right now. Alex had gone, and the rest of the team was engaged in humanitarian work with no affiliation. They had sufficient training and equipment and a letter from UNHCR confirming their bona fides. There really was nothing to fear.

She lifted her chin and walked across to examine the tent, drooping again when she pulled the flap aside. There was an air of total hopelessness about the inhabitants. They weren't begging for help; they were slumped in heaps. They'd lost the energy to care about the next fortune or misfortune coming their way. She caught the eye of a small boy. He turned away and hid his face in his mother's arm.

The first of the buses arrived in the early evening, two large coaches. The beginning of the end. They stopped and parked close to the police post, but the doors stayed shut and the police remained at their stations. The silence was bewildering.

Matt called a meeting in the minibus. Lily hadn't been at the site after dusk before. The place lit up with small fires here and there, but it felt neither cosy nor companionable. The voices populating the darkness were muted and sober. The atmosphere was so different from three months ago, and it hadn't been entirely cheerful then. More police arrived and parked their van near Lily's bus. Not quite a stand-off, but the presence of each ensured that neither could act with any freedom.

'I've spoken to Maggie again,' said Matt. 'We're going to pull out with as much gear as we can assemble and head north and up around the coast. Lily, can your guys do the inventory as we pack everything up?'

'Sure,' said Lily, wondering how she could explain the spoiled medicines. '*Damaged in transit*' wouldn't be fair on Andy. He'd not lost so much as a sticking plaster on his endless shuttling across Europe.

'We're not following the buses with the refugees?' asked one of the medics.

'To do so might be seen to express a political opinion.'

'And we have none,' said the doctor.

'Exactly. And also, we don't know where they're going.'

'Maybe Hassan knows more,' said the doctor. 'He chats to everyone. He might have picked something up.'

Before Lily could stop him, he marched across to the tent to fetch him.

'Come on,' said Matt. He grabbed her arm and pulled her off the bus.

By the time Hassan sauntered over with the doctor, they were leaning casually against the vehicle.

'Hello, Lily. Back so soon?' said Hassan.

His arrogance touched a nerve and gave her courage. 'So, Hassan, everything's changing here,' she said. 'What are you going to do?'

'I'm going to get on the buses,' he said. 'It's my best chance, I think.'

Best chances for what? She gave him her stoniest look and stepped away.

'Matt, if there's nothing else we can do this evening…'

Matt nodded and turned to the doctor. 'You take the bus back, we'll take the car,' he said, and ushered him on board, shutting the door firmly after him.

Lily banged on the door to tell the driver to go as Matt turned back towards Hassan.

'Well, if we don't see you again,' he said breezily, offering him his hand as if he didn't have a care in the world, 'I hope it goes well for you.'

'Oh, I'll be here tomorrow,' said Hassan. 'But I think you're right. It's much better if we don't see each other again. Much better if you don't come back here.'

The sudden improvement in his English brought Lily up short. She glanced at Matt.

'You aren't threatening us, are you?' asked Matt, in his most reasonable tone.

Hassan didn't deny it. He stood with his hands in his pockets, feet planted firmly. Gone was the round-shouldered refugee, scared to look authority in the eye.

'Go,' he said, mimicking Matt's mild delivery. 'Enjoy your evening together. Make the most of your time while you can.'

'Come on,' said Matt.

He pulled Lily away, before she had a chance to share her opinions about Hassan's insinuations.

'We need to call Maggie,' she said instead.

They sat on Lily's bed, hunched over a phone, trying to keep the noise down while Maggie's voice came through loud and clear on speaker. Lily let Matt do the talking. The chief exec was never going to be happy to be disturbed at that time of night, but if there was bad news to be broken, Matt had all the essential qualities – good track record, calm manner, knack of sliding the negative between such huge chunks of positive in the most freshly cut shit sandwich. Lily could never have done it. She'd been with the charity less than a year and, to all intents and purposes, had already screwed up. Matt knew how much to share. It seemed Omar's sojourn in Matt's room was something no-one else needed to know about. Not even Maggie.

'Awkward,' was Maggie's response, and she only knew half of it.

'It's blackmail,' whispered Lily. 'We keep quiet about him or he has us arrested.'

'Can he do that? Realistically?' asked Matt. 'He'd give himself away, wouldn't he?'

'Possibly. You could argue it's a sting operation and you always knew he worked for the police in some way,' said Maggie. 'That's why you cooperated and let him travel on the bus. I'll have to have a quiet word with the legal team and see if you could defend yourselves against an investigation. Should there be one. Let's hope it doesn't come to that because either way the publicity would be catastrophic.'

She paused. Lily gritted her teeth. The blow must fall soon.

'What we're not going to do is panic,' Maggie said eventually. 'We'll get Andy out first thing tomorrow with the van. I'll leave you to decide whether you go back to finish taking down the site. I'm at a sponsor lunch tomorrow so I'll only be free intermittently, but I'll keep my phone with me. We mustn't show we're worried. This Hassan may have more to lose than you think.'

Lily didn't see it. What did Hassan have to be scared about? If he climbed into a police van and disappeared, everyone else would think he'd been arrested. She, Matt and Dania would be the only ones to suspect he was catching a ride home to the police station.

'Moving forward,' said Maggie, 'minimising risk must move up the agenda. You'll deal with this in your exit report, of course, perhaps as a concern to be flagged up for future volunteer induction. And Matt, in the meantime, we'll take you out of Southern and Central Europe and post you in-house for a while, just as a precaution.'

Matt grimaced, but it had to be purely for show. To be taken off field ops was a rap over the knuckles. It could have been much so much worse. And as for Lily, well, someone had to be tasked with closing the site down, she supposed.

50

Ed

29 June 2017, 03.00

Ed left his colleagues to take selfies with the trophy and walked up the grand staircase. There was no phone signal in the hotel ballroom and it wasn't much better on the mezzanine landing. He sent Lily a picture of the award and hoped it would reach its destination at some point. The signal was patchy where she was too.

Only hardened partygoers now remained. Ed wandered outside to chat with the smokers on the pavement. While he was working out whether it was better to join the long queue for a taxi or take his chances further down the street, a minicab arrived – one of those eight-seater jobs, pre-booked by some of the team to take the East Londoners home. It wasn't going in the right direction, he lived north rather than east of Hyde Park. He protested, but he was dragged aboard, nonetheless. It wouldn't be too bad, he thought as he disentangled himself from his workmates sprawled across the back seats. If he got a lift to Angel, he could walk home from there. Someone else obviously had the same idea because when he climbed out at the top of City Road, he found himself standing on the street with Andrea, Head of Marketing, and the person, coincidentally, who had submitted his nomination.

'D'you want to share a cab?' asked Ed, feeling some responsibility for her safe journey home.

'I can walk to my house from here,' she said.

Ed looked at her feet, the silver toes peeking out from under her long hem, and hesitated. She only had a tiny bag with her, not large enough for spare shoes – unlike Lily, who usually had at least two alternatives in her backpack. He'd rather pay for a taxi than accompany Andrea as she tottered along, complaining her feet were killing her.

'They're flat,' she explained, lifting her skirt to display a shoe. 'I'm tall enough as it is. In heels, I'm a giant.'

Ed was embarrassed to admit he'd never noticed; she was always behind a desk. Now he was paying attention, he could see she was barely shorter than he was.

Her house was close by, the walk not long enough to sober him up but sufficient to feel the pressure building on his bladder. He'd have to drop Andrea and then find a discreet alleyway before carrying on to his flat. On foot. If he took a cab, he'd be home too quickly.

'D'you want to come in?' Andrea asked.

'Oh, okay.'

He hadn't thought of it but now it seemed daft to refuse. He could use the bathroom – and maybe grab a glass of water – before he continued his journey. A long walk was appealing.

It was a clear night and only turning chilly with the prospect of dawn.

Andrea showed him into the kitchen.

'This is a nice place. D'you live here by yourself?' said Ed, more to be polite than anything else.

'I live with my sister. She's a lawyer.'

That would explain how she could afford it. The area was what you'd call sought-after, but nowadays, pretty much anything with a London postcode was desirable.

'It was the same with us,' said Ed. 'I used to live with my brother, but he got married and moved out.'

'So you're on your own now?'

'No, not really... Some of the time, I suppose... Well, quite a lot of the time at the moment, but...'

'You could get another flatmate,' Andrea said. 'Someone to share the bills.'

Ed wrinkled his nose. He rambled a bit about ending up with the same problem further down the line. The prospect of Lily moving in suddenly seemed very far away.

He finished his water and continued to play with the glass in his hand. He ought to leave, but there wasn't anywhere else he could bear to be. Before he had a chance to think the matter through, Andrea moved towards him and ran her fingers across his cheek. She kissed him quickly and slipped her arms around the back of his neck.

'Do you want to stay?' she asked.

He was letting this happen to him and he couldn't explain why. His limbs wouldn't move, as if the electrical impulses from his brain weren't reaching their destination and he was watching it all happen to someone he recognised as himself but wasn't actually him. He couldn't feel her lips on his; he'd removed the part of himself that was in the room to concentrate instead on contemplating the contradictions in his existence. Being a star for the evening was great, but pointless if you were only a success during working hours and didn't enjoy living with yourself the rest of the time. He was a fraud.

He snapped back to find himself kissing her in return. It must have been going on for a few minutes and now she'd undone his belt and her hand was somewhere he really didn't want it to be. He wrenched himself away.

'Andrea, I can't do this. I shouldn't have… I'm sorry.'

'Oh,' she said. 'It's okay.'

She looked surprised but he didn't understand why. He couldn't seem to connect himself to the situation.

'It's not you,' he said hastily.

It was her, but that wasn't her fault. There was only one person he wanted to be kissing and switching in someone else didn't lessen the longing. It made it worse.

'Your girlfriend.'

'Yeah. Lily.'

He staggered back into the hallway, which seemed to have grown longer and narrower in the last half hour.

'Well, er, thanks, Andrea. See you tomorrow.'

Ordinarily, he would have offered her a peck on the cheek, but he didn't know what to do now. He lifted his hand in a half-wave as he opened the front door.

Did this make him a cheat? He stood on the pavement, straightening his clothes and struggling to make sense of what happened. He wasn't the cheating type. Nor was he self-destructive. This sort of thing had only happened to him once before, when a girl in a club had, quite literally, thrown herself at him and he'd caught her as a means of defending himself. That had been funny. This was disturbing. He yanked off his tie, stuffed it in his jacket pocket and started to walk.

He didn't look up until he reached home, and when he did, he suffered another shock. He wasn't in Kentish Town. He'd walked to Hampstead, to the house he'd grown up in, the house his father was now sharing with Samantha, the builders' board outside a sign she was making the place her own. He leaned against the garden wall, visible to anyone who cared to look out.

What was wrong with him?

He hadn't lived there for years. Truth be told, he'd left as soon as he was able. The distance brought home to him how desolate the house had become. While his boys were at university, Laurence heated only one room, cooking from one pan – when he could be bothered at all. Ed called home regularly but was never sure of reaching his father. He wondered where Laurence was sleeping, he seemed to be so rarely in the house. When the boys were back, they brought an entourage of friends and the holidays became a lengthy party, empty bottles and take-out cartons joining the grime and dust until Ed and Kit could stand it no longer and ordered a mass tidy-up. Each time the debris was removed, it revealed another layer of decay, more peeling paint and cracked window panes, curling postcards on the mantelpiece, mildew in the kitchen cupboards.

Ed had been relieved when Martin offered him his place. He couldn't get in there fast enough. It would have been impossible otherwise to move back to London without going home to his father, something he couldn't bring himself to do. The arrangement suited Martin too. He got a reliable tenant and he was able to move into the flat above the Portobello Road shop.

If Laurence felt put out, he said nothing. He and his son were close, but they didn't have that sort of relationship. Ed kept an eye out for his father and how he was living, but over time, it became harder to push the old house back into a serviceable state. He had to scour architectural salvage sites for tiles to patch up the roof and there was more filler than wood around some of the windows. The beautiful frames with their distinctive wooden mouldings deserved a bit of care. Ed dreaded the day he'd discover woodworm in the joists and imagined the Hampstead neighbours checking their party walls to make sure nothing destructive was creeping in from next door. He didn't believe his father didn't notice. Ed suspected he'd been waiting for someone else to see it and rescue him from the wreckage. Or for the wreckage to take over, whichever happened first.

Laurence, meantime, stayed in his study, ghost-writing other people's memoirs from the hours of recordings and transcripts supplied by his agent, and let life happen around him.

It was difficult to reconcile the damp and gloomy building with the warm chaos of his childhood. He might have been looking at two different families, two different lives. Well, now his father had introduced new blood and the place would get a new lease of life. It was about time. Ed doffed an imaginary cap to the house, to its loyalty and perseverance.

His phone buzzed in his inside pocket. Ed looked at the display. How did she know? Was she clairvoyant? He scrambled to his feet and set off in the right direction now, flinching each time he felt the discomfiting vibrations next to his ribs, like a kind of shock treatment, as Lily tried again and again to reach him. He couldn't speak to her yet, not in the state he was in.

He stopped for breakfast on his way home, queuing among the early commuters and late nightclubbers for coffee and an Egg McMuffin, feeling less conspicuous than he might have in his dinner jacket. He made it barely a hundred metres up the street before he had to turn off the main road into a rubbish-strewn alleyway. He couldn't keep it down.

51

Lily

June 2017, 04.00

Lily didn't want to talk anymore. Her mind was screaming for silence and her body for sleep. She was too tired to care what anyone would think if they spotted Matt leaving her room at this hour, but he kept on going.

'If I move in-house, I'll have to go to Cardiff. There's no coordinator role at Bristol at the moment.'

'Isn't that where they do the Middle East jobs – Lebanon and Jordan? It could be interesting,' she said, only half listening as she searched social media for news of Ed.

'I'm worried about you, though. You can't stay in Bristol if you're taken off the European jobs. You'd better come with me. We'll say we have to keep the team—'

At last she found what she was looking for on the *Architecture Now!* twitter feed.

'He won!' she said, and leapt off the bed. She jumped

around in a circle. It felt like forever since there'd been anything to celebrate.

'Who won?' said Matt, looking at her with that forced patience reserved for children distracted by the nearest shiny object. 'And what did they win?'

'Ed! He won his design award. That's amazing! I need to call him.' She rubbed her hands over her face to wake herself up.

'It's the middle of the night, Lily. We should sort this out first, shouldn't we? You heard Maggie.'

'Oh, he'll be up. I'm sure they'll still be partying.' She smiled again at her phone.

'I'll leave you to it, then,' said Matt.

He was sulking but she let him leave. If she tried to apologise or explain, he'd only go over it all again.

Ed wasn't answering his phone. Each time she tried, it was the same. Four rings and then voicemail. And not even his own voice, just the automated message. Right then, the most appealing thing she could think of was going home to London to hide in the old man's comfort of his flat, with its heavy furniture and thick soft furnishings muffling the drama of the outside world, but she wasn't getting a chance to tell him.

She hid under the bedcovers and closed her eyes but woke after a couple of hours, sweaty and breathless. She reached for her phone and tried Ed's number again. Still no answer. Where was he?

She messaged Kit before she left the hotel to go back to the site.

Is Ed with you? I can't raise him.

Not with me, he replied. *Did he win?*

Yes!

Wooo, came the response, followed by a bunch of happy emojis, which made her laugh despite all the rest of it.

The morning was a slog. Counting, packing, sealing tubs of medical supplies before lugging them across the dry mud to the van. Her phone rang as she was bent over a cardboard box, calculating how many packets of dressings would have to be written off.

'Hey, how's it going?' said Ed, sounding less triumphant than she'd imagined he would.

'Oh, got a few issues this morning.' She stood and took her call away from anyone else. 'But never mind me, let's talk about you. Where've you been? Were you out celebrating?'

'You saw the result?'

'Yeah. It's so brilliant. I'm so proud of you. All that grief paid off in the end.'

He laughed finally. 'It'd take more than that.'

'Were you out all night?'

'No, no. I went home. Got in about three.'

'I tried to call.'

'Yeah, sorry, I didn't see the messages 'til this morning. My phone was off.'

Ed didn't usually turn his phone off. It stayed on vibrate, buzzing on the dresser at odd moments through the night.

Lily frowned. 'But you're okay?' she asked.

'Yeah, yeah, feeling my age is all.' He was quiet for a moment. 'But, anyway, what's happening with you? Is everything all right?'

'I really wanted to talk to you.' Tears were pricking her eyes, which was embarrassing. She pinched her nose and managed not to gulp. 'Things are falling apart here.'

271

'Oh, no.' He perked up. 'Is it safe? Should you leave?'

'I'll be out of here soon as I can. Today probably. But if this project folds, I need to think about what I'm going to do. I need a shoulder to cry on.'

'You've got one. It's here, ready and waiting.'

She waited for a quip about face paint and a request she wiped her cheek before pressing it to his shoulder as it was a bugger to get out of his suit, but there was nothing.

'I needed it last night,' she said.

'I'm sorry. But you've got it now. You've always got it.'

'You aren't worried I had to use someone else's shoulder?'

'Should I be? Did you?' he said, not sounding remotely worried.

'No,' she said, shaking her head, and smiling, though he wouldn't know why. 'No other shoulders here.'

'Good. Will you be back tonight, then?'

'I hope so.'

'I could meet you at the airport.'

'Will you?' she said, lowering her voice. 'Please?'

She turned to go back into the caravan and spotted Hassan approaching from the direction of the road. The feeling of warm relief evaporated. She moved to the side and pretended to be typing into her phone. It didn't put him off. She could see him bearing down on her out of the corner of her eye.

'Still here, then?' she said.

'Waiting for my turn to leave,' he replied. 'So, Lily, it's time to say goodbye. I will miss you all.'

He put his arms out. She thought at first he was going to pat her shoulders but instead he pulled her to him, trapping her. It was the most threatening and least affectionate embrace she'd ever experienced, and bizarre too, because she wasn't scared any longer, just utterly repulsed.

'I need to go,' she said blandly, leaning away from him.

He forced his weight against her, his mouth close to her ear as he pinned her arms to her sides. It went against all her natural instincts to stay still, to refuse to fight back, but she wouldn't struggle. She wouldn't give him the satisfaction.

'Yes, please go,' he said, but he still didn't release her.

'Everything okay here?'

Matt appeared at Lily's elbow and Hassan abruptly let her go. She stumbled back, momentarily unbalanced.

'Yeah, it's all fine,' said Lily, moving behind Matt, shielding herself, resisting the urge to massage her upper arms.

Her phone buzzed in her shaking hand.

Dug up Ed, said the message from Kit. *Hes a bit rough. Didnt get in til 7*

52

Ed

12.50

The choice was stark. Falling on his family's mercy (hell would freeze over first) or grabbing his bags, racing to the airport (he might just make it) and spending Christmas alone in a cottage on a glacier. It could work. He'd buy a litre or so of whisky in duty free, light the log fire – as promised in the property description – and stretch out on the sofa (there was surely a sofa?) with a book. He'd need to get hold of a book. It would give him plenty of time to ponder where he'd gone so wrong.

Or, he could go home, shut himself in, drink himself stupid for a couple of days and go back to work as soon as possible. No-one need know he was there, and he wouldn't be subject to any customs restrictions on his alcohol purchase. That was more like it, though there was no point going yet. The wolves would start circling soon enough.

She'd been on his mind, so he called Pam.

'As it's Christmas, I thought it'd be rude not to check in and see how you are.'

'I'm fine, Ed. How are you?'

'Yeah, fine. Seems strange, you know, not to see you at Christmas. I mean, how many Christmases did we spend together? Eight? Ten?'

'More like fourteen. But we didn't exactly spend them together, Ed. I came by on Boxing Day for the pleasure of clearing up your dinner before I could start on my own.'

'I'm sure I remember you there on Christmas Day.'

'Only in the evening with my Marigolds on.'

He laughed. 'I've missed you, Pam.'

'I've missed you too. So, is it business as usual? Off to your dad's?'

'God, no.'

Now she laughed.

'I might go to Kit's. I was supposed to be going away with Lily but… What're you doing for lunch, Pam?'

'I'm boning and stuffing sea bass. I've got dinner for twelve this evening.'

'Your own or someone else's?'

'My own. But come over if you like. I've made some paté you can try.'

Ed didn't fancy the tube. The crowds at the Oxford Circus entrance resembled a rugby scrum, worse than a midweek rush hour, and he was weary of being jostled and sworn at. He'd walk the couple of miles instead. It wasn't as if he was in a hurry.

He paused at the florist beside Maida Vale tube station to pick up a large poinsettia.

'Well, this is an unexpected pleasure,' said Pam as she

opened the door to him. She placed her hands on his shoulders and kissed him on both cheeks. 'And what's this?'

'Happy Christmas,' he said, handing her the plant.

'You've never bought me flowers before. Actually, you've never bought me anything before.'

'I'm sure I bought you a magazine, once. When you twisted your ankle.'

'Mmm, maybe.'

'And how is your ankle? All better?'

'Come in before I change my mind,' she said, laughing again.

'I blame my father,' he said, once he was safely in the hall.

'Me too.'

It was years since he'd been in her flat. The place was almost unrecognisable.

'You had some work done?'

'A bit.'

She studied his face for a second and then took him through to the back of the flat, where she settled him at her vast kitchen island with a pile of toast and mackerel paté.

'So how is everything? And everybody?' She sat down with a plate to join him.

'Same as ever. Kit, Anisia and plus one, Laurence and Samantha, etc.'

He spread paté on the thinnest toast imaginable and looked around. It was a cook's kitchen with more gadgets, utensils and larder space than he'd ever seen outside a showroom. It couldn't have come cheap, not with marble in that quantity and so much soft white lighting.

'Congrats on you and Tony. You're looking very well. Marriage obviously suits you.'

Pam must be nearing sixty but didn't look it. There was no grey showing in her hair and she was still slim in her narrow jeans and satin shirt.

'It's what you do when you marry a younger man, Ed. I can't have people thinking I'm his mother. I'm surprised you noticed my eyes, though. Most people don't.'

Neither had he, he'd been looking at the new suspended ceiling. Whatever he said now would be wrong. He smiled instead.

'So, what's going on with you and Lily?'

'Fucked it up.'

Pam waited.

'I dunno, Pam. I don't know how to do this. D'you think my parents were happy? You know, before Mum died?'

'Oh Ed,' she said, rising from her stool. 'How can I answer that?'

She leaned against the kitchen counter, arms folded, but then gave the question proper thought.

'They were happy at the beginning, I'm sure they were, but then Laurence lost sight of your mother. He got a massive jolt when she was diagnosed and he panicked. He tried to put things right but the speed of it took him by surprise.'

'I'm scared I'm doing the same thing. Losing sight of Lily.'

Pam shook her head. 'You're nothing like your father.'

'Why didn't you marry him?'

'You need to ask him that. I finally got smart that I'd be waiting for him for ever. It's as if he thinks Cat died on purpose, the ultimate revenge for his neglect. He's never got over the shock.'

'So, why Samantha?'

It was the thing he understood the least. Why his dad

277

would choose someone so different, so at odds with how he lived? Unless that was the point.

'Oh, he'll tire of her, I'm sure. You know what he's like, he hates to be pinned down. He'll pay lip service to everything she asks because behind the scenes, he's doing exactly what he wants. He still calls me, you know. Invites himself over.'

Of course!

'Was he here this morning?'

Pam nodded. 'Seems the dog needed a long walk.'

It was a weird relief to know his father hadn't bought in hook, line and sinker to life with Samantha. He saluted Pam with a quarter of toast and paté.

'This is really good, by the way.'

Pam brought him some more toast. He made quick work of it. He hadn't realised how hungry he was.

'You have no idea how many excuses he made because of you and Kit,' she said. 'He couldn't commit to this or that because he had responsibilities. I soon realised you were basically parenting yourselves. With Martin's help.'

'So, they were unhappy? Mum didn't want to be there?'

He couldn't leave it alone. Laurence must have told her something.

'I didn't say that. Only that he didn't appreciate her until it was too late. What is it, Ed? What's worrying you?'

'I hope… Suppose she felt trapped by it all.'

'Do you think she was unhappy?'

'I dunno. I never really thought about it before. Laurence was Laurence, in his room, writing, coming out when he wanted something. He'd tell us to keep the noise down, we'd say, "Yeah, sorry," and move somewhere else. Mum had her studio, but the door was always open. We'd play while she worked. She wasn't bothered about noise or mess. She joined in.'

'Ed, I barely knew your mum, so it isn't fair for me to comment, but he missed her terribly after she was gone. He refused to take her pictures down. He said it was for you, but it wasn't really.'

Ed scoffed. It was more likely to be inertia than sentiment. Laurence had hardly touched the place for years, so it was no surprise that the walls remained hung with his mother's work. Not only her illustrations but all the framed images of her, starting with her art school days, when her pink mohawk haircut and silver piercings had tourists stopping her in the street waving their cameras. You could still buy a postcard in some of the souvenir kiosks off Carnaby Street. How many Japanese students had chosen her picture as their defining image of London?

'I think it was the first and only time in your father's life that things didn't go his way,' said Pam.

Ed fiddled with his rings. His own life hadn't been beset by constant struggle. It was only losing his mum that cast a shadow. Pam moved back to the table.

'You aren't like him, Ed. You work hard for what you've got and you don't take things for granted.'

'I think I might have been.'

'You mean Lily? She takes you for granted, too.'

He frowned.

'Oh, she does, Ed. If she sticks with you, life's going to be quite comfortable.'

Ed shook his head, dismissing the thought.

'You've got a good job and as long as Samantha doesn't sell off the family silver, you've got some money behind you.'

'Lily isn't like that.'

How could she think it, let alone say it? Lily refused to take anything from him. It was what they argued about most. You'd almost believe Lily was sorry his finances had improved and she preferred it when he was paying off seven years of student debt.

'And Samantha's welcome to sell the silver,' he said, 'if she can find any, because the house is in trust for Kit and me. Mum saw to that. Dad's only the owner while he's alive and he can't sell it. Not easily, anyway. It would involve a whole bunch of legal stuff.'

There were things Ed had only been half aware of when he was growing up. He'd always suspected his father played away. It was there in his embarrassment and his almost obsessive loyalty after his mother's death. His mother used to joke about how her husband ran around after his female writing students. *I'm the one he married*, she said. Ed had been too young to understand the edge to it.

He'd known the house was in Cat's name, bought with money from her parents and re-mortgaged more than once. It was why Laurence took up the ghost-writing. He'd had to generate a regular income and keep his end up in whatever deal he'd made with his wife.

But what had happened to turn the girl with the nose ring and shaved haircut from the art school punk into the capitalist investor? Perhaps she hadn't changed. Laurence always said, *She was never a proper punk, she just liked the fashion and all the attention*, and that's what he'd loved about her.

It struck him that his father was less conventional than his mother. His mother hadn't had a lot to rebel against. Her parents, North London psychiatrists who encouraged self-expression and sexual equality, were in their forties when Cat came along – an afterthought, Martin always said, not an accident. She was spoilt and indulged. But never reckless. She might have left home at seventeen to join a commune, but she didn't run away; her dad gave her a lift.

If Cat had felt caged, she created another for her family, something Ed had discovered sorting out Martin's affairs. When she knew she was dying, she tied up her assets in so much red tape it was worse than all her punk bondage straps, literally trussed for her sons. She made nothing over to her husband. That had come as a shock. Had she felt so vengeful? Or was it panic, a need to protect her boys and guarantee they'd have everything she planned for them? Was she future-proofing their lives?

Whatever else, it wasn't a fair thing to do. His mother should have had more faith. Laurence wasn't a bad man, far from it. He was a decent father, warm and funny, and he would have provided for his children properly even if his wife hadn't been to the lawyer's. Ed didn't doubt it for a second. His dad would probably have enjoyed it more if he'd had more wriggle room. And if there'd been a downturn in Laurence's fortunes, so what? They would have coped.

So it couldn't have been about trust, not in any major way. It was about control and that, Ed surmised, was the reason Laurence didn't fight back. His wife could maintain her grip on the things that troubled her. He'd do everything else his way. It was all he could do. Cat had given him no choice.

Ed thought about all the building work Samantha had set in motion and felt a sudden pang of conscience.

'Do you think Laurence has told her?'

'Who knows? But Lily has an idea. She didn't have to

move to Bristol, but she knew you wouldn't stand in her way.'

He shook his head again. 'Lily couldn't have known about it all. Not the extent of it. I didn't until this year.'

'Well, she knew if it didn't work out for her there, she could come straight back.'

He pushed his plate away. 'You're not being fair to her. It's something she's always wanted to do. She could have gone sooner but she stayed back because of Martin.'

'And she knows you'll wait while she tries all these things out, until she decides she's ready to be a wife and mother.'

Ed twitched reflexively. Was he ready for Lily to be a wife and mother? Maybe. He traced the grain of the smooth stone counter with one finger.

'Don't get me wrong, Ed. I love Lily, you know that, but I care about you too and you look exhausted. In fact, I was about to suggest you stayed here tonight. Free bed and board, you won't even have to serve the soup.'

'Maybe I should have asked her,' he said as much to himself as Pam.

Pam dismissed the suggestion with another shake of her head. 'I know why you didn't. It's what Laurence would have done. Look out for number one while pretending to give everyone else what they want.'

'You really don't like him, do you?' said Ed with a smile.

'I love him. That's why I'm so bitter,' she said. She narrowed her eyes and gritted her teeth before she too cracked a smile. 'I'm not sure she'd have had you if you'd asked her then.'

At least someone agreed with him.

'But she would have known, though.'

'She knew.'

'When did you get so wise, Pam?'

'It's spending so long failing to fix the problems in my own relationships. You get good at spotting the flaws in everyone else's.'

'So how do I fix this, then?'

'Show her how much she's got to lose,' said Pam. 'That's what kept me coming back.'

53

Lily

July 2017

Ed was making it easy for her. A holiday all planned, booked and paid for. All she had to do was jump on the plane, hand luggage only. A bit of a challenge but she'd do her best.

'You sure you don't want me to drive down with you?' she asked, more than once.

'Don't see the point if you can fly from Bristol. I'll hack down in the car and pick you up at Pisa. Travel light. I'll bring everything with me.'

He had the widest smile when he met her at the arrivals barrier. 'You made it.'

She wrapped her arms around him as he buried his nose in her neck. 'Did you think I wouldn't?' she said, though she had no right to be indignant. With everything that had happened in the last couple of weeks, even she wouldn't have put money on her getting there.

Their bikes were strapped to the back of Martin's old blue convertible. Was that his contingency plan in case she didn't turn up? It was sad he felt the need.

She stopped by the car, took Ed's face in her hands and kissed him several times. She stroked his cheek. 'You're looking very fine.'

And he did look good. He'd caught some colour on the way down, but it wasn't only that – or the sunglasses and Birkenstocks. Sandals, no less! He was looser, freer. Something had changed.

The car looked appealing too, its leather seats absorbing the summer warmth even as it sat in the shade. Lily climbed aboard, relishing the heat against her back and under her thighs, and lifted her face to the sun and the clear, blue sky. It was all so perfect. She couldn't spoil it. Her news could wait.

Over lunch at their beachside hotel, she saw the cycle route he'd planned around Tuscany.

'Is this what you've been softening me up for?'

'A few days of cycling, that's all,' he said. 'You said you wanted to see the countryside. Then we'll get back in the car and hit the beaches.'

Lily studied the road from Siena to San Gimignano. Neither of them was the type to spend seven days stretched out on a sun-lounger but... She dragged her eyes from the sea which waited, silvery and inviting, just the other side of the road.

'How hilly is it?'

'Not too bad,' he said.

Not too bad by comparison with the Himalayas, she assumed as she pushed down hard on the pedals. Either he'd been lying or they had very different ideas now of what constituted fun. At every turn of the winding road, she expected to see the town unfold before her, but it was always around another bend. The sweat poured down her back as she leaned forward over the handlebars. She was so hot all she could think about was ripping off all her clothes and jumping into the nearest fountain, but that would be far from this arid landscape and up in the town, which was around another bend and then another.

The city gates appeared at last, behind a hairpin bend at the top of a slope. Ed stopped at the side of the road and pointed silently at their destination. Lily ploughed on, groaning as she weaved a wobbly line through the arch, but the cobbled streets were too big a challenge for her burning thighs. She slid off her bike and dropped it with a clatter next to a water trough.

Ed skidded to a halt beside her and stepped off his bike. He passed her a bottle of water as he chained their bikes together and unstrapped their belongings.

'I hate you,' she gasped.

The three words were all she could muster. She never wanted to see his back view again, lean and muscled though it was in its black cycle shorts, leading her through hell with an encouraging backward glance and a *Not far now, Lovely*.

Ed wasn't talking either. Exhaustion? Or did he judge silence the best option?

'You're not going to tell me that wasn't tough,' she said when speech was possible again.

'It was tough,' Ed said. 'It wasn't supposed to be that bad.' He took the remains of the water from her and poured it over his head, shaking the drops off like a dog. 'At least you had my slipstream.'

'Slipstream! I need an ice bath.'

'What about a cold beer and an ice cream? Come on, I'll treat you,' he said.

He threw the panniers over his shoulder and took her hand, helping her up the slope and into the main square. They were both hunched and bent-legged, gingerly stretching out their hamstrings.

The queue outside the Gelateria was twenty people long, snaking the thin ribbon of shade offered by the building, and confined by a rope barrier. It was more like the queue for a nightclub than an ice-cream shop. An American woman joined the line just ahead of them.

'It's usually worse than this,' she said. 'Yesterday, there was a thirty-minute wait.'

'Why's that?' Lily asked. 'Is this the only one?'

It seemed unlikely. The country was renowned for its ice cream. She gazed blearily around the square.

'It's the most famous ice cream shop in Italy.'

'Ed? Did you know that?' Lily asked.

He was busy studying the menu of flavours. He nodded, without lifting his eyes.

She stared at him. The idea that this man might have thought it a good plan to cycle a helter-skelter in reverse for the sole pleasure of sampling the perfect ice cream seemed insane.

'What d'you fancy?' he asked, handing her the laminated card.

'How about cheese and olive? What d'you think that will be like?'

She hoped it would be horrible and she'd make him lick it off her burning, sweaty stomach, or better still, off her sore and blistered toes.

He sighed. 'Okay, I'll do it. I'll get cheese and olive as long as you get caramel and we can swap halfway through.'

'Oh, I was going to get rosemary and pine nut.' She really was. It sounded nice.

Ed wrapped his arms round her, hugging her to his sweat-soaked chest and kissing the top of her head. 'This is why I love you.' he said. 'Okay, I'll do any penance you want. Feta and lemongrass? Whatever you like, I'll do it. I'm sorry. You can ride back on my handlebars. The guide said you needed moderate fitness. You're fit enough, Lily. In fact, you're so fit, I don't know anyone fitter.'

Lily laughed as she pushed him away. 'Cheese and olive, then.'

'Cheese and olive, it is. I'll do gorgonzola and walnut tomorrow.'

'How long are we staying?'

'Until we can bear to cycle down the hill.'

On their third day, she relented and allowed Ed a free choice of flavour. They sat together on the stone steps of the Collegiata, watching roadies set the stage for an evening concert of opera in the square in front of the church and contemplated the ride back down the hill. Lily dipped her plastic spoon alternately into her pink grapefruit and his mint choc chip.

'I think I might be about to lose my job,' she said, her spoon hovering above the carton. She had to broach this at some time.

'What? Why's that?' Ed looked genuinely concerned.

'It's the problems we had in Serbia. The European programme's all a big mess.'

'That's not your fault. That's geopolitics.'

'Yes,' she drew out the syllable, 'but if the project folds, there'll be no job for me in Bristol.'

'There'll be other jobs. You've got experience now.'

'Yes, but if I want to keep this one, I might have to move to Cardiff.'

She stuck the spoon in her mouth and sucked the ice cream slowly away. It wasn't so much what Maggie had said which was worrying but what she hadn't. Matt was moving indoors but Lily's name featured nowhere in the plan. All the signs were there. She'd be the fall guy if one were needed. Matt was right. She needed to find a new role for herself and he was the only person offering one.

Ed took his time to respond. 'Cardiff's okay, Lovely. I went to uni there.'

'So, you don't mind if I move to Cardiff?'

He was choosing his words carefully. 'I'd like it better if you came back to London, but it's your choice.'

'Really?'

He switched the tub to his other hand and put his free arm around her. 'Of course. If this is what you want, we'll cope.' He pressed his chin to her hair. Other people's hair went frizzy in the heat. The body dropped from hers.

'I could help you find somewhere to live. I know all the worst places.'

She was getting that feeling again, that somehow it suited him that she had another life elsewhere. She was loath to confront it. He'd been in such a good mood the last couple of days, happier than he'd been for months. Her silence gave her away.

'Or d'you want to give it all up?' he asked.

'And come back to London?'

She thought for a second. Not as a failure, not unless you're offering me something better. Will you do that, Ed?

'No, not yet.'

It took him a few seconds to respond and when he spoke again, it was with a sigh. 'So, Cardiff will be fine, Lil. What's wrong? Do you want me to say it won't be?'

'No, but you don't have to be so rational,' she said, pushing the ice-cream tub away.

He laughed and hugged her more tightly. 'Don't go if you don't want to,' he said. 'Do you want to?'

'Yes, I think so.'

She twirled her spoon between her fingers, wondering whether to admit she probably liked the mint choc chip the best.

'Well, then.'

He stood, offering a hand to pull her up.

Ed led the ride back down at a gentle pace. Lily stopped peddling and let gravity take over, speeding past him. He laughed as she flew by but didn't try to catch her up. He wouldn't have had to try that hard, the gradient was in his favour. Lily recognised a delaying tactic when she saw one. The longer he took, the less time they'd have to talk.

They picked up the car and drove to one of the pretty pastel-coloured towns lining the blue waters of the Ligurian coast. Lily stretched as she got out of the car and surveyed the bustling restaurants lining the promenade. The evening was still warm and there was barely any breeze off the sea. Cardiff seemed a world away and if Ed wasn't going to mention the move again, she wouldn't either. Perhaps in the end it didn't make much difference to him which city she was living in if it was a different city from his.

She shoved everything else to the back of her mind and concentrated on making the most of their few days lazing in the sun. It wasn't difficult. Long, warm nights, mornings meandering hand in hand through cobbled streets, flopping after lunch on whichever beach they'd chosen as their destination for the day.

Ed lay on a lounger shaded by a huge beach umbrella and she squeezed in next to him, resting her head on his shoulder. He put his arm out to support her so she could prop her book on his ribs.

'What're you reading?' he asked, eyes half closed.

'It's a history of the development of surgery,' she said. 'It's really interesting.'

The book jiggled as he laughed. 'When we agreed one book each on the bikes, that was the one you chose?'

'It's probably less gory than yours.' She pointed at the Nordic noir thriller that lay pristine and unopened in the bag. 'Shall I read you a bit?'

As he dozed next to her, she read him hair-raising descriptions of early clinical experiments and pioneers in anaesthetics and post-operative care.

'I can't believe they did that,' he said. 'You'd stand a better chance if they left you alone.'

When her eyes were tired of squinting against the sun, she put the book down and he wrapped his arms around her, nuzzling her hair as she slept against him.

'D'you really have to go back on Saturday?' he asked when she woke again. 'If we change the flight, can you stay a couple more days?'

She measured her fear of being away against her fear of going home. What was being said in her absence? What were they planning?

'Can you?' she murmured.

'I think I can swing it. I'll say I fell off my bike and my medical treatment was in the hands of a former clown with a manual on nineteenth-century surgery and excellent hand-eye coordination. Things got worse before they got better.'

'Idiot,' she said, pressing her cheek into his warm, bare chest as she wriggled back under his arm, somehow not minding the sweat sliding off her ribs.

'I could stay,' she said. 'I'll drive back with you.'

'Good,' he said. 'You need a bit longer to blend in your cycle short tan line.' He ran his finger across the top of her thigh.

She lifted his sunglasses to get a better look at his expression. It was a bit of a trek back up to their hotel.

He grinned at her. 'Swim?'

She wasn't the only one watching Ed as he wandered along the shore in his beach shorts, long enough to cover his own white lines. Anisia always said that she'd married the handsome brother, but from what Lily knew, the rest of the world didn't agree. It wasn't just the women leaning up on their elbows. She padded down the baking sand to join him at the water's edge, sliding her hand into his.

'Did you see that girl checking you out?' she asked, kicking the water up with her toes as she fell into step beside him.

'Which one?' he said, not bothering to look around him. He pushed his sunglasses to the top of his head. 'These aren't prescription lenses. I can't see much beyond you. And that's all I need, isn't it?'

He scooped her up to carry her into the sea, wading through the shallows, the sea so relaxed and flat, the waves lacked the energy to do more than a languid lap at the shore.

'I'm not going to scream,' she said.

'Oh, go on. For the viewers at home? It's no fun if you don't.'

He carried her out, dipping her back in the water as he went, until they were beyond the line of inflatables and basking holidaymakers and Lily could only just touch the bottom with her big toe. She screwed up her face each time her hot skin breached the surface, refusing to squeal. When he finally released her, lowering her gently into deeper water, he handed her his sunglasses and submerged, resurfacing after a few seconds, scraping his hair back off his face as the water ran down his cheeks.

'That's better.'

Lily closed her eyes against the splashes before wrapping her arms round Ed's neck to stay afloat. He slipped his hands into the waistband of her bikini bottoms, pulling her close and kissing her as they bobbed in the water.

She must have told him she loved him once an hour on the drive home. Each time she said it, she wondered if what she was really asking was whether she was doing the right thing. She didn't ask him that. Whatever he answered wouldn't be what she wanted to hear. She didn't know what that was. Perhaps only that he loved her.

Her eyes were wet when they said goodbye at Paddington Station. Ed wiped a stray tear from her cheek with his thumb before he kissed her. She clung to him.

'It's only two days, my lovely Lily. It'll be Saturday before you know it.'

'Will you come early?'

'Early as I can.' He nudged her towards the barrier. 'Don't miss the train. I want you home before dark. Call me the minute you're in.'

She pulled her bag through and paused at the other side of the gates, already feeling the draught at her side.

'Two sleeps, Lily, that's all, though I don't know how I'll get to sleep without you.'

54

Ed

15.00

'Okay, so I kissed her.'

He didn't bother with an introduction. She knew it was him. At least she'd picked up this time.

'Andrea? Or are there others?'

'Andrea. What do you mean, "others"? There aren't others. You know that.'

'I knew you were lying. That's what I knew.'

'I don't know that I'd characterise it as lying, Lily. I told you nothing happened and nothing major did. She kissed me and then I left. I didn't want it to happen and I felt sick about it.'

'That's lying, Ed.'

It was the same thing. Just like the kissing. He'd let that happen when he could have resisted. He could let this happen, too. Or he could stop the slide and fight back.

'Whatever. I'll tell you what I did lie about. I knew you called. My phone was ringing in my pocket, ringing and ringing, and I knew it was you and I didn't answer and that was wrong.'

He paced Pam's sitting room, one hand to his skull, the other clamping his phone to his ear as he made his confession. This was the thing he felt worst about, ignoring her, when she knew by some magic connection he didn't believe in that all was not well and he hadn't respected her instincts.

'Why would you do that?'

'Because I couldn't tell you and I couldn't lie.'

'So, you waited until you could lie?'

'No, no! Not like that!'

'I was really worried. I thought something was wrong.'

'Something was wrong, Lily. With me.'

'I could have helped.'

'I was too angry with myself. And to be honest, I was angry with you too. For not being there.' He was getting louder as he continued to pace. He lowered his voice. He didn't want Pam coming in to check on him.

'So, it's my fault?'

'No, of course not!'

Lily sighed. 'I wanted to be there that night, Ed. I really wanted to speak to you. You have no idea.'

He thought he did. He went for broke. 'So, tell me, Lily, who have you been kissing?'

Did she take a breath? Maybe not. She was quick enough with the comeback. 'Not so fast, Ed. We're still talking about you.'

'I've told you everything there is to tell. It's ancient history. It happened once and it was ages ago.'

'Six months.'

'I've told you I'm sorry.'

'No, you haven't! You said you were sorry you didn't pick up the phone. Not sorry you kissed someone else and lied about it.'

Sorry didn't quite cover how he felt. Sorrow was more accurate. Raw and whole-hearted. The industry award was still stuffed in a carrier bag under his desk. Whenever he caught sight of it or knocked a toe against the heavy glass, all he saw was vomit in an alley, splashing off fly-postered walls onto his shiny black boots. It would be hard to find a more effective aversion therapy. It was one kiss and it was never going to happen again.

'You had so many chances to tell me,' she said.

'I know, I know, but all you could talk about was moving to Cardiff and the timing was all wrong.'

He'd wanted to tell her. It had been burning a hole in him. He'd wanted to show her it might even have been a good thing. It forced him to his senses and within days, he'd cleared the remainder of his uncle's belongings from the flat. Every form that needed signing, witnessing and returning had been sent off. He'd turned a corner, got a grip, however you wanted to describe it. There were only a couple of nasty moments, like when he came across a couple of his mother's sketchbooks. Then he sat on Kit's bed, turning the pages with bloodless fingers until his pulse slowed again. It was a while since he'd looked properly at any of Cat's illustrations. Seeing the little doodles in the corners of the pages was more powerful than hearing her voice. It threw him right back, snapshots of his childhood flying into his mind from all directions. He'd taken the books into the living room to sit quietly for a while before tucking them into the shelves. Everything else had to go, but the drawings could stay. Now it was done and he wasn't going to think about any of it anymore. He'd cleaned up his act. Had Lily really not noticed?

'You're blaming me again,' she said.

'That's not what I meant. I'm sorry. I was sorry at the time and I'm sorry now. It shouldn't have happened and I want to wipe it from my memory.'

'And how are you going to wipe it from mine?'

'Well, my lovely, how about you tell me something? Like why you were so keen to speak to me at that hour of the morning?'

Funny how his conversation with Pam had made him bolder.

'I don't want to have this conversation over the phone.'

'How else are we going to do it? As you aren't planning to come to London, do you want me to come to Cardiff?'

The clipped tone had crept in again, although he didn't mean it. Yesterday he might have resisted the idea of spending Christmas in Lily's top-floor flat. Now, compared with a weekend with only a record player and a bottle of Chivas Regal for company, Cardiff seemed the ultimate in desirable destinations.

Lily hesitated. This time he was sure of it.

'Where are you?'

'I'm at home.'

'Alone?'

'Matt's here,' she said quietly. 'He brought lunch.'

'Oh, that's nice. I'm glad you had a good lunch.'

'He was just being kind. There's no food in my house.'

Ed could find no words. Nothing arrived in his head that

would be any use in the circumstances. She was in Cardiff with Matt. How could he have misread it so badly? His knees buckled. Perhaps she'd never left Cardiff and all her tales of missed trains and lost luggage had been an invention, buying time while she found the guts to tell him she wasn't coming. He grabbed a fistful of his hair, almost pulling it from his scalp.

'Well, I guess that's it then,' he managed. 'Happy Christmas, Lily.'

'Ed, wait—'

He hung up before he crumpled.

'All sorted?' asked Pam when he made it back to the kitchen.

'You could say so,' he answered, chest still tight. He fumbled his way back into the parka and picked up the bag with his leather coat. 'I'll get going.'

'Here,' said Pam, holding out the other carrier.

'It's just Christmas stuff,' he said. 'Maybe you can use it or re-gift it.'

Pam looked inside. She pulled out the sweater and examined it through its cellophane wrapper. 'Nice colour. It will suit Lily.'

He didn't trust himself to speak.

'Keep it,' said Pam, placing the bag in his hand. 'I bet she'll be wearing it by New Year.'

Ed lacked the energy to contradict her.

'Apparently, my education's lacking because I can't tell cashmere from viscose. D'you think, if she'd lived, my mother would have imparted all those useful bits of knowledge to me?'

He'd never thought of his mother as a cashmere jumper

sort of person, but perhaps she was. Or would have been. In most of his memories she was in a T-shirt, a pair of his father's old jeans and covered in ink, raking her hand through dyed black hair.

'I doubt it,' said Pam. 'I think your mother looked at you and Kit, wild boys that you were, and decided the best she could do was make sure you used cutlery and had clean underwear. But you didn't turn out badly.' She hugged him. 'And she taught you how to love, Ed, and that's the most important thing.'

She showed him to the door.

'Keep in touch.'

55

Lily

October 2017

Lily could think of so many things she'd rather do than sit opposite Samantha studying a restaurant menu. It wasn't the food (the chef had books out) or even the place – which was lovely. Round tables with heavy white cloths and just enough noise that you had to lean in close to have any sort of conversation with the person alongside. Perfect if you were looking for excuses to whisper in your neighbour's ear, but there wasn't a lot of chat going on. It felt less like a birthday celebration than an uncomfortable job interview. Lily didn't believe Samantha had assembled her new stepsons and their partners solely so they could wish her husband many happy returns. They could have done that over Sunday lunch at the Freemason's Arms. As they usually did.

She lifted her wineglass to her lips.

'Don't swallow,' muttered Ed, sitting to her left.

Lily hid her smile with her hand. She knew what he meant. At any moment, someone might fall to the floor clutching their throat. It was that sort of atmosphere.

The seat next to Kit was empty again. Anisia had spent most of the evening outside, wandering the quiet streets off Piccadilly in her heels and lace dress, soothing her wailing daughter. Lily had a wild desire to wrestle the baby from her friend and fight it out for a turn pushing the pram up and down the pavement. Anything to get away from the table. She gripped the edge of the chair to stop herself.

It was a relief when the waiters cleared their plates and handed round the dessert menu. They were on the homeward straight.

Laurence placed his menu card on the table. 'Guys,' he said, lifting his reading glasses from his nose and examining the lenses. 'We've been thinking about Christmas, Samantha and I. Wondering how to arrange things this year.'

Lily gulped at her wine to hide her shock. This couldn't have been Laurence's idea. Lily would lay bets he rarely gave Christmas a thought until the day before. Organisation wasn't his thing. He liked to do exactly as he pleased on the spur of the moment, and if anyone's plans were put out, he'd blame poor memory or pressing work deadlines.

She fixed her gaze on the white space between the words *pannacotta* and *tarte tatin* and tried to look disinterested, all the while checking Ed from the corner of her eye. He was staring straight ahead, showing her his perfect profile as he scanned the list of liqueurs. There was nothing to indicate he'd even been listening. Nothing except the way he flicked the ring on his little finger.

'It's barely October,' said Kit.

'Things like this need to be considered,' continued his father smoothly. 'It's our turn to host Christmas and—'

'Your turn?' interrupted Kit again. 'Who are you taking turns with?'

'I should have explained. We want to invite Sam's children, make a long weekend of it, have a proper Christmas. If they all stay, we'll be tight on space.'

'Well, you've got our rooms. We don't need them, do we, Ed?'

Ed didn't respond. Lily switched her gaze back to Laurence, still stunned at the fakery of his offering his new family a 'proper' Christmas or pretending there was any shortage of space in that huge shambles of a house.

Anisia returned, weaving her way between the tables, hugging her sleeping baby to her chest. Kit jumped to his feet and rushed to help her out of her jacket, cradling his daughter with a hand of his own as he pulled the garment away one careful arm at a time.

'What have I missed?' she said, sliding into her seat.

Lily shrugged helplessly. She was an experienced performer, trained to carry on in all weathers in front of a tough crowd, but she wasn't up to this.

'What d'you think?' Kit asked, mild tones at odds with his pleading eyes. 'Are we staying at home for Christmas or...?'

'Maybe we can pop over in the morning?' his wife said slowly, choosing her words like stepping stones over a rushing torrent.

'What about you?' Samantha turned to Ed, offering him the sweetest of smiles. She'd once been a pharmaceutical rep. Lily didn't know why, but it always seemed relevant. 'You'll come for lunch, won't you? I'm sure we can squeeze you in.'

Ed put his menu on the table and fidgeted again with the heavy gothic rings, the ones his mother used to wear. Lily reached across, covering his hand with hers, squeezing his knuckles as she racked her brain for something helpful to say. Samantha wasn't extending a hand of peace; she was throwing down the gauntlet, challenging Ed to commit to her new world order or maybe lay claim to the house which was still as much his as hers. It was very unfair. It was due to him that the place was still standing.

"Fraid I can't come for Christmas this year but, you know, thanks, anyway,' said Ed.

Lily nodded to herself. It was a neat sidestep but he didn't have much room to manoeuvre.

'Oh?' said Samantha.

'Yeah. We're going away. Lily and me.'

Lily dropped his hand and quickly grabbed it again. He could have warned her he was going to do something like that.

'Where are you going?' said Samantha, her smile noticeably tighter.

'Iceland,' said Ed. 'We thought it would be suitably Christmassy – festive spirit and all that.'

'Iceland?' His stepmother frowned and turned her cool, blue gaze to Lily. 'Really?'

'Hmm, yes,' said Lily. 'I've had a yearning to go since my geology GCSE. All those rocks and volcanoes. And, erm, fish?'

At that moment she couldn't confidently place Iceland on the map. Her imagination ran wild as she shifted an island here and there around the North Atlantic.

Fortunately, a waiter arrived, carrying a huge, nut-

304

encrusted cake, emblazoned with candles. The conversation ground to a halt. Was Samantha going to make them sing? That would be excruciating. Laurence would hate it, or would have in the old days. He usually skipped pudding and carried a brandy outside to swirl around as he rocked on his heels and smoked a cigar.

'Iceland?' Lily echoed when, hot on Kit and Anisia's heels, she and Ed made their excuses and left.

She started running as soon as her feet hit the pavement, party shoes no challenge for someone used to stilts.

'Yeah,' said Ed as he chased after her.

He stopped to catch his breath when they reached Piccadilly, the lines of queuing traffic and red buses reassurance that nothing had changed in the past couple of hours, despite the storm brewing down the street.

'You didn't do geology,' he panted, hands on his knees.

'She doesn't know that.'

'What d'you think?'

'Why there?'

'I don't know. Somewhere with no buildings or people, all wide skies and landscape. No-one to hear you scream. And it might be nice, reindeer and snowmobiles and so on. You will come, won't you?'

'Yeah,' she said.

She was already dreading telling her mum.

56

Ed

15.20

Ed checked his watch. His flight would be airborne, racing north without him. He glanced up, squinting for contrails in the overcast sky. Ridiculous. The plane would hardly be trailing a banner.

If he'd known earlier what he knew now, he'd have made better plans, and they would not have included trudging the streets of North London filling the hours of daylight with random activities before he chucked in the towel and went home.

Perhaps he should swing by his dad's and see whether Samantha had managed to pull his mother's pictures down. Was it the reason she'd brought in the builders? A less than subtle way of hiding all Laurence's belongings in one of the upstairs rooms while she remodelled downstairs. When it was finished, she'd look at her perfectly plastered white walls

– the ones that remained after the living areas were opened up – and shrug (un)apologetically that there was no space for the old things. They wouldn't sit right with the new design scheme.

If he picked up another plant and a bottle of something sparkling, Samantha might accept a truce and let him in to have a poke around. She hadn't asked his opinion about her plans – and he hadn't offered – but he wouldn't mind seeing what she was doing to the old place. From a purely professional standpoint. Had she asked, he'd have recommended gutting it, starting with the back of the house. It would mean demolishing his mother's studio. The perfect party venue and games room, large and empty with high ceilings and a paint-spattered floor, it had provided good service over the years. Sadly, its loyalty hadn't been repaid by its users. Its corners were damp and spidery, and the huge windows onto the garden were rotting out of their frames. It was time to put it out of its misery, and the person to do it was Samantha. No-one else would be brave enough. She had to do it if she wanted to continue to live there, though why she'd want to wasn't at all clear.

Or Laurence, for that matter. He was clever; he could have unravelled the trust. He could also afford to leave, with the income from his books and even a pension, thanks to Cat. If he'd been in his father's shoes, he'd have left long ago, and now Samantha had given him the perfect excuse.

Ed stopped suddenly and looked around. He hadn't been paying attention to his surroundings, putting one boot in front of the other, ambling along in the general direction of home. It took a moment to recognise the perimeter of Regent's Park, the route he would have cycled but certainly not the shortest on foot. He turned slow circles on the pavement, finding his bearings, working out the quickest way to Kit's.

Why hadn't it occurred to him before? Laurence was waiting for permission to leave. It had nothing to do with the house; he'd never cared about that. If he did, he'd have looked after it better. He stayed because he thought he had to. It explained so many things, including why he hadn't tied the knot with Pam. He must have promised his wife. They'd all made promises to her. Ed and Kit still wore her rings, now rubbed thin and brittle, and moved from finger to finger as their hands grew. Laurence had kept to the deal long after he needed to, hanging on until his sons had finished their almost endless professional training and made their own lives. Kit was now settled, and Laurence must have been as sure as everyone else that Lily was there to stay. Well, Ed wouldn't be the one to disillusion him.

He called his brother.

'Can I pop by with a present?'

'Yeah, sure. Anisia's not back yet so we have a window as it were. D'you still need the car?'

'No, er, not now.'

'It gets better and better.'

57

Lily

November 2017

Cardiff made Lily anxious. Not the city, or the people. They were lovely. It was the sense of imminent tragedy. Her working hours were filled with examples of human frailty. It was her job to immerse herself in the detail – the studies predicting the most likely sites of natural disasters for better planning of aid delivery, updates from think-tanks on strategic engagement and prospects for conflict resolution, reports on medicine shortages, limited budgets and mortality rates. It was like reading the plans for doomsday. She wanted to believe the world was a fundamentally sunny and good place, but instead she spent her days preparing for disaster.

Since the day she'd joined Matt on the Middle East desk, she'd been working towards a single goal – establishing a catch-all centre in Turkey to offer emergency treatment for the people streaming out of Iraq and Syria. It was Maggie's brainchild, a pilot to develop a virtual medical base, concentrating on harnessing local skills from neighbouring nations and building a network of on-the-spot response teams, each cell with a central coordinator, whose role was to assemble the manpower and expertise. Next time there was an earthquake in Turkey or Iran, they would be ready. At least, that was the plan. If it were that easy to negotiate all the competing interests in the region, Lily was sure it would have been done before.

It didn't get to Matt in the same way, or maybe it did and he was better at rationalising it. *It can't be wrong to be ready, can it?* This project played to his strengths – flitting about on planes, organising conference calls between parties in three countries, easing the way, and then returning with another list of people for Lily to contact and permissions to obtain. The closer they got to the launch, the further from ready they seemed.

Lily had come to dread Mondays. Even if she and Matt booked out their mornings, Maggie would slide a meeting into their schedule. She couldn't be avoided. They'd hear her trainers on the stairs seconds before she burst into their office. *Any news on a date?*

There weren't many more ways to say the same thing. A project as ambitious as this was bound to have stumbling blocks.

This Monday had started badly with a summons to the boardroom. It was only the second time Lily had been called in. Maggie was already there when she and Matt arrived, sitting at the head of the table, flanked by two of the trustees.

'We've made a decision. We go live with what we've got,' Maggie said, almost as soon as they'd sat down.

Lily looked at Matt. What had they got? The virtual

network was disappearing further into the ether, battered by flare-ups in the regional conflicts which were the very reason for its inception.

'The static medical centre's more or less ready,' said Lily slowly. 'We can open that and use it as a platform to introduce the other thing.'

The virtual thing that still had no name, that changed shape and identity every day.

'That's definitely the way to go,' said Matt, taking up the slack, the master of smooth. 'It'll draw people in, re-establish our presence and our credibility.'

'Can you launch on 1 January?'

'That might not—' started Lily.

'Not a problem,' Matt jumped in. 'We'll go out the week before, nail down all the final details and open the doors.'

Lily rested her chin on her hand and let the rest of the conversation wash over her. She felt as if she were being propelled to the end of a diving board and every attempt she made to get back to dry land was headed off. No-one seemed concerned about whether what they had was viable or would sink without trace. She waited until they had shuffled back through the doors and out into the corridor.

'It's not possible. We won't have time to send everything out,' she said. It was an effort to control the tremor in her voice.

'Why not? It's the same as every other site we've worked on. Send the vans out early. We'll meet them there, get it all stocked, ready to open.'

'We can't send the vans out the week before New Year. That's Christmas, in case you've forgotten. And I can't go then, you know I can't.'

'Can you reschedule?' said Matt. 'Iceland will still be there.'

'But Christmas won't. I can't leave Ed in Iceland to go to Turkey.'

Matt didn't ask *Why not?* but it was all over his face. He leaned against the wall, hands in his pockets. 'Surely when you spend so many months working on something, you want to see how it works out?'

'I've been out to the site three times already,' she said. 'And I'll do the evaluation once it's up and running. I won't be missing anything.'

'Don't you want to be there to see the first person cross the threshold?'

'You can video it for me,' she said over her shoulder as she walked away, down the stairs and out of the building. She needed some air.

Why was he doing this? They were so far from ready. He was making it into a contest that no-one could win.

She sat outside on the smokers' wall and composed a long email to him, her thumbs racing over her phone keyboard, typing, deleting, redrafting. He could get Maggie to push the launch date back to the following week – if he tried. They were already four months late, four or five days more would make no real difference, and they'd stand a better chance of getting celebrity endorsement and decent photo opportunities if they avoided a national holiday. If there was one thing she understood, it was that the size of the crowd depended on the day of the week and the pull of the competition that day. Wouldn't it be better to launch when the world was back at work and they had support available, IT for example, in case, God forbid, anything went wrong?

Matt came out and sat next to her. 'Lily—'

'I've sent you an email.'

'Wouldn't it be easier to talk about this?'

She shook her head. Her hands were shaking too. 'You need to have it in writing that, as the person in charge of logistics, I have severe concerns about delivery. And also, as you know, I've got plans for that week.'

'I know, but disasters don't wait for working hours, Lily. The date's symbolic. We're ready, so what are we waiting for? Let's do it!'

She stared at him, his bright smile, his enthusiasm. Yes, he'd kept her in a job, and she owed him something for that, but it didn't stretch this far. He might never switch off, but it didn't mean she had to do the same.

'They want to book our tickets. I could get you something for the 27th,' he said.

'I'm not going then,' said Lily, refusing to look up from her phone.

'You know, as we have to travel via Istanbul, it's actually easier to go out at the weekend. I might even go out on Christmas Day.'

'Who does that? No-one does that, Matt.'

'Boxing Day, then?'

'Not me. I'll fly out a week later. I'll buy my own ticket if I have to.'

'Up to you,' he said, 'but you need a success.'

It stung, but he wasn't being unkind, merely stating the obvious. It was always in the air, the tiny question mark over her competence. She felt it too, the niggling fear that without Matt to pick up the pieces, she'd be bound to let the side down, but it wasn't fair; this was a job she could do – if they'd only let her.

She should speak to Ed, but that was another thing she wasn't going to do just because Matt wanted her to. It could wait until Friday even if it was a shame to spend their time together talking about her work problems and worse that she had no other plans for her days off. Their weekends had become so horribly predictable, barely more than a chance to eat and sleep before the working week came round again. If Ed came to her, he arrived before lunch on a Saturday and stayed until Monday morning, scrambling out of bed to catch the first train back to London. When she went to him, he met her off the train at Paddington late on Friday night and took her back to the station on Sunday evening. Whichever way round, he still made it to the pub after work on a Friday while she'd be still at work until the cleaners threw her out. Funny that.

Matt was still speaking. 'I think it's important to remember what this project means to you.'

'And to you,' she reminded him.

He'd want her there to witness his triumph. He couldn't pretend he didn't. If they managed to pull this thing off at all.

'Well, yes,' he conceded. 'But that shouldn't be your main consideration.'

'I'm not cancelling on Ed to go to Turkey earlier.'

'I know you're conflicted.'

'I'm really not,' she said. 'But if I get my bag ready, will you take it out with you, so all I have to do is get a plane at New Year?'

'You'll miss the launch.'

'I'll be there.'

'You'll miss the set-up.'

'You'll cover for me.'

314

'And if I can't?'

He held her gaze for longer than necessary and the anxiety started to creep back. She shook her head against it.

'Okay. Your decision,' he said.

58

Ed

17.00

Kit opened the door of his Stoke Newington flat. He was in shorts and bare feet, his daughter balanced on his hip.

'For the baby,' said Ed, handing him a bottle of Chivas Regal. A good one, in a box. 'I would have got you a plant but couldn't trust you to water it.'

'Ah, mate,' said Kit, examining the label. 'I've been thinking the same thing. We'll toast him at midnight. You in Iceland, me in London. Send him wishes from two continents.'

'Same continent, bro. And I'm not going to Iceland.'

Kit stared at him. 'We need a Christmas pint. If we go now, she won't be able to stop us.' He held the baby out to Ed. 'Grab her while I get her coat.' He dashed into the back of the flat with the urgency of a crash team call.

Ed dropped his bags and took his niece. 'Hey, Kitten.'

He touched the tip of his nose to hers, which was a thing

he'd learned she liked as she could grab the frames of his glasses and smear baby goo over the lenses.

Kit reappeared, buckling the belt on his jeans and carrying a jacket and a snowsuit for his daughter. He sat on the stairs and dressed the little girl while Ed pulled the pram from where it rested against the wall, tugging it open and fiddling with the clips and locks until it looked stable enough.

'Can you strap her in?' asked Kit, handing the baby over again, while he stuffed his feet into his socks and deftly laced his boots.

Ed placed his carrier bags into the tray underneath, admiring how neatly they fitted into the space, and opened the front door. There was something wrong – the giant bag of infant paraphernalia that Kit usually hauled from place to place was missing.

'Do we need to bring something for her or can she get a drink at the pub?'

'Good point,' said Kit. He rushed back inside and returned with the bag. 'Milk, juice, water, pureed something or other, I've got the lot. Quick, let's go.'

Ed watched his brother wheel the pram one-handed.

'They're quite well-designed, really,' Ed said, indicating the tray underneath. 'You can fit a lot of stuff in there.'

He was looking for common ground, building a bridge for what he was about to suggest. Kit was generally quite chilled, but you never knew. Everyone had no-go areas.

'It would be better with panniers on the side,' said Kit. 'Like a bike. Wouldn't have to bend down so much.'

With panniers on the side, the contraption would be as wide as a car, but Ed wouldn't quibble.

Kit stopped in the middle of the pavement. 'I just realised

what's different about you. I knew there was something, but I couldn't work it out. Where's your coat?'

Ed pointed to the carrier bag. 'Don't panic. I thought I'd try a different look for a while.'

'Why?' Kit shook his head.

'Oh, I dunno. It's quite comfortable, not as heavy on the shoulders, decent pocket depth.' He pulled open a pocket to show his brother.

'Hmm, not bad.'

'I got these too.' He lifted a foot to show his brother. 'Do I look rugged?'

'Not as rugged as me. I got my baby wipes and my nappy cream. I'm so rugged, you'll have to do some very manly things to catch up. You'll also have to do your laces up.'

Ed nodded at the truth of that.

Daylight was just clinging on as they reached the pub. Kit went to find a table out the back, away from the smokers and under a patio heater for the now sleeping baby while Ed went to the bar. He returned with a pint for each of them.

'So why no Iceland?' asked Kit. 'Now you've got your Arctic explorer starter kit.'

'We broke up.'

'No way! What happened?'

'I've been really dumb, Kit. There's this guy she works with and she's with him. In Cardiff.'

'Ah, mate, that's so wrong.' Kit frowned, his mouth hanging open. 'I can't believe it. Not Lily.'

'I must've been blind. It happened under my nose and I didn't notice. I even encouraged her.'

'You encouraged her?'

'I encouraged her to go to Cardiff.'

'Oh, right, but that was different. You can't stand in someone's way.'

Ed turned the beermat between his fingers. If he told the rest of it, Kit would understand, for sure, but he'd tell Anisia and she, most definitely, would not. On the other hand, if Anisia heard it from Lily first, that would not be a good look. He dithered too long. Kit had started one of his musings.

'She's always had a bee in her bonnet about her charity thing. She's still trying to get Anisia to volunteer for her.'

'Yeah, well, her "charity thing" saves lives, Kit.'

'Well, if it's a competition to save lives, Ed…' Kit grinned. 'You know, when you first told me Lily was moving to Bristol because she was tired of being a living hedge, I thought it was some sort of psychological state. Or a metaphor, like a doormat or a scapegoat. I didn't get what was so wrong with it. It sounded kinda nice, you know, organic and environmental, a habitat to protect endangered species… I even googled it, to see if I was missing something and being a human hedge was really a terrible state of mind to be in.'

Ed was already laughing, head in his hands. 'Tell me, what did you find?'

'A website to hire party entertainers.'

'Are you sampling the drugs you should be injecting into your patients? How do they let you near real people?'

'I'm book smart, as they say,' said Kit, unconcerned, 'and I have a good bedside manner.'

'Ooh er, missus,' said Ed without enthusiasm.

'Yeah, well, it's all they want in an anaesthetist. But even now, I don't see that being a living hedge is that bad of a deal.'

'I think it's that there's limited scope,' said Ed, humouring him, as he always did. 'I mean, you can put flowers in your

319

hair and roller skates on your feet and find different ways of interpreting the essence of shrubbery, but ultimately you're waiting for someone else to book you for a gig. The challenges are all physical, not mental, and there's no career progression. You don't start as a hedge and finish as a Scots pine.'

Kit nodded sagely. 'So being a living hedge is a metaphor for being stuck in one place, looking pretty but disguising your true self. Have we invented a new syndrome?'

Ed raised his glass to clink it against Kit's. 'Good job.'

'Still doesn't sound so bad to me. Anyway, whatya gonna do for Christmas? D'you wanna stay with us? It would make me happy.'

'That's nice, Kit, thanks. But I'll pass. Maybe I'll go to Iceland after all. I could make it the start of something, take a bit of time off, travel for a while.'

'On your own?'

'Whatever I do now, I'm on my own.' He took out his phone and scrolled up and down, pretending to check flight times.

Kit tipped his chin to the side and reached across the table to clutch Ed's hand. 'Well, don't forget, you'll always have a home with us.'

'That your bedside manner?' said Ed, pulling a face and yanking his hand away.

'Never fails.'

Their laughter drained away as a shadow fell across the table.

'So here you are,' said Anisia.

'How does she know?' Ed leapt to his feet, although he had nothing to feel guilty about. At least, nothing immediate.

'GPS,' said Kit, and tapped his phone. 'How was work, Darling?'

'Do you want a drink?' said Ed. 'Port and lemon? Dry sherry? Half a stout?'

'Diet Coke,' said Anisia. 'It's a bit early for a G and T.'

'Half five? Not necessarily,' said her husband.

'It's Christmas after all,' said Ed.

'Oh, go on, then. What are we celebrating?'

'We're not,' said Ed, and went inside to the bar.

When he returned, Anisia was feeding the baby a bottle and scolding Kit for letting her sleep so late in the day.

'Kit, listen,' said Ed, interrupting, before Anisia had a chance to ruin his brother's good mood. 'I've been thinking. How would it be if we let Dad sell the house?'

Kit glanced at Anisia and back again. 'We've been thinking the same.'

Ed could sense Kit's relief and the echoes of other conversations going on out of his earshot – Anisia's *Talk to him*, Kit's *Yeah, all right, in a minute*.

'You know how things are with us. We need more space, but you can't afford to buy me out of the flat – not unless you sell it – and we couldn't make you do that. It wouldn't be right.'

'But if we sell the house and split it between the three of us, everyone gets what they want,' said Ed. 'I buy you out, you two get something big enough to live in and Dad can move on.'

He clinked his glass against his brother's and Anisia's. They could do this communication stuff.

'Shouldn't you speak to your dad first?' asked Anisia.

'Oh, he's wanted out of there for years,' said Ed, now certain that was the case.

Whether it was the time alone or the slow walks around the capital, he felt like he was seeing things clearly for the first time in a long while. Life might have been better if they'd got rid of the place sooner. Their mother's hold on them was strong; she didn't need to tie them up financially too.

Ed bent to retrieve his bags from under the pram, turning his face from the others. When he stood, Anisia stood too and gripped him in a tight hug. That didn't happen often.

'Ed, I'm so sorry. I thought you and Lily were made for each other.'

'Me too,' said Ed, feeling exhausted suddenly. 'I mean, I hold my hands up to some stuff. I didn't ask her to marry me or anything and I never tried to get work in Bristol. But I thought she felt the same and she'd let me know when she wanted to talk about that. Drop a few hints.'

'And she never did?'

'Not that I know of. Not like you. You left wedding magazines lying all around the flat.'

'I did not!'

'And you told me to make sure Kit noticed which pages of the jewellery catalogues had the corners turned.'

'Okay, that,' said Anisia.

'And if Lily wanted me to know something, she'd have told you.'

'Yes, I'm sure she would. Or Kit.'

They both looked at Kit.

'She didn't say anything. Nothing specific. I would have remembered that, wouldn't I?'

Kit didn't seem sure, but if Lily had wanted to pass on a message, she wouldn't have relied on him. Neither was it fair to pull his brother into the mess. It was no one's fault but his own. Something else occurred to Ed.

'Anisia,' he said, almost unable to give voice to it. 'D'you think Lily told you about Matt because she thought it would get back to me? She didn't have the guts to tell me herself.'

Anisia shook her head. 'Lily didn't tell me anything about Matt. All she said was one of the guys she worked with in Serbia had come back to the UK and she was going to Cardiff to work with him. But that doesn't necessarily mean—'

'You thought it did,' said Ed.

'I didn't really,' said Anisia. 'I—'

Ed picked up his pint from the table to finish off the dregs and put it down again untouched. If Lily moved to Cardiff because of Matt, it made everything untrue. He'd been living a lie. He needed to change the subject quickly, push away the old thoughts with some new ones.

'I'll be off, guys. I'll see you at New Year.'

'Where are you going?' asked Kit.

'Not sure yet. I'm free as a bird for a week, I can go wherever I want.'

He kissed the top of his niece's head, kissed Anisia and Kit in turn, and stepped slowly out of the pub garden, clanging the gate behind him.

It was too dark to see any birds in the sky or whether they were enjoying their liberty. It was overrated as far as he could see. He hadn't asked to be set free. He still belonged to her, even if she didn't want him anymore.

59

Lily

17.00

Lily stared at her phone as if it was the thing that betrayed her, summoning her with its treacherous ringing only to break her heart. The truth was no comfort. Not at all. She'd been hammering her palms on that door for months and now it had given way, she wished she'd walked on by because whether it was one kiss or fifty made no difference.

If it even was the truth. If he'd held on to that little secret for so long, what else was he hiding? She'd been feeling sorry for him on his own in the flat, but he hadn't been alone. Or not as much as he made out. Andrea! Of all people! The only thing she had going for her was that she was on the spot. In London. Near him. In the office. With him. How could she? How could he?

'Everything okay?' called Matt.

She hadn't meant to scream. She got up from the bed

and went back through to the kitchen. Her pulse was racing. When she felt her forehead with the back of her hand, it was clammy. She ran a glass of water and sipped it slowly.

'Couldn't sleep?' he asked.

'What time do we have to be at the airport tomorrow morning?' she asked.

'Ah.' He put down his phone, tipped back on the wooden chair and smiled. 'Five-thirty should do it.'

'Did you print my ticket?'

'Seemed a bit presumptuous. I'll do it now, shall I?'

She handed him her laptop. 'Do I need to pack anything?'

'Not much. Your bag's on the van.'

So, Christmas without Ed. How to do this? She ran back into her bedroom, yanked her wardrobe doors open and started throwing items on the bed.

Breathe. Take charge of how you're feeling.

Loss. That was it, that burning feeling welling up into her throat and sending tears into her eyes. Or indigestion. She kicked the door shut with her foot. Seriously, fucking pissed off. That was it. It wouldn't feature on Matt's lists, but it was how she felt. And broke. Where was her credit card? Hidden somewhere under a pile of photos and books.

'Making a statement?' asked Matt when Lily re-emerged in her silver snakeskin leggings and velvet top.

'Christmas Eve at my mum's,' she said, tightly. 'Starting as I mean to go on.'

She stood at the counter, chin up, back straight, and emptied her rucksack, silently checking off each item against a revised packing list. Matt handed her the boarding pass and she tucked it in to her plastic wallet. What to do with her Christmas jumper? It was in a very sad state, but until she was reunited with either of her bags, she was short of outside layers. She crammed it in the top of the bag.

'Okay, let's go.'

60

Ed

This was Christmas as it really was. The windows of every corner shop, café and restaurant decorated with twinkly coloured lights where every fourth or fifth bulb had blown, the Merry Xmas signs in green and red foil drooping as one corner peeled away from the glass. The bins wouldn't be emptied until the morning and overflowed with plastic bottles and fast-food wrappers. The tang of deep-fat frying (forget roasting chestnuts) clung to the damp air. There was no point dreaming of a white Christmas. It wasn't even cold enough to do up his coat.

Ed's phone buzzed in his new pocket. His heart leapt and then settled back into its usual cavity. Not Lily, but Laurence.

Sorry I missed your call. Have a great Christmas with your rocks and geysers. Catch up when you're back. Love to Lily. Dad xx

Iceland then. He'd fly out early on Christmas Day and avoid all the palaver. The smart thing to do would be to collect his bag from the hotel and go home for the evening. But home was full of Lily's stuff – her shampoo, her breakfast cereal, ten pairs of shoes. Present and absent at the same time. Better go straight to the airport and spend the evening in a bar, preferably one which showed sport all night. He'd work it out as he went along.

His pace slowed as he neared Victoria. The new boots pressed painfully against his heels and his stomach ached for food. None of the fast-food outlets – and fair play, there were a decent number of them – looked tempting. Too many bright lights and unidentified items in a crispy coating. He bought a bar of chocolate and some fruit juice from a newsagent, deriving some bizarre comfort from the smell of damp newspaper near the door. Fresh, shiny and successful wasn't in reach of everyone at Christmas.

The receptionist at the hotel unlocked the luggage cupboard and stood by as Ed gathered his bags together.

'The bar's for residents only tonight, sir,' he said, hospitably.

'That's okay. I'm not staying.'

'It's only people staying tonight who are residents.'

'That's not me then, I stayed last night.'

'I expect it'll be okay, then. Just give the barman your old room number.'

Ed frowned. It was worth trying. He carried his belongings into the bar area and dumped them next to a table.

'I'll have a whisky, please,' he told the barman. 'Scotch, preferably. And some peanuts.'

'Double?'

'Why not? One for yourself?'

'I'll save it for later if that's okay. Soda?'

'On the rocks.'

'I'll bring it over.'

The man took his time, especially as the only other customers were a couple in the corner working their way down a bottle of Prosecco. Perhaps he was having a quick check of the hotel register.

'Doing some shopping? Seeing the lights?' the barman said, placing the coaster on Ed's table.

It must be the coat. If he looked as if he didn't belong in his hometown anymore, there were endless possibilities for reinvention.

'Yeah, passing through,' said Ed.

He lifted his glass to the company and took a large slug of his drink followed by a handful of peanuts. It's going to be fine, he thought, and unlocked his phone for some internet searching. There were no direct flights to Reykjavik on Christmas Day, but he could get there via Frankfurt if he took the first flight out from Heathrow. The price was eyebrow-raising but when weighed against the cost of the eco-cottage and reindeer safari… Insurers didn't cover broken promises or broken hearts.

With a boarding pass, he was no longer a person without a future. He was headed somewhere. He'd even treat himself to a window seat, somewhere near the back of the plane with an empty seat alongside. It seemed appropriate in the circumstances.

61

Lily

December 2017

Lily sat at her first-floor window and waited. The early morning sun had swiftly vanished into grey clouds and torrential rain, along with her hopes of spending the day outside, wandering the Christmas markets. Doing something. Anything. The only daylight she'd seen all week had been through the windows of her office.

Ed arrived at lunchtime, dripping wet, and went straight into the bathroom to towel off his hair.

'Man, it's cold in here,' he said, when he emerged. 'Why don't you put the heating on?' He was still hoarse from the cold they'd passed between them. He bent his head to kiss her.

'It's on,' she said.

What had seemed a cute and cosy space when she arrived in the summer now felt cramped and damp. Ed ran a hand down the radiator and then went to the kitchen to fetch a spanner from her bicycle pannier.

'Not sure how much difference I can make with this,' he said as he set about bleeding the radiators.

'It's fine, Ed. Let's leave it and go out.'

She hid in the kitchen, legs folded under her on an awkward wooden chair, listening to the sounds of tools clanging and Ed coughing, composing a speech in her head. How would he feel about postponing their Christmas trip? Going later in the year or going somewhere else instead?

'Best I can manage,' he said, when he finally gave in. 'It's a bit better, might be warm enough in your room to sleep without your coat on.'

'It's never that bad,' she said, not looking up.

'What's wrong?'

'Can't we go out?'

'And go where?'

'I don't know. Skating? Or the cinema?'

Somewhere fun. Something unimportant with no repercussions for anyone.

'We can watch a film here.'

When she glared at him, he sighed and went back to the bathroom to retrieve his still-damp coat and the hat Menassi had given him, but Lily wore more often than he did.

'Come on, then.'

He trudged into town with her and refused to express any preference about the films she suggested, falling asleep halfway through her choice.

Lily woke early. It was cruel to be so tired and yet unable to sleep late. She pulled on a hoodie and went into the darkened kitchen to eat breakfast by herself, as she did on every weekday morning. By the time Ed joined her, her mood had settled on her like a shroud.

'Why are you up? Come back to bed.'

'We never do anything anymore,' she complained.

He sighed. 'What is it you want to do, exactly?'

'I dunno. There's loads we could do. I mean, what's the good of you coming across here every other weekend if it stops us doing other things or making new friends? I can't live my life holding out for Saturday if when Saturday comes, it's so... so nothing. I mean, we used to put in so much effort.'

'Okay,' he said slowly, brow furrowed. He reached across to grab hold of her hand. She started to pull her arm away but checked herself just in time. He kissed her fingertips. 'Can't we just hang out together?'

'When was the last time we got tickets for something?'

He sat down next to her and tugged her towards him. 'Each time I do, I end up reselling or giving them away because your plans change.'

He started to rub her shoulders and she forced herself to relax. It would be low to be picking a fight on purpose.

'Your plans change too. You travel as much as I do,' she said, and hated how sulky it sounded.

'Okay, so, next time I have an overnight, come with me. I've got something in Madrid in January, we could build a weekend into it if you like.'

She turned to stare at him. His hands remained suspended in mid-air, where she had shrugged them off.

'I can't go to Spain with you, I'm going to Turkey,' she said slowly. 'As soon as we're back. Have you forgotten?'

'I meant after that,' he said. 'It was just an idea.'

'You could come to Turkey to see me?' she said, glimpsing an opportunity.

'Mm,' he said. 'Hold that thought. What about lunch? Shall we go out?'

Ed was nodding but he wasn't really listening. His eyes were on his phone, where a flurry of messages filled the screen.

'Sorry,' he said, tossing his cutlery aside and picking up his phone. 'I've got to call the engineer.'

Lily pushed her plate away but stayed at her table by the window, watching Ed walking up and down the pub car park, talking into his phone mic and making calming gestures with his hands. He finished the call and dialled another number and then a third, continuing his pacing and talking. If he mouthed, *Sorry, two minutes*, at her one more time, she'd get her coat and leave.

Night arrived early in December and it was almost dark by the time they paid the bill. They detoured on their way home to take a wintry walk past the floodlit castle. Ed put his arm round her shoulders but stopped to check his phone each time it buzzed in his pocket. It was a shame the city had got rid of the moat. It would have been so satisfying to chuck the handset in and watch it sink without trace. Lily wriggled out of Ed's arm and carried on walking. He could catch her up if he liked, or not. She really wasn't bothered.

Lily curled on the sofa under a fleece blanket and spread the remaining third across Ed. She wouldn't let him freeze. As she tucked the blanket in, she searched for the words to start the conversation, but she was tired and it was so much easier to let it sink back down inside. If Ed noticed her silence, he said nothing.

They went to bed and he reached for her in that familiar way. His hands felt like the hands of someone she recognised but no longer knew. She edged away and turned to face the wall.

'You okay? What's wrong?' he asked.

He really could not have avoided it any longer.

'You ignored me all afternoon,' she said.

'I didn't. Okay, it's true, I did ignore you for about half an hour, forty minutes tops. I'm sorry, I wasn't ignoring you in particular, I would have ignored anyone. It's my biggest contract.'

'I thought dealing with the clients was the associate's job.'

'He's away, so it's down to me. I couldn't let it go, there's too much at stake. We can't lose a big client like that. It's all next year's work.'

His rationalisation was even more unbearable.

'It's as if you come here for sex and nothing else,' she said, surprising herself by the strength of her reaction.

Ed looked genuinely shocked. Had she gone too far?

'Would you rather I went somewhere else?' he asked after a beat, his voice quiet, strained.

'Don't be horrible,' she said.

'I come here to see you, to be with you. But do I come here to have long, meaningful discussions? Honestly? Not always. Not really. We can do that on the phone.'

He was still staring at her – but without his glasses. He usually put his glasses on when he wanted to see things properly, when he was concentrating. It was almost more insulting. He thought he knew what he was seeing. He didn't need to take a closer look.

'You don't talk to me.'

'What are you saying? We talk all the time. Don't we? Every day?'

'Not as much as we used to.'

'Maybe we message more. I dunno, we're busier than we used to be. I thought it was great how we let each other get on with work and make the most of our time together.'

'Is that what we do? Let each other get on with it?'

'I thought so.'

He shook his head and rolled away from her.

She knew he didn't sleep because neither did she. She lay on her back looking at the ceiling, listening to his breathing and waiting to see if he'd say anything else. He stayed quiet, his body rigid beside her, his warmth just out of reach. When his alarm rang at 05.30, it was almost a relief. He shut it off after two rings.

'Ed? Don't go yet.' She leaned over and put an arm around him.

His back stiffened. 'I can't stay, I've got a meeting.'

'Get the next train. Please?'

'It's too late, Lily. I'm going to have to work on the train as it is.'

He did at least kiss her before he left. He paused in the doorway, rubbing his forehead with his fist as he stared at her.

'If you want out, Lily, you only have to say. I don't, though, just so you know.'

After he left, she turned her face into her pillow and let the tears slide silently down her cheeks. She had her excuse now if she needed it.

62

Lily

20.00

Matt drew up outside her mother's house. It didn't disappoint. Icicle lights cascading top to bottom, illuminated reindeer in the garden and a huge sparkly wreath on the door.

'This okay, yeah?'

'Thanks,' said Lily. 'I appreciate it. Really, I do. Everything you've done for me.'

'Not a problem. Getting you to your mum's is my good deed for the day. Christmas is about families.'

'You've changed your tune. Thought you wanted to work through Christmas.'

'That's different. Anyway, Reading's on my way.'

Lily glanced towards the front door and her laugh dried. She puffed out her cheeks. 'Better get on with it, then,' she said, fumbling with the door handle. All the energy seemed to have left her.

'Go on. You'll miss all the fun,' said Matt, leaning across to help her with the door.

'That's the idea.'

'I thought you loved Christmas – all the decorations and tinsel, all the dressing up.'

'I do, but—'

'And I thought you felt bad about missing Christmas with your mum.'

'I said it was hard for her to understand I wouldn't be there. It's not the same thing.'

Matt waited. He was doing that thing, giving her time and space to express herself, but why did she need to explain? Ed understood because he felt the same way.

'It's different if your Christmases haven't always been happy,' she said finally, more to please him than anything else.

'What do you mean?'

'It's complicated. My mum makes such a thing about my dad having left us at Christmas.'

'Oh, Lily. I'm sorry. I had no idea.' He rubbed her shoulder and she recoiled. He looked horrified. 'Sorry, I didn't mean…'

'No, no, I'm sorry,' said Lily. It wasn't personal, just that everything hurt. 'I don't know why I did that.'

'It's my fault. I didn't mean to pry,' he said.

She shook her head. 'It's fine. Thing is, he didn't leave at Christmas, he went in November, and it wasn't unexpected, it was planned. He wanted to go back to Hong Kong. He'd been trying to persuade my mum to go for years, but she refused. She wouldn't even apply for our passports so we could visit.'

Matt was watching her again. Why was he making her do this?

'So, she's got this thing about getting us all together. She

337

used to try to get my dad to come over for Christmas with me and my brother – but he never would. It became this huge issue. He basically stopped answering the phone between the end of October and January because he couldn't deal with the blame.'

There were times Lily had dreaded Christmas morning and the compulsory gathering around the house phone to call her dad. It felt treasonous to pray he wouldn't pick up so she wouldn't have to go through the agony of speaking to him while the others listened in. Sometimes he'd call back later, when everyone else had lost interest, and she would get to sit on the stairs, phone pressed to her ear, whispering all her school news. Even thinking about it brought her out in a cold sweat.

She could pretend to her mum that signing up to Ed's holiday plans was a wrench, but it wasn't so difficult. Anything to escape the claustrophobia.

'And now I've got to tell her about Ed,' she said. 'A break-up at Christmas. It's not the best present I could give her.' She flicked the car door open and swung her legs out.

'Lily? Is that you?'

Lily jumped as a pale face loomed out of the shadows. 'Nana? What're you doing out here?'

'Never mind about that,' said her grandmother, emerging from behind the hedge. 'Who's this?'

'It's Matt. From work. He gave me a lift.'

'Well, you don't want to stay out here,' she said, pulling on Lily's arm. 'Come in, both of you.'

'We mustn't hold him up,' said Lily. 'He has plans.'

'It's okay,' said Matt. 'I'd like to wish your parents a happy Christmas.'

Lily's grandmother tucked her hand into the crook of

Matt's arm and escorted him up the path. Lily hung back. With luck, Nana would make the introductions before she had to explain herself. Or before Matt filled her mum in about Ed, which was a thing she couldn't allow to happen. Nor could anyone else get to Ed before she did because whatever else had been going on, she had not been kissing other people when she could have been with him. If this was the end, it wasn't going to finish with that thought planted in his head. She ran up the path and into the house.

'Hi!' she called, and poked her head into the sitting room, where Mick and her brother were drinking beer with a couple of family friends. She leaned across to kiss her stepfather.

'Hello, love, glad you could make it. Hi, Ed, how—?' Mick turned to greet the new arrivals and the smile slid from his face.

'It's Matt,' Lily explained. 'From work. He gave me a lift.'

Mick leapt to his feet. 'Let me get you a drink.'

He ushered them down the hall, squeezing past the guests crowding the doorway, to the extended kitchen, where his wife was pulling a tray of mini chocolate puddings from the oven.

'Jo, it's Lily,' he said. 'With Matt from work.'

Lily opened her mouth to explain and then closed it again without uttering a word. Her mother put the tray on the counter and removed her oven gloves. She turned with a smile and a hand extended to shake his.

'You must be hungry,' she said, and passed Matt a plate.

'It's very kind, but I really shouldn't. I need to do justice to my mum's cooking.'

Lily and her grandmother observed the tussle. Jo was persuasive, but Matt had better training.

'He's very nice,' said Nana.

'Yes.' Lily nodded.

Matt was nice and he was certainly attractive, with his sweet smile and tousled hair, the blue of his eyes picked up by the colour of the shirt he'd thrown casually over a washed-out festival T-shirt. And yet, no.

She walked him to his car.

'Will you make it to the airport by yourself?' he asked. 'Or shall I come back and get you?'

'I'll be there,' she said, and added a fist pump for good measure.

'Well, happy Christmas.' He placed a hand on her shoulder and Lily tensed for the kiss.

'You didn't say anything to my mum, did you?'

Matt stopped short before his lips made contact with her cheek. 'Course not. And I don't want you to think I'm assuming—'

'No, no—'

'And while we're in Turkey, we're not... I mean, we'll be working.'

That he was even giving breath to any of it made her cringe. These things that had been unspoken for the past couple of years.

'Good. I mean, that's good to know,' she said, and tried a smile.

Her mother had appeared in the doorway. Lily backed away from the car. She had enough explaining to do as it was.

'See you in the morning.'

'Don't be late.'

'I won't,' she said, smiling again and succeeding on her second attempt.

'You're going away with Matt?' asked her mum as she passed her on the doorstep.

Lily went to sit on the stairs. She hunched over her knees and picked at the polish on her nails.

'It's a work thing.'

'What happened?'

Lily shook her head, but her mum would never be put off so easily. She sat down next to her. Lily leaned against her shoulder.

'You'll feel better if you have something to eat,' said Jo.

Lily knew she wouldn't. This was the sort of feeling, the gut-churning sense of betrayal, that would get worse before it got better.

'What about a chocolate pudding?' said her mother.

'There won't be any left,' said Lily.

'I'll put more in,' said her mother, using the bannister to pull herself up.

Her brother passed by on his way to the bathroom.

'Seriously? Couldn't you have waited?'

Lily took her phone from her pocket and ran up the stairs to her mother's bedroom, dialling as she went. She shut the door behind her as the line connected.

'Why did you let me go to Cardiff?'

Ed sighed. 'Could I have stopped you?'

'You could've tried. You thought I'd find out what happened that night.'

'Nothing happened that night!'

He was clearly keeping his voice down, but why? If he wasn't at home, where was he?

'You want the details? Okay, here goes. She kissed me, I kissed her and then, I don't know, I was really drunk, but

341

suddenly her hands were in my trousers and my head was screaming, woah, woah, woah, and I had to make her stop.'

'Why didn't you tell me that before?'

'Because I felt like an idiot, Lily. I'm a grown man and I got myself into a situation like that. I even felt kind of violated, I can't explain, and I was the one apologising to her, saying no, no, I can't do this.'

'Oh my God, Ed.' She sat on the bed with a thump. It got more shocking, each time she heard it.

'It's no big deal.'

'It is! How could you? How could she? Can't you report her to someone?'

'You're getting this all out of proportion. I behaved like a dick. End of. And it's hardly news, is it, that I'd rather be with you than anyone else?'

'Why didn't you tell me? I would've—'

'What, Lily? What would you have done? I thought if I told you, you'd go.'

'I did go.'

'Exactly.'

'But you never asked me why. Weren't you interested?'

'You went because of Matt.'

'I didn't! Why would you say that? I had to go somewhere else. I couldn't stay in Bristol.'

'Why not, Lily?'

'Because... Because there was this thing. With Hassan.' She heard the intake of breath. 'I see.'

'You're not making this easy.'

'Oh, I'm sorry.'

'Ed! It wasn't just me. Other people were affected too. Some of the doctors. It was so scary and what they do is so

342

brave…' Every time she thought about it, her throat tightened. 'And you were right about Hassan. He was police, hanging around the migrant camp. I don't know what he was up to and we didn't stay to find out. It was all getting a bit nasty.'

'What do you mean, nasty?'

Her phone beeped. Another call was trying to force its way through. Menassi again. She couldn't speak to him now. Couldn't he tell she was busy?

'He could've had us arrested.'

'How? What for?'

'There was a mistake, Ed. You know how transporting migrants is an offence in a lot of countries? Well, Matt and I were in charge of the van and—'

'So, you were in trouble?'

'Briefly.'

'And you didn't tell me.'

'I couldn't. Because of the others. They told me not to talk about it. To anyone.'

'Who did? Who told you?'

Matt. It was Matt who told her.

'Maggie was worried about the publicity.'

He said nothing for a moment. 'I wish you'd told me.'

He sounded so far away. Where was he? Had he gone away without her? She rubbed her hands over her eyes, clearing the tears, glad that her mum's room was so dark and no-one's Christmas would be wrecked witnessing her meltdown.

'So do I,' she said. 'I thought I couldn't, but I was wrong. I'm sorry, I felt so trapped. It was like go to Cardiff and pretend nothing's happened or stay in Bristol and take the blame.'

'You could've come back here,' said Ed, helping her out with his impatience.

343

'Could I?'

'Lily, you know you could. I would've helped you. You could've come back if you wanted to.'

His tone had changed, as if the words were no longer meant for her. As if he'd reached a conclusion.

'I would have if you wanted me to.'

'Really? I always wanted you to.'

'You never said.'

'I thought you knew. You must've known. I thought if I asked you to give it up, you'd say no.'

'You didn't ask, though. You never ask me anything important.'

They lapsed into silence again.

'Did you want me to ask, Lily?' he said finally. 'Do you want me to?'

He was so quiet, so distant.

She nodded. He couldn't see that, though. Tears filled her eyes and her throat.

'Exactly,' he said, and hung up.

63

Ed

21.30

If he didn't pick up, Menassi would just keep ringing.

'She's at her mum's,' Ed told him, cutting the preliminaries. 'Call her there. And then she's going to Turkey. Some work thing.'

'That's wild,' said Menassi. 'So are we!'

The battery on his phone was showing red. Ed rummaged deep inside his parka and pulled out his charger. He found a socket on the wall under the round, glass-topped table.

'Another drink, sir?' called the barman.

Ed checked his watch. Nine-thirty, still early.

'What the hell? Why not?'

Something buzzed under the table. His thumb hovered over the answer button. There couldn't really be anything else to say.

'You know, I always thought we'd be together for ever.'

Where was she going with this?

'Ed, did we miss the moment?'

'Which moment?'

She'd caught him so easily. He kissed his teeth.

'The moment when we should've made a decision about us.'

'I thought we'd reach that place in our own time, when it was right for us,' he said, batting away the memory of Kit and the bridal magazines.

'Maybe we reached it and walked on by.'

'What do you mean? When? How?'

'That one was down to you.'

'What? What are you talking about?'

He'd never had any walking to do. He'd always been at that place. Waiting for her. No decision to make.

'You're the one with a ring in your pocket, carrying it everywhere with you and never saying a word.'

'But that's not…'

Through the soft haze of the whisky, things were beginning to make sense. He knew she must have seen the box – she was forever diving into his pockets for keys or small change – but she couldn't seriously think he would give her that monstrosity.

'It's something Martin gave me.'

'I know.'

'He should have sold it, though I can't believe anyone would've bought it off him.'

'I think he thought—'

'Whatever he thought, you can't just toss someone a ring and expect them to do something with it. A truly horrible ring, by the way, one that's only fit for melting down. It's not a ring for you.'

'Why not?'

'Because it's ugly and I do not believe you would have thought it okay if I'd presented you with one of Martin's cast-offs. It lacks respect. It would be like tying up the future with the past and there's been too much of that in my family. Martin, of all people, should have known that.'

It took a lot to rile him, but now he was there, it occurred to him that it might have been helpful if he'd got a lot angrier much sooner.

'I see.'

'Lily, can we talk? I'll come to you, to your mum's.' He checked his watch again. He could still get a train.

'Jo wouldn't cope.'

'Did you tell her?'

'What d'you think? I'd never be forgiven. Or you. Can you meet me somewhere? What about Paddington?'

'Paddington?'

He couldn't believe she was even suggesting it. Hadn't this been punishing enough already?

'This isn't over, Ed.'

'That's good.'

'I mean, you've got some talking to do. This isn't over.'

He smiled into the phone. It could be the alcohol, but little chinks of hope were starting to appear in that huge, black cloud of despair.

64

Lily

22.00

Lily lingered in the darkened room, testing how she felt about that small laugh, the sound of his voice, the familiar sensation stabbing away somewhere beneath her ribs.

It was obvious, really.

Mick was back in the sitting room when she went downstairs. She dropped her rucksack onto the floor and slid into the seat beside him.

'Is there anyone sober enough to give me a lift to the station?'

'Already?'

'I'm meeting Ed,' she said quietly, kicking off her patent high heels and lacing her feet into her hiking boots.

'What time will you be back?' said Mick, giving her a long look.

It was unlike him to question anything she did.

'Don't worry,' said Lily, smiling and patting his arm. 'There'll be no tearful calls at 3am. I am definitely, one hundred per cent, flying out in the morning. You'll get your Christmas lie-in, I promise.'

Mick surveyed the assembled company. 'Okay, I'll do it. Say your goodbyes while I turn the van round.'

'So soon?' said her mum, rushing out of the kitchen.

Lily glanced at Mick, standing by the front door, rattling the car keys. She wouldn't say anything if he didn't. She owed them a peaceful evening.

'It's just that a cab to the airport will cost the earth,' she said. 'It's easier if I get a train and the last tube.'

'Okay...' Jo sighed and wrapped her in a hug that smelled of hot chocolate, garlic and Chanel No. 5. 'Call me when you get there. And take care, for heaven's sake.' She loosened her arms but kept her hands on her daughter's shoulders, smoothing her top and picking a stray hair from her sleeve. 'I'm sure you'll work it out, darling. Just... you know.'

'Mmm,' said Lily.

'And have you got everything? Am I going to find your passport or your make-up lying around somewhere tomorrow?'

'Will you stop? I don't do that anymore,' said Lily. She tugged Mick's arm. 'Can we go?'

65

Ed

22.30

Ed ordered another whisky and messaged Kit.

She's coming back. We're going to talk

Thats so bad, was his response. *You cant jump between people like that.*

What are you saying? I should call it a day?

Course not. Be cool. Dont massage her feet for a bit

Ed winced.

Your relationship not mine

Lily called at the very moment the barman placed the drink before him. Further evidence of her sixth sense.

'I get in at 11.15. Will you meet me?'

He nodded. 'Lily…?' He swallowed. Even if it was too late and it would make no difference, she ought to know. She had a right. 'I didn't put up a fight when you went to Cardiff – or Bristol for that matter – because it could never change how I felt. But I thought it might make a difference for you.'

'It did.'

'Well, then.'

'But not in that way. You didn't seem to want me there.'

'I wanted you there, but I was a mess.' It wasn't, after all, that hard to admit. 'It wasn't fun viewing.'

'I wouldn't have minded. You thought you could do without me.'

'I never thought that, Lily. Ever.'

He shook his head, becoming more expressive with each sip of his drink. He reined it in a little. It wouldn't do to be identified as a non-resident and ejected onto the pavement. He needed a place to wait for half an hour.

'D'you think I take you for granted?' he asked, lowering his voice.

'No, no. There were just things I couldn't tell you.'

'Why not?'

His heart was sinking again. Pam was right. Lily could keep her secrets because she knew he'd always be there. Waiting. Like a…

'And what things?'

'Not those sorts of things,' she said. 'Work things. You weren't always there for me.'

'And Matt was?'

'Well, obviously he was there, physically. I see him every day.'

'I see.'

'Ed, he's a friend, a colleague. That's all.'

Why was she getting impatient? He was only asking. He had a right to ask, surely, without her going off the deep end. Or getting off the train.

'Lily, don't get off the train! Don't go back to Cardiff again.'

She laughed. 'I won't. I want to see you.'

'Okay, I'm going to ask.' Every word felt charged, its impact potentially fatal. 'Every day?'

'Yeah, every day.' She was quiet now.

'Like Matt?'

'No, not like Matt. Jesus, Ed!'

And she was gone. He'd overshot the mark. He punched himself on the forehead. Try again.

'A friend, yes?'

'Yes!'

'You don't…?'

'No.'

His chest felt so tight. Alcohol was supposed to be a relaxant. 'Help me out here, Lily. Why did you run back to him if—?'

'I didn't. He gave me a lift.'

'A lift. Okay, a lift…'

It sounded reasonable. Friends gave each other lifts.

'And Turkey?'

'It's work.'

'But Lily—?'

'Leave it, Ed. Meet me at the station.'

One last attempt.

'Don't go with him.'

'I love you. Can't you just accept that?'

He ought to be able to. It had always been enough in the past and, given recent events, he should probably feel relieved. So why, now, did he need more?

'I love you too, but…'

He was talking to himself. It must be a long tunnel,

or perhaps she was waiting for a sign from him because she didn't call back. He logged back on to the Lufthansa website and bought the airline seats beside him for her. It was a competition now. Should he buy refundable? It was undoubtedly less risky, but the optics were wrong. All or nothing. He sent her a screenshot of her boarding card, leaned back and waited for his phone to ring.

The knot in his stomach had loosened a little but his head was hurting. So were his feet. And he was tired. He pushed his glasses up to his hairline and massaged his eye sockets with his free hand. At least the chair was comfortable. Nice to come across a decent wing-backed armchair. Martin would have appreciated it.

66

Lily

23.00

Lily dug the wireless battery charger from the bottom of her bag, gave thanks for the thoughtful boyfriend who'd supplied it and decided not to tell him she'd neglected to charge it again. If she was lucky it might have enough left in it so she could call Ed back and point out that if she was going to Turkey, it was because she had a job to do. A job which couldn't wait. She wasn't chasing some guy around. Why did people find it so difficult to believe?

The handset vibrated as soon as she plugged it in.

'Hey, Menassi,' she said, sounding as unenthusiastic as she could manage.

'Lily! At last. Where the hell've you been? I need your help, babe. Sooo bad!'

'Sorry, Men. Whatever it is, I won't be able to do it. I've got some issues right now.'

'You haven't heard about this yet,' he drawled. 'You are going to love it.'

'Yeah, well, I'm kind of busy.'

'I know. Ed said. This is for when you come back. In fact, it's the job you were made for. Guess where we're going?'

It was textbook Menassi, never rushing a punchline, drawing people in with a slowly spreading smile. He was giving it the works. She'd seen it all before.

'I'm not doing the drum roll. Just tell me.'

'Okay, okay, wait for it. We're going to Turkey. Just like you! Can you believe it? That's what I want to talk to you about.'

He'd done it again. Unbelievable.

'Go on.'

'I knew it. Sooo, Lillee, we are going on a world tour!' He paused for the applause, but he'd be waiting a while. He gave up. 'Yeah, we got talking to a couple of people who've been putting on shows for children in refugee camps. One's a teacher and she got all her friends together and raised money to send proper entertainers to places like Jordan and Turkey because it's making a real difference to the kids. It's helping them communicate and behave more normally. Behave like kids, basically. They're looking for experienced clowns and entertainers with a good rep and reached out to us.'

'You hate charity gigs.'

'It's for the kids, Lily.' He managed to sound reproachful.

'And how are they going to pay for this?'

'See? You get it already. They've raised loads of money. They also need a proper coordinator, someone who knows how to get visas and permissions and shit. I said I knew exactly the right person.'

'Is that me, then?'

'It's the perfect gig, Lils. Learning circus skills is helping kids get their childhoods back. We'll be doing good and getting paid. You wouldn't even have to paint your face. You could be manager. I'll give you the diary… How's that as a sign of my respect for you?'

'How long's it for?'

'S'long as you like. There's money for office space and stuff. It'll probably take a few weeks to get it all organised and then it's up to you. What d'you think? Can I give them your number?'

Her phone died before she could answer. It wouldn't bother Menassi. He'd have handed over her number already. His only embarrassment would be if they spoke to her before he did. Even then, he wouldn't be that concerned. Ed, though, was more of a worry. If he didn't hear from her, would he wait? Suppose he couldn't get over how she'd turned to Matt. He'd accuse her of playing them off against each other and he'd be right. Ed had lied and Matt was manipulative, but what she'd done was cruel. And not like her. Matt knew the score – even if he pretended not to. He was amazing at what he did, and he deserved all the praise he got, but she wasn't one of his Mattellites.

Ed was different. He didn't need anyone's approval. He knew who he was and how to live his life. Please God, let it not be without her.

The train clanked into the terminus and squealed to a halt. Lily was first onto the platform, hitching her bag onto her shoulder as she ran towards the gate.

She'd wanted to exist in Ed's space almost from the moment they met. She could remember his expression as he opened the door that first evening, the flash of interest as he looked her up and down, starting with her face and moving swiftly towards her thighs. *Here we go*, she thought, but it wasn't her legs that caught his attention. He was looking at her bike. *So what was wrong with her?* As he led her back down the stairs, he canvassed her views on brakes and gear sets and which worked better on a lighter frame. He seemed genuinely interested and when she saw his bike, she understood why.

'You built this yourself?'

'Yeah.' He was almost embarrassed. 'With a bit of help. But I'm thinking of making some changes.'

It was rare she found someone who would dance without pawing at her or missing every beat and crashing into her knees and toes. As they sat on the tube together on that first evening, she had to resist the urge to take hold of his hand.

'You seeing anyone, Ed?'

She'd waited almost the whole journey to slip it into the conversation.

'No. You?'

She shook her head. He nodded. She couldn't find anything to say for a while. Neither, it seemed, could he.

Her only clear thought when they returned to his flat was that it was too soon to say goodnight. Their shared disappointment at the mess that greeted them crystallised things, as if the tempo that had driven them all evening had stalled suddenly, the needle scratching its way across the vinyl into an unhappy crackle. She wanted him to smile again, the way he'd been smiling all evening, and did the first thing that came to mind. She stepped into the space between them, placed a hand on his cheek and kissed him. Her other hand was curled round the back of his neck, the black polythene of the bin liner draped across his shoulder and down his arm like a cape.

After a second or two, when he might have pulled away, he tightened his arms around her back and committed himself fully to the kiss, his tongue opening her mouth wider. She couldn't read his face then; she was better at it now. He looked surprised, impressed, moved – kind of how he looked the first time he saw her perform.

There was no way she was going home that night, but Ed insisted on a performance of modesty and good behaviour. He put her to bed in his room, where she waited, propped against a pile of white pillows edged with antique lace and cutwork, wondering if – no, hoping – he'd change his mind and come knocking. Should she creep into his room instead? She opened the door a crack and squinted at the room across the corridor, unable to tell if his light was on or off. Suppose he wasn't that bothered, anyway? That would be excruciating. She padded into the living room and looked around, picking up an object and examining it before going to the wall to switch off the light. She felt her way back to the table, lifted her bare foot and carefully kicked the chess board to the floor. Maximum impact, minimum damage.

Lily didn't have strongly held views either way about one-night stands, but this was different. If this was her future, and she had a disturbing sense it could be, it might as well get started right away. And if it wasn't, well, at least they'd both know and could move swiftly on.

Their first time was rushed. His rings caught in her hair and her back stuck against the leather of the sofa. He apologised, but the urgency was hers too.

'And Anisia might come home with Kit,' she reminded him.

Fear flashed across his face. He untangled his legs from hers and stood. 'Let's get out of here,' he said, and tugged at her hand, but she was too sleepy and stayed where she was.

She watched him walk naked to the bathroom, lean and strong, easier, less aggressively muscular than the boys she lived with, and then closed her eyes, opening them only when he returned to fetch her.

The bath was huge and Victorian with claw feet. Ed had filled it three-quarters deep and the water rose dangerously close to the top as he climbed in with her.

'Shall we light the candles?' he said.

'Candles?'

Ed pointed out the niches in the black-and-white-tiled wall. 'This was my uncle's flat. We have loads of weird shit like that.'

'Do you usually light them?'

'Me? No, never. But we could.'

'Go on, then,' she said, and helped him light the tea lights in the antique brass holders as if they marked the start of an ancient rite.

It must have made a difference because in low tones by the dim, flickering light she told him things she'd never admitted to anyone but her very closest friends, certainly not to all those people who still saw her as the stage-school kid who'd turn up at some point as a casualty in a medical drama. Ed listened. He took her seriously.

She stretched out in his vast mahogany bed, luxuriating in the thick white cotton bedlinen.

'You like this?' he asked.

'I do.'

'We have drawers full of it. Most people think it's over the top.'

'Could be why I like it.'

She held his hair away from his face as he pushed into her. She wanted to see his eyes, the eyes Anisia said were too round, but then she rarely saw him without his glasses. Without the solid frames, his eyes were soft and brown, not at all owl-like.

'Thanks,' he said, and turned his head to kiss her palm as he started to move inside her.

She rolled onto her side to face him, pulling one of his fine feather pillows under her head. He propped himself on his elbow, trailing his fingertips across her stomach, still giving her goose-bumps even as she tried to stop her belly rumbling.

'I can't find anything to dislike about you,' he said.

She felt the same, but she toughed it out.

'Seriously? Is that what you do first?'

'No, of course not, but when it's literally all pluses, you worry you're missing something. Too dazzled.'

'What sort of thing?'

'Oh, I don't know,' he mused, 'like working for building control or listening to nothing but Britney. Obviously, we'd find a work-around, but it's good to know.'

She thought back to when he'd answered the door to her. 'I know almost nothing about bikes,' she admitted. 'My brother chose the spec for me.'

Ed considered it. 'That's not necessarily fatal. Does he look like you?'

'I look more like my dad. He's a bit of everything –

Malaysian, Scottish, you name it. He's in Australia now. He likes to think he's an adventurer.'

'Mine too.' Ed nodded.

'Really?'

'Oh, yes. He makes it to the Heath and back pretty much every day, I think.'

She laughed and pushed him back against the pillows, leaning over him as she traced his eyebrows, his eyelids, his nose, his mouth, with her fingers. It was still one of her favourite things to do.

'You know, Ed, if there's ever a competition to find a face for a new coin, I'll vote for you,' she said. 'You have the best profile. Maybe if you design some amazing buildings, they'll put your head on the money – Edgar Black, architect and engineer.'

'Something to aim for,' he said, and pulled her on top of him to kiss her again.

No-one had ever made her feel like that, as if desire could be enhanced by the promise of love. As if real, true love were not only possible but present in the room, waiting for the taking.

But if you start like that, where do you go?

'I'm in love,' she told Adam, when she immediately refused work with him to spend time with Ed.

'Again?' he scoffed.

'When have I done this before?' she asked him.

There'd never been anyone else like that, but was it possible that they'd lived their whole love story already – start to finish – and somehow skipped the happy ending? That would be so unfair. She wasn't ready to be out of love with Ed. She wanted her fairy tale back.

But where was he?

She stood on the station concourse with her bag clutched to her chest. Ed couldn't have missed the train. He didn't do things like that. She had told him the right time, hadn't she? She moved nearer to her usual platform and turned in a circle, searching for a glimpse of his black-clad figure and upright stride. There were still people about, but her fellow travellers were looking more and more unreliable, drunk and disorganised, the sort who missed their last train and would still be trying to get home at ten on Christmas morning. With her air-dried hair and mismatched holiday clothing, she was starting to blend in.

67

Ed

Christmas Day, 00.00

'Mr Black?'

Ed pulled himself into consciousness, not immediately recognising his surroundings. Fear replaced disorientation and he leapt out of the chair.

'What time is it?'

'It's eleven-thirty, sir. We're closing the bar now. I'm afraid you'll have to leave.'

The barman was accompanied by the suspicious concierge. The barman was more conciliatory.

'Do you have somewhere to go, sir? Is there anyone we can call?'

'Yes, I mean, no, I have somewhere to go.' He checked his pockets and then ducked down, scrabbling about on the floor for his phone charger. 'Could you get me a taxi?' he asked, gathering his bags with shaking hands.

The concierge sighed and strutted back to his desk. Ed could him muttering as he picked up the phone.

'It'll be twenty minutes. You're better off finding a cab in the street.'

He escorted Ed out of the main door and locked it firmly behind him. Ed stared up and down, searching the oncoming traffic for an illuminated 'For hire' sign. It must be one of the busiest nights of the year for cabs, but suddenly they'd all disappeared. He wandered across the road and back, alternately checking the cars and his phone as he tried to get hold of Lily. Would she wait?

A yellow light appeared in the distance. Ed leapt into the street, both arms raised to flag the driver down.

'Paddington,' he said, as he jumped in the back. 'Fast as you can.'

'Train to catch? You'll be lucky. Think you've missed the last one. It's Christmas, in case you hadn't noticed.'

'Thanks for the heads-up,' said Ed.

He fished a handful of notes from his wallet and readied himself to dive out of the door as soon as the driver stopped his snail's pace circling of the station cab rank.

Lily had never had to wait for him before. It wouldn't help his cause or her mood. If she was there, which didn't seem to be the case. She wasn't in her usual spot. He widened his search. The place had become a bit of a home from home, he'd spent so many hours there. He knew the locations of the platforms and exits, the bathrooms, the coffee shops, but it was of no use now. Everything was shuttered and padlocked, and the only people loitering were the cleaners and a couple of transport police. Kind of funny that he'd missed Lily because for the first time ever in their relationship, he'd been late. The one time it really mattered. Why hadn't she called him?

He squatted on his case. Of all the plausible explanations for her silence, the most likely was that her phone had died. It wouldn't be the first time, or even the fifty-first, that she'd been MIA because her battery had run out. Every device he'd ever given her worked perfectly well as long as she charged it. The other possibility was not one to be contemplated. She couldn't have changed her mind again. She loved him. She'd said so.

So where was she?

If he could only think straight. He should have stopped at the second whisky. If Lily went looking for him, where would she go? He ran his hands over his skull. There were only two possibilities, but if she'd gone to the flat and found he wasn't there, she'd have called him, surely. He messaged Kit.

Lost Lily again. If she turns up at yours, let me know

Next question: should he look for her? Where, though? If she'd got tired of waiting and bailed on him, she could, quite literally, be anywhere.

Two police officers were moving towards him, slowly but purposefully. He sprang upright and headed for the entrance to the tube. If Lily thought he wasn't going to show, what would she do? She'd go to Turkey, that's what. With Matt. The last time they'd spoken, he'd begged her not to go and then he'd let her down. Who'd blame her if she cut her losses and headed off for the airport? That was where he'd find her enjoying an early breakfast in the departure lounge.

He'd have to run if he wanted to make the last tube.

68

Lily

Christmas Day, 00.00

The boards at Paddington Station were empty. Every train that was due had arrived. Still there was no sign of Ed.

If she'd known he'd treat her like this, she would not have bothered. No doubt he was lounging on his sofa, swirling the ice in one of Martin's crystal tumblers, nodding to himself and waiting to see whether she came back or not. Okay, she'd take his stupid test. She'd go to the flat and they could have it out there. At least she could charge her phone, though it would take some effort not to climb into Ed's comfy bed, close her eyes and hope it all went away. He'd have to do a lot of making up before she'd let him join her, though.

An inspector blocked her path to the bus station, shepherding her away with widespread arms.

'It's all finished,' he said.

'No night buses?'

'It's Christmas. Everyone gets a night off.'

He moved across to scoop up another couple of stragglers and waved them all outside.

Lily trudged back up the ramp to Praed Street. There must be a way to contact Ed and let him know she wasn't coming, that she'd wanted to, but time had run out. She had to find someone to lend her a phone.

The inspector was back, barring her way into the station and pointing her in the direction of the taxi rank. She joined the back of the queue, fumbling in her wallet for her credit card and hoping there wouldn't be a four times surcharge on the fare. What a way to spend Christmas Eve!

'Where to, love?' asked the driver as she hopped into a cab.

'Heathrow, ultimately, but…' It hadn't sounded like Ed was at home. The buzz in the background – bland music and muted voices – was more like a restaurant or bar. It wouldn't hurt to check. 'Could we go via Victoria?'

'Anywhere in particular?'

Lily reached for her phone and sighed. The address of the hotel – plus map, this was Ed, after all – was on a message. What was the place called again? It was the name of a painter, wasn't it? Renoir? Or was it a composer? She glanced at the tourist ads for inspiration and caught a glimpse of a fleeting figure in khaki leaping out of a taxi and haring into the entrance.

'Can we start at the station?'

Victoria was closed with notices posted outside, listing the holiday opening times.

'What now?'

The name would come to her, she was sure of it, if the man would stop drumming his fingers on the steering wheel for a minute and give her time to think.

'I'll get out here,' she said. 'What do I owe you?'

'Thought you wanted the airport,' the driver said, totalling the fare.

'Yes, but there's something I need to do first.'

She tapped her bank card against the card reader and climbed out before he asked any other awkward questions. Her mission made no sense, but not much of what she'd done recently stood up to scrutiny. Finding the hotel would add nothing, this day-too-late tribute to her boyfriend's romantic imagination, except rub a little more salt into her wounds and delay the moment she stepped onto a plane and separated them.

There were only a couple of people hanging around the station, but they looked in greater need of help than she was. She put her hood up, cast her eyes to the ground and carried on walking. Two police officers were patrolling near the coach station. They looked considerably more approachable than anyone she'd seen so far.

'You okay there?' the female officer asked.

'I'm looking for a hotel.'

'There are a few over there,' she said, and pointed in the direction of Buckingham Palace Road.

'I'm looking for one in particular,' said Lily. 'I'll know it if I see it. Is there a list anywhere?'

'Tourist Information's your best bet,' said the other officer. 'It's closed now, but if you're desperate, the bus station's open all night.'

Lily took a step back. Things had hit a really low point if the best she could hope for was a bench to crash on.

The hotel on the corner was called the Rembrandt, but there was something not quite right about it. Too modern and yet not modern enough for Ed. She passed the Buckingham Gate Hotel and the Victoria Palace, alert to every noise behind her. This time of night, the city had lost its glow. The gutters outside the pubs stank of urine and vomit and wouldn't be cleaned until the morning, while bundles of humanity curled up in doorways in stained sleeping bags.

This was pointless. She stepped off the curb to flag down a black cab and glimpsed a sign on a building set back from the street. *Hotel Elgar.* That was it!

She ran across the street and pulled at the external door, which stayed firmly locked. A bit of arm waving and the uniformed receptionist behind the desk finally spotted her and sauntered across the tiled floor.

'Did you forget your key?' he asked, unlocking the double doors.

'No, no,' she said. 'I had a reservation last night, but I've been a bit delayed. I wanted to see, I mean, I'm sure he isn't, but is my boyfriend still here?'

The man looked at her critically as if her tardiness must have been caused by getting stuck for hours in the hedge she'd been dragged through backwards.

'Mr Black?'

Lily's heart leapt. 'Yes! Mr Black. Is he here?'

He shook his head. 'Left a couple of hours ago.'

'D'you know where he went? Is he coming back?'

'Didn't say. He was a bit strange, to be honest.'

'What d'you mean?'

'Wanted razors in the middle of the night. Bad sign, usually.'

'Razors?' she said, keeping her voice light. 'That is strange.' And alarming. She'd never worried about Ed before. Not in that way.

'D'you really have no idea where he went?'

'None at all, but he left in a hurry.'

She was halfway down the road before she realised she should have asked the man if she could use the phone.

69

Ed

02.00

Ed stood in front of the departures board and hazarded a guess. There was only one flight to Turkey out of Terminal 2 that morning and that was at 07.05, destination Istanbul. It was leaving at the right time but going to the wrong end of the country. Could that be it? There was no way to check. Jo would hardly welcome a call from him.

He took a brief tour of the check-in desks, dragging his bag behind him. Moving at all was painful. The boots had become shackles and he had the beginnings of a hangover. Even thinking hurt. It wasn't worth the effort. The airport was emptier than he'd ever seen it. If Lily was there, he'd have spotted her – her silhouette, her walking speed, her fidgety impatience in any queue.

They must have removed all the chairs as there was nowhere to sit. No way was he walking in circles for hours until his own check-in opened. He put one carrier bag inside the other and headed for security. If his case was too large for the cabin, they could take it off him at the gate. He really wasn't bothered.

The departures lounge was filled with stereotypes of people who might be prepared to spend Christmas in an airport – students heading home whose transfers had been delayed or cancelled and tourists taking advantage of a cheap deal. It was pleasantly sleepy. The more adventurous, escaping London for a long-haul, tropical destination, were leaving from a different terminal.

Ed found a space to sit, dropped his bags on the floor, and turned his phone off and on a few times to make sure it was working. If Lily still hadn't made contact by the time he was called for boarding, he'd get on the plane. Or go wait at her gate. Or contact the police. Would they think he was an idiot?

He sent her a message. *Missed you. See you at the airport?*

He topped it up with one to Kit. *If Lily calls, I'm at Heathrow (T2).*

His phone rang straightaway.

'She still not turned up?' asked Kit.

'Why are you awake?' Ed could barely keep his own eyes open. He would certainly not be up at this hour by choice.

'You keep messaging me,' said his brother.

'Sorry. Who else would share my pain?'

'It's cool, some kind of entertainment while I pace the floor with the sleepless child. Did you know babies couldn't blow their noses?'

'I've never given it much thought, to be honest.'

'It's a massive design flaw.'

'I see you've opened the whisky.'

'Supposed to be good for a cold. It does, actually, seem to have helped.'

'You. Not her.'

'Obviously. I'm a doctor, remember? But seriously, Ed, when all this is over, I'm gonna recommend some apps so we never have to go through this again.'

'Why do I need an app? What's wrong with good, old-fashioned trust?'

At least they were both laughing.

'See you tomorrow, yeah?'

'You never know,' said Ed, and rang off.

The two women at the end of the row moved away, so Ed stretched out over the three seats, lying down before he toppled into the space. He balanced his dangling feet on his case and cushioned his head on his shopping bags. This was not a comfortable place. It was cold, yet also airless, and every surface was hard and shiny, but it would take more than that to keep him awake. He pulled up his hood to block out the announcements and tucked his phone in his inside pocket next to his heart. He wouldn't miss it if it rang.

70

Lily

02.00

Lily marched down the road, exuding enough confidence and hostility, she hoped, to deter attention from any of the stumbling drunks being hustled out of nightclubs. If the bus station was open all night, it could only be because the buses were running. They'd have power sockets too.

The shallow ramp into the coach station gave no warning of the heaving mass of people within. The streets of London had emptied, but only as far as the bus station, it seemed. Every spot on the rows of chairs was taken and people leant against the walls or squatted on their luggage. There was a small bank of payphones in the corner, half-hidden by the crowd. Lily rushed towards them, but only two were working and both were in demand. Lily joined the shortest queue, behind three women who were alternately snatching the receiver from each other and arguing over how to pay for a call.

'Why won't it take the money? It's supposed to take coins,' said one.

'Maybe it's full,' said another.

Lily leaned in. 'Try a card,' she said.

'We're trying,' said the first one, shooting Lily a dirty look.

'If it's not working for you,' said Lily, waving her credit card, 'would you mind if I had a go?'

All three grabbed the handset protectively. Lily stepped away to wander the rows of seats looking for a plug socket that wasn't in use or blocked by a sleeping stranger. Would any of these people lend her a phone? She'd have a better chance without the guy on the other side working his way along in just the same way and asking for handouts of change. A bus inspector watched on, flicking glances between him and a jumble of a person sleeping on the benches in the corner, surrounded by carrier bags tied together with string.

A group of backpackers, Canadians by their accents, sprawled on a row of seats, feet propped on their rucksacks. One had his phone plugged into a portable charger. Lily looked back at the payphones, where the women were still arguing and the queue had grown longer. At worst they'd refuse.

'So sorry to bother you,' she said, giving the young men the full beam smile.

She held out her own phone and charger for inspection. The backpackers took a moment to register her presence, slowly suspending their noisy teasing of each other to look at the objects in her hand.

'Would I be able to charge my phone for a minute? Would that be possible? My charger's dead and I can't get in touch with my boyfriend.'

They turned their attention to her face.

'Sure,' said the one on the end, unplugging his phone and offering her the charger.

Lily squeezed down beside him, cringing as her phone screen stayed resolutely dark.

'He was supposed to meet me,' she said. 'It's really unlike him. Something must have happened.'

The man gave her a half smile, simultaneously sympathetic and wary.

'Oh, here we are,' she said as the phone slowly emerged from its sleep. 'Soon be there.'

Her phone rang immediately.

'Lily? Oh, thank God. Where are you?'

'Hi, Anisia,' she said, gritting her teeth. 'Look, d'you mind if I call you back? I need to find Ed.'

'I know! That's why I'm calling.'

Lily's stomach turned over. 'What's happened? Is he okay?' She could hardly get the words out. Could it be that all the disaster planning that filled her working hours had been no use when it mattered, and the one time Ed needed her, she wasn't there?

'He's looking for you. He's had us up all night with it. You're not leaving him, are you?'

'What? No, no, course not.'

'Because you'd be mad to. We should talk about this.'

Lily wasn't prepared for the abrupt change of direction. Or to have this conversation with Anisia. She cast her eyes round the draughty waiting room, searching for an escape route.

'But is he alright? Do you know where he is?'

'He's at the airport.'

'Gatwick?'

'No, Heathrow. That's right, isn't it, Kit? Kit?' There was the sound of a thump followed by a mumble. 'Yes, Terminal 2.'

Gorgeous, clever, Ed. He'd been listening. Lily hung up as fast as she could and leapt over the outstretched feet to reach the bus inspector.

'Buses to Heathrow?'

'Next one in twelve minutes. Bay 5.'

'Tickets?'

'Machine.' He pointed in the direction of the street.

She ran back to the entrance, fumbling for the credit card in her pocket, dialling frantically as she went.

71

Ed

04:00

Ed woke with a start. His heart was pounding and his throat so dry he had to swallow several times to get some moisture into his mouth. Embarrassing to have crashed so completely. He sat up and ran a hand over his face as he reached with the other for his phone.

Fuck it. She'd called and he'd slept the hell through it. He circled his head, trying to get some movement back into his neck and dialled her number. Straight to voicemail. At least she'd made contact. He typed out a message, another version of the same *Call me please* message he must have sent her fifty times in the past twenty-four hours, and added some gifs and a couple of songs. Some people might consider it a bit much.

He scrolled down his phone in case anything else from Lily had slipped through without him noticing. But why would he need a word from his girlfriend when he had a nine-part missive from Anisia, detailing all the things that were wrong with the way he'd approached this and the necessary corrective action? *Yeah, yeah.* He pressed delete on each message until he came to the last one.

I found her, said his sister-in-law. *She's on her way to the airport. Looking for you. You're still on. Don't screw up xxx*

God bless Anisia. He leaned back in his chair and forced his eyes to stay open.

72

Lily

04.00

He'd be waiting outside the terminal building, checking his watch. Not pacing; he didn't do that. She'd speak first. She knew what to say. She'd planned it all out on the bus.

Ed wasn't at the entrance. He wasn't anywhere at check-in either. None of the desks was open yet and there were only a handful of people milling around.

Anisia must have got it wrong.

Her phone battery was low again, which meant she'd have to make sensible choices, which wouldn't include returning all the Christmas wishes filling her home screen. They were sweet, but they'd have to wait until she'd located Ed and told him that, once again, she seemed to be in the wrong place at the wrong time. She clicked on his name, flicking through his last communications while she composed what had to be the most miserable message she'd ever sent.

Frankfurt? Why was he going there? She took a closer look. He wasn't going there. She was. The boarding pass was in her name. Okay!

She ran to the nearest departures board. Gate announced at 05.15. Twenty minutes. She redrafted.

I'm coming

The staff manning security weren't brimming with Christmas cheer. Lily took a tray and unpacked her laptop while an official intoned a list of forbidden items. She dumped her rucksack into a second tray and was about to push it onto the conveyor belt when she remembered the batteries sewn into her jumper. She snatched the bag back, tore the casing out of the seam and dropped it in the bin.

'Happy Christmas,' she called as she passed through the security arch. It cut no ice. They sent her back to take off her boots.

'Must be the glitter laces,' she said, handing over each item separately before stepping into the X-ray machine in her socks.

'Whose is this?' called an officer, pointing at the single tray passing over the conveyor belt. He diverted the bag to the side.

Lily padded across. This was so unfair. Compared to every other trip she'd ever taken, she had almost nothing with her.

'Can you tell me what's inside?' asked the man, pointing a blue plastic-gloved finger at her rucksack.

Lily screwed up her face, trying to remember. 'A week's worth of underwear, clean T-shirt, hair straighteners, spare boots and some juggling balls.'

'There are wires,' he said, sternly.

She reached inside the bag and the officer stepped back.

'It's a jumper. Can I show you?' She eased the grimy sweater from the bag, gently turning it inside out to show the roughly sewn-in connections.

'It looked better before,' she said, as a couple more sequins dropped on the counter.

'Okay,' said the man. 'But in the circumstances, we'll have to ask you to go back to the X-ray machine. With the jumper.'

'Where are you going today?' asked a female officer as she stepped into the scanner for the second time.

It was a good question, but it was now ten past five and not the time for a heart-to-heart. Lily pulled the boarding pass from her back pocket and showed her the destination.

'Istanbul?'

She gathered her belongings and trotted back to grab her bag. Ed had a point, she thought, as she pulled out her patent boots and slipped her feet into them. No time for zips, buckles or bows. She threaded a lace through the top eyelet of each walking boot and tied them together like a brace of ducks, slinging them over her shoulder along with her bag. The jumper she tossed in the nearest bin. She was so done with Christmas.

The departure lounge was busy. Escaping the holiday must be more popular than she'd thought. It would soon be over. Just a couple more days. The shops were already preparing, every storefront emblazoned with 'sale' signs alongside the snowflakes.

Lily spotted a table near a coffee shop with access to two power sockets and rushed over, narrowly avoiding colliding with a pair of huge grey boots which hung over the end of the benches while the owner of the feet lay comatose, cocooned in his coat.

Two minutes until their flights were called. Her fingers couldn't type fast enough for her.

I'm here. Right place, right time. Where are you?

Her phone rang immediately.

'You're early,' Ed said. 'And I was late. I'm so sorry, Lily, I fell asleep. I don't know what happened.'

'It's fine. You're here now.'

He laughed. 'If I'd known you'd enjoy this, I'd have done it sooner.'

'Really, not that much.'

She unplugged her phone from the wall and walked as she talked, searching the departure lounge for him. 'Look, I've got to do something quickly. Will you wait for me at the gate?'

'You're coming?'

'Of course.'

'Lily, if it means you'll lose your job—'

'It's fine. See you in a minute.'

He must be queuing at one of the concessions for his caffeine fix because she still couldn't see him. She'd spotted Matt, though, wandering onto the concourse in his blue down jacket, perfectly relaxed, as if he was off for a week's skiing. She waved and he strolled over.

'Hey, you're bright and early.'

He kissed her cheek and then looked down at her silver-clad legs. He raised his eyebrows, a thing Ed would never have done.

'Have you come straight from the party?'

'More or less. Can we go sit down?'

She pulled his arm and took him over to a row of stools by a bar which was a few hours away from opening.

'Is this what I think it is?'

'Yes,' she said, starting briskly, hoping it would discourage him trying to dissuade her. 'I'm going with Ed. I'm sorry to do this to you.'

Matt nodded, lips pursed.

'You've been a really good friend to me and I appreciate it, I really do, but I've got to do this.'

He nodded again and inhaled sharply. 'It's okay, I understand.'

'You can't help who you love.'

'True,' he said.

And you can't keep people apart, or fence them in, or fill their heads with doubt about the only thing they're certain of, she would have added, but she was in a hurry.

'I know I'm doing the right thing.'

He still wasn't making eye contact. She touched his arm.

'Get over yourself, Lily,' he said, pushing her hand away gently, 'and go get on your plane.'

'Come here.' She got to her feet and pulled him up by the elbow into a hug. He lifted his arms and put them awkwardly around her. All the times he'd laid a hug on her. It felt good to be back in control.

'If I sort this out with Ed, can you be happy for me?'

'Course I can,' he said. 'But if I—?'

'Hook up with every girl in the Western hemisphere? Yeah, sure, I can be happy for you. Go for it.'

He pulled a face. 'That's not what I meant.'

'Oh, I know, Matt. Whatever. I've heard the stories.'

'Listen, Lily.' He was frowning now. 'I don't want this to be a thing between us.'

'It won't be. I'm good if you are.'

'Yeah, course, we're friends, aren't we?'

Lily nodded but she knew that if Ed wasn't around, she couldn't be friends with Matt. Ed was the reason she and Matt got on so well. Her heart was safe; it was with Ed.

'What about your clothes?'

'I'll cope. I've got everything I need.'

He smiled at that, and this time when she hugged him, he hugged her back.

'I'll see you in a week – if I've still got a job.'

73

Ed

05.45

Lily flopped into the seat beside him.

'Hey,' Ed said. His heart was racing. 'Where've you been?'

'Ah, you know,' she said, pulling his face round to plant a kiss on his lips. 'Stuck at work, dead phone, the usual.'

''Scuse the whisky breath,' he said. He couldn't keep the smile off his face. He wouldn't even try.

'Really not a problem. Hang on,' she said, reaching into her rucksack. 'I've probably got some mints.'

'Course you have.'

He shook his head, laughing now. He pulled his portable charger from his pocket with one hand, held out the other for her phone and connected the two. Her phone beeped with more incoming messages. Lily tipped the screen towards her to take a better look as she nestled in against him.

'Don't read mine,' he begged. 'They're not representative.

It was two in the morning and I was getting a little desperate.'

'Ah, yes. The razor,' said Lily, stroking his cheek and kissing him again. 'You shaved. What a relief!'

'It wasn't that bad!'

'It wasn't bad at all. Otherwise, are you okay? All in one piece?' She patted her hands up and down his arms.

'I am now.'

'And this? What's this?' She tugged at the hood of his parka. 'What are you wearing?'

'I might say the same to you,' he said. He pulled at a woollen pompom that, rather randomly, had attached itself to the Velcro on her coat, and pointed at her feet. 'You do know where we're going? You'll ruin those boots.'

She was still thinking, scrunching up her face to concentrate. 'Where've I seen that coat before? Or is everyone wearing green parkas today?'

Travellers were forming a queue at the desk, shuffling their feet and bags into position. Ed was in no hurry. Not now that she was with him.

'You told me I don't make an effort. So,' he said, lifting a sore and heavy foot to show her, 'I did something about it. New coat, new boots.'

'You don't need to change for me. I like you as you are.'

He looked at her over the rim of his glasses, the sort of look she called professorial and made her thump his arm and accuse him of being patronising. 'You sure?'

'I'm sure. I love you.' She held his glance as he leaned in, smile widening as the distance closed between them.

'That's good, that's good,' he said, touching his lips to hers. 'You too. There's a couple of other things I need to tell you, though.' He threaded his fingers through hers and held her hand tight, swallowing the lump in his throat. He was feeling a bit teary.

'Me too,' she said.

'Good things?'

She nodded. 'But they'll save. I'm starving. You got anything to eat?'

He bent to retrieve the chocolate from one of the shopping bags and passed it to her. 'This is it. You?'

She offered him the choice of an apple or satsuma. He chose the apple. Lily peered inside the carrier bag. 'What else have you got in there?'

He let her rummage. She examined the package of make-up through the cellophane wrapping.

'You need to look pretty for me,' he said.

Now she thumped his arm. 'And you were doing so well.'

He lifted a hand in defence. 'Look, if I'd known you were going to turn up with nothing but breath mints and a satsuma, I'd have got you something more useful. Now, though, might be the time to introduce you to the concept of knitwear. You'll catch cold dressed like that.' He passed her the sweater.

She handed it back with a smile. 'It's lovely, but I won't need it.'

'Oh?'

She couldn't have changed her mind again. Not so soon.

'I thought we were doing this... Aren't we going? It'd be a shame to waste the coat. The boots, though, I'm happy to ditch.' He studied her face. Was it one joke too far?

'Sure, but I won't need the jumper. You promised to wrap me in your love. Remember?'

He ran a hand across his face. 'Yeah, I did say that, didn't I?'

It seemed so long ago.

'Promise me you will?'

'Promise.'

'Always?'

'Yeah, always.' He put his arms tight round her and kissed the side of her head. 'Let's do always, Lily. Please?' He inhaled deeply. 'Never would kill me and sometimes is driving me insane. I'm tired of living my life in two halves. I want to live with you in one place, I don't honestly care where, Cardiff, Turkey, wherever you like... I want one door key and one toothbrush. I really want to do always.' He ground to a halt. It was a long speech for him.

'Menassi's offered me a job. In London.'

'You're coming back?'

'I haven't sorted out all the details yet, but—'

'You don't have to. I can sell the flat or rent it out.'

She rummaged in one of his deep outside pockets. 'We'll talk about it later. Is it still in here?'

'What?'

'The ring.'

'It's here,' said Ed, pulling the box from an inside pocket. 'But you're not having it.'

'Why not?'

'Because any ring I give you should be beautiful. It should symbolise what I feel about you, what you feel about us. This,' he said, opening the box, 'is an ugly pile of crap.'

'I like it.'

'I don't believe you. You see, this is what you do. You say you like things when you don't.'

'It'll do for now,' she said, grabbing the ring from the box and cramming it on her finger.

'Lily, you're not taking this seriously.' He tugged at her finger. 'No wife of mine… I'm not saddling you with my family's hideous relics. Let me design something better, something fresh, that's only for us.'

'Okay, later,' she said, distracting him with kisses. 'Anyway, I like your family.'

The last of the passengers was heading to the gate.

Ed stood, offering Lily his hand. 'So, we're definitely doing this? All of it?'

'Definitely,' she said, letting him pull her to her feet. 'It'd be a shame to miss your snowmobiles.'

'You got snowmobiles?'

She nodded.

'I knew you'd do reindeer.'

'Yes.'

Author's note

One thing you realise when you write and research a book is how generous people are with their time, knowledge and expertise. I need to thank Trevor for walking round London and Cardiff with me location spotting, Cameron for sharing details of his architecture training and all the refugees who have shared their stories with me. Then, there are the writers who have read and provided opinions on the various drafts, especially Amanda at Retreat West, the New Writers' Scheme at the RNA, my writing group and my book club. Your help has been invaluable.

This is a work of fiction and none of the events described have happened.